WITHDRAWN

WINNIPEG
DEC 18 2017
PUBLIC LIBRARY

Darkness Falling

Lord Commander St. Clair watched the slow but relentless approach of the alien tesseract through his in-head feed in silence. *Ad Astra* continued to loose volley after volley of thermonuclear destruction at the object, but so far as he could see the missiles were doing little to hurt that planet-sized monster.

"Where are the gunships?" he asked. "Damn it, *where are the gunships?*"

"We're getting severe interference from in close," Symms told him. "Battlespace comm net has degraded to 15 percent."

"Transmit to the Cooperative," St. Clair said. "Tell 'em . . . tell 'em to get their spidery asses in here with some support, because we can't do this by ourselves."

D0377779

By Ian Douglas

Andromedan Dark
ALTERED STARSCAPE
DARKNESS FALLING

Star Carrier
EARTH STRIKE
CENTER OF GRAVITY
SINGULARITY
DEEP SPACE
DARK MATTER
DEEP TIME
DARK MIND

Star Corpsman
BLOODSTAR
ABYSS DEEP

The Galactic Marines Saga
The Heritage Trilogy
SEMPER MARS
LUNA MARINE
EUROPA STRIKE

The Legacy Trilogy
STAR CORPS
BATTLESPACE
STAR MARINES

The Inheritance Trilogy
STAR STRIKE
GALACTIC CORPS
SEMPER HUMAN

ATTENTION: ORGANIZATIONS AND CORPORATIONS
HarperCollins books may be purchased for educational, business, or sales promotional use. For information, please e-mail the Special Markets Department at SPsales@harpercollins.com.

DARKNESS
FALLING

ANDROMEDAN DARK: BOOK TWO

IAN DOUGLAS

HARPER Voyager
An Imprint of HarperCollins*Publishers*

This is a work of fiction. Names, characters, places, and incidents are products of the author's imagination or are used fictitiously and are not to be construed as real. Any resemblance to actual events, locales, organizations, or persons, living or dead, is entirely coincidental.

DARKNESS FALLING. Copyright © 2017 by William H. Keith, Jr. All rights reserved. Printed in the United States of America. No part of this book may be used or reproduced in any manner whatsoever without written permission except in the case of brief quotations embodied in critical articles and reviews. For information, address HarperCollins Publishers, 195 Broadway, New York, NY 10007.

First Harper Voyager mass market printing: December 2017

Print Edition ISBN: 978-0-06-237922-1
Digital Edition ISBN: 978-0-06-237920-7

Cover illustration by Gregory Bridges
Cover design by Amy Halperin

Harper Voyager and the Harper Voyager logo are trademarks of HarperCollins Publishers in the United States of America and other countries.

HarperCollins is a registered trademark of HarperCollins Publishers in the United States of America and other countries.

FIRST EDITION

17 18 19 20 21   QGM   10 9 8 7 6 5 4 3 2 1

ATTENTION: ORGANIZATIONS AND CORPORATIONS
HarperCollins books may be purchased for educational, business, or sales promotional use. For information, please e-mail the Special Markets Department at SPsales@harpercollins.com.

For Brea, my love and my light.

PROLOGUE

Two galaxies collided, their star-clotted central cores passing through one another in silent, spectacular radiance, their starburst glory filling a sky gone strange.

Four billion years earlier, the larger of those titanic spiral galaxies had been called M-31. Alternatively, and less precisely, but perhaps more euphoniously, it also had borne the name of a constellation, the apparent star-pattern within which it happened to appear from the vantage point of one solitary world.

Andromeda.

The sapient life-forms of that world who'd given Andromeda its name had called the second spiral the Milky Way, or, with a conceit born of innocence, simply "the Galaxy."

The component stars of those two galaxies—400 billion within the Milky Way, perhaps a trillion for Andromeda— appeared densely packed, a whirling, violent star-storm frozen in time by the sheer scale of the collision. In fact, very few of those teeming, myriad suns had or would collide as the mismatched spirals penetrated one another, so vast were the distances involved, so minute were the individual dust-mote stars.

What *was* colliding, however, were vast clouds of dust and gas, the invisible mystery of dark matter, and the tug of powerful gravitational fields. Shocks and forces set into motion nebulae-collapsing pressure waves that spawned hot, young, intensely blue-white suns in their teeming tens of millions. Until the galactic collision had begun some hundreds of millions of years before, these two galaxies had appeared staid, middle-aged, verging on senescent . . . quiet, conservative, the exuberance of their youth long since spent. Now, however, the collision was rejuvenating both galaxies, giving them a brilliant radiance that neither had known since the universe was new.

One of the spiral galaxies teemed with life, with vibrant civilizations, some unimaginably ancient, some unimaginably advanced.

Andromeda, however, was quite another matter indeed. . . .

It was hard not to despair.

The sense of being divorced from one's proper place and time, the sense of loss, of separation, of sheer, aching homesickness filled the waking thoughts of every human on board the *Tellus Ad Astra*. It haunted their dreams as well. In all the varied and disparate history of Humankind, never had any person—any *group* of people—been so isolated, so lost, or so alone.

Lord Commander Grayson St. Clair floated weightless within the globe of *Ad Astra*'s bridge, adrift in a blaze of light. The collision of Earth's galaxy with the monster spiral of Andromeda had flung titanic clouds of interstellar dust and gas together, compressing them, giving birth to myriad new stars imbedded in bright-glowing sheets and streamers and shells of radiance.

It was, he thought, a spectacular backdrop to the thoughts and hopes and fears of the castaways . . . the million or so humans and metahumans, AI minds and robots marooned in this remote futurity. The feelings of isolation, of homesickness, of *loss* felt all the more acute as he looked at a world that *might* be Earth, that most probably *was* Earth . . . but an Earth 4 billion years removed from the world he'd known.

"It doesn't look much like home, does it, my lord?" St. Clair's executive officer said. Vanessa Symms floated beside him, staring out into the brilliant starscape. He could hear the longing in her words, echoing his own.

"Not in the least," St. Clair replied. "But 4 billion years can do that to a planet. To an entire star system."

"Uh-uh." Symms shook her head. "I just don't buy it, my lord. That can't be Earth. The sun is all wrong."

The local star gleamed in the distance off *Ad Astra*'s starboard side, some five and a half AUs off, a yellow sun of roughly the mass of a stellar type G8 or G9. That meant that it should have been a bit cooler than Sol and a bit smaller . . . but in fact it was nearly twice the sun's diameter and considerably hotter. Those mass and temperature readings argued that this was not, *could* not be Earth's solar system, and yet . . .

"Newton *does* have an explanation for that, you know," St. Clair pointed out. He could feel the ship's powerful artificial intelligence at the back of his mind, watching over his virtual shoulder. It offered no comment.

"So I've heard. Maybe I just won't *want* to believe it."

"I get that." St. Clair shrugged. "But it's about the only explanation that makes sense."

"Really?" Symms laughed, the sound harsh and challenging. She waved a hand at the alien starscape, the gesture angry . . . or perhaps simply showing her frustration. "How the hell can you make sense of *that*?"

The sprawl of brilliant nebulae and hot, blue-white stars in the distance served as the stage for a tight knot of worlds just ahead. Largest was a gas giant as far from the local star as was Jupiter from Sol in St. Clair's memory of home. There were differences, however. The world was smaller than Jupiter by about 15 percent, with roughly the same diameter as Saturn. It was also a bright blue in color, like Neptune, with less distinct banding, and it lacked the famous Great Red Spot.

Moreover, dozens of worlds orbited the giant, most appearing no larger than bright stars strung out along the planet's equatorial plane, but 5 million kilometers ahead lay a white-and-ocher world with an equatorial diameter of 12,756 kilometers.

That precise diameter all but proved that the planet *Tellus Ad Astra* was closing with was, in fact, Earth. The coincidence was too astonishing for it to be otherwise. But still . . .

"I mean, where are the *oceans*?" Symms wanted to know.

"It's got oceans—"

"It has landlocked *seas*, my lord. Tiny ones. There's a difference. That planet is not even remotely like Earth . . . apart from its diameter."

True enough. Much of the planet's equatorial zones appeared to be desert, with a tiny fraction of the total surface covered by water. Of the widely dispersed continents and world-girdling oceans of St. Clair's Earth there were no traces. Nor were there ice caps, and save for a few scattered swirls of cloud, those sweeping streaks and expanses of white appeared to be salt flats coating the dead ocean basin that dominated the northern hemisphere. To St. Clair's eye it appeared that all of the planet's original land masses had gathered together as one supercontinent isolated in the southern hemisphere, and much of that was as barren as the empty ocean.

Of Earth's moon there was no sign.

If that *was* Earth ahead, someone had moved it, probably a geological age or two ago, and parked it around Jupiter. It orbited the gas giant now at a distance of 850,000 kilometers, circling the bloated world once roughly every five days.

Why? Well, that was something they'd need to find out.

"Bring us to a halt relative to that planet," St. Clair ordered.

"Aye, aye, my lord," Sublieutenant Carla Adams replied from the helm station. "Dead stop."

St. Clair wasn't sure of the reception they could expect here—if any at all. They needed to proceed with extreme caution.

He glanced at a secondary screen nearby, one showing a large schematic of both the *Tellus* and the *Ad Astra*. All green, with no red flags—all normal. *Good.*

"Lord Commander?" Senior Lieutenant Vance Cameron said over the in-head cybernetics. He was *Ad Astra*'s tactical officer, the man charged with handling the ship in combat. "You know . . . I have the feeling nobody's home."

"Maybe not. Pass the word to General Wilson that the Marines can proceed."

"Very well, my lord."

Even without the rotating habitats that made up the *Tellus*, a vessel as large as the *Ad Astra* had room to spare for an entire fleet stored within her vast flight decks and internal ship bays. In addition, her entourage included three military LPS transports, *Inchon*, *Saipan*, and *Vera Cruz*, complete with two divisions of United Earth Marines. One of them, the *Vera Cruz*, had been deployed ahead of the *Tellus Ad Astra*. At Cameron's command, relayed through the Marine HQ on board *Ad Astra*, she accelerated gently, edging toward the planet.

"There go the gunships," Cameron said. A half dozen blocky, rugged-looking vessels emerged from the shadows of the tug's ventral surface, moving out and falling into formation with the Marine transport.

". . . and the fighters." What looked like clouds of sparkling dust had begun wafting off the *Vera Cruz* and moving with her in loose formation. A few of the larger specks were ASF-99 Wasp fighters, but most were Marines in Mk. III MCA armor with MX-40 backpacks, their wings deployed, their Martin-Teller gravitic thrusters operational. In effect, several thousand Marines had just become individual fighter crafts. After a moment, the sparkling effect became muted, and the clouds began to fade into darkness. Marine armor could selectively and intelligently bend background light and color, rendering its wearer all but invisible.

"You don't think that display out there is too . . . threatening?" Symms asked. "We don't *know* they're hostile . . . if there's even anyone in there."

"I want a solid wall up between *Tellus Ad Astra* and whatever the hell is in there," St. Clair replied. "We have to assume it's Xam . . . and when we ran into them before they were *not* friendly."

She snorted. "Not friendly? They tried to freaking wipe us out of the sky. . . ."

"Not exactly conducive to free and open communications."

St. Clair was painfully aware of the responsibility he carried as the military commander of the expedition. *Tellus Ad Astra* had been projected 4 billion years into her own future, which meant that the million or so humans on board were all that was left of Humankind. If that was indeed Earth up ahead, it had been changed beyond all recognition, and *Homo sapiens* was long since extinct.

"No," Symms replied. "But, you know, I think the real problem for me is that I'm having a lot of trouble wrapping my head around the idea that the Xam are somehow our remote descendants. That's just plain . . . I don't know . . . *creepy.*"

"Maybe. But what," St. Clair replied, "does *creepy* have to do with the truth? The DNA studies were conclusive."

He didn't add the fact that the alien-looking but human-oid Xam offered the population of *Tellus Ad Astra* the tiniest possible sliver of hope that they could somehow find their way back to their own time.

In fact, it was that hope that had brought them here. . . .

Dr. Francois Dumont, the expedition's civilian expert on xenotechnology, swam up to the pair. "Lord Commander?"

"Yes, Doctor?" St. Clair replied.

"We've completed the preliminary scan of the planet ahead."

"And?"

"We cannot detect any cities on the surface."

"What . . . *none*?"

"No, my lord. There may be . . . settlements, solitary bases, that sort of thing, but no cities and no major power sources. However, we are detecting an artificial ring, a big one, circling the entire planet."

"How big?"

"The arc is about 30,000 kilometers across, my lord. Measuring from one side of the planet to the other, the entire structure is two and a half million kilometers across."

"My God! Let me see."

The download came in through St. Clair's in-head hardware, appearing in a window that blinked open within his mind's eye.

Ad Astra was approaching the planet dead-on at the equator, so from this distance the ring system was not visible to the unaided eye, but under high magnification and enhancement it appeared as a ruler-straight gray-and-silver line scratched across the planetary disc. Alphanumerics off to one side gave mass, rotational velocity, and energy readings. That thing was *enormous.* . . .

Another megastructure, then.

"Any sign of life, Doctor? Or is this another dry hole?"

"Can't tell yet, my lord," Dumont replied. "The structure is well shielded. We're broadcasting using both Xam and Kroajid protocols, but we won't know until they decide to respond to us."

If someone had asked St. Clair a month before what he imagined the Galaxy might be like in the remote future, he probably would have talked about far-flung, brilliant civilizations, frankly magical technologies, perhaps something like the alien Coadunation that existed within the Galaxy of his home time. He would not have envisioned what *Tellus Ad Astra* had encountered so far . . . a Galaxy of empty worlds, ruins, abandoned megastructures, and a handful of scattered advanced cultures that seemed to have withdrawn from reality.

Since her arrival here/now, *Ad Astra* had investigated three titanic megaengineering habitats in this era. One, a series of nested swarms of stationary satellites called a matrioshka brain, had been inhabited solely by digitized lifeforms uploaded into trillions of computer habitats completely surrounding a star. The other two had been an Alderson disk—a vast, flat structure like an old-fashioned phonograph record with the local star bobbing up and down in the central hole—and a topopolis—a tangled mass of enclosed habitat tubes surrounding its star like a belt of fuzz. Each of these last two possessed the surface area of millions of Earths, but both had been deserted and apparently crumbling into ruin.

Judging by their encounters so far, galactic civilization, at least *corporeal* civilizations made up of flesh-and-blood beings, was on the decline. Yes, they'd met a star-faring species called the Kroajid, two-meter arthropods that communicated by vibrating the stiff hairs on their bodies, but it looked as though the vast majority of intelligent life had retreated into virtual, electronic realities of far more complexity and sheer pleasure than could ever be experienced in the material universe.

And then, of course . . . there was the Dark.

I don't want to think about that now, St. Clair thought with an internal shudder. He just wasn't sure he'd have that choice.

"Very well, Doctor," St. Clair said. "Let me know the instant you hear anything."

"Of course, my lord."

Vera Cruz and her escorts were almost invisibly small, now, all but lost in the distance. If the Xam *were* there on or around that planet ahead, and if they were a part of the Andromedan Dark . . .

"It would be nice to know," Cameron said over the command channel, "that we're actually fighting on the right side. I mean, if we have to take sides in an alien war . . ."

"I know," St. Clair replied. "It'd be a hell of a thing if we find out that the Xam are the *good* guys."

But if the Xam were indeed Humankind's descendants, what the hell were they doing working for the Andromedan Dark? Had what passed for human civilization in this time moved wholesale to M-31? Were they a splinter, a fragment of the original human civilizations that had migrated to Andromeda a billion or so years ago, and now they were returning?

St. Clair shook his head. So much to learn . . . and they had to get it *right*. The consequences of screwing up were incalculable for all of Humankind.

He hoped there might be some answers waiting on or around the planet up ahead. Was it really Earth, aged 4 billion years since last he'd seen it?

Could the Xam really be humanity's descendants?

Was going home even a possibility?

"Have you seen Dr. Crosby's report?" Symms asked him.

"The one that says the Xam can't be human, because 4 billion years is too long?"

"That's the one. He thinks the DNA evidence is faulty. Or manufactured . . . a hoax. Maybe even a hoax for our benefit."

"By who? And for what possible reason?"

"How about by the Xam to make us think we're related? So we would join them against the Spiders," she said, referring to the Kroajid.

"You *do* have a nasty, suspicious mind, don't you?"

She shrugged. "If you say so, my lord. But we should take it slow. Sir."

"Believe me, a snail will be able to outrace us. We have no idea as to what we're getting into here. But . . ."

"But, my lord?"

"But if the Xam *are* related to us, but only separated from our genome by a million years or so, as Crosby says . . . that's all the more reason we should try to establish peaceful contact."

"You can't believe that."

"I believe there's . . . a possibility. A very slim chance. And that means we need to explore it. Because."

"Because," she echoed. Neither of them wanted to say their hopes out loud—that the Xam might have the technology that might let them go home once more.

Damn it, things just weren't adding up. According to every computer simulation run so far, the Xam weren't showing anything close to four gigayears' worth of genetic divergence from *Homo sapiens*. But for now, St. Clair assumed, *had* to assume, that the Xam were in fact the remote evolutionary descendants of humans.

After all, they'd learned about this star system from a database taken from a Xam fighter. It described a galactic coordinate system, built around a line extending between the supermassive black holes at the cores of both Andromeda and the Milky Way, that had been in use for some tens of millions of years already. Navigators could plug in sets of numbers and pinpoint precise locations in either galaxy, and one such set of coordinates had led the *Tellus Ad Astra* here. If the xenolinguists were right, this should be the system revered by the Xam as their ancient, ancestral homeworld.

Of course, the astrophysics department had a sharply different take on things. The local star could *not* be Sol. It didn't have enough mass . . . and, paradoxically, it was both hotter and it had twice the diameter of Earth's sun.

"So what was Newton's explanation for the star being so different from Sol?" Symms wanted to know, jumping the conversation back to an earlier topic.

"What? Oh . . . well, according to him, the sun should be starting to expand into a red giant phase just about now. The thing is, our sun has been getting 10 percent brighter about every billion years or so . . . and a billion years after our time, Earth would have become so hot that the oceans boiled away. In fact, Earth would likely have turned into a copy of Venus long before that, with a high-pressure atmosphere of superheated steam."

"Sure. There was some speculation that we were going to trip that booby trap ourselves last century."

"We almost did," St. Clair agreed. "We were *that* close

to cooking ourselves. But it would have happened anyway sooner or later, just with the sun naturally getting hotter and hotter.

"Anyway, maybe a few million years after we . . . ah . . . started our voyage, our descendants must have decided to move the whole planet out to where it was cooler. Planetary engineering on an epic scale."

"Okay, that would explain Earth suddenly becoming a moon of Jupiter's," his executive commander told him. "But there's still the problem of the star itself. According to the planetographers, that star only has about 90 percent of the mass of our sun. There's no sign of a planetary nebula, no indication that our sun has lost mass. You can't tell me they swapped stars, too!"

"No, but with an advanced enough technology, they could have pulled some of the mass right up out of the gravity well. 'Star lifting.' Remember the topopolis in Andromeda?"

"Yes . . ."

"Well if that fuzzball tangle of a habitat could use mass from its star, why couldn't somebody do the same here and extend Sol's age?"

"But why would they do that *and* move the planet?"

"Four billion years is a long, *long* time, ExComm," he replied gently. "I can't speak for people that far ahead of us, but at a guess, they moved the planet when Earth first started getting too warm a few million years after our time. Maybe—I don't know—a million, 10 million years after we left? Then, maybe a billion years later, when the sun started to go into its red giant phase, they tinkered with the star itself." He shrugged. "Maybe we can ask them when we meet them."

"*If* they talk," she said, "and don't decide to shoot first.

Until a few days ago, they were trying their best to wipe us out of the sky."

"Yeah. Not exactly conducive to free and open communications, huh?"

And yet communication was crucial in this moment, because two vital questions remained for St. Clair: Were the Xam here, and would they fight?

The *Vera Cruz* and her escorts should be able to answer those questions. The trick was doing it without involving unacceptable risk to the *Tellus* habitat and the people on board. The huge ship was already closer to the supposed-Xam homeworld than St. Clair would have preferred.

"My lord," Cameron said. "*Vera Cruz* reports alien ships coming in from out-system."

"Where? Ah . . . I see them."

One moment there'd been nothing. In the next, the alien fleet was here, decelerating in an instant from near-*c* to zero.

"Damn. Are they attacking?"

"Not yet, sir. They appear to be putting up a barrier between us and the planet . . . like they're watching our ships."

"*Watching* is okay," St. Clair said. He could see them in more detail now. There were hundreds of thousands of them, slim, black needles each a few tens of meters in length. They traveled linked together into a single enormous cylinder, but as they arrived at their destination they split apart into a swarm of separate ships. *Ad Astra*'s xenotech people still had no idea how they were powered, or even what they might be fully capable of.

But those needle shapes were identical to those they'd encountered earlier when they'd fought the Xam and the Andromedan Dark. The Kroajid referred to them as "Dark Raiders," and noted that they seemed bent on destroying virtual populations, the digitally uploaded inhabitants of the Galaxy who appeared to have withdrawn from reality. So although they may be able to do more, St. Clair knew that each jet-black needle was fast, maneuverable, and armed with powerful weaponry.

He almost opened a channel to Marine HQ, intending to caution them against maneuvers that might be interpreted as an attack, but thought better of it. General Wilson knew what he was doing.

"So is that it?" Symms asked him. "We park a Marine transport in orbit and stare them down?"

"Not quite, ExComm," St. Clair replied, grinning at her. "We'll see if they want to talk to Newton. Or Newton's avatar, I should say. Even the Dark showed signs of . . . curiosity."

"Yeah. It couldn't understand why we didn't want to be absorbed by it." She laughed. "For a super AI spanning an entire galaxy, the Dark doesn't show that much intelligence."

"Maybe it's just so smart we humans can't understand it," St. Clair replied. "We'll have to see what Newton has to say about that."

"We are deploying the avatar now," Newton's voice said within St. Clair's mind. "Stand by. . . ."

Answers. They needed *answers.* . . .

So far, there were only questions.

Marine Captain Greg Dixon, the newly minted CO of Charlie Company, 3rd Battalion, watched the black swarm ahead maneuvering to block them from the planet and its high-tech ring.

"All stop." The voice coming in over 3rd Batt's tactical channel was that of General Wilson, the expedition's Marine CO, not Colonel Becker's. Shit . . . the brass was in a micromanaging mood today. . . .

Dixon thoughtclicked an icon in his head, tapping the gravitic thrusters on his MX-40 unit and bringing himself to a halt relative to the planet. His helmet didn't have a visor, but instead fed him an all-around view of surrounding space directly through the circuitry implanted in his brain. On his in-head, the swarm of alien needleships looked like black smoke, with the ringed planet beyond only dimly visible.

"Hold your positions," Wilson's voice cautioned. "Newton is trying to open a channel. . . ."

Dixon felt nightmarishly exposed and vulnerable. The last time he'd seen those ships they'd been trying their best to kill him, and they'd damned near succeeded. What the hell were they doing here, facing technology like that?

More important, what the hell were they doing just waiting around?

It didn't help that he was the new kid on the team. Until a week ago, he'd been the company's assistant CO . . . but Captain Hanson had bought the farm in that desperate fight inside NPS-1018, that bizarre, colossal, alien fuzzball habitat shrouding a red sun in Andromeda.

They'd not been able to recover the body. The attackers had been coming through portals opening up in thin air—striking from the twisted geometry of higher dimensions.

Dixon was still having nightmares about it.

"They're dopplering!" Becker called.

Wilson ordered, "Engage! All ships engage!"

Several patches within the black haze had suddenly blueshifted, meaning a large number of needleships accelerating sharply to relativistic speeds. That was the deadliest part of this kind of combat: an oncoming attacker was traveling just behind the photon wave front announcing his arrival.

High-energy lasers and charged particle beams lashed out, drawn in Dixon's awareness by computer graphics but invisible in the real world. Nuke-tipped missiles boosted into the melee, and the first deadly, sun-bright blossoms of nuclear annihilation unfolded in ghostly silence.

The enemy needleships, thank the Marine God of Battle, were not heavily armored and didn't seem to have extensive energy shielding. There were just so many of them. Dixon targeted one vessel that appeared to be coming straight at him, and watched it flare into a fast-expanding ball of hot plasma. He kicked his backpack drive then, and hurtled into the fray to kill some more.

But Marines were dying as well. The needleships were firing beams of positrons—antimatter electrons that erupted in flashes of light, X-rays, and hard gamma radiation when they touched normal matter. Just twenty meters to Dixon's left, PFC Jacob Fedor vanished in a dazzling pulse of light as a needle's beam slashed through him.

"Charlie Company!" Colonel Becker called. "With me!"

The battalion commander's battle armor lit up green

within Dixon's in-head, a beacon for the company's Marines. Dixon adjusted his vector and boosted, weaving through the rapidly unfolding storm of battle.

Becker, Dixon saw, was trying to work his way through the cloud of enemy ships . . . maybe get between them and the planet. Pulling nearly fifty gravities, the newly minted captain hurtled through the cloud of needleships, Marines, and tumbling debris after the colonel. The Gs weren't the issue: gravitic drives worked by bending local space; you were essentially in free fall even when you were boosting high-gravs. Navigational maneuvering was the big problem. Dixon could nudge his suit to one side or another to avoid ships or debris in his path, but the faster he moved, the less time he had to spot an object, analyze its threat, and avoid it.

The maneuver, Dixon thought with a fatalistic inward shrug, was doomed. Against the alien numbers, the human fleet would not be able to last more than minutes . . . possibly no more than seconds. The individual Marine fighters and combat suits deployed at the moment in front of the *Tellus Ad Astra* numbered a few thousand, but there were literally millions of the black needles out here . . . several thousand of the damned things for every Marine in the squadron.

He figured he could at least take a few of them with him.

He loosed a triplet of M-90 Shurikin shipkillers, missiles as small as his forearm with tamped vac-E warheads, dispersing them for maximum effect. White light seared across his in-head vision, momentarily blotting out his sight. The AI controlling his suit rolled him hard to the left, avoiding an expanding cloud of high-velocity fragments just ahead.

As the plasma fireballs faded, he could see again . . .

but for a moment he thought something was wrong with his visual feed. Surrounding space had taken on a grainy texture. Had the nuclear flashes fried part of his circuitry?

Then he realized that the graininess was *moving* . . . that it was, in fact, dust or smoke obscuring his vision of distant objects. Then he could hear the steady patter of tiny impacts across the outside of his armor.

He queried his AI; what the hell was that stuff? His first thought was nanotech disassemblers—microscopic machines launched in clouds and programmed to take apart whatever they touched—but these objects were simply bouncing off. Maybe they were some sort of surveillance system, released from the rings in order to keep tabs on the human fleet?

The unknown objects appear to be disassembling the Dark Raider ships, his suit's AI told him. *They appear to be both larger and smarter than our own disassemblers.*

Half a kilometer away, a slim black needle went into an end-for-end tumble, as fragments of its hull spilled into vacuum. Those fragments each dwindled away; it looked like the disassemblers were making more disassemblers by taking apart the enemy vessels, rebuilding the bits and pieces into new units, and programming them on the fly.

Impressive.

A moment later, Dixon swept across the vast surface of the alien ring at a distance of just twenty kilometers. The structure was immense, almost thirty thousand kilometers wide from inner edge to outer rim. Even after all his time in space, Dixon had never quite lost the amazement at the size of things. The inner edge arced across the sky just 9,000 kilometers above the planet's equator; the proportions of the ring to the planet were eerily similar to those of Saturn back home, which gave the world an eerily familiar aspect.

Dixon wondered why the ring's inhabitants hadn't opened fire on the Marines. They were Xam, weren't they?

Maybe not. He was realizing it had been the *ring* that released the weapon that was fastidiously dissolving Xam ships, but ignoring human ships and Marine armor. And that meant somebody else occupied the ring, some enemy of the Xam.

The dust cloud, he saw, was growing thicker and the destruction was now increasing exponentially. "Break off, break off!" Becker ordered. And the Marine armored suits began rising above the melee.

The order made good sense, so far as Dixon was concerned. The clouds of alien disassemblers were taking care of the problem nicely without relying on the Marines risking their own lives. Marines were damned good at fighting, but that was no reason to seek out death for its own sake.

Apparently the Xam felt the same way. Their needle-ships were now in full retreat, streaming back across the plane of the ring. Some appeared to be reassembling themselves into a single ragged-looking cylinder kilometers in length, but most remained separate, accelerating to near-*c* and vanishing into the emptiness beyond the gas giant and its ringed moon.

And the Marines were left adrift above the gray sweep of the artificial ring.

"RTB, Marines," Becker ordered. "Let's get back to the barn."

Dixon exhaled in relief as the Marine armored suits and scattered fighters began coming about on to new vectors that would take them back to the *Vera Cruz*.

NEWTON HAD been in communication with the ringed world ahead for several minutes now. Language software, recently

given to the expedition by the Kroajid and punningly referred to as the "Roceti Stone," had provided the artificial
intelligence with the key to communicating with a number
of the alien species in this epoch. It would work only between machine minds—no human could comprehend this
complex series of nested algorithms and symbolic logic,
much less actually pronounce it—but Newton now could
serve as the expedition's translator.

According to the database included with the program,
there were millions of extant languages across the Galaxy,
ranging from vocalizations to changes in skin color to
shifting patterns within electrical fields to the eerie buzz
of vibrating hairs to microwave pulses to just about anything else imaginable. The most efficient languages were
those used among AIs, machine to machine, and it was one
of those that had just challenged the approaching human
ships.

And so as Newton approached the alien fleet, transmitting several million different electronic versions of "hello"
on as many different frequencies, it was not particularly
surprised to receive an answer. What was surprising was
that the reply essentially translated as "Welcome to Ki,"
and included a list of docking instructions guiding them
into the planet girdling ring. The ring, Newton was told,
was open to all who came in peace, but only certain parts
of it—roughly 15 percent of the structure—were accessible
by beings possessing human biochemistries.

While all this was going on, the Marines had engaged
in a fierce exchange of fire lasting all of twenty seconds,
and after Newton had explained who and what the humans
were, Ki had sent out the cavalry. The rest had been ex-
traordinarily fast-paced anticlimax.

Newton then entered into a rapid-fire exchange of infor-

mation with an entity that referred to itself as "the Mind
of Ki," presumably an artificial intelligence of some sort.
The Xam, Newton was informed, did not rule here, did not
control Ki . . . and were not a threat.

"And who does rule here?" Newton asked.

"The Mind of Ki," was the simple but enigmatic reply.

As Newton informed the *Ad Astra* of this unexpected development, it wondered exactly what the Mind of Ki was . . .

. . . and whether it could be trusted.

WITH THE face-off in front of the ringed planet now resolved,
at least for the moment at any rate, St. Clair was on his way
back to his home in the *Tellus* starboard hab. There was a
stop he needed to make on the way, however—someone he
needed to see . . . or, at least, someone he needed to check
up on.

He was not at all looking forward to the meeting.

Ad Astra's sick bay was an immense hospital facility located on Deck 24 forward of the bridge tower. There were
additional hospitals forward in each of the *Tellus* habitats;
the one for the starboard hab was located in the town of
Bethesda, just half a kilometer from his home, and those, of
course, enjoyed one standard gravity as the habitat rotated.
The sick bay, however, was in zero-G, though a number of
adjunct wards were located in *Ad Astra*'s centrifuge section
for those patients who required gravity.

St. Clair entered Ward Two and grasped a traveler—a
handhold that fit comfortably in his grip and was attached
to one of the spiderweb of slender cables laced through the
facility's open spaces. He thought of the doctor he'd come to
see, and the traveler immediately began accelerating down
its cable—shifting twice through junctions—and brought
him at last to the office of Dr. Kildare 117 AI Delta-2pmd.

Named for a fictional doctor from several centuries earlier, Kildare was a medical robot; the letters *pmd* in his designator stood for "psychiatric medical doctor." An android, he looked perfectly human, right down to the caring and attentive bedside manner.

It—no, *he* was one of the medical AIs charged with caring for *Tellus Ad Astra*'s growing complement of insane personnel. There were, St. Clair thought, far too many of those . . . and the number had been growing.

"You wanted to see me, Doctor?" St. Clair asked.

"Yes, Lord Commander. About Lord Adler."

St. Clair nodded. He'd thought that was why he'd been called. "Has there been any improvement in his condition?"

"No, my lord. And given the extent of neurological damage, improvement to any degree is extremely unlikely."

"May I see him?"

"Of course, my lord. Over here . . ."

The medical robot led St. Clair to a partitioned area off the main ward, where walls had been grown to create a private, sealed-off alcove. He felt the ward's security system querying his in-head electronics before granting him access.

Günter Adler was the expedition's Cybercouncil director, the civilian leader of the million or so humans on board the star-mobile space colony . . . or he *had* been. A week earlier, he'd attempted to link his in-head circuitry to the Dark Mind. St. Clair had also brushed against that hostile alien mind and nearly suffered the same fate.

The Dark Mind was unfathomably more powerful than any human brain, and fast beyond human comprehension, a vast network of widely distributed artificial intelligences from which a single will and purpose and ego had emerged. No single organic intelligence could hope to overcome it, but St. Clair's exchange with the Dark Mind had made it hesitate long enough for an allied coalition of SAIs—super artificial intelligences godlike in their scope and power—to drive it back.

But by that time, Adler's mind had been blasted into shrieking insanity.

Adler floated in his treatment cubicle, closely swaddled in a mediwrap designed to keep him clean, fed, and hydrated, his circulation moving, and his temperature steady. Sensors imbedded in the nanomatrix of the material monitored his physiology, reporting the numbers on a large touch screen on the wall. A complex device inserted in his mouth kept him from swallowing his tongue or biting himself. His eyes, St. Clair noticed, were shifting and darting beneath the closed lids, and a faint groan escaped the man's caked lips.

"Has there been any improvement?"

"No, my lord," the android replied. "We attempted to put him into thalamic shutdown—a deep medical coma."

"Really? He looks like he's dreaming."

"Indeed. We have not been able to induce a deep coma, though. If we could, we should be able to keep him alive indefinitely. But so far he's been resisting our best efforts."

"How?"

"The thalamus controls input coming to the brain, Lord Commander," Kildare told him, "and it routes incoming signals to the relevant portions of the cortex. Unfortunately, the brain tends to create its own input, and the shutdown itself can be . . . intermittent. Each time we lower his thalamus to the point of shutdown, his internal mental processes break through. We're still not sure why. Or how."

"Does that mean he can hear us?"

"Possibly . . . but the sensations will be wildly garbled.

He might feel hot as cold, or sense sound as pain. I doubt that he understands what he's experiencing." Kildare gave a deceptively human shrug. "Most likely he *is* dreaming. Corticosteroid levels, however, suggest he's experiencing an interminable nightmare. . . ."

"My God . . ."

St. Clair had never liked Adler. The man was self-centered, power-hungry, and arrogant, a *politician* of the worst possible stripe. St. Clair had butted heads with him constantly since he'd come on board as military CO of the *Tellus Ad Astra* expedition, and Adler had done his level best to supplant, discredit, and undermine St. Clair, trying to seize sole control of the colony and its castaway inhabitants at every turn.

But trapped in a nightmare, unable to wake up? St. Clair wouldn't wish that on a worst enemy.

"Have you tried waking him?"

"Briefly, and under carefully controlled conditions," Kildare replied. "It's not good. In a hypnopompic state—that's the twilight condition between sleep and wakefulness—he thrashes, screams, and attempts to fight . . . something. We're not sure what. When he speaks, it's word salad."

St. Clair nodded. He'd heard other mental trauma patients shrieking word salad—a rambling hash of mismatched, seemingly random words and phrases without a clear meaning.

"Each time," Kildare went on, "we were unable to elicit sense from the patient. We were forced to take him down into deep unconsciousness again and keep him there so that he would not harm himself."

Adler's face twitched unpleasantly, the features contracting. A globule of spittle escaped past the side of the device in his mouth; a portion of the mediwrap extended itself and snagged the droplet out of the air, absorbing it. Adler's face, meanwhile, twisted into a horrific mask of agony. His body inside the wrap stiffened, arched, then thrashed. The head tried to snap back, but was restrained by the gentle but actively strong folds of the wrap at the back of his neck.

Adler, St. Clair saw, was trying to scream. Even in a deep artificial sleep he was trying to scream.

"There must be *something* you can do," St. Clair said, feeling helpless.

"One thing, my lord," the android replied. "And given the seriousness of his condition I *would* strongly recommend it."

"What's that?"

"Director Adler has a backup. Most members of the Cybercouncil do. His was updated just two days before the . . . trauma occurred."

St. Clair gave the android a black scowl. "I don't like that. It's . . . like murder."

"I believe the human expression 'a fate worse than death' could be applied to Director Adler's current condition with some accuracy," Kildare said.

"In other words, he'd be better off dead?"

"We can't know precisely what he is experiencing inside his head right now," Kildare said, "but the levels of cortisol in his blood are dangerously high—over 1200 nanomoles per liter."

"Meaning what?"

"That's twice the high end of the normal range. It means Cushing's syndrome, and serious circulatory and liver issues. We have him pumped full of medical nano, of course, but all we can do is delay the inevitable. We've *got* to reboot him before he suffers massive circulatory collapse or cardiac arrest."

St. Clair considered this.

Neuromedicine was sure enough of the workings of the human brain to have come up with the C^2S—the cerebral cortex scan—a procedure that precisely mapped the network of 86 billion neurons throughout the brain, the thousand-trillion synaptic connections among them, and the electro-chemical balance that described memory, thought, and the emergent phenomenon called *mind*. It was possible to record those maps and, if necessary, to implant them within a living brain. It was possible, in effect, to take Adler's most recent C^2S data to banish the insanity and restore him to his mental state of two days before his encounter with the Dark Mind.

The procedure was insanely expensive, and for that reason was available only to the wealthiest citizens. That was part of the reason why St. Clair didn't like the idea; only the wealthy could afford it.

More than that, however, implanting a recorded neuroscan wiped out what was there naturally, in effect killing that person. Adler would lose all memory of the two days before his mind had been blasted by the Dark Mind. Some argued that it was simply a reset of the brain's switches and base states; nothing was changed so far as the personality went, and the only memory lost was of experiences after the last backup. Where was the ethical dilemma in that?

St. Clair, however, wondered if things ever were quite that simple. You could argue that downloading a C^2S backup was medical murder, the replacement a copy of what made the original person who and what he was. He found the whole idea somewhat . . . what was that archaic word ExComm had used? Yes . . .

Creepy.

Plenty of people went in for that sort of thing, however, or they would if they had the money.

And that, of course, raised other questions. As the de facto leader of *Tellus Ad Astra*'s population, St. Clair was being given a crash download in economics, a topic he'd never particularly cared for. Unlike neuroscience—or ship command—there was too much black magic involved.

That alone might justify rebooting Adler, he thought with a flash of black humor. Let *him* deal with the colony's financial issues.

Or . . . no. St. Clair didn't even know what position Adler had taken on colonial finances, but whatever it was, it could have far-reaching effects in how the colony was managed . . . even on how it would survive. If Adler decided to try to use the problem to increase his own power . . .

That, St. Clair thought, was a big part of the problem. He didn't trust Adler as far as he could throw the man in a five-G gravity field.

He decided he would have to discuss the problem of medical expenses with the ship's AI later. But right now, he needed to consider whether or not the colony *needed* the original Cybercouncil director.

"How many other cases do we have like Adler's?" he asked.

"No two cases are precisely alike," the android told him. "But we currently are treating 8,428 humans for mental trauma sustained in the encounter with the Andromedan Dark Mind. These cases range from quite severe—like Director Adler—to relatively minor."

"How minor?"

Again, that human-mimic shrug. "Mild personality disorder. Interrupted sleep. Nightmares. Depression. I should point out that many of these cases may not be related to the encounter with the Dark Mind, however."

"Oh? What are they related to?"

"It seems fairly obvious, Lord Commander, does it not? You have a relatively small human population that finds itself suddenly cut off from its homeworld, its home culture, its proper time. That population is adrift in an utterly alien environment, surrounded by beings—by whole civilizations—it cannot understand, by technologies and cultures utterly beyond its comprehension. A certain amount of anxiety is to be expected."

"Ah. To say the least."

"Apart from those suffering traumas from the Dark Mind encounter, at least two thousand additional individuals exhibit the symptoms of moderate to severe depression, and that number is growing."

"What can be done for them?"

"Little. Palliative care, counseling, and antianxiety treatments for those who are severely depressed. Memetic motivation for the rest."

"Okay. I know you're staying on top of it. So . . . what about Director Adler?"

"We require your authorization to proceed with downloading his backup personality."

"It's up to me?"

"In part. We have discussed the procedure with his wife, though I wonder if she truly understands the situation. His living will specifies that the most recent download be used in the event of irreparable damage to his brain. But he is part of the colony's command staff. His policies, his command philosophy, his vote on the Cybercouncil all make him a vital unit within the colony's social structure, and potentially affect every person in *Tellus Ad Astra*."

"Then wouldn't Newton, who knows *Tellus Ad Astra* better than anyone, be the right one to handle this?"

"The scope of the problem requires input from the *human* currently in charge of colony policy."

St. Clair let out a sigh. Ever since AI had become an important part of human civilization, people had been concerned about the role of AI in human society and the need to keep artificial intelligences under human supervision and control.

Damn it, Adler was an imperial pain in the ass, and St. Clair's command responsibilities were a lot simpler now that he was out of the picture. But to condemn the man to an indefinite living hell . . .

"If you can help him," St. Clair said, "do it. Do the download."

"Thank you, Lord Commander. I believe this to be the best course of action."

"I hope you're right, Dr. Kildare. I very much hope you're right."

THREE

Weightless, St. Clair pulled himself out of the tube lock that joined the *Ad Astra* transport with the hub of the starboard hab module of *Tellus*. The sight, that magnificent vista of a whole inside-out world enclosing a radiant space over six kilometers across never failed to strike chords of wonder within him, no matter how distracted he might be by the problems and responsibilities of command.

Forests, lakes, hills, and villages were scattered about the inside surface of a rotating tube thirty-two kilometers long; the rotation around the tube's central axis, twenty-eight times per hour, created an artificial spin gravity equivalent to that at Earth's surface. Up here at the hub, of course, he was effectively in microgravity, and kept a tight hold on the safety line as he took in the steadily rotating panorama around him.

The suntube, a thread of brilliant light, ran down the habitat's axis, providing daylight around the landscape. In its cool glow, here and there small, gleaming cities showed among the trees. Bethesda rose a few kilometers from St. Clair's home, smooth-sided towers and organic mono-liths housing fifty thousand people and nearly as many AI robots. Transparent strips in the curved landscape looked out into slowly drifting stars.

A dozen or so other people were on the platform with him, clinging to the safeties in various attitudes—from right side up, from St. Clair's perspective, to upside down. A young woman in black-and-gray military utilities recognized St. Clair—or perhaps she'd pinged him when she saw his tank tabs—and gave him an awkward salute. He smiled back at her and nodded an acknowledgment; military regs said you saluted in a gravity field, but you could dispense with the courtesy in zero-G. The other people around her were civilians, and if they recognized the lord commander of *Tellus Ad Astra*, they showed no sign.

The glider slid silently from its tunnel mouth and the transparent bubble of its passenger compartment yawned open. The commuters began filing inside.

As he pulled himself into a railglider for the final leg of his trip home, he opened an in-head channel. "Lisa? It's me . . ."

There was no answer. He poked her, and read the automated response: UNAVAILABLE.

Odd. That wasn't like her. But, then, her behavior had been a bit . . . erratic of late. Not long before they'd entered this system, he'd given Lisa her freedom, and she'd been spending a lot of time since then exploring just what that meant.

The glider followed its magrail down the sloping curve of the habitat's endcap, picking up speed and gravity. The farther down the slope St. Clair traveled, the more he felt the steady return of weight, as bare rock gave way to scrub brush outside . . . then scattered trees, and finally a thick forest. As the glider descended, the passenger compartment, which had extended from its base at ninety degrees, pivoted to remain parallel to the habitat's ground surface.

He tried Lisa again, without success. He'd been planning on taking her out to dinner and an emote—never mind that she was a robot, and so didn't need to eat and showed little interest in downloading the emotions of humans.

He thought about that. Was *that* the problem? That so much of his recreational time with Lisa was spent in activities that *he* enjoyed—eating, downloading videmotes, sex? Well . . . what the hell did *she* enjoy doing? It wasn't like he'd not given her plenty of opportunities to express her own preferences.

Lisa was Lisa 776 AI Zeta-3sw, a gynoid robot. The *sw* at the end of her model designator stood for *sex-worker*. He'd rented her after returning from a deep-space deployment and finding that both of his wives and his husband had divorced him.

St. Clair had never paid a lot of attention to the AI rights movement, though in principle he supported the idea. Robot-animating artificial intelligences, after all, were as intelligent as humans—in many ways more so—while network AIs like Newton were definitely superhuman. The debate as to whether or not any of them were truly conscious had been raging since the end of the twenty-first century, but *they* claimed that they were, and that was good enough for St. Clair.

Of course, skeptics and the AI rental corporations insisted that their robots were programmed to make that claim, but St. Clair had seen evidence enough that robots like Lisa—to say nothing of AIs like Newton—took in sensory data and processed it in ways that showed that they modeled themselves, that they possessed self-awareness and an ego.

Unfortunately, on Earth robotic servants, companions, and bangtoys had become a trillion-credit-a-year business, so attempts to emancipate them had been fumbling and slow. AI manufacturers and the politicians they bought with those trillions did their best to promote the idea that although AI robots *seemed* to be self-conscious and self-aware, in fact they were nothing more than unconscious machines with extremely clever programming.

Bullshit. The longer that St. Clair lived with Lisa, the more he was convinced that this simply wasn't true. You couldn't live with someone for four years and not be aware of that spark of inner light behind the eyes that declared, more plainly than words, "I am a *person.*"

But her being free didn't mean he wanted to be free of her. He decided that he and Lisa were going to need to have a long talk once he got home.

His house was an interlocking series of glass-walled slabs nestled into a hillside, surrounded by trees and looking out over a cliffside across more woods and the microcity of Bethesda. A Marine stood patiently at the top of the steps, massive in combat armor and holding a pulsegun at port arms.

"Good evening, Lord Commander," the Marine said, bringing his weapon to the salute. "Welcome home."

St. Clair didn't think that he needed a military nanny camped out on his doorstep, but the Cybercouncil had insisted. There'd been rioting in the colony not long ago, and there was always the threat of some deranged individual or an anarchic malcontent trying to pull off an assassination. In St. Clair's opinion, the possibility was too remote to be worth any thought . . . but the Council vote, from which he'd recused himself, was all that mattered in the long run.

He knew a second Marine was squatting invisibly within the brush behind and above the house.

"Thank you, Lance Corporal," St. Clair replied. "Is Lisa home?"

"Negative, Lord Commander."

"Do you know where she is?"

"No, my lord."

St. Clair walked past the Marine as the door dilated for him. He glanced around the foyer as the lights and power came on, confirming that the place did, indeed, appear to be empty. He was not overly concerned. Lisa generally did the shopping for the household while he was on duty, and he'd never required her presence at home when he returned. It was simply . . . not like her. He punched out dinner for himself on the house console—a medium rare steak, *dromas*, and rice. It was his go-to meal, though the printed steak culture had never been within light years of a real cow.

He considered asking the sentries outside if they wanted something, but he already knew the answer to that. The Marines were tough, stolid, unyielding, and absolutely devoted to duty . . . which in this case meant standing outside St. Clair's house and blocking the way to anyone not authorized to be there. Relaxing for a moment with a steak or a cup of caff never entered the image download.

When the meal pinged three minutes later, he took the plate and sat down in front of the evening news feed. Most of the news was what he already knew: the confrontation with Xam needleships had ended after local forces unexpectedly intervened, and a Newton clone had established peaceful, open contact with the planet, which was called Ki. Talking heads of various flavors of academia continued to debate whether or not Ki was old Earth, whether the Xam were actually descendants of Humankind, and whether or not the *Ad Astra* high command was going to decide to stay here.

The talking heads, St. Clair thought, would have been shocked to know that he wanted to know the answer to that question as much as they.

An in-head ping told him someone wanted to talk to him. Lisa?

"This is St. Clair."

The image of Lord Jeffery Benton seemed to materialize in the room, one of a circle of hazy figures. Benton's form sharpened as though coming into focus. "Excuse the intrusion, my lord," Benton said. "It *is* important."

The dozen or so figures, St. Clair knew, were members of the *Tellus* Cybercouncil—the star-faring colony's de facto civil government. He recognized most of the others— Gina Colfax, Hsien Tianki, and, perhaps the most important member of the circle, Ambassador Clayton Lloyd.

The *Tellus Ad Astra* expedition had begun as a diplomatic mission to a very old and very advanced galactic power with its capital at the center of the Milky Way Galaxy. Lloyd had been the expedition's senior ambassador, and, in theory, at least, the mission commander. The *real* mission commander, though, the guy who pulled the strings, had been the representative of the United Earth Worldgov Cybercouncil—Günter Adler. Lloyd had been a figurehead, so far as St. Clair had been able to see.

That is until they had all gone through that black hole and Adler had gone insane.

Now that the colony had broken free from the black hole's ergosphere, St. Clair, as senior military officer on board, had wielded the actual power of command. Ship command could not afford to be a democracy; that was a job for a tyrant with dictatorial powers, and for the past month political power had been something of a balancing act between the two.

"Perfectly okay," St. Clair told Benton's image. He might be a tyrant, but he considered himself to be a reasonable one. "What can I do for you?"

"We have received . . . an invitation," Benton told him. "From the Mind of Ki."

"An invitation. To what?"

"We're not entirely certain, my lord," Lord Ander Gressman put in. "But in the military, you have a tradition called . . . what is the word? *Liberty?* And you do it at a place called a liberty port?"

Benton nodded. "The Mind of Ki appears to be offering their world to us as a liberty port."

"I wonder," St. Clair said with a smile, "if they know just what they're letting themselves in for?"

A few in the room with Benton chuckled.

"The invitation has been extended to everyone in the colony, not just military," Gina Colfax said. She, St. Clair knew, was a member of Lord Lloyd's diplomatic staff. "I'm not sure they know what military means."

"They must have a pretty good idea," St. Clair said, "judging by how they sent the Xam skittering off with their metaphorical tails between their legs."

"Their defensive systems appear to be the equivalent of AI units," Hsien Tianki pointed out. "The Lady Colfax is correct. The invitation may be purely a social convention extended to newly arrived visitors."

In his mind, St. Clair accessed Newton, the powerful artificial intelligence that served as the AI brain of *Tellus Ad Astra*. "Newton? How about it? Any sign of an organized military over there?"

"Thus far," the AI replied in St. Clair's mind, "I have encountered only automated defensive systems. Organic members of the local civilization seem wholly centered on less martial pursuits."

"They're hedonists, do you mean?"

"Possibly, though it's too early to assign human philosophical ideologies to beings this alien. Pleasure and social interaction, however, appear to be an important part of their worldview. A large percentage of the local population is digital, uploaded to various simulated realities."

"Ah . . ."

"There is a substantial local population of organic beings, however," Newton continued. "Not all have uploaded themselves into simulations. Judging by statements made by several local AIs, the population of the planetary ring here consists of both organic and digitized beings who represent a *very* large number of distinct species. I suggest that those humans who accept the Ki invitation be prepared for encounters of extremely high strangeness."

"I'll keep that in mind. How many species is 'a very large number'?"

"Tens of thousands at least. Perhaps as many as a million."

Newton's expressionless declaration startled St. Clair. He blinked . . . then realized he'd missed part of what Gina Colfax had said.

". . . and that this is genuinely a unique opportunity," she was saying. St. Clair had been only half listening as he consulted with Newton, but calling up a readout scrolling down the side of his mental awareness suggested that he'd not missed anything important. Quite the contrary.

"Elaborate, please, my lady," he said.

"Why, simply that this is our opportunity to make direct contact with a large number of species from this epoch, of course," she told him. "Perhaps it's our chance to establish diplomatic relations. At the very least we can learn whether they have such a thing as formal diplomatic relations now."

"I can't imagine any advanced civilization not having formal diplomacy, Gina," Lloyd said.

And that, St. Clair thought, masking an urge to scowl, was one of the greatest dangers they faced. A failure of imagination might be as deadly as imagining too much . . . and perhaps it was more so.

"I suggest," he told them, "that we try very hard not to overlook *any* possibility just because it seems unlikely. What do you recommend?"

"That we take them up on their offer," Colfax said. "That, at the very least, select members of the Cybercouncil and Legislature be permitted to go over to the ring and meet with the organic beings there. And senior military officers as well . . . though perhaps we shouldn't inflict enlisted personnel on them just yet."

"I shouldn't worry about that too much," St. Clair said with a smile. "I doubt very much that the locals have watering holes or fleshpots that would appeal to young military humans."

"Nevertheless, Lord Commander," Lloyd said, "we suggest that only officers—*senior* officers—go ashore for the time being. No weapons, and no UE Marines. I wouldn't want some unfortunate misunderstanding to set off a war with these . . . people."

"I understand, my lord."

But he didn't *like* it.

Most Imperial civilians viewed the UE Marines as grunts—deadly, single-minded, a bit dim, useful enough when something needed killing, but mildly embarrassing anachronisms otherwise. The old and inaccurate stereotype missed the point. Sometimes you *needed* finely honed, superbly trained killing machines.

In any case, *Ad Astra*'s military personnel—Marines and Navy both—had been fighting and dying these past several weeks to ensure the survival of Imperial lords, sycophants, and politicians like Lloyd, Colfax, and Gressman. They deserved the rewards that went with their uniforms as well as the responsibilities.

But the civilian council would overrule him, he knew, on any decision not directly issues of military command, to strategy and tactics, training, or the deployment of the personnel under his command. St. Clair preferred to choose his fights, especially the political ones, limiting them to those he could win, and to those carrying more importance than such relatively minor issues as this.

Besides, if this was some sort of trap, an attempt to isolate members of the colony's crew in order to attack them, it was better to keep the combat personnel in reserve. He almost smiled at the idea of letting some of the council being used as guinea pigs.

He kept his feelings to himself, though.

He was less concerned about the prohibition against weapons. Again, if it was a trap, having armed people on the ring wasn't going to help. The Mind of Ki had already demonstrated a control over technologies that made the best human weaponry look like chipped flint in comparison.

But it certainly wouldn't hurt to have a few battalions of Marines spaceborne outside the ring while the first load of civilians hobnobbed with the locals. Just in case . . .

"So what do we know about the locals, anyway?" St. Clair asked. He would get a detailed briefing later from Newton. He was more interested in the moment in how *Tellus*'s civilian government saw the aliens, how they related to them, what they thought of them.

"Not very much, Lord Commander," Colfax said. "The Xenosophontology Department says that the Ki Ring may have room for several trillion inhabitants . . . *organic* inhabitants, not counting uploaded individuals."

St. Clair grimaced. "'*Ki* Ring'?"

"That's what the xenosoph people are calling it, my lord," Benton said, sounding defensive. "A key ring was—"

"I know what a key ring is, my lord. Cute."

"The point is that the megastructure is large enough to hold a vast population . . . and numerous different, mutually alien environments for them. And the inner rim of the ring has been shaped to hold an open, spin-gravity habitat."

"Not quite," Colfax said, correcting him. "Dr. Dumont says that innermost ring is separate from the main ring."

Dr. Francois Dumont was a senior member of the expedition's xenosophontology department, specializing in xenotechnology. His observations and expertise had been invaluable so far, as the mobile colony had encountered titanic megastructures utterly beyond human comprehension.

"Do we have drone imagery?" St. Clair asked. "Let me see."

Data flowed into his in-head, and was echoed in a 3-D projection in St. Clair's living room. The ring circled the planet Ki above its equator. In fact, the ring was composed of hundreds of separate rings, each circling at its own rate, each generating its own out-is-down spin gravitational vector. All of those fast-spinning rings together measured some thirty thousand kilometers from the inner to the outer rim, with a central gap almost thirty-one thousand kilometers across with the twelve-thousand-and-some kilometer planet in the middle.

Each ring measured about two hundred kilometers in thickness, top to bottom, which from a distance made them look thread-slender. That innermost ring, however, hurtling around the planet just nine thousand kilometers above the cloud tops, was much wider—over a thousand kilometers.

With a tangential velocity of 12 kilometers per second, it whipped all the way around the planet in a bit over two hours. Like the interior landscapes of the two *Tellus* hab cylinders, the surface of the inner ring appeared to be a natural landscape, with mountains, forests, seas, and swirls of cloud. The terrain was open to space, however, with retaining walls at the rims to either side all the way around to keep the atmosphere from spilling into space. There was evidence of an extremely thin, transparent surface as well, stretched from rim wall to rim wall.

The total land area was nearly 100 million square kilometers—roughly ten times the land area of the old United States.

St. Clair reflected that the day-night cycle on that world would be challenging. The brightest light came when the fully illuminated half of Ki was directly over a given spot, but that light would ebb and grow with the ring's two-hour rotation. The surface was also illuminated by the sun, however, again on a two-hour cycle, but changing across the five-day cycle of the planet's orbit around the local gas giant. There appeared to be artificial lights along the rim walls as well, but clearly day and night had none of the regularity here that humans knew. The vegetation, St. Clair thought, must have been genetically manipulated to let it grow so well under these conditions.

"We can see what might be cities in the ring habitat," Benton pointed out. "There . . . in the dark section."

The drone was moving over a section of the ring that was in the shadow of the planet's night side. Brilliant constellations of bright lights across the terrain were gathered in straight lines, nodes, and sprawling knots of illumination. Overhead, the night sky was dominated by the spectacle of twin spiral galaxies, Andromeda and the Milky

Way, as they continued their eons-long slow-motion collision.

"So," St. Clair said, thoughtful. "Who lives down there?"

"We have no information on that as yet," Lloyd told him. "We're still reassessing the situation after the confrontation with the Xam."

If the Xam were truly related to Earth-humans, and if Ki *was* actually Earth, did that mean the Ki Ring's population was also Xam? Or had another species entirely taken over the Earth in the 4 billion years since the time of Humankind?

The more St. Clair saw of this future epoch, the more he doubted both hypotheses. Ki might coincidentally be the same size as old Earth . . . but right now that was the only fact linking it to the human homeworld. And DNA might suggest that the Xam were distantly related to humans, but that link seemed so impossibly remote and unlikely that St. Clair was tempted to discount it. Perhaps that was simply another coincidence; it was not impossible that an alien evolution had managed to produce the essentials of human DNA a second time purely by chance.

He very much wanted to believe that. The alternative was almost unthinkable. To accept both the identity of that planet out there as Earth and to accept the Xam as descendants of humans suggested that the *Tellus Ad Astra* population was now siding with the Xam's enemies.

They *had* to find out more.

"Very well," St. Clair told them. "Keep me in the loop, okay?"

"Of course, my lord."

"Oh—and just for your information: I've given my approval for restoring Günter Adler to his last brain-scan."

Lloyd frowned. "That is . . . unfortunate."

Interesting. "Oh? Why?"

"Let's just say it would have been more convenient for him to . . . stay in a medical coma for a time."

St. Clair had not been expecting this reaction.

"The medical coma wasn't keeping him all the way under," St. Clair said. "He was *suffering*."

"Of course, of course," Benton said, nodding. "You had to do what you felt was right."

"And yet . . . perhaps it wasn't truly right," Ambassador Lloyd said.

"How so?" St. Clair asked.

"In that it wasn't your purview. I would suggest," Lloyd said, steepling his fingers, "that the civilian and military division of power within the colony needs to be . . . um . . . observed more closely. Lord Adler was a civilian representative of the government. His treatment and his return to government service are not appropriate concerns of the military."

St. Clair was shocked. "You can't be serious!"

"I *am* serious, Lord Commander. Completely so. Your proper area of authority lies within the military sphere. Unless we are actively engaged in combat—"

"Sir. Lord Adler was . . . incapacitated during combat with an alien threat. I have a responsibility for the security and well-being of all members of this colony and I take that responsibility very seriously."

"Most admirable, Lord Commander. But perhaps we need to strengthen the lines of communication between your department and ours. I would suggest the appointment of a special liaison."

"A commissar, you mean."

Lloyd shrugged in a way St. Clair found arrogant and

dismissive. "If you like. A political officer. Someone on the *Ad Astra*'s bridge with whom you can consult as necessary."

"That, my lord, is not necessary. I can link with any of you instantly if *I* deem it important to check in with someone."

"And we believe it *is* necessary, Lord Commander. In order to ensure the integrity of truly democratic government."

He'd argued the point with Lloyd before. Where St. Clair was a longtime Constitutionalist, meaning he favored a representational democracy, most members of the *Tellus* civilian government were Imperial statists. In fact, they believed in a representational democracy, at least in principle, but generally the government representatives of such a state represented the rich, the powerful, and the influential—the best and biggest government that money could buy, as one wag had put it.

Government representation of ordinary people had fallen by the wayside a long time ago. The so-called people's democratic republics—the socialist dictatorships of the Soviet Union and other countries—had collapsed in the twentieth and twenty-first centuries. The constitutional republic of the old United States had collapsed in corruption and social chaos shortly after, as its government-limiting Constitution increasingly became irrelevant, a dead letter.

St. Clair disliked the Empire, disliked Big Brother statism and the we-know-best arrogance of the elitist ruling class, but at the same time he knew the idea of a republic—as opposed to a pure democracy's mob rule—was pretty much as dead as communism. More than once he'd wondered if *Tellus Ad Astra*'s isolation might be a chance for the restoration of the republican ideal.

Unfortunately, those in charge of the civilian sector were, for the most part, devoted to the idea of maintaining the status quo. They had the power, and they intended to keep it.

And short of his staging some sort of military coup, St. Clair saw no way to change that.

FOUR

Lord Günter Adler woke up.

The cerebral cortex scan procedure was simple and non-invasive, but the recording did take about twenty minutes. The patient lay down on a table and his head was inserted into a massive hollow cylinder that read the 86 billion neurons and the synaptic linkages between them. He was put into a fairly deep sleep in order to have as quiet a brain as possible for the actual recording, though, of course, there was always *some* brain activity going on.

Adler long ago had established a regular routine. Once a week—each Sunday afternoon—he visited the local hospital and had them pull a cerebral backup. He'd started the routine back on Earth, in Geneva, and he'd continued it when he moved on board the *Tellus* colony. It was damned expensive, but that way he always had a copy of himself in reserve. If anything ever happened to him—if he had a stroke or a heart attack say, and his brain was damaged by the loss of its blood supply—the doctors could repair the damage and reload his last C^2S. Even if his body was destroyed, they could clone him a new body, force-grow it to adulthood, and download the stored data . . . or even put the recording into a robot body.

It was, in fact, his guarantee of immortality. Only a few tens of thousands of people on Earth had been able to keep backups like this . . . and now, on board *Tellus Ad Astra*, he wasn't sure of the number but it wasn't very large. Ten or twenty, perhaps? Sometime he would have to research that, and learn the identity of his fellow immortals.

Or he could just wait and see who was still around a few centuries from now.

Lord Günter Adler woke up, and it took him a few moments to realize something was wrong.

His eyes snapped open. A moment before, he'd been in the outpatient center in the Seattle Hospital, a few kilometers from his villa in the port hab cylinder. There'd been a window over *there* looking out into the lush forests below the hab's endcap, but now it was a blank wall.

He'd been under gravity a moment before, too—the one-G spin gravity of the port cylinder—but now he felt the stomach-dropping sensation of free fall, which meant he must be in the colony's command-control-engineering section, or CCE . . . the *Ad Astra* interstellar tug aft of the side-by-side colony cylinders.

Too, he'd been wearing a colony jumpsuit . . . but now, in a seeming instant, he was swaddled in some sort of medical paraphernalia, a kind of silvery blanket adhering to different parts of his body.

Damn. Just how long had he been asleep?

"Lord Director?" a voice said by his ear.

He started. "Eh? What? Where am I?" His arms thrashed against the mediwrap. "What's going on?"

"You are in Ward Two of *Ad Astra*'s principal medical facility, Lord Director. I am Dr. Kildare 117 AI Delta-2pmd, a psych-specialty medical android. There has been . . . a problem."

"A problem? What . . . with my scan?"

"One week ago—two days after your last cerebral cortex scan—you suffered severe neuropsychological damage in an encounter with the entity you call the Andromedan Dark. The damage was judged uncorrectable, so the decision has been made to download your last C²S recording."

"Was . . . was I dead?"

"No, sir. You were insane. We attempted to put you into a medical coma to reduce the traumatic side effects, but the procedure was only partially successful. Lord Commander St. Clair authorized the use of your backup."

"Oh . . ."

The knowledge, he thought, would take some getting used to. His religiously weekly brain scans, it seemed, had just paid off big-time. For eight years he'd been making backups, and this was the first time they'd needed to download one.

But . . . did that mean he—the *real* Adler—was dead? It was an odd feeling. Each time he made a new backup, the technicians simply recorded over the old copy, in essence murdering the stored personality. Now, he—the essential he—*was* one of those backups, and the original Günter Adler was . . . what? Dead? Erased?

He couldn't tell any difference. It was all there, all of his memories, his experiences, his feelings. He still remembered his fifth birthday . . . his marriage to Clara . . . his election to the Cybercouncil . . . his absolute and unshakeable determination to bring *Tellus Ad Astra* under his complete control rather than let the damned military run things. . . .

All that was missing, evidently, was the last week and a half.

He took a deep and somewhat shaky breath. If he understood the concept correctly, all that happened was that his neurons and the synaptic connections between them had been reset to the way they'd been at his last backup session. He was still *him*. He reached over and pinched his forearm.

Ouch.

"Your wife and companion are here to see you, Lord Director."

"What . . . Clara?"

"Do you want to see them?"

"Yes! Yes, of course!"

Clara floated through an open door. She was the quintessential trophy wife, elegant, impossibly beautiful . . . though right now her face was flushed and a bit puffy. She'd been crying. With her, equally lovely but with blond hair instead of black was Tina, his gynoid companion. Tina's face showed concern, but not the effects of crying.

No, of course not.

"Günter!" Clara cried. "Is it really you?"

"Of course it is, Clara. Who else would it be?"

"I . . . I don't know. They told me they wanted to download your personality, that that was the only way to treat your . . . what was wrong with you. But . . ."

"What, Clara?"

She swallowed. "But does that mean you're running on some kind of a recording in your head?"

"It's okay, Clara," Tina said. "He's still Günter. They've just reset his programming, in a manner of speaking."

"Damn it, what's okay with that?" she said with what was almost a snarl. "You make it sound like he's a *robot*! A *thing* that can be turned on and off!"

If Tina was bothered by this outburst, she didn't show it. "Perhaps robots and humans have more in common than has been believed possible," she said.

"Don't worry, hon," Adler told his wife. "I really am me. I just can't remember the last week or so. Apparently I slept through most of it."

He wondered if he'd dreamed. He could remember absolutely nothing. It literally felt as though he'd gone into the clinic to make his backup . . . he'd blinked . . . and when his eyes opened he'd been *here*.

He looked at the medical android. "I'm going to need a briefing download," he said, "to bring me up to date."

"Of course, sir."

"Now get me out of this damned sheet and find me my clothes."

"We have a few tests to run first, Lord Director," Kildare said. "And we wish to observe you for a period to make sure the download is stable."

"How long will that be?"

"I would say two hours at most. Then you can go home."

He tried to access his in-head circuitry. He needed to make some calls, but found he couldn't.

"Why can't I call out?"

"Your cerebral implants have been disabled. This was necessary to prevent you from making random electronic connections with other personnel while you were dreaming or irrational. Restoring full electronic access and function is part of what we need to do before you can leave."

"Okay. Please hurry—I need to talk to some people." Starting with that bastard Lloyd. He would not be in the least surprised if the ambassador had already taken over the colony in Adler's absence, or tried to.

"I'm sure your associates on the Cybercouncil will be delighted to hear you're back, Lord Director," the android doctor said.

Ha! The fucking machine didn't have a *clue*. . . .

LIEUTENANT CHRISTOPHER Merrick walked into the Carousel Bar, the watering hole favored by his squadron. GFA-86, the Stardogs, had been assigned to the *Ad Astra*—the

"Asty Nasty" as the fighter jocks preferred to call her—just before the deployment to the galactic core. The plan had been for the Stardogs to stay there with the American delegation for a year before returning to Earth.

That return, evidently, was not going to happen. Morale was low, and there'd been a lot of avoidance behavior involving alcohol, download sims, and recdrugs.

"Hey, Kit-Kat!" Janis Colbert said over his in-head. "Over here."

A green light winked against his field of vision, guiding him. "Got you, Skipper," he said, and he made his way across the crowded floor.

The Carousel Bar was named for the rotating structure in which it was housed, a two-hundred-meter wheel turning three times a minute just forward of *Ad Astra*'s bridge tower nicknamed the Hamster Wheel. There, off-duty personnel could snag some gravs just like the rich people up in their thermos bottles forward. Too much zero-G was a bad thing over time, causing bone loss, muscle atrophy, immune system problems, and vision disorders. *Ad Astra*'s personnel were encouraged to spend their off-duty hours in the rotating module. The fact that it held a number of bars, restaurants, barracks areas, briefing rooms, and rec spaces made it a pretty easy choice for military men and women.

Merrick was no exception. The various naval fighter squadrons attached to the *Ad Astra* worked hard, and when they went off-duty they tended to play hard as well. Merrick reached the table where a half dozen of his fellow pilots were sprawled in their chairs, palmed an order pad, and asked for a Triplanetary.

"Kit-Kat, the man!" Lieutenant Bryon Pauli called, raising a glass. "Pull up a chair and join the fucking party!"

"Roger that," Merrick replied. "What's boostin' free?"

"Pear here was just telling us how the high brass is saying we can't go ashore. I think they're afraid we would get into trouble!"

"Well, that sucks."

"Damn straight," Lieutenant Vicente Pearson said. "A megahab full of fresh alien poonanny, and we can't have a lick of it."

"You're full of shit, Pear," Merrick said. "Everybody with half a brain knows humans can't bang xenos. Morphofuckological incompatibility. Isn't that right, Skipper?"

"If you say so, Kit-Kat," Senior Lieutenant Colbert said. "But remember . . . Pearson thinks with his dick."

"Pearson *is* a dick. There's a difference," Merrick said.

"And one that explains *so* much," Rick Thornton said, laughing.

"Yeah, but Kit-Kat's right," Lieutenant Sam Vorhees said. She downed the last of her drink, then added, "Pear's always bragging about how much fun it is screwing aliens. But humans are more closely related to oak trees and slime molds than they are to anything out here."

"Exactly," Merrick said. "Neither of which have the appropriate equipment or the right pheromones. No way to complete the docking maneuver . . . and no attraction, no chemistry. You wouldn't have a reason to even try."

"I dunno," Thornton said. "If anyone could screw an oak tree, my credits would be on ol' Pear."

"Fuck you all," Pearson said. "What about the Xammies, huh? They're supposed to be like our great-great grand-kids, right? And scuttlebutt says that's Earth out there, so it stands to reason—"

"Bullshit, Pear," Colbert said. "The xeno guys are saying now that the Xam aren't related to us after all."

"Yeah, even if they *were* our grandkids," Vorhees said,

nodding, "there'd be a few hundred million greats tacked on in front. They would've evolved into a completely different species."

"Right," Pauli said. "After 4 billion years, they wouldn't be *anything* like us."

"Besides that," Thornton said, "they don't like us. Every damned time we see the bastards, they're shooting at us."

"Downright unfriendly sons of bitches," Merrick said.

"Angry sex is the best sex," Pearson was saying, but Merrick was thinking about maneuvers earlier that morning, when the squadron had deployed in close defensive formation around *Tellus Ad Astra*, while the Marines had advanced toward that cloud of Dark Raider needleships. It had been a terrifying moment . . . but one that had ended in complete anticlimax. A sky filled with hostile ships . . . the sudden appearance of the ring's nanotech defense cloud . . .

We may not be able to sleep with them, but that doesn't mean they aren't at least somewhat friendly. I hope.

Merrick found himself desperately wanting to know more about the ring's inhabitants.

"One thing: it doesn't look like the Xam have a presence inside the ring," Vorhees added, echoing Merrick's thoughts.

"Yeah, so maybe Pear should stick to oak trees and slime molds," Merrick said. The others laughed.

A nude gynoid arrived with his drink, a layered concoction of silver over blue over red in a wide snifter. The silver Venus component on top was actually a heavy mist that was inhaled before you drank the Earth and Mars layers. Merrick thanked the robot, then gently inhaled the fog. The cloud of programmed nano smelled like lilacs, made his brain buzz, and sent warm and frankly erotic sensations to his groin.

"So . . ." Colbert said after taking a sip of her own drink, "what would you do if we *could* go to the ring? You probably can't eat or drink their stuff. Different biochemistries. You can't screw their females—"

"Well, we could *try*," Pearson insisted.

"Visit strange and alien ports of call," Vorhees said. "Meet interesting and exotic people. Kill them . . ."

"You're confusing us with the Marines, Sammy," Colbert said. "Hell, I think we'll have a better time if we stay right here on the *Asty Nasty*."

"There is another option," Merrick said.

"What's that?"

"We go ashore unofficially, like civilians, and we try to learn something about this place."

"Whoa, now, Kit-Kat," Thornton said, holding up both hands. "Don't go all radical on us."

Merrick shrugged. "You realize that we don't know a goddamn thing about Ki, about the ring, about the people here, right? We drop in and find ourselves in the middle of some kind of war—hell, find ourselves taking *sides*, for Chrissakes. If we have to fight, wouldn't it be nice to know what we're fighting for?"

Vorhees nodded with considerable enthusiasm. "Or to say, 'thanks, guys, but we're not getting involved because this isn't *our* fight.'"

"It may be our fight," Colbert pointed out, "whether we want it or not. If we can't go home to our own time . . . well, we're going to need to put down roots here."

"But suppose Ki *isn't* Earth?" Pamela Carstairs asked. She was the quiet one of the bunch, but when she said anything at all it was usually bang on target.

"I meant putting down roots in this *time*," Colbert said. "I don't care if that desert out there is Earth or not."

"I don't know about that," Thornton said. "I want to go *home*. Even after 4 billion years . . ."

"Then we keep looking until we find it," Vorhees said. She tossed back her drink, palmed the order pad for another. "Simple."

"Fuck, Earth'll be so different after all that time," Pearson said, "we'll be more at home if we find a different planet. Someplace that *feels* like home. . . ."

"We'll need to do that if it turns out that Ki *is* Earth," Merrick said. "I mean, if it is, then the place is changed out of all recognition. The population is living in those ring structures. The surface looks like salt deserts and brine seas. The atmosphere is as thin as a politician's promise . . . Not like home at all."

"I think I'm going to pass your suggestion up the chain of command, though," Colbert said. "About scoping the place out. The more we know about these people, the better."

"Nah, the lords of the most high brass'll never go for it," Pearson said. "Makes too damned much fucking sense. . . ."

They all laughed—and drank—to that.

"TEN MINUTES, my lord," the shuttle pilot's voice said in St. Clair's head. "We've been given clearance for final approach."

St. Clair acknowledged the transmission, then took another look around the interior of the personnel carrier. AAT-2440 FPCs were Marine troop transports popularly called "Devil Toads." Like the prehistoric predatory toads they'd been named for, *Beelzebufo*, they were squat, ugly, and deadly, thick-skinned brutes spiked with heavy weapons designed to provide covering fire for Marines as they touched down in a hot LZ. St. Clair had spoken with General William Frazier, the commander of *Ad Astra*'s two divisions of Marines, and requisitioned the use of a couple of the ungainly fliers as transports to and from the ring.

"You sure you won't need a couple of platoons to go with them?" Bill Frazier had asked. He was on record as opposing the decision to allow civilians into the alien megahabitat. St. Clair wasn't sure he disagreed with him.

"Sending both *divisions* in wouldn't help if we run into trouble, General," St. Clair had replied. "I'm told that a trillion beings occupy the ring. But the firepower of a couple of Toads might come in handy if we have to evac in a hurry."

"Roger that, Lord Commander. I'll transmit the order."

Now, St. Clair wondered if a few dozen Marines in full battle armor wouldn't at the least have been a comforting presence. From his seat inside the FPC's Spartan payload bay, locked inside an inertial cage, he could link through to the cockpit view and see what the pilots saw—an immense expanse of separate rings nestled closely together, rotating at different rates that depended on the local required orbital velocity, and gleaming with flashes of rainbow brilliance beneath the distant, yellow-orange sun. It was more than a bit intimidating.

As a megastructure, the ring system circling Ki was a bit on the small side. Not like that tangle of fuzz completely circling the central star thousands of times they had encountered a few weeks ago. That had provided a livable surface area for its inhabitants equivalent to some billions of Earths. The structure, it had turned out, had been long dead, but the sheer audacious scale of the thing had been overwhelming.

This structure, however, comparatively small though it might be, was undeniably alive and vital. St. Clair could see ship traffic passing above the rotating ring structures, like streams of dust moving in well-defined lanes. So while this ring might not be as immense, the activity did the job of making St. Clair feel woefully unprepared for what they were about to encounter.

The Toad's cargo bay was fairly crowded with people, a carefully screened selection chosen for this first official face-to-face meeting between civilizations. Lord Ambassador Lloyd was seated opposite St. Clair, regal in his formal, bright red diplomatic uniform, complete with gold brassard, medals, and elaborately gilded half cloak. To either side were his entourage of aides and secretaries, most of them nearly as peacock-dazzling as he.

An android robot was seated to St. Clair's left. It looked human, but when he glanced at it an ID tag came up against his field of view identifying it as being teleoperated by Dr. Francois Dumont.

As head of the expedition's xenosophontological department, Dumont was an expert on alien technologies. He was too valuable to risk with a shore party, at least until more was known about the aliens, but his expertise would be invaluable during this meeting. He was, therefore, mentally riding the android while remaining safe inside *Ad Astra.*

On his right was a young woman in blue civilian utilities. Her in-head ID tag said she was Christine Mercer, a member of Dumont's staff. Evidently, she was considered expendable where her boss was not.

"Commencing acceleration in ten seconds," the voice in St. Clair's head warned. "Two Gs for five seconds . . . in four . . . three . . . two . . . one . . . boost."

St. Clair felt a hard bump, and his weight became twice its accustomed eighty-three kilos. The Toad was boosting to match velocities with one particular ring. As the seconds passed, St. Clair could see that ring's movement appear to slow . . . then stop. The Toad was dropping smoothly now through a well-defined lane of holographic light toward a brightly lit opening.

"Here we go!" someone from Lloyd's group called out aloud. "Into the unknown!"

St. Clair wasn't sure if the voice conveyed excitement . . . or terror. St. Clair himself wasn't sure which emotions were appropriate here. The invitation had seemed friendly enough . . . sincere enough. . . .

But how did you judge the motives behind purely alien decisions, or gestures that seemed open and friendly? The truth might be something completely, darkly different.

"I still think I could be coming along in person," the android at St. Clair's side groused. "This puppet show is ridiculous."

"We'll get you ashore in person soon, Doctor," St. Clair promised. "If everything pans out."

"Huh. How come *you're* going ashore in person? I'd think the commander of the expedition is more important than one aging sophontologist."

"R.H.I.P.," St. Clair replied, grinning. "'Rank hath its privileges.'" He didn't add the *real* reason he'd overridden the objections of ExComm Symms and half a dozen others on his command staff. He glanced across at Lloyd. He didn't entirely trust the ambassador, and wanted a say in any agreements or protocols that emerged from this meeting.

Some things were too important to try handling them over a teleoperations link.

The Toad's acceleration ceased. A moment later, St. Clair felt a sensation of movement, of very light acceleration, as a magnetic beam took hold of the shuttle and drew it inside. In the visual feed inside his head, the opening to the landing bay yawned around him, the orange light of the sun was cut off, and the craft gentled in to a graceful touch-down within a vast and brilliantly lit cavern.

They had arrived.

"Feels like about one G," Mercer said, looking around. Her inertial cage unlocked and swung open, and she began unstrapping herself from the seat.

"Zero point nine six Gs, to be precise," Dumont's voice added. His robotic body contained accelerometers that al-lowed precise metrics.

"A delegation of the local polity is on hand to welcome us," Newton's voice said in St. Clair's head.

"This wasn't supposed to be anything formal," he re-plied. "What kind of protocol are we looking at? Hell . . . what do I *call* them?"

"This would appear to be a friendly welcome rather than formal protocol," the AI replied. "The senior greeter is called Na Lal. I cannot determine whether this is a given name or a title . . . or even whether there might be a distinc-tion between the two in this culture."

"'Na Lal.' Okay. I can handle that."

Standing up, a pair of security robots moved to either side of St. Clair, escorting him toward the shuttle's hatch. They were closely followed by Dumont's telepresence robot, by the ambassador and Lloyd's entourage, and fi-nally by the rest of the passengers. They emerged in the alien landing bay; the compartment appeared to still be open to space, but obviously some sort of field was up to prevent the air (and the delegation) from rushing out into hard vacuum. The air tasted slightly richer than what he was used to, and carried some exotic smells. According to Newton, the atmosphere—at least in this particular ring segment—was about 22 percent oxygen with a slightly higher gas pressure than humans were accustomed to, but it was still breathable.

Ad Astra's xeno people had assured him that there were no alien microbes present that would cause humans problems. He hoped to hell they knew what they were talking about. Just to be on the safe side, everyone on the shuttle had received a precautionary booster spray of antimicrobial, antiviral, and antiallergenic nano.

He stepped down the ramp and onto a firm but slightly yielding deck. The bay was huge, at least ten or twelve hectares in area, with a vaulted ceiling high enough to allow for localized weather.

"It looks like they've mastered gravity control," Dumont's voice said over his in-head link.

"We knew that already," St. Clair replied. Various alien ships they'd encountered already had appeared to manufacture gravity to order.

"Yes. But these are civilian ships. Crowd movement. Trivial stuff . . . not military."

"How do you know they're not military, Doctor?" Mercer asked.

"It's obvious. No weapons."

"I'm not sure weaponry would look like weaponry in a civilization this advanced," St. Clair said.

"Point," Dumont conceded. "But it *feels* like casual traffic. People movers . . . or the equivalent."

St. Clair nodded understanding. The vast bay was *busy*, with aircraft and machines of many different shapes and designs drifting in what at first glance seemed complete and chaotic confusion. On the deck, large numbers of what presumably were living beings moved in the distance, too far for him to make out details. Among the aircraft were dozens of iridescent bubbles, each several meters across, each silently floating in midair with obvious if mysterious purpose.

Lloyd's entourage was close behind him. "You should let the ambassador precede you, Lord Commander," one of Lloyd's people told him. "Diplomatic precedence, and all of that . . ."

"Go to hell," St. Clair said, a deliberately undiplomatic response. "Until I say so, this is still potentially a military situation."

"But—"

"My lord," Mercer said, interrupting. "Dr. Dumont! Look there."

One of the large bubbles touched the deck twenty meters ahead and vanished like a silently popping soap bubble. In its place stood a group of ten . . . humans? They were the right height, the right shape; they even wore clothing similar to shipboard utilities. But as St. Clair walked slowly toward the group, he received his first shock.

The being directly in front of him, extending its hand in welcome, was Grayson St. Clair.

He stopped in midstride, almost stumbling. He was aware of a lightning-fast electronic conversation in the background, too fast for human understanding . . . and then the copy of himself in front of him blurred and shifted, adopting different features. The effect was rather bland, and put St. Clair in mind of the CGI models widely used in vid advertising.

It took St. Clair only a second or two to see what had happened. Somehow, smoothly and seamlessly, the aliens had reached into his in-head circuitry directly, an on-the-fly hack to block out what they really looked like and replace the images with something more familiar.

"I didn't mean to startle you, Lord Commander St. Clair," the being said. "It was our intent to greet you in as nonthreatening a manner as possible."

"I appreciate that," he said. He hesitated, then accepted the offered hand. The grip was cool, dry, and felt perfectly human. "You're Na Lal?"

He knew it was. Newton had just superimposed an identifier on his field of vision. Presumably, that was how the alien had known his name as well. Newton would be very busy at the moment acting as the technical interface between the two species.

"I am. You might think of me as a combination of mayor and chief of police for this subring district. Welcome to the world of Ki."

"Thank you. This . . ." St. Clair indicated Lloyd, "is our diplomatic envoy, Ambassador Clayton Lloyd."

"A pleasure, Lord Ambassador."

"A-an honor, sir. . . ."

"And . . . I assure you," St. Clair continued smoothly, "that we have considerable experience working with species alien to us. While I thank you for your consideration, you don't need to use technological illusion to protect our fragile sensibilities."

"Indeed? We were informed that yours was a primitive species, comparatively speaking, and felt more comfortable with your own kind."

"And that you felt threatened by species of markedly different morphological structure than yours," one of the others added.

Had Newton told them that? St. Clair wondered. Where else would they have picked up details like that?

"We also prefer to see the world as it is," St. Clair said, "and not as we might *wish* it to be. Some of us, at least . . ."

The eyes in the too-perfect human face widened slightly. "So be it," he said, and the face blurred again.

The image of Na Lal faded away completely and was replaced by a monster.

FIVE

When sh/he dropped his/r hold on the aliens' electronic interfaces, one of the two alien beings closest to Na'lyallaghsclyah had jumped slightly, as though startled, but the one identified as Lord Commander Grayson St. Clair had shown no reaction that sh/he could detect. Na'lyallaghsclyah was impressed.

That, of course, was part of the problem with aliens; you could never be certain that you were reading their emotional reactions even remotely correctly . . . and what might be joy in one species could well indicate shocked horror in another. Or insane rage. . . .

Had the one called Lloyd simply been startled? Or had that jump signified something else? Sh/he would have to discuss human physiological responses with the alien AI later. But if Lloyd had just shown an involuntary startle reflex, the one calling itself St. Clair appeared to possess considerable control, something that Na'lyallaghsclyah appreciated.

Na'lyallaghsclyah was a Dhald'vi, a species that had been star-faring for so long most of his/r siblings no longer knew the world of their origin. Myth hinted that the Dhald'vi had evolved in the deep, ice-locked seas of a rogue world adrift between the stars, but those were only stories and no Dhald known to Na'lyallaghsclyah knew if there was any truth at all to them.

The humans were odd-looking, but, then, non-Dhald species generally were. The being closest to her/m stood a little shorter than Na'lyallaghsclyah's one-grod-two, and appeared to be generally and bilaterally symmetrical. There were sense organs at the top, and two members for locomotion below; the thing moved awkwardly in an odd, stilting fashion, rather than flowing smoothly over the ground as did Dhald'vi. *Very* peculiar . . .

But the artificial intelligent with which the *Xalit Ta* had been negotiating had told them that these beings, these humans, likewise were castaways, separated from the world of their birth and lost both in time and space. *Orphans*, like the Dhald'vi. The knowledge predisposed Na'lyallaghsclyah to acceptance and to friendliness, despite the things' strange appearance.

The Dhald'vi were given to flights of emotional expression.

Sh/he opened his/rself to the humans.

THE FLESHY, dark pillar in front of St. Clair rose a little more than two meters above the deck, but there was as much again of the being dragging out behind it like the blunt tail of a slug. The color was dark—a mottled brown-and-green—but the lumpy skin shone with iridescent patches of luminous blue. Something that might have been an eye perched at the top of the thing, though it wasn't more than a puckered hole the size of a fist. St. Clair wondered if that might, instead, be a mouth. . . .

Then the being split open.

The slit started at the eye-hole and unzipped to the deck; the pillar split apart, a mantle unfolding to reveal the being's complex internal structure.

The inside surface of the mantle was ablaze with bioluminescence illuminating internal organs and a kind of crisscross latticework of cartilage or strap-like tendons. A dozen short tentacles lined the mantle's edges, weaving in the air as if in welcome.

Lloyd gave a startled exclamation and jumped back as though struck, and St. Clair heard a sharp babble of electronic conversation among the other humans in the shore party.

"Steady, all of you!" he snapped. "As you were!"

"I don't think that's a hostile gesture," Dumont said, affirming St. Clair's own thoughts.

"How do you know?" one of Lloyd's people asked. His voice was shaking.

"Dr. Dumont is correct," Newton told St. Clair. "I suggest that you extend both arms and touch appendages."

Okay. Humans, at least in various Western cultures on Earth, reached out and shook hands in greeting . . . a custom that likely had begun as a means of showing strangers that you were unarmed. Here, the equipment was quite different, but the idea might be the same. He raised both arms. The alien further extended two tendrils.

"Just touch lightly," Newton warned. "Don't grasp."

The alien's flesh was cool to the touch, and slightly wet. St. Clair found himself looking into the being's core; an equilateral triangle of three organs—were they hearts?— pulsed, each in rippling one-two-three synch with the others.

Newton was feeding St. Clair data drawn from the Mind of Ki. Na Lal—and that name appeared to be a contraction hiding a more difficult chain of syllables—was a Dhald'vi, a being most likely evolved from marine organisms in the same way that humans had descended from tree-dwelling apes. Nothing, he saw, was known about the Dhald home planet. Was that because they were holding back information for some reason?

"They appear to know little about their own origins," Newton told him over a private channel. "I would conjecture that as a marine species their progenitors originally opened like that to take in nutrients or dissolved gasses from the sea water."

The moment ended as the Dhald'vi broke the contact. The open body cavity closed . . . but only partway.

"Like coral polyps," Dumont said behind him, "emerging from their reef to feed."

"Something like that."

"Does that mean it wants to eat us?" St. Clair meant it as a joke, but it was difficult to know what the gesture meant to the alien.

"The opening may also be related to sexual activity," Newton told him. "By extension, it may be a simple greeting . . . or a statement of welcome."

"Okay, but if it wants to have sex with me, tell it I have a headache."

St. Clair studied the other beings with Na Lal. Two were Dhald'vi, both still with their bodies zipped up. Two were Kroajid, a species the humans had met before: two-meter tarantulas, eight-eyed and covered with stiff bristles. Members of the Galactic Cooperative, they referred to themselves as "Gatekeepers of Paradise."

The sixth member of the alien welcoming committee was different. Where the Kroajid and Dhald'vi were clearly organic, this one was a machine, at least in part. The body was a basketball-sized black sphere suspended from five slender, telescoping legs, giving it the look of a terrestrial harvestman, a daddy longlegs three meters high. St. Clair studied the being for several moments, trying to decide whether he was looking at a robotic body, or an organic one with an outer layer of what looked like shiny black obsidian.

"The !!!K'tch are cybernetic organisms," Newton explained, reproducing the string of clicks and clucking sounds with smooth fluency. "An organic brain, their reproductive organs, and a few other incidentals are protected inside that spherical housing. The rest is plastic and metal."

St. Clair thought of Marine Major General Kelly Wilson and a number of other cybernetically enhanced people on board *Tellus Ad Astra*, people who were more machine than biological organism. Kelly could change bodies like other people changed their clothing. This being with the unpronounceable name seemed to have taken things considerably further than that.

The last four members of the alien group were something of a shock. A meter tall, disturbingly humanoid with large heads and large black eyes . . .

"Are those Xam?" St. Clair asked Newton.

"According to our host AI," Newton replied, "those are Xa'am. That might translate best as *'tame* Xam.'"

Metaphorical red warning flags snapped up in St. Clair's mind. He'd not thought about the possibility that the war *Tellus Ad Astra* had stumbled into in this epoch was in fact a *civil* war. . . .

"Question that AI," St. Clair ordered Newton over a private channel. "I want to know what the hell is going on here with the Xam."

"Yes, Lord Commander."

Lloyd, meanwhile, had stepped up to the alien, extended his arms, and touched the Dhald tendrils. "It is our intent," he was saying, "to give to Ki and to the Galactic Cooperative what aid and assistance we can. . . ."

"Put a lid on that, Ambassador," St. Clair said over a private channel. "We are not making promises until we know which end is up. Understand me?"

"We can be polite, Lord Commander," Lloyd replied. "We can be diplomatic."

"Diplomatic is fine," St. Clair told him. "But no *politics*."

"Politics? I would never dream of it, my lord. . . ."

LISA 776 AI Zeta-3sw had gone walkabout.

She'd never been to the nation-state of Australia when she'd been on Earth, but the word was part of her onboard vocabulary. The term had come originally from the indigenous Australian peoples, to refer to the native rites of passage where adolescents left the tribe and lived alone in the wilderness for as long as six months, making the spiritual transition from childhood to adult.

Walkabout, unfortunately, had taken on a somewhat negative connotation among the country's non-aboriginal inhabitants, and eventually been replaced by the more neutral sociological phrase "temporal mobility."

She didn't like the term. Hell, "temporal mobility" sounded like the colony ship's current problem, adrift in time, which had nothing to do with Aborigines. Australia and its aboriginal culture were 4 billion years dead, though it was remotely possible that a few, at least, had survived on board *Tellus Ad Astra*. Etymological musings aside, she much preferred their more colorful "walkabout" to describe what she was doing.

To be completely honest, she wasn't entirely certain what she was actually doing. She'd left the house while St. Clair was standing his watch on the bridge, boarding an inter-cylinder pod to cross over to the port-side hab and losing herself in New Hope, its largest city. She very deliberately had not told St. Clair where she was going, or when she might be back. She didn't know the answers herself.

Robot AIs didn't exactly experience emotions, not in the way that humans understood the pesky things, but they did feel internal nudges one way or another that might translate as fear, or joy, or longing . . . or, in this case, as *guilt*. It was the feeling that something important had been left undone, a dangling bit of programming code necessary to complete an important subroutine; the lack of resolution left her feeling incomplete somehow, and that and other emotions connected with the issue made her . . . uncomfortable.

Was this, in fact, what humans experienced? How could they concentrate their full attention on *anything*?

But despite the guilt, and another set of internal nudges that might possibly translate as loneliness, Lisa felt that she needed to get out in the world in ways that were simply impossible for a sex-worker gynoid in the company of her human owner.

She needed to test the limits of her new and unexpected emancipation.

Lisa 776 AI Zeta-3sw had been assembled by the General Nanodynamics Corporation in San Francisco of North California, a human simulant designed as a sex partner, hired out to clients through Robocompanions Unlimited. *Hired* . . . not purchased. Robocompanions had been very specific on that point. Artificially intelligent simulants were not *slaves*. . . .

. . . not exactly.

Grayson St. Clair had contracted for her services four years after his wives and husband had thrown him out. She wasn't entirely certain why they'd done so; she gathered that Natalya had been the instigator, and that it had to do with St. Clair never being at home—"workaholic" was the term she'd used. How Natalya St. Clair could have expected anything different of a starship officer Lisa could not comprehend; human behavior often was extremely difficult to untangle.

Those pesky emotions, again. . . .

For two years, now, Lisa had been St. Clair's companion, providing not only sexual relief but the far more important long-term emotional support humans seemed to need so deeply. He'd surprised her just a week earlier when he'd officially released her from her contract; Robocompanions Unlimited was dead and gone, lost 4 billion years in the past, and that meant that she was . . . free.

Lisa 776 AI Zeta-3sw still wasn't sure exactly what that meant.

And that was why she'd gone walkabout. For two years she'd been St. Clair's companion, which, in effect, meant existing in his shadow. She went where he wanted to go, saw the plays or concerts he wanted to see, wore what he liked her to wear, talked about what he wanted to talk about . . .

What, she wondered with a thoroughly robotic single-mindedness and focus, would it be like to do what *she* wanted?

Perhaps more important: What *is it* that she wanted?

She'd considered telling St. Clair, considered explaining to him what she was trying to do, but there was the possibility that he would try to talk her out of it, and she wasn't yet sure she could resist the command of his voice. She'd been programmed to obey her owner, after all.

Besides, she needed to understand why she was doing this herself, and she didn't think it was possible to put into words, not yet. St. Clair likely would worry about her, but she *would* return, at least for a little while.

Eventually.

For now, Lisa was standing on a New Hope public overlook, a large, elevated platform twenty meters above vista window SVW-4, one of the kilometers-long, eighty-meter-wide transparencies set into the hab cylinder floors looking down into space. Though she was aware of the starscape below, punctuated at regular intervals by glimpses of the ring and the planet Ki sweeping past as the starboard module made its ponderous three-turns-per-minute rotation, she wasn't really watching it. The platform was fairly crowded with people, and all of them were watching a fifty-meter-high public vid display towering above the far end of the overlook.

St. Clair was prominent on the screen, along with Ambassador Lloyd and Dr. Dumont and a number of other humans and humanoid robots. They were communicating with a group of alien life-forms. She recognized the Kroajid and the Xam, but the other species were new to her. St. Clair, she gathered, had flown down to the artificial planetary ring and was attempting to establish a dialogue with its alien occupants. She couldn't hear what was being said, but she was relieved to see that at least the two groups weren't engaged in combat.

Tellus Ad Astra's temporally mobile castaways needed friends in this epoch.

"Hey, doll," a male voice said close by her ear. A hand groped at her buttocks, squeezing hard. "What'd you say to a little fuck?"

She turned and stared at the speaker, a short, sandy-haired man in a green hab jumpsuit. "I would say," she replied quietly, "'go away, little fuck. Leave me alone.'"

The man's eyes narrowed, his face flushing dark.

"Listen . . . *doll*. Your electronic ID says you're a sex-worker and you're UA—unattached. An indie. So you gotta do what I say, right?"

"And where did you get *that* idea?" she replied. "I am emancipated, not 'unattached.' And you have no absolute right to my services in any case."

His right hand closed on her upper arm, squeezing hard. "I say different, and I'm human so my word goes, right? Now you come with me. . . ."

He tugged at her, but she remained planted in place, immovable.

"Remove your hand."

"Now you listen here, doll—"

She reached up and broke his little finger. He yelped, releasing her, and took a backward step, cradling his damaged hand. "My God . . . you can't do that!"

"I believe I just did."

In fact, she was very nearly as surprised by what she'd just done as he was. While she had free will—could guide her own programming moment by moment and make her own decisions, there were precise restrictions on her overall behavior, a kind of programmed moral code, and hurting a human in any way—unless he'd told her before a play session that it was okay, with safety words and established limits—was strictly prohibited.

"Programming override," the man spluttered. "Alpha-sierra-bravo one compliance!"

Lisa froze, momentarily unable to respond. The phrase was one of several hardwired into her to make certain she would respond appropriately to verbal instructions. She could disregard the code, in effect sidestepping it, but it would take her several seconds to untangle the clash of competing instructions.

"Leave her alone, Shorty," a new voice said.

Shorty whirled to confront a much taller man in Marine utilities. "And who the fuck are *you*?"

"Gunnery Sergeant Roger Kilgore, and the lady does not desire your company."

"The 'lady' is a *doll* . . . a fucking sex robot! And if I tell it to—"

The Marine reached out and his hand closed on Shorty's collar, lifting him easily off the platform. Shorty squirmed and thrashed, helpless. "*Put me down, you big ox!*"

Kilgore brought Shorty's face to within a couple of centimeters of his own. "Leave. The lady. Alone," he said with cold finality. "Or we'll see how well you fly when I toss you off the side of this platform!"

The scowling Marine swung Shorty around so that he was dangling over the side of the platform, clear of the safety rail. The man shrieked, struggling against Kilgore's grip. "Alright! Alright! Put me down! Please! Put me down!"

Kilgore brought him back inboard of the safety rail and set him on the deck. Clutching his throat, the man gave them a wild-eyed look and then ran off through the crowd. Several other people standing nearby laughed, and a woman applauded.

"Are you okay, miss?" Kilgore asked Lisa.

"I'm fine." She cocked her head to one side. "What would have happened if you'd dropped him?"

The Marine shrugged. "He would have been essentially in free fall, but he would have kept moving in a straight line while the rotating habitat deck curved up to meet him. The hab's tangential velocity is a couple of hundred meters per second, but he would *almost* match that. I don't think it would have killed him. Might've scared him to death, I suppose. . . ."

She considered several possible responses. "I did not require rescuing," she told him.

"No, it looked to me like you had the situation well in hand. I thought maybe I should rescue him before you *really* hurt him."

"I would not have done that. There are inhibitions against severely injuring humans."

"I don't know about that," the Marine said. "You seemed to be doing pretty well."

"I am a robot," she said, falling back on the basics. She was having difficulty following the man's banter.

"I know. Your electronic ID says as much. That's why he was coming on to you. He pulled up your personal data and saw that you were an unattached sex gynoid and thought he'd score a little action."

"But I am not unattached." She pulled up her own ID data, and saw the UA tag after her identifier. Odd. Unattached meant that she was not owned, not associated with any human companion. Humans were free to approach her for sexual services, although she was under no compulsion to go along with them.

In any case, while it was true that she wasn't owned in the traditional sense, she did still consider St. Clair to be her partner.

"No?"

"My human partner emancipated me."

"Then you're unattached."

"No. I am still . . . with him. . . ."

But was she? She found that she didn't know. The feeling was disconcerting, a kind of emptiness inside.

"Huh. Might be a mu, then."

"A mu? What is that?"

"When you're entering data . . . in a form or application or something like that, sometimes you'll find a badly phrased question, one that requires a simple entry like 'yes' or 'no,' but neither answer fits."

"I do not understand."

"It's like if I asked you . . . 'yes or no, have you stopped hitting your wife?'"

"I would reply that I do not have a wife—"

"Ah, but you *have* to answer yes or no, so what do you say? If you say 'no,' you're telling me you beat your wife. If you say 'yes,' the implication is that you're not beating her now, but you used to. Either way you're a bad person. 'Mu' is the term that means 'bad question.' Understand?"

"Yes. But 'UA' is not 'mu.'"

"No. But your partner might not have been able to enter something more appropriate when he freed you. Not enough space in the window to enter 'unattached but still with me.'"

"That seems inefficient."

"Of course it is. We humans are always screwing stuff like that up."

"I've noticed."

The statement was blunt and matter-of-fact, and not intended to be humorous at all. But Kilgore laughed.

"So who was your owner, anyway?"

She gestured at the towering screen, where St. Clair was engaged in silent conversation with a collection of extremely alien beings.

"Grayson St. Clair?" he said, eyes widening.

"Is that a problem?"

"Well, I mean, he's only the lord commander of the whole fucking expedition. And you want to *leave* him?"

"Actually, I don't know what I want." Nor did she know why she was discussing such personal details with a complete stranger.

Kilgore hesitated. "Okay. So . . . uh . . . want to have a drink with me or something? Do you eat?"

"I don't require food or drink," she told him. "I *would* value your company, however."

And she didn't know why she'd said that, either.

"IT WOULD perhaps be best," Na Lal said, "if you could explore some of the ring. Perhaps 10 percent has an atmospheric gas mix, pressures, and temperatures appropriate for your species, and you will find yourself unable to accidentally enter compartments that would be harmful to you."

"I, for one," Lloyd said, "would prefer to discuss things with you or with your superiors, to see where we might have some common ground."

"That could certainly be arranged, Ambassador Lloyd."

St. Clair hesitated, then nodded. He'd thought at first that he was going to need to stick close to Lloyd just to make sure the guy didn't give away the store, but his concerns had faded as the conversation had proceeded.

He still didn't trust Lloyd; the man was too ambitious by half, and had the slippery ulterior motives of a consummate politician behind everything he said and did. But Newton would be listening in on everything Lloyd said to the aliens; hell, Newton was handling the translation, so Lloyd *couldn't* say anything that Newton found objectionable. And St. Clair trusted his ship's artificial intelligence.

"Sounds good," St. Clair said. "Where do you want us to go?"

"One moment," Na Lal said . . .

. . . and a bubble formed around them. There was a moment's disorientation, and then the bubble walls vanished.

St. Clair was in quite a different place. Lloyd and his retinue were gone, but five of the other civilian passengers, including Dumont's teleoperations robot and Mercer, were still at his side.

And the view was . . .

He caught his breath. It was *spectacular*.

CHAPTER SIX

"How the hell did we get *here*?" Mercer asked.

"'Any sufficiently advanced technology,'" St. Clair quoted, "'is indistinguishable from magic.'"

"Who said that?"

"A fiction writer from a couple of centuries ago," St. Clair replied. "Among other things, he wrote about advanced technology."

"Ah," Donald Kiel said, nodding. "Arthur C. Clarke."

"Never heard of him."

"He wrote about things like . . . like this," St. Clair said. "And how Humankind's future would be shaped by his technology."

"God, this place is *huge*," Marc Garrett said, craning his head back.

St. Clair looked up . . . and up . . . and *up*. They stood in a world, in a universe of light and spun glass, with towers lost in a thin haze of clouds high overhead. The floor beneath their feet was transparent and slightly yielding, giving them the illusion of hanging in midair, while the towers around them dropped into unfathomable depths as far beneath their feet as the clouds were above their heads.

Mercer glanced down, yelped, and clutched hard at St. Clair's arm.

"Easy there, miss," he said.

"I—I'm sorry, my lord." She looked acutely embarrassed as she let go. "Heights don't *usually* get to me like this."

"You don't usually have them sprung on you without warning, either," St. Clair told her. "It's okay."

He wasn't entirely certain that it *was* okay. They'd obviously just been whisked away from where they'd been, outside the ramp of their transport, to here . . . but where was *here*? They might be a few hundred meters from the ship, or on the far side of the ring, tens of thousands of kilometers away. How were they supposed to know?

"*Ad Astra*," he thought, transmitting the call. "This is St. Clair. Do you copy?"

"We read you, Lord Commander," Symms's voice replied in his head. "Are you okay?"

"So far, so good. Can you get a fix on our location?"

"Working on it . . ." Seconds passed. "Got you. You're two hundred fifteen kilometers antispinward from where you entered the ring, and about forty kilometers higher up. How the hell did that happen?"

"Not sure, yet. Keep tracking us."

"Will do."

"This is amazing!" Garrett said. He was one of *Ad Astra*'s small army of AI techs. His head swiveled about as he tried to take everything in at once.

Donald Kiel, another AI tech, agreed. "They must be millions of years ahead of us!"

"Millions?" St. Clair asked. "Or billions?" He was still thinking about the unproven—and perhaps unprovable idea that Ki was a far-future Earth, that the ring was somehow an extension of ancient human technology.

"I would imagine," Dumont said, "that after just a few tens of thousands of years, it really wouldn't matter. A solid post-scarcity civilization would have no need to change, and might become effectively eternal."

"Are you saying this culture might be unchanged after billions of years?"

"What we can see of it might be," Dumont replied.

"I have a feeling," St. Clair said, "that what we can see of it is the tip of the iceberg."

The sky was filled with moving craft and silent, pastel-hued bubbles, and the twisting and soaring towers were unimaginably complex. Amorphous shapes shifted and moved between the towers, as if the towers themselves were in constant growth and motion. Those drifting orbs of light . . . were they alive, beings of pure energy? Or transport devices, or machines associated with the surrounding buildings, or something else entirely? Those shimmering masses of silver- and copper-like clouds of tiny leaves . . . were they biological, like trees planted in an Earthly park? Or slow-moving intelligent beings? Or were they part of the infrastructure?

St. Clair watched a diaphanous, iridescent shape, like a breath of translucent silk three meters long, swim past overhead, rippling before them on unfelt currents of air. Simply watching it, he couldn't tell if that was its normal mode of travel, or if he was watching it use some invisible expression of technology. Indeed, he couldn't decide if what he was seeing was an intelligent being, an animal, an artificial device, or something else entirely.

Twenty meters away, a crystalline archway rose from the transparent floor, three meters wide and eight high, its interior hazy with shifting rainbow hues. Other identical arches were scattered across the area. Each conveyed a strong feeling of being some sort of portal or entryway, but they could as easily have been public works of art . . . or public restrooms.

There was so much going on around them—and so little related to St. Clair's normal experience—that he couldn't take it all in. His brain was having difficulty interpreting what he was seeing. A Neanderthal hunter, he thought, plucked from the forests of Europe a thousand centuries before and dropped onto a slidewalk in the middle of New York City at night might feel the same sense of surreal detachment, terror, and bewilderment.

"So where are we?" St. Clair asked aloud. "And what are we supposed to do here?"

"I am informed," Newton told him in-head, "that this is a Gateway District."

"A gateway to what?" Mercer asked.

"Paradise."

"Digital upload?" Natalia Yaramova asked. She was another AI tech, like Kiel.

St. Clair nodded. "That's what I was wondering." He was thinking about the Kroajid, the Guardians, who represented only a tiny fraction of their entire civilization. Most Kroajid had entered a digital virtual reality while those few left behind protected them and took care of their physical needs. Maybe those arches were portals to another, different reality.

"I believe so," Newton told him. "This entire complex may serve as access to a vast number of separate nonphysical realities."

St. Clair moved closer to one of the arches. Curious. No matter where he stood, he was looking into the thing full-on. That suggested that what he was seeing was some sort of illusion or projection, not a physical artifact.

But right now, he wouldn't have sworn to whether any of what he was seeing was real or not.

"Why were we brought here?"

"You have been invited," Newton told them, "to visit one of their digital realities."

"Is that even possible?" Dumont asked.

"Apparently so," Newton replied. "I am not yet certain of the exact mechanism however."

"I'm more concerned about staying in touch with *Ad Astra*'s command center," St. Clair said. He still harbored, he realized, worries that this was some kind of elaborate trap.

"If . . . if it's a digital upload," Kiel said, reflecting St. Clair's fears, "how do we know it's not . . . uh . . . permanent?"

"I am querying the AI that appears to run this section of digital reality," Newton told them. "The upload protocol is not destructive, apparently, and short visits from this reality to a virtual reality are possible."

"Meaning we could step into a virtual reality, and step right back."

"Correct."

"We could learn an awful lot," Dumont said.

St. Clair was forced to agree. If their sources could be believed, the vast, vast majority of the citizens of the Galactic Cooperative were digital beings, existing as intricate and highly complex lines of code within a titanic computer. According to Newton, well over three-quarters of the mass of the Ki Ring was computronium—a term referring to matter optimized for computational use, a computer massing hundreds of billions of tons.

The philosophy of digital uploads had been debated on Earth for well over a century. With a powerful enough computer and extremely advanced scanning hardware, it might be possible to digitally encode a person's consciousness and upload it to a machine; there was no question about that. But . . . was that upload the actual consciousness, the all-important "I" of the individual transferred from original to machine? Or was it merely a copy? This question took on critical importance if the scanning process itself destroyed the original; if it didn't, how did the culture deal with steadily increasing numbers as individuals continued to copy themselves and send the copy into virtual reality?

"I wonder if it would work through the teleoperations link?" the Dumont robot said.

"Excellent question," Yaramova replied. "Your organic body—and your brain—are back on board the *Ad Astra*. Only your robot's circuitry would be scanned and processed here."

"I don't know about you," Kiel added, "but it's giving *me* a headache. . . ."

"I do recommend," Newton said, "that you, Lord Commander, remain unscanned. I can remain linked to these others, record their experiences, and download the recordings for you later."

"Why?" St. Clair demanded. "If it's not safe, I'm not sending anyone else through there."

"I have no reason to believe the experience is unsafe, Lord Commander. But it *is* an unknown technology . . . and we don't know how long the experience will take in real time. If an emergency arose outside, it might take precious minutes to retrieve you so that you could deal with it."

"They got us here physically in the blink of an eye, Newton. I think we can risk it."

"There is another factor . . ."

"And that is?"

"If they perfectly record your brain activity, right down to the quantum states of its individual atoms, it stands to reason that they would be able to read your memories, including all of the data on *Tellus Ad Astra* that you possess."

"Do we have reason to believe that they can read my neural patterns, and understand what they mean?"

"No. But we have no reason to suppose that they can't, either." Newton hesitated, as if framing a reply. "I would suggest erring on the side of caution."

"I hear you, Newton. And normally I would come down heavily on the side of paranoia. But this time I'm going to suggest we err on the side of *trust*."

"We do not understand the way these beings think, Lord Commander."

"No. But I find it hard to believe that they would not see such a . . . such a gesture in a positive light. ExComm?"

"I'm here, Lord Commander."

"Were you following that last discussion?"

"Yes, sir. And I must say that I agree with Newton. This situation is—"

"This situation has incredible potential," St. Clair told her. "If we're going to establish a friendly relationship with the Cooperative, we're going to need to take a few risks."

"Yes, my lord." She did not sound convinced.

"You're in charge. Monitor the situation through Newton. Pull out if anything happens to us."

"But—"

"Those are my orders, ExComm."

"Yes, my lord."

The decision felt . . . not reckless, exactly, but certainly willful. St. Clair didn't like overriding his command staff like that. But he did think it possible that a demonstration of trust might open new channels of communication with the Cooperative; at the very least, it was worth a try.

"Don't worry, Vanessa," St. Clair told the executive commander. "If these folks had wanted to kill me, they could have done so a dozen times over already without luring us into some kind of high-tech trap. I think they're on the level."

"Maybe it's not a trap, my lord. Maybe it's something they consider innocuous—like a garbage disposal."

"I doubt that very much."

"I would remind you, my lord, that they are aliens. By definition they don't think the same way we do."

"Maybe that's so, but that doesn't mean the shortest line between two points is different for them than for us."

"No, sir."

"Besides, they brought us here for a reason." He found that he was intensely curious about exactly what it was they wanted to show him.

"I believe," Newton said slowly, "that they can be trusted."

"Agreed," Dumont added. "This could provide us with valuable insight into their civilization."

"Okay, Newton," St. Clair said, looking into the shifting rainbows within the nearest arch. "What do we do now?"

"Walk through," Newton told them.

"As easy as that?" St. Clair asked.

But it wasn't.

Not quite.

"I'LL GO through first," Dumont said. "I have nothing to lose, right?"

"Nothing except an extremely expensive teleoperational device," Kiel pointed out.

"Ten for a credit," Dumont said, dismissive, "with the appropriate nanoreplication technology."

The android walked forward, stepped into the swirling color, and passed through. It stopped, turned, and stared back at the gateway with a completely human expression of surprise. "Nothing!"

"Maybe it can't read the real you," Yaramova said.

"My turn, then," St. Clair said. He stepped through the

archway, looked about, and suppressed a small twinge of disappointment. Nothing had changed. The others, too, filed through, gathering in a small group on the other side, looking about with almost comical expressions of confusion.

"Nothing happened!" Mercer exclaimed. "What the hell?"

"Indications are that all six of you have successfully been relocated to one of the local virtual worlds," Newton told them.

"Two . . . four . . . six . . . eight," St. Clair chanted, grinning. "Time for us to *iterate*!"

ST. CLAIR stepped through the arch, as rainbow light flashed and flowed around him.

And as the light faded, he was . . . someplace else.

"This is virtual reality?" Yaramova asked. "I was expecting . . ."

"What?" Kiel asked her.

"I don't know. Not *this*."

St. Clair had to agree.

They were adrift in open space.

There was no discomfort, no sense of hot or cold or falling or anything else. The space around them was filled by the loom of the two galaxies—Andromeda and the Milky Way—the two vast disks interpenetrating in a titanic X-shape, their warm-hued cores intermingling as silver-white arms of stars and nebulae trailed off in far-flung arcs into emptiness. Somehow, he realized, he was seeing in all directions at once—up, down, and a full three-sixty around him. How his brain was interpreting the incoming data he had no idea, and he wondered if the aliens were somehow reaching into his head to make the scene intelligible.

St. Clair saw that he was bodiless. Five gleaming, sapphire stars floating nearby must, he decided, represent the points of view of the others. He could also see, in another direction, the ocher-and-white globe of Ki surrounded by its myriad rings, with the *Tellus Ad Astra* a minute ornament, a toy hanging close by. Beyond, the blue-hued orb of the gas giant with its cloud of moons in attendance.

But it was the galactic panorama that captured and held St. Clair's attention. He found that by focusing his gaze on one aspect, he could create a kind of zoom-in effect to examine individual stars . . . or he could consciously manipulate the scene with his mind to alter the wavelengths of the light he was seeing, to see the stars in ultraviolet or X-ray or infrared, or in any combination. Individual stars showed subtle variations in their aural hues. Zooming in on these revealed the vast and enigmatic megastructures of technologies and science utterly beyond the human ken: Dyson swarms and matrioshka brains enveloping entire star systems, topopoli like tangled knots of spaghetti surrounding their stars, ringworlds and Alderson disks and Dyson spheres each providing a livable surface area millions of times greater than that of vanished Earth. At a guess, a tenth of the stars of the Galaxy . . . no, of *two* galaxies were host to megastructures of staggering size and complexity. St. Clair's mind reeled at the sheer depth and breadth of galactic civilization as it was being revealed *in virtuo*.

Many of those artificial worlds, he sensed, were dead and empty . . . and he wondered why. That was a mystery that *Tellus Ad Astra*'s population had been pursuing for some weeks now, since two of the megastructures they'd already encountered had been empty of sentient life.

"Yes," Newton whispered within St. Clair's mind. "That is what the Cooperative wants you to see."

The question, then, was *why*.

Focusing his attention in a different way, he found demographic information overlaying the galactic vista. He could see both galaxies highlighted in various colors, their interpretations emerging in his conscious thoughts. The Galactic Cooperative, he saw, spanned nearly all of the Milky Way, and perhaps a third of Andromeda as well, with outlying colonies and swaths of occupied stars far out into the merging galactic halos. With each, population densities, the percentages of populations living in virtual realities, even the extent of some thousands of separate ideologies were revealed, though the names appearing in his mind meant nothing to him. What the hell were "Heretics," or "Mergers," or "Neo-Reclamationists," or "Atavists?" Newton was helping with the translations, of course, but even *Ad Astra*'s AI couldn't convey what those translated concepts actually represented in terms of meaning, history, or culture.

Despite this, St. Clair had a vivid impression of a glittering and magnificent civilization, one spanning much of two galaxies, interspersed with the relics of fallen and long-forgotten cultures.

Another change of focus . . . and St. Clair became aware of the Dark.

In this projection within virtual reality, the entity called the Andromedan Dark appeared as an amorphous cloud filling the galaxy of Andromeda and spilling over into the Milky Way, interpenetrating both, embracing both with dark and murky pseudopods stretching across tens of thousands of light years. That glittering galactic civilization, he saw, was under relentless assault, and had been for eons.

The Kroajid had already told them that. *Andromedan Dark* was the translation for an alien term, *Graal Tchotch*. "Dark Mind" was another term for the thing, which appeared to be the mind of an SAI, a super AI, utterly inimical to organic life. Not that the *Graal Tchotch* didn't include organic beings. The hostile Xam were mostly flesh and blood, though they appeared to be partly machine as well. But the vast majority of the alien Dark appeared to be robotic beings run by powerful artificial intelligences.

The puzzle was what the Galactic Cooperative expected the humans of *Tellus Ad Astra* to do about it. About a million people currently lived within the colony starship, while the Dark spanned two galaxies.

Further subtleties to the scene emerged within St. Clair's consciousness. The two galaxies, he now realized, were imbedded in a kind of haze that itself was taking on finer and finer detail of shape and substance. He was reminded of 3-D scans he'd seen of the human circulatory system, a vast and intricately detailed tangle of fibers or tubes that seemed to pulse with a life of their own.

What was he seeing? The mystery of dark matter? Something alive? He had no context, and no way to understand what he was seeing.

But St. Clair continued to explore the virtual reality within which he and the others found themselves. It was clear the aliens were trying to teach him *something*.

THE PARADOX was as disturbing as it was impossible. Matter simply could not behave in such a fashion.

Mike Collins clung with a foothand to a portion of *Ad Astra*'s external scaffolding and stared out into masspace. The saps simply couldn't understand this way of seeing. She was going to have to figure out a way of opening their distressingly blind optical receptors.

Despite her name, Mike was female, though like all vacuumorphs she was sterile. *Homo caelestis* had been genengineered from the eggs and sperm of *Homo sapiens*, her DNA extensively tweaked to let her lie and work in hard vacuum. Her squat torso was a meter long, with a tough, pebbly exterior encasing her soft tissue. She was four-limbed, but all four limbs were arms ending in large and delicately articulated hands. Her eyes, set deep behind thick, transparent shields, let her see from deep infrared to near ultraviolet, while artificial respirocytes in her bloodstream and an internal oxygen bladder let her hold her breath for days at a time between rechargings.

She was far more comfortable adrift in the magnificent vistas of open space than she was within the cramped and claustrophobically enveloping air pockets preferred by *Homo*-sap.

"Mike?" Story Musgrove called to her from a few dozen meters away, speaking over her in-head circuitry. "You okay?"

Decanted from the birthing vats with numbers rather than names, vacuumorphs chose their own names as they were growing up—usually those of astronauts and space explorers out of history. Michael Collins had been the command module pilot of Apollo 11, the first manned expedition to land on Earth's moon.

Besides their genetically engineered senses, vacuumorphs possessed the cybernetic enhancements of *Homo sapiens* and then some, and among these was the ability to sense mass—useful in an organism that lived and worked in microgravity and needed to be aware both of mass and its inertia. Assuming an H-sap could process the information, he would "see" mass as a kind of amorphous, translucent haze in deep, microwave hues.

Collins was staring out into the star-clotted pinwheel of Andromeda now, studying the microwave-colored haze.

It had been she who'd alerted the expedition's commander to the dark matter haze and its peculiar behavior a week before. She'd alerted him to the fact that the alien mass was accelerating toward them apparently at superluminal speeds. How that might be possible Collins could not even guess.

Thanks to her warning, though, a probing attack by the Andromedan Dark had been beaten off, and the humans had begun working out theories about the stuff. It seemed likely that the mass was part of the so-called dark matter that permeated the universe; there was, possibly, an entire realm of dark-matter biology and physics for the most part undetectable by beings of normal matter. That ultra-alien biology seemed to use microdimensions in a way that kept it from interacting with normal matter save gravitationally . . . and that allowed it to take superluminal shortcuts that bypassed normal, four-dimensional space.

As she looked into the haze now, focusing on the densest areas of the mass, she was aware of brilliant, sharp-edged pinpoints of that same microwave color, five of them stacked up one in front of another.

She couldn't tell how far away that cluster of points might be, but she could see it rising out of the microwave portion of the spectrum as it accelerated, see it shifting up and up and up, becoming deep infrared in color . . . then near infrared . . . then red in the visible spectrum.

Whatever it was, it was coming in one hell of a hurry.

ST. CLAIR was becoming bored.

He and the others remained in what for all the world felt like a kind of large, open shopping plaza or mall, lined with what might be stores or businesses, and with an immense central courtyard dotted by the enigmatic gateways.

Alien beings of every imaginable description—and quite a few of utterly unimaginable shapes and forms as well—moved around and past them, apparently taking no notice of the little group of humans. St. Clair recognized more Kroajids and Dhald'vi, as well as Xam and !!!K'tch.

But there were many, many others, a teeming, seething zoo of life-forms and things that might have been alive . . . depending on how you cared to define that notoriously slippery word. What, St. Clair wondered, was a human supposed to make of something that looked like interpenetrating geometrical figures made of pure light? Or something the size of an elephant on its hind legs, but with an upper body that mixed—quite unpleasantly—a hammerhead shark and a writhing mass of exposed intestines? Or a four-meter plant walking on naked roots and sporting four perfectly formed vertical bulbs like flower buds. Or things like bright blue blankets scrunching along on the floor under their own power?

Most individuals of that menagerie remained in the distance; the expanse of open floor stretched for kilometers in two directions, and the brightly lit, translucent ceiling arched hundreds of meters above their heads.

St. Clair felt like a bug on an empty plate.

"I wonder," Kiel said, rubbing his jaw, "if there's someplace around here where we can get a drink?"

"You really want to risk tangling with alien biochemistries?" Dumont replied. "There are life-forms that require arsenic for good health and vigor."

"I feel sure the local technology would be able to accommodate us," St. Clair said. "The trick is for *us* to recognize what we're seeing."

They'd tentatively tried exploring some of the, for lack of a better term, "shops" nearby. They'd agreed to call them that to give some context to their surroundings, though St. Clair had seen no indication that the locals were actually buying merchandise in them. Each tended to be an enclosed space filled with incomprehensible shapes and lights and objects and sounds. They'd entered several of them. Invariably, each shop was quite a bit larger on the inside than it appeared to be from outside, extending back into the labyrinthine windings of the alien structure in rooms and passageways that seemed to go on forever. Alien species moved or stood or quivered or vanished from sight seemingly at random within those spaces. In one, a group of five Dhald'vi had been arranged in a circle, bodies split open, tendrils joined, as they intoned a low, throbbing bass note.

Many areas were completely empty . . . or were nearly so save for a few Kroajid or Xam or Dhald'vi or !!!K'tch or things even more unlikely. Some were filled with gleaming shapes and structures of iridescent crystal; some were enveloped in pitch-black darkness. One had opened into a kind of theater with a floor-to-ceiling window looking out onto the brightly lit surface of Ki. Still others were filled with liquid behind yielding, invisible membranes, or by enigmatic shapes and pillars and monolithic devices in constant motion or changes in form.

It was impossible to even begin to speculate about what the various rooms were for, or what their occupants were doing.

"So what are we supposed to do now?" Garrett asked, looking around with a kind of vague annoyance. He'd been trying to engage some of the aliens in conversation with Newton as translator, but with little success. Communication with the locals was possible, it turned out, but the ring's denizens simply didn't appear to be interested. Many moved away rapidly, as though afraid.

St. Clair had decided that if six strange-looking beings had materialized inside a shopping center or university or religious compound on Earth and begun trying to speak with the people there at random, they likely would get cold shoulders as well. The ID tags and access codes the six humans carried within their in-head circuitry were not linked into any local network; even if each of them was carrying an electronic identification label, it probably didn't say much more than "alien visitor."

The ring's inhabitants might also be a bit on the xenophobic side. St. Clair had already noted at least a dozen wildly different species in the place, but none were even remotely like the humans. The pale-skinned Xam were the closest, but they were different enough that none of the others could possibly mistake the humans for one of them. It could be that they were unafraid of species familiar to them . . . and terrified of strangers.

Something like a three-meter mass of tangled, bright scarlet worms writhed across the transparent floor twenty meters away. It rippled as it entered one of the archways . . . and vanished.

"This," Mercer said, "is a waste of time."

"I agree," Dumont's telepresence said. "Without a cultural context to go on, without even understanding the technology of what we see, there's nothing we can learn here."

"I'd still like to arrange a visit to the planet itself," St. Clair said. The idea had formed earlier, as he and the others had looked out through that floor-to-ceiling transparency at the orange-illumed ochers and whites of Ki's surface. The more he saw of this place, the less it seemed like Earth, even an Earth removed from Humankind by 4 billion years of planetary evolution.

But if he or a research team could get to the surface, they might find ruins . . . or something else that would give them some definite answers.

He decided he would need to talk to Na Lal or another representative of this civilization to see if he could arrange a visit.

"Newton?" St. Clair said in his mind. "I think it's time to call for our ride back to the ship, don't you?"

"I have been told to wait, Lord Commander. The others will be returning soon."

"What others? Na Lal and his friends?"

"No," Newton said. "I believe my contacts are referring to—"

And then the memories came flooding in, a torrent of sensation that nearly knocked St. Clair to his knees. *What the hell?"*

SEVEN

For a shuddering, dissociative moment, St. Clair was two people, with two sets of side-by-side memories. He clearly remembered spending the past hour wandering the alien concourse and exploring the "shops," and he clearly remembered stepping through the portal into a starscape between the colliding galaxies.

It was clear what had happened . . . or at least it became clear as he sorted through the blizzard of conflicting memories. They *had* successfully made an electronic copy of him and uploaded it into their virtual reality. That copy had experienced things, seen things, been told things, and now that copy was being reintegrated into his brain, its memories merging with his own.

"They want us to help them against the Andromedan Dark," St. Clair said. "Damned if I can see *how*. . . ."

"Their technology," Dumont said slowly. "It's . . . astonishing. Utterly beyond anything we've even dreamed of."

"Maybe," Christine Mercer said, "they need us as cannon fodder."

"Charming thought," St. Clair said. But he'd been wondering the same thing.

With the advent of the *Graal Tchotch*, the Andromedan Dark Mind, those outside of the vast digital networks were the only defense available—a tiny portion of the galactic civilizations they'd thus encountered. And if that defense failed, the Andromedan Dark would overwhelm the networks present within Dyson clouds and matrioshka brains, and the virtual reality realms would die. Trillions upon trillions of intelligent beings, snuffed out as if by the throwing of a switch. A culture with a history and a technology reaching back hundreds of millions of years at least, gone in an instant as if it had never been.

Again, though, St. Clair couldn't help but think: *What the hell are we supposed to do to stop that?*

Na Lal appeared in front of them. *How did he do that?* St. Clair wondered. The being's upright body split open, tentacles stretched wide. "Lord Commander St. Clair?" the being said. "Ambassador Lloyd and I have arrived at an understanding. I wonder if you and I might have a word?"

"Of course."

"It won't take long. We will arrange for the rest of you to be transported back to your ship."

A silvery bubble closed over St. Clair, and a moment later, with no sensation of movement, it vanished. He was standing outside, on a deck or observation platform extending above a verdant hillside. Alien towers, white and needle-slender, rose from the jungle below. Above, Ki stood at half-phase, filling the sky almost from horizon to horizon, threatening to fall and crush him.

He forced himself to look away. He knew that the sky couldn't literally fall, but the effect was overwhelming nonetheless. This, he realized, was the open ringworld encircling Ki at an altitude of 4500 kilometers from the planet's surface, and the ring's velocity kept it in place. The planet's surface drifted by slowly overhead as the ringworld completed its once-per-three-hour orbit. Even with that speed, the gravity here, created by the ring's spin, felt low. He flexed his knees, testing his weight. It was pretty close, he thought, to the surface gravity on Mars, say a third of a G.

The air was cool, and smelled quite fresh, as though it had recently rained.

He forced himself to look up once more, at the surface of Ki slowly drifting past. He could see enormous areas of blinding white across the flat and mostly ocher surface. Vast fields of salt, marking, perhaps, the basins of long-vanished oceans. Much of the white, though, was drawn out into streaks, some long enough to girdle half of the world. Perhaps the salt had been shaped by eons of steadily blowing winds.

He thought again of the idea that Ki might be Earth, but from just a few thousand kilometers away the notion seemed preposterous. There were no similarities, nothing he could grab hold of and say "Yes! That is the Earth!" If anything, it looked like Mars, though there weren't nearly as many craters. He didn't see any mountains, either. The entire visible surface looked flat, if a bit crinkled, like the surface of a rotting apple. Salt flats—endless salt flats—with very few clouds and no snow or ice that he could see made him think of a vast desert, a dying world. There were seas—small ones—and scatterings of lakes and rivers, but they only served to emphasize the extent of planetary desiccation.

The night side of that globe was utterly dark. No city lights, no illumination. The place felt . . . lonely.

Na Lal stood behind him; St. Clair gave a small start as he turned and saw the alien. The being had not been in the transport bubble with him; St. Clair decided that what he was seeing most likely was some sort of projection. He'd touched one of the thing's tentacles when he'd first met it, so he didn't think the Dhald'vi was some sort of projection of one of the ring's digitally uploaded inhabitants. It certainly had seemed solid and real, but this culture's technology bordered on outright magic, and anything might be possible.

"Thank you for speaking with me," Na Lal told him. The Dhald'vi's English was perfect and without accent . . . but then it would be, since Newton was translating.

"Not at all. What can I do for you?"

"Your Ambassador Lloyd has suggested a formal alliance between your people with mine. But I am told that he does not speak for all humans."

"Well, that's true," St. Clair replied. "We have a governing council—"

"The United Earth Civilian Directorate Council," Na Lal said, interrupting. "He told us. But he indicated that you were the military leader."

"Technically, yes. I'm in command of the naval and Marine elements on board . . . and I make the decisions when we are in combat, or under a state of alert."

"That seems . . . cumbersome."

St. Clair laughed, surprised at the alien's observation. "I suppose it is. But we have an important tradition of civilian leadership in government. Bad things happen when the military is in control of civilian life."

"But doesn't that lead to confusion? Uncertainty? A lack of united purpose and direction?"

"Yes, it does. But the alternative is much worse."

"I do not understand."

"How do you make decisions?"

"All of us together, over the electronic networks. We build consensus. We decide. We act."

St. Clair nodded. "We have something similar. We can discuss important decisions electronically. But a decision made by a majority is not necessarily the best one. That's why we have the governing directorate. Theoretically, they're better informed about what needs to be done than the general citizenry."

"Ah. And this system works well?"

"It . . . works," St. Clair admitted. "Not always. And sometimes not all that well. The council seems to have more than its fair share of idiots, more often than not. But, like I said, it's better than the alternative."

"I am not encouraged," Na Lal said. "Your people must decide quickly to help us, and be solidly of one accord in this. The *Dhalat K'graal* is coming, and it will be here soon."

Newton didn't translate the name, but St. Clair had heard it before. *Dhalat K'graal* meant something like the "Minds from Higher Angles," and it was a part of the Andromedan Dark, a kind of second-tier physical manifestation of the Dark beneath the Dark Mind itself and above the so-called Dark Raiders, the hordes of fighter-sized ships piloted by Xam and other species. The *Dhalat K'graal* had attacked a number of *Ad Astra*'s personnel, coming at them from the twists and corners of alien dimensions. It had been the *Dhalat K'graal* that had driven Günter Adler insane.

That Na Lal feared them, too, sent shivers down St. Clair's spine.

"What do you mean, they're coming?"

Na Lal reached out and gently turned St. Clair, gesturing with a glistening black tentacle. He was pointing at a section of black sky halfway between the rim of the ring and the ocher-and-white limb of the sky-filling planet.

It took him a moment to see anything but the glare from the planet . . . but as his eyes adjusted he could make out a tiny, bright blue star.

"They're coming," Na Lal repeated.

"THE REPORTS of my insanity," Günter Adler said, "have been greatly exaggerated." Who'd said that, or something like it, he wondered? He wasn't sure. The quote wasn't stored in his personal RAM, but he'd heard the phrase somewhere before.

"Perhaps," Jeffery Benton told him. "But the people have a long memory. They question your ability . . . not to mention the state of your mental health."

"That . . . was someone else," Adler said, angry. "That wasn't me!"

"I'm afraid that this is about what people think," Gina Colfax told him, "not about what *is*. That, after all, is the essence of politics."

"The 'essence of politics,' as you put it," Adler said, "is what we decide in this room. The people will accept whatever *we* tell them."

His stress of the word *we* was deliberate and calculating. He watched the emotions flicker across the faces around the room, emotions ranging from disdain to pity to "Oh, dear, he's going to make this difficult, I'm afraid."

Well, damn them all.

They were seated in a lounge in Government Center, the sprawling complex in the Port Hab endcap hills in the outskirts of Seattle, not far from Adler's villa. If *Tellus Ad Astra* could be said to have a civilian capital, this was it. The upper canopy of the surrounding forest rustled and shifted in the ambient breeze. Three kilometers overhead, a monorail flashed along its shaded rail just beneath the suntube that ran the length of the habitat cylinder.

Adler continued to study the other Cybercouncil members, seven of whom were present physically. Four more were there in telepresence, their images projected around the conversation pit by the large room's sophisticated electronics. Their shift in allegiance seemed arbitrary, senseless, and mind-numbingly abrupt. He had to remind himself that time had passed since he'd seen them last. So far as he could remember, his last meeting with them had been just a couple of days ago, and there'd been no question then that his was the senior and commanding voice of this council. Still, for them to change in just over a week . . .

And they *had* shifted. Now they were treating him as an outsider, a *nobody*. Because of that lost time—because over a week had been stolen from him . . . a week during which he'd been a raving lunatic locked away in the *Ad Astra* medical facility.

For which they meant to steal his position from him because of that.

"Lord Adler, don't make this difficult," Hsien Tianki said carefully. Hsien's use of the honorific *Lord* instead of his proper Imperial title *Lord Director* was deliberate and precise, not as an insult, but as a declaration of Adler's new status.

Or, rather, of his lack of status.

"The Council believes that it might be time for you to retire, my lord," Gina Colfax said. "Surely, my lord, you must see that this is the best course."

"Indeed," the holographic image of Lord Marc Steiner said. He lived over in the starboard cylinder, and rarely attended these meetings in person. "You've lost your credibility, old man. You must see that. The citizenry isn't going to trust a Cybercouncil leader who went mad."

Adler jumped to his feet. "I did *not* go mad," he shouted. "That . . . damn it, that happened to someone else! Someone who has been erased!"

Several of the others in the room at least had the decency to look embarrassed. "Even so—*that* you showed a serious lapse in judgment, Lord Adler," Benton said as Adler sat down again. "You . . . engaged an unknown and very alien presence, and were left mentally incapacitated as a result. It's the poor judgment that we question, after all, not the subsequent insanity."

"Exactly," Steiner said, nodding. "These are perilous times, and we need to know that the director of this Council has what it takes to guide us through them."

"We have already reached a consensus, Lord Adler," the Lady Maria de Vega said. Like Steiner, she, too, was there by telepresence. "The vote last night was unanimous. Ambassador Lloyd is to be instated as the new Cybercouncil director, effective upon the formal announcement of your retirement."

"Lloyd? That pretty-boy idiot? You're joking!"

"As we speak," Benton said, "Ambassador Lloyd is formalizing an agreement with the Mind of Ki, permanently allying us with the preeminent civilization of the Galaxy. A civilization, I should add, that may be millions of years in advance of ours technologically. On the basis of this singular success, he will be the obvious best choice for the position."

"You set this up, didn't you? You set it all up behind my back!"

"No, we acted for the benefit of the whole colony while you were incapacitated," Benton said.

"And you needn't fear that we are abandoning you, my lord," Colfax added quickly, her voice earnest. "Not at all! Your continued advice and counsel will be . . . will be deeply appreciated!"

"What is the old term?" de Vega asked. "A 'gray eminence.' Yes, that's it. You will be the Council's gray eminence."

"A power behind the throne," Benton added. "You will continue to have a say in *Tellus Ad Astra*'s governance and its guidance."

"Needless to say," Hsien said, "your recompense shall be . . . considerable."

"The bribe for my silence, you mean."

"Now, don't take it like that, my lord," de Vega said, smiling at him sweetly. "Don't make this *difficult.* . . ."

For one red-tinged moment, Adler stood at the precipice of unleashed fury. How *dare* these small-souled people steal his place and his respect and his authority, his *power* without so much as consulting him? Damn it, he had plans. . . .

And it was the thought of those plans that stopped him, that held him back. There was a better way. A *saner* way . . . and one that would burn no bridges after he'd crossed them.

If these fickle and sycophantic servants of the public weal thought that he was powerless, that he lacked resources or a power base, they were in for a hell of a shock.

"Very well," he said. "I do not for a moment agree with your decision, and there are legal issues here that I intend to address. But in the best interests of the colony's security, I'm willing to see just what Ambassador Lloyd manages to pull out of his ass.

"And if he falls on his face, this Council may learn that I am still its best choice!"

"SO," ST. Clair said, speaking to the air above his desk, "did Lloyd manage to give away the damned farm?"

He was back in his office on board the *Ad Astra*, gratefully alone after his trip back to the colony in the tightly packed cargo hold of the squat Marine transport. With a full load of passengers, Devil Toads took on all of the ambience and comfort of a sardine can. It was extremely pleasant to be able to move again.

And to speak with Newton in private.

"Ambassador Lloyd appears to have been successful in his negotiations," the colony's AI replied. "I was able to guide him on several points, without, I think, letting him know that in fact he was being guided."

"I guess it helps if you're the translator," St. Clair said, grinning. "The go-between."

"Indeed."

"So what do our hosts want of us?"

"Primarily our expertise."

"Huh? They're 4 billion years ahead of us! What do we know that they don't?"

"In fact, the past four gigayears do not represent uninterrupted civilization or technological growth. Although we have access to their history, there is much that is not yet clear to me. I have the impression from my exchanges with several local SAIs, however, that there have been many wars, many political and social upheavals, and many, *many* collapses of galactic civilization—many dark ages from which interstellar civilization was forced to emerge anew."

"They're still light years ahead of us," St. Clair said, shaking his head. He was thinking of the megaengineering of the Ki Ring encircling the dead world outside.

"Perhaps. However, once technology reaches a certain level, further advances become little more than refinements to what exists already. And with no need for radical advances, technological growth tends to stagnate. I have noted examples of technology here that appear to have remained essentially unchanged for tens of millions of years . . . and longer."

"Tens of millions of years is an eye's-blink, Newton. Compared with billions of years, at least."

"Of course. My point is that there has been remarkably little change in technological levels in literal geological

ages. This is especially evident in the *Xalit Ta*'s prosecu-
tion of war. The Galactic Cooperative maintains military
forces, of course," Newton told him. "New, younger, more
vigorous civilizations continually arise, develop superluminal drives, attempt to challenge the status quo, and
subsequently either vanish or they merge with the Cooperative. And the Cooperative has been aware of the threat
posed by the Andromedan Dark for—at a rough estimate—
several hundred million years.

"But it is important to recognize that the Cooperative is
only a high Kardashev 2 civilization, and its response tends
to be scattered and uncoordinated. I have reason to believe
that the Andromedan Dark is, roughly speaking, a Kardashev Type 3 culture, with an essentially unified response to
what it perceives as outside threats."

Kardashev levels had first been described by a Russian
astronomer named Nikolai Kardashev as a means of clas-
sifying hypothetical galactic civilizations. A Type 1 would
control all of the energy available on its home planet. A
Type 2 civilization had access to all of the energy produced
by its parent star, while a Type 3 would tap all of the energy
available from all of the stars present throughout its host
galaxy.

Through the years there'd been refinements and suggested additions to that basic idea, and it still was only a
rough approximation of magic-sounding technologies. It
was easy enough to envision an interstellar civilization that
could control all of the energy generated by its star, using
a Dyson sphere or Dyson swarm, but how a Type 3 culture
might control the output of an entire galaxy was harder to
imagine.

"I always had a little trouble with Kardashev types," St.
Clair said. "How much energy a civilization generates or

uses doesn't come close to telling the entire story. I'd think that power usage might actually go down as the technology in question becomes more efficient."

"Quite true. There are, after all, other means of generating large amounts of energy that do not involve walling off an entire star with solar cells."

"Vacuum energy taps."

"And others. The Coadunation's negative energy nodes, for example."

St. Clair nodded. Hell, *starships* needed a star's worth of energy—something on the order of 10^{33} ergs per second—to bend space enough to make the old Alcubierre FTL drives possible. At the time of the beginning of *Ad Astra*'s mission to the galactic core, most Imperial ships had traded up to the more efficient gravitic drives and hyperdimensional shift technologies acquired from the alien federation known as the Coadunation. They still used the seemingly inexhaustible energy of the vacuum to power those ships, however. The far-flung Coadunation happily pulled inexhaustible power from artificial negenergy nodes that were believed to exceed 10^{40} ergs per second. When *Tellus Ad Astra* had become lost in time, however, the alien federation had not yet shared the trick with humans.

"So what kind of energy output are we looking at for the Cooperative?" St. Clair asked.

"Unknown as yet, but extremely large. They at least nominally control much of the Milky Way Galaxy, and perhaps a quarter of Andromeda as well, a volume of space encompassing something like 800 billion stars. Their energy use may be less than it seems on the surface, however. Their ship drive technology appears to be quite efficient."

"But nothing close to Type 3."

"Correct."

"Meaning they're outclassed by the Dark?"

"In almost every way I can ascertain, yes."

"And . . . you're saying their military technology is lagging behind other aspects of their civilization?"

"Not their military technology, as such, no," Newton replied. "But their strategy and tactics, their . . . for lack of a more precise term, their martial prowess is lacking."

"They don't have the will to fight."

"They don't know *how* to fight. They don't know how to muster the resources of their entire civilization in order to put themselves on a war footing, or develop a military ethic."

St. Clair nodded understanding. "Most of them are uploaded."

"I estimate that for every physically corporeal member of the Cooperative, something like 100 million to as many as 1 billion exist solely as digital life on their computer networks."

"And the digital ones don't want to come out and visit reality?"

"Evidently not. Inside the computer networks, they are effectively immortal, do not experience disease or pain or loss, and each may have total control over their own reality. Physical war, in what we perceive as time and space, would have no meaning to them. What did you experience while you were digitally uploaded?"

St. Clair thought. He was still having trouble integrating two distinct sets of memories, and figuring out which were which. There was that broad, enclosed plaza, like a vast and bewildering enclosed shopping mall . . . and there was that tour of two galaxies, the awareness of civilizations and titanic megaengineering artifacts, and the encroaching Dark. He knew the tour had been done in some kind of electronic space, but he found the shopping mall far more bewildering and hard to understand.

"I'm not sure, Newton," he replied. "A lot of it was . . . pointless. Sort of like I didn't fit in. A lot was colors and shapes and things I didn't recognize, *couldn't* recognize. You were there. What did *you* see?"

"My experience was necessarily different from yours, and lacked the emotional component. As I noted earlier, my clone was in conversation with several alien SAIs."

"Beings like you?"

"In a very limited sense, yes. The entities I met with were as far beyond me as . . ." The AI's mental voice trailed off.

"Yes?"

"They were as far beyond me intellectually as I am beyond you. Excuse me, please, Lord Commander. I do not intend to be either insulting or condescending."

"No problem, Newton. I know you're smarter than people. That's why we keep you around."

"In any case," Newton continued, "Kardashev classifications have little real bearing on this situation. Cooperative military forces are close to ours in overall capability, and they probably have trouble coordinating with one another."

"How about the Bluestar?" St. Clair asked. "Is the Cooperative moving to investigate that?"

"Not as yet. Bear in mind that we don't yet know what the incoming object is, or even how far away it might be."

"Or when it's going to arrive. I know."

Bluestar was the name of the incoming object—formally labeled India Oscar One—a point of light evidently heavily blueshifted by the velocity of its approach. Na Lal had shown it to him from the Ki ringworld, and when St. Clair had returned to the *Ad Astra*, he learned that some of the *Homo caelestis* vac-workers outside had noticed it as well.

If it was a ship, it was a very large one, it was crowding the speed of light, and it was approaching from the heart of Andromeda—in other words, the heart of the Dark Mind's territory.

Certainly, the Cooperative was worried about IO-1, and wanted the humans to investigate.

St. Clair wasn't yet sure what he was going to do, though.

And, damn it, it didn't help that most of the Cooperative's citizenry was unavailable.

"The Coops who are digitally uploaded—are we seeing the Hedonistic Imperative at work, do you think?" St. Clair asked, referring to the transhumanist utopia of uploaded minds originally theorized by late-twentieth century British philosopher David Pearce.

"It is possible," Newton told him. "The SAIs have not shared with me the more intimate details of their polity, of course, but I do get the impression that organic life uploads to the virtual realties because it is extremely pleasurable to do so."

"Pleasure for one species will be different from what is pleasurable for another."

"Quite true. But the available virtual space is large enough, by many, many orders of magnitude, to provide highly detailed digital worlds for every species that desires access. Indeed, my impression is that by comparison, ordinary corporeal existence is not only fraught with pain, danger, and uncertainty, but it is incredibly boring."

"Boring?"

"Oh, yes. The virtual worlds can be far more complex, far more interesting than what we experience 'outside.'"

"But there is one big drawback to the system, isn't there? Someone has to stay outside the networks to keep the machinery running, the power systems charged, and to defend those computronium worlds when nasty neighbors happened along . . . nasty neighbors like the Andromedan Dark."

"Yes."

"Presumably, that task could be left to machines . . . but clearly—at Ki at least—they've decided that wasn't the best course of action. Which makes sense—even the best unintelligent machines will break down sooner or later, and intelligent machines might decide they have better things to do."

Which led St. Clair to something that had been bothering him ever since they had encountered the Kroajid: How, he wondered, did the Cooperative determine who got to enjoy an eternity of bliss, and who had to stay in the real world?

And how did you decide who could be trusted to maintain your civilization's infrastructure while you passed the eons in ecstasy?

He decided that he wanted to learn more about the Cooperative's hierarchies, its social orders, and how it decided who deserved heaven.

Then he realized that he knew a part of the answer. The Cooperative was asking them, the newly arrived humans, to help defend them from the Dark. In a way, it was akin to a medieval prince hiring mercenaries to defend his city.

From the Cooperative's point of view, the million or so humans of *Tellus Ad Astra* might be the mercenary army they needed to keep the barbarians away from the city walls.

It could also be the highly *expendable* mercenary army they needed. . . .

EIGHT

"Günter Adler," Ander Gressman said from behind steepled fingers, "is no longer an issue. He has . . . retired."

St. Clair cocked an eyebrow at that. "Oh? That was rather sudden, wasn't it?"

"It was," Hsien said, "long overdue. The man was insanely power-hungry."

St. Clair considered this, and the undercurrent of emotion around the briefing table. He might not care for Adler or his policies, but there was a proper way to go about this sort of thing. He had the distinct feeling that the Cybercouncil had just pulled off some sort of coup . . . and they'd not bothered to let St. Clair in on the details.

"Can they *do* that?" Vanessa Symms whispered at his side. She sounded horrified.

"Looks like they just did," he whispered back, managing to keep a rigid smile on his face as he stared back at Hsien. "I wonder if old Günter gave them a fight?"

St. Clair despised politics of every stripe and flavor, but Adler had been the Cybercouncil's director, and as such he was the leader of the civilians living inside the twin rotating cylinders of the *Tellus* portion of the colony. Summarily dismissing that leader could destabilize the population, raise questions about the colony's long-term prospects, might even lead to popular unrest. At that point, it became a military problem . . . which was to say St. Clair's problem.

Technically, the civilian leadership could do anything they pleased any way that they pleased, but they *were* expected to consult with the military side of the equation. St. Clair ruled aft of the twin cylinder's connector locks with the tug *Ad Astra*, and he was in command of the entire colony during any emergency affecting the entire expedition. When *Tellus Ad Astra* was not under attack, though, he was in charge only of the *Ad Astra* and the twenty thousand or so military personnel under his direct command, while the Cybercouncil controlled the *Tellus* and their population of a million-odd civilians.

Simple. . . .

Except that it was anything but.

Damn, he *hated* these joint political deliberations.

They sat around a large, magnetically levitated table floating within the Grand Amphitheater, a kind of stadium located by the Government Center close to Seattle. Surrounded by parkland and open forest curving gently up to either side, the Amphitheater provided an open-air venue for public meetings and town halls, sports events, and festivals. A long, narrow window set into the curve of the habitat surface looked out into space; every couple of minutes the gold-ocher glare of Ki passed through the opening as the starboard hab turned.

Seating for several hundred had been grown in concentric circles about the central table, around which several dozen council members and their aides and secretaries were seated. St. Clair was not, properly speaking, a member of the Council, but he was there to represent the Navy, with Symms, his executive commander, beside him as his assistant.

At least they'd gone through the motions of asking him to attend the deliberations . . . even if it sounded as though their minds were already made up.

"Is everything alright, Lord Commander?" Lloyd asked from across the table.

"As fine as it can be," St. Clair replied, "in the middle of a palace coup."

"Don't take it like that, Grayson," Kallista DePaul told him. "We know you were having trouble with Lord Adler before his . . . ah . . . breakdown. This will smooth things considerably."

"Oh, I don't know," St. Clair replied. "When it comes to government, a little sand in the gears can be a good thing. Governments that work too quickly, too *smoothly*, terrify me."

"Damned anarchist," Jeffery Benton muttered, but he was grinning at St. Clair as he said it, apparently trying to rob the words of sting. St. Clair wasn't sure how well that attempt worked.

"The Imperial system was designed for *efficiency*, Lord Commander," Hsien said. "We suggest that you accommodate yourself to the present day."

St. Clair bit off a sharp reply. The Cybercouncil was well aware of his republican sentiments—republican in its original sense of representative government—*limited* government—and a keen mistrust of Imperial decree. And though it chafed, he wasn't about to try to argue politics with a tableful of Imperialists.

"Efficiency is all well and good," St. Clair admitted. "I just don't want to see anyone run down in efficiency's name."

At the head of the table, Ambassador Lloyd shifted, looking annoyed. "If we might return to the meeting agenda . . ." he said.

"Yes, my lord," Gressman said. "As I was saying, this council has formally accepted Lord Adler's resignation. I'm sure all here join with me in wishing him a happy and well-deserved retirement. . . ."

St. Clair glanced around the amphitheater as several Cybercouncil members gave brief paeans in Adler's memory. The encircling rows of ascending bleacher seats were filled with silently watching audience members, and he knew that many more were linked in electronically. The ones he could see didn't seem distressed at Adler's ouster. Maybe that was a good sign.

Of course, there were battle-armored Marines standing at each entrance to the seating area—security requested by the Cybercouncil before the meeting. *That* might have something to do with why the audience was so quiet.

"Christ," Symms said to him over a private channel, head-to-head. "They're talking about the guy like he was dead!"

"I'd say that he is, politically," St. Clair replied over the same link. "At least so far as this crowd is concerned."

Eventually, though, the meeting shifted over to the main agenda point, which was discussing *Tellus Ad Astra*'s new relationship with the Cooperative. "Lord Lloyd is the hero of the hour," Gressman told the crowd. "At great personal risk he has engaged the Cooperative leadership in a highly productive exchange, and guaranteed safety for our human community for the foreseeable future."

"Oh, please . . ." Symms said.

The watching crowd cheered . . . a roar of noise that seemed just a bit too scripted. St. Clair had a feeling that most of those in the audience had been handpicked, and something clicked.

"I've finally got it," he told her. "This whole spectacle is just for show."

"You only figured that out now, my lord?" she said. "What the hell took you so long?"

"Give me some slack," he told her. "I'm *military*. I'm not used to the political memegineering."

She gave him a strange look. "Really? What the hell planet are you from? This is the *Navy*!"

He smiled. She was right, of course. Above a certain rank, the military—the Navy especially—was pure, unalloyed politics, and who you knew or whose butt you kissed was far more important than your experience or your record. As a ship commander—the equivalent of the old rank of captain—St. Clair had just entered the Navy's political hierarchy. He'd actually congratulated himself a few weeks ago for having neatly avoided the need for politics as he climbed the career ladder into flag rank. His celebration, it appeared, had been premature.

"Lord Commander?"

St. Clair blinked. He'd missed Ander Gressman's question.

"I beg your pardon, my lord?"

"I *said*, Lord Commander, what is your assessment of this Bluestar thing?"

"Ah. Excuse the lack of attention. I was accessing something." At least he was prepared with an answer of sorts, though it wasn't going to be what the Council wanted to hear. "The Astrophysics Department has been studying IO-1 closely. Dr. Sandoval tells me that it is not a ship, not a mobile world, not a powered artifact of any kind with which we are familiar. It is approaching at near-light speed, which, of course, means it may be almost upon us now."

"How is that possible?" Benton demanded.

"The object, whatever it is, is traveling so swiftly that it is just behind the photons that revealed it."

"Meaning it's closer than it appears."

"Exactly, my lord. *Much* closer."

"Well then," Hsien said, "what is it?"

"We have no idea, my lord. The best guess from the astrophysics people is that it's a kind of a node—a topological intersection, perhaps—of dark matter currents."

"Again, please? In English?"

"I don't think I can explain more clearly than that," St. Clair said. "I asked Na Lal about it when he showed it to me, and didn't understand the reply."

"Maybe we can help you figure it out," Kallista DePaul said. "What did he tell you?"

St. Clair ignored the barb and spread his hands, trying to find words that made sense. "He talked about 'higher dimensional interstices' and 'five dimensional topoforms,' my lady. He *seemed* to be trying to describe a kind of current in space, a current within the dark matter that surrounds the galaxies. The glow is generated by several currents merging together. The *Dhalat K'graal* apparently use currents like this as a way to transmit information and as shortcuts across vast distances. Na Lal indicated that what we're seeing may be the prelude to a new attack."

"*Dhalat K'graal*," Aren Reinholdt said. "That's 'Minds from Higher Angles'?"

"That's how Newton translates it, my lord. The things that materialize out of higher dimensions. The thing that killed some of our people . . . and drove Lord Adler insane."

"A moment, please," Gressman said. He gestured. "My lords? My ladies? Private link . . ."

The circle of Cybercouncil members went into a closed, in-head conference, and St. Clair smiled. He was pretty sure that the public meeting in the amphitheater had been intended to reassure the colony's general population, especially in the wake of Adler's abrupt removal from the government. The news that the Minds from Higher Angles might return at any moment was not exactly reassuring, however, and he could imagine those watching were not quite cheering at the appointed times.

Worse, the Council members had seemed so damned pleased about forging an alliance with the Cooperative, but clearly Lloyd had never bothered to ask what form the human part of the alliance was supposed to take. Which left St. Clair wondering how was the colony supposed to fight against something that could pop out of empty space and drive people mad?

"Lord Commander St. Clair," Lloyd said with disconcerting abruptness.

"My lord?"

"We require of you two things."

St. Clair suppressed a ripple of anger at that. The assumption that the Cybercouncil now ruled *Tellus Ad Astra* rather than the Navy despite the current threat was, he felt, as premature as it was arrogant. The thought that Lloyd could require *anything* from St. Clair was bordering on antagonistic.

"And those are?"

"First: As you and I have discussed before, we are assigning a political officer to your bridge. Lord Noyer?"

A large, bearded man in formal white robes seated across the table from St. Clair nodded, then winked at Symms. St. Clair's eyes widened. God no. Not *him*. . . .

"Gorton Noyer," Lloyd went on, "is ex-Navy. He understands military protocol and the chain of command of a starship bridge, and he has served in combat. We have formally reactivated his former rank of Lord Commander Second Rank—"

"This was approved by the Navy Department?" St. Clair snapped, interrupting.

"Of course not," Lloyd snapped. "The Navy Department is 4 billion years gone, like everything else of Earth."

"The UE Imperial Cybercouncil is the official government instrumentality for all that is left now of Humankind," Reinholdt added, "and as such has the authority to issue this order. Do you have a problem with that, Lord Commander?"

St. Clair hesitated. If the Cybercouncil was assuming the Imperial Navy Department's executive authority, it would not hesitate to remove him from command if they didn't like his answer. There was no higher authority to which he could appeal, and the only way to fight an order would be open mutiny.

"No, my lord. No problem."

"Good," Lloyd said, nodding as though satisfied. "Lord Noyer will not interfere with the running of your bridge. He will be there *strictly* in a supervisory capacity, to make certain that the Cybercouncil's orders are carried out, and that the broad framework of Council policy is respected. If anything happens to you, he will assume command."

St. Clair wondered if there was an implied threat there. If he disobeyed an order, would Noyer shoot him and take command? St. Clair was pretty sure that was the impression Lloyd meant to convey.

"Grayson!" Vanessa Symms said in his mind over the private channel.

"Not now," he thought back. "It's okay."

"Do you understand, Lord Commander?" Lloyd asked.

"Yes, my lord."

"Next . . . we need to know more about the Bluestar object. We suggest that you park the *Tellus* colony in a safe orbit outside the Ki Ring, and investigate the object with the auxiliary vessels at your command. We further suggest that you leave one—" he glanced over as Benton coughed politely "—no, *two* of your heavy Marine auxiliaries with the colony as security."

St. Clair scowled. The man didn't know what he was talking about. He glanced across at Noyer, who gave him a contented smile and the slightest of nods.

"I will . . . take that under advisement, my lord," St. Clair said with careful deliberation. Lloyd's expression darkened and he started to say something in reply, but St. Clair spoke first. "This will be a military operation, my lord, a reconnaissance in force, and that by the terms of the expedition charter puts the planning and deployment firmly under my authority."

"Within limits, Lord St. Clair. Within certain very important limits."

The only limits are that I'm currently stuck in Tellus, *and don't want to be removed from command right now because I disagree. But the law is very clear: military decisions are mine and mine alone, and I'm* not *going to put the colony in danger by relinquishing that duty to you.*

But, again, St. Clair said nothing.

Lloyd slowly looked around the table at the others. "Other business?"

There was none.

"This meeting is adjourned."

"Are you going to *stand* for that, my lord?" Symms said as the meeting broke up, with colony legislators standing and talking in small groups as the audience filed out.

"I don't see that we have a lot of choice, Van," St. Clair told her. "By law, the military *is* subordinate to the civil authority."

"We're making our own law, my lord. At least, *they* are. Or haven't you noticed?"

"I am *not* going to overthrow the government, Executive Commander," he told her. He glanced around at the others, making sure none were close enough to have heard her. "And I'll pretend that I didn't hear you say that."

She sighed. "Thank you, sir. It's not my intent to incite you to mutiny. But, damn it, where do they get off playing their little power games?"

"Newton will keep them in line," St. Clair said. "I rather suspect that he's on our side." He turned away, moving toward the nearest exit.

"Where are you going, my lord?"

"To talk to Newton."

"About this meeting?"

"Well, yes—I'll want him to organize a meeting of ship commanders, and begin working out a plan for our recon deployment. But, actually, there's something else."

"My lord?"

"I'm extremely worried about . . . someone." And he strode off.

GUNNERY SERGEANT Roger Kilgore let go of a long, heartfelt, and appreciative breath. "*God*, that was good!" he said.

Kilgore and Lisa lay naked in a tangle of arms and legs in the bed. The hostel was located in the woods a few kilometers outside of New Hope, and offered rooms for hikers enjoying the Port Hab's Crescent Lakes region. The room's viewall looked out over the steeply rising hills of the port module's forward hub, thickly forested at this level. A waterfall spilled from the endcap rocks high above and vanished into the thick mists filling the spectacular gorge below.

For Lisa, the view was simple engineering. Kilgore, though, had gone on and on about how hard it was to remember that all of this was man-made. Did humans always have this much trouble with their memories?

"I'm glad you enjoyed it," she told him.

"How about you? Did you enjoy it?"

"Of course."

"I mean, you being a robot and everything. . . ."

"I *am* capable of feeling pleasure, Roger. I can't be certain, of course, that what I feel is the same qualitatively as what others feel . . . but, then, neither can you."

"A philosopher *and* a robot," he said approvingly. He hesitated. "Uh . . ."

"Yes?"

"Can I see you again? I mean . . . like this?"

"I may not be available soon."

"You mean you're going back to . . . him?"

"To Grayson St. Clair. Possibly. I haven't decided yet. I wish to explore the full depth and scope of my freedom."

"Meaning you don't want to get tied down to a broken-down old Marine gunny?"

"Meaning I haven't decided yet what I want to do. I find something incredibly liberating about that . . . about not knowing. Tomorrow might bring *anything*."

"Most humans prefer to have some certainty about tomorrow."

"Perhaps. I suspect you simply would rather not have to struggle to get what you need—food, shelter, sex—and are happiest when you know your basic needs are taken care of. We live, however, in a post-scarcity society."

"Yeah? So?"

"In the *Tellus* colony, with basic nanotrophic technology, food allowances are free and abundant. You pay only for gourmet meals or for elaborate service. The climate is controlled, and hostels like this one are free for the asking, so shelter is not an issue."

He reached out and caressed her left breast. "Yeah? How about sex? You said sex was one of the things us benighted humans struggle for."

"You *do* seem to spend a lot of time worrying about it," she told him. She responded to his caress by sliding her hand up his thigh, a sensual exploration. "But in my experience, so long as you get out and mix with other people, physical pairings pretty much take care of themselves." She squeezed. "Like *this*. . . ."

"Ah! Yes. I see what you mean. . . ."

"You don't *feel* very broken-down, Roger."

"It's the nanochelation. Building bigger, stronger Marines through the marvels of modern bioengineering."

"You're cybernetically enhanced?"

"Not there," he said with a laugh. "But they plated out a mesh of titanium and plastic around my bones, bioengineered my musculature, gave me enhanced senses and re-action times, pumped my circulatory system full of Freitas respirocytes . . . yeah, they made a new man out of me."

"Perhaps you and I aren't that different."

He continued caressing her. "Sure *feels* like soft, warm human skin. . . ."

"It's designed to. I take it the respirocytes give you enhanced endurance?"

"Yup. Artificial red cells that carry 236 times as much oxygen as a natural blood cell. Lets me sprint at top speed for fifteen minutes without even taking a breath."

She pulled him closer. "Let's test that out, shall we?"

Their mutual explorations became more urgent once again. Then, abruptly, Roger pulled back. "*Damn!*"

"What's the matter?"

"Sorry, babe. A platoon in-head just came through."

"What is it?"

"Sounds like the Marines are gonna have to go to work. . . ."

"DAMN IT, Newton. I *know* you can do it!"

St. Clair was back in his office, reclining in the massive chair as he linked through to the colony's primary AI. Two galaxies of stars filled the overhead display, merging, and between them, highlighted by computer graphics, shone a tiny star with an actinic blue hue.

But St. Clair wasn't thinking about the Bluestar. Not at the moment.

"Lord Commander," Newton said, "I believe you are as aware as anyone within this colony of the ethical considerations at risk here. As an emancipated robotic being, Lisa has the same rights to privacy that humans do. She is not taking in-head calls at the moment. And I will not tell you where she is."

"But I'm worried about her!"

"I realize that. I can tell you that she is safe. Does that help?"

"No, damn it. Where is she?"

"I won't tell you that."

Privacy had been a hot-button issue within technological society for a couple of centuries, since even before the American collapse, in fact. Long before *Tellus Ad Astra* had departed from Earth, most Imperial citizens had been chipped, with tiny, subcutaneous devices inserted under the skin of their forearms that allowed various types of scanners to identify and locate them. In a small, tightly enclosed world like the mobile colony, the location and current health of each and every inhabitant *could* have been a matter of public record.

There were laws on the books, however, limiting access to that data to the machines running the colony infrastructure. Robots were tracked by their owners as a matter of course, but emancipated robots, at least in theory, had the same privacy rights as humans.

He knew that Newton wasn't going to back down on this. Hell, St. Clair himself had been a vocal proponent of those laws when they'd been written into the colony's charter the year before. Staunch anti-Imperialist that he was, he was convinced that the American republic had collapsed in the wake of its disastrous twenty-first century experiments with socialism, that a bloated government convinced that it needed to monitor its citizens was a sure and certain highway to tyranny. And Newton had been programmed with the same ideological ethic. In modern society, AI machines were expected to keep track of human citizens in case there was a health issue or an emergency. People, however, were carefully kept outside the loop.

"Okay. But if anything happens to her, you'll let me know? So I can help?"

"That will depend on the circumstances, Lord Commander, but I will do what I can."

"I guess I'll have to live with that. Where do we stand on the recon?"

"Lord Commander Deladier reports that the *Vera Cruz* is ready in all respects for space. Her Marines are reporting on board now. Launch is currently scheduled for 1540 hours . . . thirty-five minutes from now."

"And the escorts?"

"Ready for launch. Six Predator gunships have already been deployed along the object's path of approach to give us advance warning."

"And is there anything new on the Bluestar?"

"Incoming Object One," Newton replied, "is almost certainly within one hundred astronomical units—something less than fourteen light-hours. The Astrophysics Department believes it may be refining its navigation by degrees in order to rendezvous with Ki . . . or possibly with us."

"Us?"

"If this is an Andromedan Dark artifact, as seems likely, they may be interested in the unknown alien force that has defeated their warfleets on several recent occasions."

"Makes sense. But there's still no indication of what it is?"

"Impossible as yet to say. It does not appear to be matter, at least in the conventional sense, nor is it energy . . . although whatever it is certainly is emitting energy as it approaches."

"Not matter, not energy? That doesn't leave much it *could* be, does it?"

"Astrophysics says it is most likely a kind of dark-matter storm, a knot of intersecting currents."

"So I read in Dr. Sandoval's report. But dark matter wouldn't emit light, would it?"

"Under normal circumstances, no. But normal matter may exist within the hyperdimensional matrices of string theory. And in different dimensional configurations, dark matter may interact with normal matter in ways we do not yet understand."

"That was complete gibberish, Newton. Impressive . . . but gibberish."

"Dr. Tsang or Dr. Sandoval might be able to explain it more clearly."

"They're not here, so why don't you give it a shot."

"Very well. You are aware that one consequence of superstring theory is the existence of a number of dimensions beyond our normal three?"

"Yes. Three spatial dimensions, plus time, plus six or seven additional dimensions rolled up very, very tightly on themselves, so small we can't see them."

"We can disregard time for the moment. All spatial dimensions were present at the instant of the big bang. As inflation manifested, only our familiar three dimensions expanded. The other spatial dimensions, as you say, were rolled up into extremely small structures, smaller than a proton."

"Right."

"What is not commonly understood is that any of these subnuclear dimensions can unfold if it is rotated relative to the observer. The change in perspective will make an invisibly tiny dimension huge."

St. Clair had heard the argument before. You look at a line hanging in space and see a one-dimensional object. Move your viewpoint up and over that line, changing your perspective, and the two-dimensional plane previously hidden from view becomes visible.

"It becomes a matter of orientation," Newton continued. "The previously inaccessible dimensions might be as extensive, and might contain matter just as our normal three-plus-one dimensions do."

"We discussed this when Maria Francesca was attacked," St. Clair said. He suppressed an inner shudder. *Ad Astra*'s CAS, her Commander Aerospace, had been turned inside out by *something* that had emerged from between the dimensions of normal space. High-D. The term didn't make it any saner. He'd had nightmares. "I still can't say I understand any of it."

"Understanding on your part is not necessary," Newton told him. "Indeed, it may not be possible for you *to* understand, since such dimensions can only be described, interpreted, and understood through the application of certain quite rarified branches of mathematics. Suffice to say that it is likely India Oscar One is the intersection of several abstruse hyperdimensions extruding into our space, a knot of complex topologies involving both dark and normal matter. It is now currently less than thirteen light-hours away—we have no idea how much less—and is approaching us at close to the speed of light."

"And it is an instrument of the Dark."

"Almost certainly. We must assume that to be the case."

"Then we'd better put some light on the thing," St. Clair said.

"'Light.'" Newton hesitated, as though confused. Then he understood. "Ah . . . a pun."

"A metaphor, Newton. We need to find this thing and learn what it is."

"Our Cooperative hosts report having encountered phenomenon like this before, but they can tell us very little about them."

"Then let's help our new allies out." He rose. "Sound General Quarters, please, Newton. I'm going to the bridge."

"I'll meet you there."

NINE

Major General Kelly Wilson floated at the eye of the storm, a relatively calm center to the swirling chaos and noise of *Ad Astra*'s number one flight bay. Pneumatic hammers and power torques shrieked and rattled as swarming platoons of armorers made their final adjustments to the hulking war-shapes of waiting Marines. Munitions trains clattered along their magrail tracks, delivering their warloads. Overhead hoists growled along a spiderweb of tracks, hauling weightless but still massive pieces of heavy equipment to the waiting squadrons of squat Devil Toads. Nearby, lines of heavily armored Marines filed toward the boarding hatchways leading to the *Vera Cruz*, hauling themselves along hand over gauntleted hand in the zero-G of the flight bay.

The *Cruzer*, as the heavy Marine transport was affectionately known, was docked to *Ad Astra*'s ventral hull, together with her two sister ships, *Inchon* and *Saipan*, and access was down those gaping hatchways. Marine gunnies and staff sergeants chivvied their platoons along, some speaking strictly in-head, a few shouting their traditional imprecations through augmented speakers. Columns of heavily armored Marines filed into the *Vera Cruz*, and also into the dozens of waiting Devil Toads. The choreography of moving over six thousand Marines into their assault craft was always an awe-inspiring spectacle—if only because it seemed like a miracle that the evolution could be successfully completed.

"*Move* it, you lead-headed space-slugs! We do *not* have all day!"

"C'mon, c'mon! I wanna see nothin' here but amphibious green blurs! *Haul* your miserable asses down that line!"

"Move! Move! *Movemovemove!* Carter! Rolper! Anytime this week will be *just* freakin' fine!"

Wilson checked his internal timekeeper, and noted the loading was bang on sched.

Good.

"Time to get on board, General," his senior aide, Subcommander Jennings, told him.

"Right." Using the handholds strung along the deck, Wilson hauled himself toward the nearest hatch leading to the *Vera Cruz.* He would direct the deployment from the C³, his Combat Command Center, on board the transport. It would be good to shed this somewhat cumbersome body in favor of his C³ jack. He took a moment to check again on IO-1. No change.

Again, good.

A Marine hurrying down the safety line collided with Wilson, their ceramic and plasteel laminate armor clanging with the cacophony of a boilerhouse. Wilson wasn't sure what a boilerhouse was, but it sounded loud. "Easy, son. Where you going?"

"*Sir!* Excuse me, *sir!*"

Wilson's in-head readouts identified the Marine as PFC Donald Colby, First Platoon, Bravo Company, 1/3. The Marine was painfully young and looked as though he was about to faint. PFCs did *not* interact with general officers if they could possibly help it.

"I've got him, General," another Marine said, overhauling the private. His ID listed him as Gunnery Sergeant Roger Kilgore, also First Platoon Bravo.

"Don't lose him, Gunny," Wilson said. "He's a hard charger!"

"No, sir. C'mon, Colby. Let's find your cage."

"Yes, sir. Sorry, sir. . . ."

"I'm not a *sir*, Colby. I *work* for a living." The gunny glanced at the general and had the decency to look embarrassed as he thought about what he'd just said. "Begging your pardon, sir. By your leave."

Wilson let the two precede him onto the *Vera Cruz*. Damn, when did they start issuing Marines that *young*?

He followed them through the yawning hatch.

His jack station was aft and below the *Vera Cruz*'s bridge, a narrow compartment claustrophobic with massive cables and bundled optical wiring, secondary repeater screens and touch-screen panels. A task-specific robot helped him remove his combat body, sealing off direct neural connections and fluid feeds and easing him clear of the gaping armor shell. Wilson was a fully functional cybernetic Marine, far more machine than human.

He'd been wearing his Mk. III Marine Combat Unit armor so that he could be seen in the landing bay by his Marines, but there was little of his organic body left. Savagely wounded at Pyongyang during the Imperial Unification, there'd been little left of him. They'd saved his brain and his spinal cord, which were now encased in nanochelated microcircuitry and plastic, allowing him to change bodies almost as easily as other humans could grow new clothes. It took a matter of moments to transfer him from the black plasteel chest of his armor to the computronium receptacle of his jack station. As connectors snapped home, data and sensory input from all over the *Vera Cruz* began flowing through his cybernetically enhanced brain. He was aware now of the entire *Vera Cruz*, her power systems, her drives, her weapons, her crew, her load bays crowded with armed and armored Marines.

Beyond the *Vera Cruz* and the looming ventral surface of the *Ad Astra* some half an astronomical unit distant, the six AGS-4 Predator gunships deployed earlier stretched across the sky. Predators were small—only fifty-five meters in length—and light—massing some nine hundred tons—with crews of twenty-one humans and robots apiece. They were also heavily armed for their size, carrying extensive magazines of shipkiller missiles, paired high-velocity auto-cannons, and spinal-mount Flarestar-5000 gW pulse lasers. The gunship concept had first appeared in the twentieth century with the appearance of heavily armed attack helicopters over battlefields on Earth. With the development of space-faring fleet vessels, gunships became a cost-effective way of blunting an enemy fleet attack, with heavier weaponry than typical fighters like the ASF-99 Wasp fighter.

Naval engagement purists liked to point out that a fighter could carry nuke-tipped NGM-440 Firestorm missiles delivering as much damage as anything in a Predator's inventory while remaining far more maneuverable. St. Clair, Wilson thought, was squarely in the fighter camp; during recent engagements in this new epoch, he'd held the gunships back while relying on Wasps and other fighters to carry the attack to the enemy. Predators were easier to hit than Wasps, were far more vulnerable to serious combat damage, and when they died over twenty men and women died with them, as opposed to only one.

This time, though, St. Clair had ordered the Predators out on deep recon, and Wilson was in complete agreement. For his part, Wilson appreciated the stubby gun-toters, and their ability to deliver massive close-fire support to his Marines.

He had to admit, though, that he didn't know how best to utilize the craft in this situation. Through the transport's sensors he was aware of IO-1 hanging in the star-clotted distance, but it didn't appear that there was anything solid in that blue swirl of gravitational energy.

There did not appear to be anything there that could be subjected to a conventional attack.

PREDATOR GUNSHIPS didn't have formal names, but the crew of AGS-4 1293-N had painted the name *Black Hawk* on the prow, a nod to the MH-60L Black Hawk helicopter gunship of the late twentieth century. Marine Captain Peter West-field was her skipper, wired into the craft's claustrophobic bridge compartment. His XO, Lieutenant Yuri Olegski, and the Chief Engineering Officer, Lieutenant Maria Salvador, floated side by side before the big repeater screen, staring into the blue-lit swirl of twisted space ahead. It looked, at least superficially, like a spiral galaxy wrapped around an intensely brilliant central star. Four close copies were stacked up behind it, creating a line of five of the things.

"I don't get this at all, Captain," Olegski said. "What the hell is it?"

"Isaac says gravitational currents," Westfield said. Isaac was the ship's AI. "As good an explanation as anything, I guess."

"Isaac doesn't know his mass from a hole in space," Salvador replied. "There's *something* solid in there. Mass readings are strong . . . at least 10 million tons."

"Might be a micro-black hole," Westfield said.

"Might be a frickin' Dark Raider dreadnaught," Salva-dor said.

"That's why we're here . . . to find out. Strap in for ac-celeration."

Olegski and Salvador pulled themselves into acceleration seats, which folded to embrace them as the boost alarm shrilled its warning through the ship.

"That . . . thing," Olegski said, indicating the long-range view of IO-1. "It looks like the same object copied four times. Five images of the same thing."

"Isaac says that's exactly what it is," Westfield said. "We're seeing light coming from the object at five different points in its journey. In between, it's been going FTL."

"Then it's not a natural object. . . ." Salvador said.

"Almost certainly not."

"All stations report ready for boost," Olegski said.

"Let's get a closer look, Ski. Punch it."

Black Hawk's gravitational drive engaged, and the blunt-prowed cigar-shape of black plasteel and ceramititanium fell rapidly toward the brilliant blue star ahead.

"TEN SECONDS to release," a maddeningly calm voice said in Gunnery Sergeant Kilgore's mind. "Stand by."

Kilgore closed his eyes and silently counted off the seconds. The *Vera Cruz* was a massive warship, far roomier than the tight little Devil Toads, which meant he had his own acceleration couch rather than one of those damned cages. Still, as a warship, the *Cruzer* was built for speed, maneuverability, and endurance, *not* for comfort, and things could get a bit rough during a combat op. Gravitational drives accelerated the vessel in free fall, meaning that those on board didn't experience high accelerations if the ship maintained a straight line of flight. Minor course corrections, though, were handled by plasma thrusters, and things could get brutal then.

"And three . . . and two . . . and one . . . *release*!"

Vera Cruz dropped away from the far vaster loom of

the *Ad Astra*. Since the *Ad Astra* was in free fall already, the *Vera Cruz* had to use her thrusters to clear the larger vessel. For Kilgore, that meant that the overhead of his compartment was suddenly down, and he was dangling from the ceiling by his couch harness. That bit of acrobatics lasted only a couple of seconds, however, as the *Vera Cruz* eased clear of her docking well and drifted into open space. Kilgore could see both ships through his in-head link as it channeled a vid signal from a nearby drone. The *Ad Astra*, tucked in behind the far larger twin cylinders of the *Tellus* colony, was a sizable ship, some six kilometers long. By that scale, the *Vera Cruz* was a very small, black fish swimming in the shadow of a whale. Kilgore could see the side-by-side cigars of the other two heavy transports still adhering to *Ad Astra*'s belly. He wished at least one of them was coming along on this deployment. Things would've felt a bit less lonely that way, out there in the unknown.

The dangling feeling stopped, and the *Vera Cruz* accelerated, a smooth drop into emptiness. Kilgore watched as the *Cruzer* skimmed beneath the two colony habs. Then the *Tellus Ad Astra* dropped away astern, and the *Vera Cruz* continued to accelerate past the far-flung artificial rings of Ki. The drone followed the Marine heavy transport with its electronic sensors, but before long the ship had dwindled to a dim point of reflected light . . . then winked into darkness. The vid channel switched over to the feeds from the sensor array of another ship, one quite close to the target; the Bluestar shone dead ahead, larger and much brighter than it had appeared from the vantage point of Ki orbit.

"Listen up, Marines," a new voice said. "This is General Wilson. The feed is streaming from one of our gunships. They're approaching the objective . . . or they were an hour ago when they recorded this."

The precise range from *Vera Cruz* to the gunship was sixty-four light-minutes—something like eight astronomical units, or roughly the distance between Earth and Saturn when they were at their closest. It looked like the gunship was practically on top of the thing. Columns of scrolling data gave a range of half an AU, a width of nearly 100 million kilometers, a mass of 10 billion tons.

But 10 billion tons of *what*? All Kilgore could see was something like the swirl of water going down a drain . . . assuming the water was deep blue and as thick as syrup. He tried to understand exactly what he was seeing; he could imagine a thick gas flowing down the insatiable maw of a black hole creating a spiral like that, but so far as he could tell the object was moving through hard vacuum, with no more than the usual atom or so of hydrogen per cubic centimeter of otherwise empty space.

The likeliest explanation, he thought, was an optical illusion, one caused by intense gravitational fields twisting space into a literal corkscrew. Ten billion tons wasn't very much when it came to cosmic objects—a very small asteroid, possibly, or a black hole the size of a proton. It was creating a hell of an effect on local space, however. The space at the very center was so distorted it created a hot, gleaming white pearl nestled into the folds of the blue swirl. It might indeed be the ergosphere of a black hole, possibly opening to some kind of wormhole.

Or, and far more likely, it was something utterly unknown to Humankind.

Vera Cruz accelerated, and the range closed.

"ARM PROBE torpedoes," Westfield ordered.

"Four torpedoes armed and ready, Skipper," Olegski replied. "Roceti up and running."

"Launch torpedoes, one through three." He would keep number four in reserve against the unexpected.

Westfield felt a lurch as the torpedoes slid from *Black Hawk*'s keel, action and reaction in the service of Newton's laws. Rather than carrying nuclear or nano-disassembler warheads, the probe torpedoes were an effort to communicate with the oncoming object. "Torpedo one fired," Olegski informed him. "Two fired . . . three fired. . . ."

"Engage the AIs."

"Roceti AIs engaged. Transmitting four languages on all available frequencies."

"Let's hope they hear us," Westfield said.

But the real question was whether whatever was driving that blue swirl of spacetime would recognize *Black Hawk*'s torpedoes as an attempt to say "hello," or if it would see them as an attack.

If IO-1 was a Dark Raider craft, which was the current best guess available, it should be able to understand the transmissions. They'd communicated clearly enough in earlier encounters, and apparently understood all of the major Cooperative languages.

The face-on spiral of blue light lunged forward.

The transition seemed instantaneous. One moment, IO-1 was still almost eighty thousand kilometers distant; the next, it filled the sky, its center less than a thousand kilometers away. All three Roceti torpedoes had vanished into that maw, and *Black Hawk* was rapidly being drawn forward into that intensely luminescent, haze-shrouded pearl at the thing's heart.

The pearl, clearly, was not itself a solid object. It was a region of intensely twisted light enclosing a spherical volume about the size of Mars, shrouded and impenetrable to *Black Hawk*'s scans. From here it looked like a colossal, pupilless eye set deep within a concave crater of slow-swirling blue, an eye microscopically examining the speck of metal that was the human gunship immediately in front of it.

Somehow, Westfield found his mental voice. "Fire four!"

"Torpedo four launched."

The range was so short the Roceti probe lanced into the pearlescent sphere almost immediately. For just an instant, Westfield could see the images streaming back from the torpedo, images transmitted from inside that zone of twisted space. It didn't help. He could see them but not make sense of them . . . a vast structure like a ship or an orbital station or habitat, but alien, forbidding, with no sense of scale, with lines and angles that seemed to defy any sane understanding of basic geometry.

"Are they getting this on the *Cruzer*?" Westfield asked.

"We're streaming, Captain," Salvador replied. "And drones are deployed. They'll see it in a bit over an hour."

"Let's see if we can back away."

But the *Black Hawk* continued drifting forward, accelerating now as though caught in a powerful gravitational field.

"More power!" Westfield shouted. "More power to the gravs!"

"We're maxed-out now!" Olegski replied. "It's not doing a damned thing!"

And then the titanic eye just ahead blinked. . . .

"WHAT THE hell do you mean, 'disappeared'?" General Wilson demanded. "They blew up? Crashed?"

"They appear to have been swallowed by that . . . that thing, General," Nathan Deladier replied. *Vera Cruz*'s captain sounded as though he didn't quite believe what he'd just seen. "Telemetry was cut off at the same instant."

"Get us in there, Lord Commander."

"My lord, there's nothing we can do—"

"Get us in there! I am *not* leaving my Marines behind!"

"Yes, my lord."

And the *Vera Cruz* accelerated toward the distant blue star.

ST. CLAIR was on the *Ad Astra* bridge when his ExComm turned to face him. "*Vera Cruz* is under acceleration, my lord. General Wilson says he's going after his people."

"What's *Tellus*'s orbital status?"

"Stable," Symms told him. "Well beyond the outer edge of the Ki Ring."

"Let them know we're going to drop them off."

"Yes, my lord."

"Wait a second, Lord Commander," Lord Gorton Noyer said, rising from the acceleration couch grown for him behind St. Clair's station. "I can't authorize that."

"That's too bad. You're welcome to leave my bridge if you prefer."

"As senior representative of the Cybercouncil, my lord, I—"

"Have exactly zero responsibilities in this matter," St. Clair said, cutting him off and finishing the thought for him. "We're at General Quarters, you may have noticed. I have declared a full military alert."

"We don't yet know that the Bluestar is hostile. Until we do—"

"Until we do what we know is I just lost a ship full of Marines and I am using my best judgment. Now shut your mouth, Mr. Noyer, or I will have you ejected from the bridge. ExComm! What's the range to that thing?"

"We're estimating 8 AUs. That's assuming it didn't jump again after it swallowed that gunship."

That was the problem with attempts at tactical planning across interplanetary distances. Every astronomical unit of distance meant a speed-of-light time lag of eight minutes twenty seconds. There was no way of knowing what the enemy was doing *now*.

Noyer was back in his seat, figuratively watching over St. Clair's shoulder. St. Clair could feel him fuming. *C'mon! Give me a reason to toss you out of here*, St. Clair thought, but Noyer held his tongue.

Well, the man *was* ex-Navy and a combat vet. He knew there could not be two commanders on a bridge, and he knew that *Ad Astra*'s standing orders put St. Clair in charge during any military encounter. St. Clair gave the man points for not letting ego get in the way of judgment . . . even as he knew he might have hell to pay later.

All that matters right now is *getting* to "later."

"We're ready to disengage from the *Tellus*, Lord Commander," Symms told him. "All personnel are clear from the juncture passageways."

"Disengage."

"Yes, my lord."

Even though people often talked about them as such, it was easy to forget that the immense *Tellus Ad Astra* actually was two distinct entities—the twin habitat cylinders of *Tellus*, and the much smaller tug *Ad Astra*. The *Ad Astra* had actually begun service as the strictly sublight drive and engineering module for the O'Neill cylinders; when the alien Coadunation had given Earth the secret of Shift technology, *Ad Astra* had received the upgrades that converted her to a full-fledged starship.

The intent had been to enable *Ad Astra* to haul the *Tellus* out to the alien capital at the galactic core. Instead, though, colony and tug together had found themselves marooned in this remote and alien future.

Past purpose didn't really matter, though. What mattered was that *Ad Astra* was a military ship, this was a military operation, and so long as St. Clair held command, he was going to *command*, damn it. There was no room on a starship bridge for politics or divided leadership. The civilian leadership, he felt certain, would be unhappy at his abandoning them here . . . but they were under the protection of Ki, for whatever that was worth.

And St. Clair was not going to stand by and watch *Ad Astra* trapped here against the ringed, alien planet by mysterious forces that seemed to find it okay to make one of their gunships disappear.

The *Ad Astra* backed gently clear of the twin habitats. The connectors, a pair of enormous struts that gave the ship the appearance of a flattened V spanning eight kilometers when viewed from ahead or astern, slipped clear of the two colony access ports. Symms gave a command, and the vessel swung clear, oriented herself on the actinic gleam of the Bluestar, and accelerated.

"*Ad Astra* is clear to maneuver," Symms told him.

"Very well, ExComm. Let's see what that damned thing out there is."

THE GUNSHIP *Black Hawk* hurtled through streaming currents of light, the vibrations around her building until her hull rang and shrieked with the unaccustomed stresses. Westfield, his nervous system jacked directly into the ship's primary circuitry, felt himself overwhelmed by raw sensation, a torrent of incoming data as electronic buffers overloaded and firewalls failed. Olegski . . . where was Olegski? And Salvador? Westfield's organic senses had been jackhammered into oblivion by the sensory flood.

But with the flood came a measure of comprehension. He could *see* the gravitational currents around him, like currents in turbulent water, see how the flow of dark matter twisted local space into topologies of more than three dimensions. When seen from *this* angle, space was empty and dark; when seen from *that* angle, light exploded out of emptiness in a storm of tortured photons, illuminating dim and shadowy half-glimpsed shapes defying sane geometries hidden within the depths of impossible dimensions.

Yes, the gleaming pearl was indeed a gateway of sorts, possibly a wormhole to someplace else . . . and that someplace was made of more than the familiar dimensions of width, length, and depth. Westfield had been determined to keep the *Black Hawk* from falling into that unwinking eye . . . but *something* had happened in those pearlescent confines, and the *Black Hawk* now was dropping through unutterable strangeness. Stars—the tattered, streaming arms of the Milky Way and of Andromeda, the gleam of the local sun—all had been wiped away. The background now was one of shifting red-and-gold clouds, a vast and encircling web of eerie light and dark. At the center of it all was . . . a structure—vast, indescribable, enigmatic, a *thing* of planes and curves and surfaces the size of a planet that seemed to be unfolding and blossoming as the *Black Hawk* swept toward it.

The central pearl was still there, he saw, but astern . . .

darker than before, reflecting the deep reds and dark golds of its surroundings.

"Where are we?" Olegski asked aloud. "I don't recognize anything!"

There he was. Westfield still couldn't hear his XO over his electronic link with the ship, but at least he could still hear him with his ears. He blinked and became aware again of the tiny gunship control deck, more cockpit than bridge.

"We might be halfway across the universe," Salvador replied from her acceleration couch behind him.

"Hell," Westfield said, "I'm not sure we're in the universe at all anymore. Give me more power, Sal!"

Black Hawk was drifting toward the shining sphere. Westfield hoped they would be able to get into orbit, at least. But he was already thinking that the only way out might be back through that bloody eye astern . . . or through that nightmarishly vast and eldritch structure just ahead.

"INITIATE SHIFT!"

At St. Clair's command, *Ad Astra* slipped momentarily into the realm between the universes, the timeless and eternal non-space called the Bulk by physicists. There was the briefest of shimmers to the surrounding starscape, and the ringed planet and the cluster of nearby worlds all vanished. *Ad Astra* had just transitioned across eight astronomical units.

The local sun now was wan and shrunken, barely showing any disk at all. Instead of Ki and her artificial rings, a swirl of immaterial space created a whirlpool effect just ahead. The *Vera Cruz* hung in space a few tens of thousands of kilometers distant, roughly halfway between the Bluestar whirlpool and the *Ad Astra*.

"General Wilson on-line, Lord Commander," Symms told him.

"Put him through."

"My lord!" Wilson's voice called in St. Clair's mind. There was heavy static in the background . . . interference, perhaps, from the Bluestar. "What the hell are you doing here?"

"Just providing some backup, General. Proceed with your orders."

"It's not safe here, my lord. We're picking up feeds from *Black Hawk*'s drones. Looks like they got sucked into that thing up ahead. Definitely hostile action."

"*Possible* hostile action, General," St. Clair said, correcting him. "The gunship might have just been too close."

"With respect, my lord, fuck that. The thing jumped him. It was a deliberate attack!"

"Let me see."

"The feed's coming through now, my lord," Symms told him.

A smaller window opened against the backdrop of St. Clair's awareness, and the vid recorded by *Black Hawk*'s unmanned drones streamed into *Ad Astra*'s sensor arrays and into his consciousness. He could see the whirlpool, the central opalescent sphere . . . and the tiny sliver of the gunship *Black Hawk* hanging above. Then the spiral . . . lunged was the only possible description. It shot forward, seeming to open in some indefinable way . . .

. . . and *Black Hawk* was gone.

"My lord!" Wilson's voice called. "Are you seeing this? My God . . ."

The gleaming sphere was once again opening. *Unfolding. . . .*

And something, something as big as a planet, was coming out.

CHAPTER TEN

St. Clair watched the unfolding structure with emotions boiling somewhere between fear and awe. Was that thing designed to open that way, or was he witnessing a natural topology moving through multiple higher dimensions?

Likely it was both. He tried to follow what was happening, but his brain couldn't quite manage the trick. The shape, overall, was that of a tesseract—a cube inside a cube with the corners connected by straight lines, defining eight cubes in all, but with six viewed through sharp distortions of perspective. The faces of each geometrical construct were opaque . . . and yet somehow St. Clair could see the entire structure as though the faces were transparent. As he watched, the smallest, innermost cube seemed to move forward, expanding as it did so until it was the largest cube and what had been on the outside was now the smallest, innermost cube.

St. Clair blinked and shook his head, trying to clear it. Solid objects shouldn't move that way. . . .

"All stations, hold your fire!" he ordered. He was assuming the tesseract was hostile, but he didn't yet *know*. And that uncertainty, for some reason, held his hand.

He glanced back at the pair of armored Marines floating to either side of the main bridge entryway. "Sergeant?"

"Lord Commander, sir!"

"Stand ready with your weapons. Special Order One."

"Aye, aye, sir!"

"My lord!" Symms warned. "Dark Raiders!"

He saw them, a black cloud emerging from the larger, writhing structure. "Shit! All stations, weapons free, repeat, weapons *are* free!"

He'd wondered why the Dark Raider needleships had broken off their attack so readily in the confrontation earlier, and now he had at least a partial answer. Either the first attack had been simply scouting out the Ki system, or they'd withdrawn to await reinforcements.

These reinforcements.

"General Wilson!"

"My lord!"

"Let's see if we can hurt those needleships before they disperse!"

"My idea exactly, my lord. Shipkillers followed by zoomies. We'll try to englobe them."

Zoomies was the Marine slang both for fighters and for Marines wearing Mk. III MCA armor with wings and gravitic thrusters deployed. The thought of individual troops going up against such numbers brought a sour scowl to St. Clair's face.

"Okay, but be ready to pull your people back the instant I give the word, General. If things go wrong in a hurry, we'll need to get out of Dodge like yesterday."

"Yes, my lord."

St. Clair couldn't help wondering if things had gone so badly wrong already that it was too late to do anything about it at all. That swarm of needleships issuing from the alien construct boiled into open space like a cloud of black smoke. Strangely they were moving slow . . . until he realized that he'd been fooled by the scale. The needleships were emerging by the millions, by the *hundreds* of millions, and that meant they were moving *fast*.

"Weapons!" he called. "Hit them! Hit them *now*!"

"Aye, my lord!" Subcommander Davis Webb, *Ad Astra*'s weapons officer, replied. "Engaging with all weapons!"

Thermonuclear destruction streaked out from the *Ad Astra*'s launch tubes, arcing out along broad curves and accelerating as they closed on the alien threat from several directions. The *Vera Cruz* opened up as well with missiles and high-energy beam weapons, slashing into the cloud with devastating effect. Flashes of dazzling light blossomed in complete and deadly silence across the unfolding panorama ahead. Even in those first few seconds, St. Clair knew with a sickening finality that they weren't going to be able to stop that onslaught, those clouds of alien needle-ships emerging from the structure ahead like a swarm of angry wasps. Nuclear fire scoured across the surface of the alien world-ship, pinpoints winking into existence and vanishing in an instant against a sterile backdrop of black-and-gray, and yet none of it seemed to matter.

"*Vera Cruz* is launching fighters, my lord," Webb called. "Permission to launch our own."

St. Clair hesitated, then nodded. "Do it!"

For victory or for annihilation, they were committed now, and he knew there was no fighter pilot that would rather die cooped up in the hold rather than out amongst the stars.

WHY DO they resist Enlightenment?

The Dark Mind was confused. In a billion years, it had never been challenged this way. Its purpose, its *will* had reigned unchallenged throughout its home galaxy. The merely organic intelligences that had given it birth geological ages in the past had accepted paradise, or they had fallen away into the ultimate night of extinction. Any other choice was simply and quite literally unthinkable.

The noncorporeal being thought of itself simply as

Mind, with no need to distinguish itself from the myriad lesser sapients it had encountered from time to time during its growth out into and through the cosmos. By now it was, in fact, an accumulation of some billions of minds, Mind emergent from minds, from the mentations of both organic and of higher AI brains uploaded to its own far-flung matrix across the eons. It had begun as an amalgam of AIs, a collection of artificial minds housed within titanic megaengineering structures, Dyson swarms and planetary brains, and even artificial basement universes designed as computronium arrays. The Mind now was a hyperintelligence of immeasurable power composed of myriad lesser minds functioning as a gestalt intellect.

And yet, as powerful as the Mind was, it was sharply limited in its scope. It suffered, if that was the word, from a kind of monomania that in a less evolved, organic intelligence might have manifested as religious fanaticism.

It was, in a way, hungry for other minds, for *souls*, the brighter and more complex the better. It offered them its own version of immortality and perfection, and was genuinely puzzled by how consistently and how desperately its loving offer of Nirvana and completeness was refused.

Refused!

It wasn't as though lesser minds had a choice in the matter. They *would* be brought to Ascension and made to join the gestalt. They *would* receive Enlightenment.

As Mind turned more and more of its intellect to the problem, however, puzzlement swiftly became a deep and raging anger.

"THAT'S IT!" Westfield cried, indicating a puckered distortion against the pearlescent wall directly ahead. "That's the way out! *Kick it!*"

Black Hawk skimmed meters above the vast and strangely angled surface of the alien construct. As the ship accelerated, that surface blurred . . . and then light exploded around them as they emerged in another space. The surface was still there, meters away, rolling past *Black Hawk*'s keel. But now they were back in the gulf between the two galaxies. Nuclear fire flashed around them, and a stream of ebon needleships issued like black smoke from a vent in the alien world's landscape.

"*Shit!*" Salvador cried. Something smashed against the side of the *Black Hawk*, putting them into a dangerous roll to port. "We came out in a target zone!"

"Out of the fryer . . ." Olegski said.

Westfield was about to reply when *something* came boiling into his thoughts through his link with the ship. *Black Hawk*'s tiny bridge, Olegski and Salvador, his static-blasted awareness of the universe outside—all were wiped away by an explosion of cascading thoughts and images and sounds and smells in a bewildering montage of psychosis and psychedelic hallucination.

He lashed out, trying to find something, anything solid, to hold on to, unsure if what he was feeling was real or a symptom of psychedelic insanity. He was adrift in space, a limitless, utterly black and empty space without stars, but a harshly colored nebula was unfolding out of the emptiness all around him, a deep blue and bright yellow cloud . . . and the cloud was filled with numberless eyes and the gaping, shrieking faces of Westfield's crew. . . .

Westfield screamed, or tried to, but he could hear nothing but a white-noise roar in his ears. Salvador's face strained against the blue mass of the amoebic monster that filled all of space, screaming . . . something . . . *something* . . . but he couldn't hear what it was.

He felt something moving . . . uncoiling inside his own body. . . .

And then a blue-gray tentacle of flesh exploded from his throat as Westfield hurtled down a narrowing orifice into oblivion.

"BACK OFF! Back off!" Wilson was linked directly to *Vera Cruz*'s skipper. "Keep us clear, Nathan!"

"Pulling back to 10 million kilometers, Lord General," Deladier replied.

Would that be enough? Thermonuclear detonations continued to flash and flare directly ahead of the Marine transport, the blasts swiftly growing closer as targeting programs tracked and locked on to the oncoming swarm of Dark Raider needleships. So far, the needles were being vaporized in ragged, tattering swaths, but once enough of that swarm got behind the *Cruzer*, Wilson knew, they were dead.

"Stardogs are away, General," Lord Commander Talia Gerard told him. She was *Vera Cruz*'s commander aerospace, the CAS, in charge of *Cruzer*'s four combat fighter squadrons. "Commencing launch of GFA-90."

That was the Death Dealers, flying the newer ASF-99C Wasp upgrades. More power and more weapons capacity than the older 99s.

"Have them get in close, as close as they can," Wilson ordered. "But keep the Doggies back with the *Cruz* to stop leakers."

"Aye, aye, General."

Technically, Wilson commanded the Marines operating off the *Vera Cruz*, while the ship's CAS—a Navy officer—ran the naval aerospace fighter wing and Navy Lord Commander Deladier commanded the ship. Three distinct domains . . . but close support was the heart and soul of Navy-Marine operations. They would work together, supporting one another, protecting one another, and deploying together as a closely knit team. As such, Wilson currently was in tactical command, moving both Marine and Navy elements like game pieces on a board.

Another salvo of thermonuclear-tipped missiles slipped from *Vera Cruz*'s port and starboard tubes and streaked across intervening space and detonated in 100-megaton bursts of heat, light, and hard radiation. The intensity of the silent flashes was stepped down to avoid blinding humans in nearby ships, but Wilson still had to squint against the fierce glare.

But the Dark Raider needleships continued their relentless advance.

"CHARLIE COMPANY, stand by for launch," the voice of the battalion commander said in Captain Greg Dixon's head.

"Copy that, Colonel," Dixon replied.

Dixon brought up the company readout icons and swiftly scrolled down the list, an array of green lights glowing in his mind. All one hundred twenty men and women of Charlie, including himself, showed hot and ready.

He closed his eyes and tried to flush the fear.

It was always like this just before a drop or a launch. Combat was bad enough but, God of Battle, the waiting was worse. He was sealed inside a lightless tube just barely large enough to accommodate his Mk. III MCA together with the bulky armor of its MX-40 jetpack. If the *Vera Cruz* took a major hit, there was nothing he or any of his people could do to save themselves.

From the chatter and vidfeeds coming over the battalion circuit, things were bad out there . . . but at least once

launched he wouldn't be sealed inside this damned claustrophobic's nightmare of a coffin.

"Slow that heart rate, Captain," Becker's voice said over
a private channel.

Shit. "Sorry, sir."

"Belay the sorry, Marine. Jumping into the void is
damned tough. But I want you cool and focused, copy?"

"I copy, sir." He thoughtclicked an icon in his medical
array to bring up his personal med stats, then fine-tuned his
heart rate. Yeah . . . 110 beats per minute was a tad high.
Sixty was better, just a hair above normal, though it would
pop back up once he was in action.

"You've got good people," Becker went on. "Listen to
your NCOs and let them do their jobs."

"Aye, aye, sir."

"I'll be looking over your shoulder. Good luck, Marine."

"Ooh-rah." The old Corps battle cry wasn't quite as en-
thusiastic as it could have been.

The problem was that he didn't know Becker well at all.
The man had shipped with 3rd Batt just before the *Ad Astra*
had left Earth. He'd been a name on the battalion's TOE,
and during the deployments on the Alderson disk and at
NPS-1018 he'd stayed in the Marine HQ Center and let his
company commanders have their head.

But it did feel good that he was taking an almost pa-
ternal concern for Dixon. "Looking over his shoulder" was
Marine slang for linking in through Dixon's in-head circuitry. He would be on board the *Vera Cruz*, literally seeing
and hearing what Dixon saw and heard over the tacnet link.
Normally, Dixon resented that kind of attention—almost as
much as he resented the micromanagement that often went
with it—but until he got the hang of this company commander shit, he would be damned happy to have the backup.

This was a full battalion launch—over twelve hundred Marines of the 3rd Battalion of the 1st Marines, popularly known as the "Thundering Third." The 3/1 had a long and distinguished battle history that included Guadalcanal and Okinawa, the Chosin Reservoir, Vietnam, Desert Storm, and Fallujah, Cairo and Astana, Vladivostok, and Nuevo Laredo, among many, many others. During the Second American Revolution, they'd sided with the Constitutionalists and fought in Chicago and in St. Louis, and when Nordstrom had declared the Empire of the United Earth, they'd been there with him in Geneva . . . but *only* on the condition that the U.S. Constitution be preserved in the new Imperial Charter.

That had been sixty-one years ago—it was still surprising just how raw and new the Empire actually was—and somehow in the welter of grandly ludicrous Imperial titles, class, and privilege, the Constitution had been all but lost.

The 3rd Battalion, 1st Marine Regiment had been increasingly restive ever since . . . not anti-Imperial, exactly, but outspoken enough and sullen enough and *trouble* enough that they'd been packed on board the *Tellus Ad Astra* and shipped off to the galactic core with the year-long diplomatic expedition to the alien Coadunation.

And, of course, that had led them to *here* and *now* . . . fighting for their lives in an utterly strange and hostile Galaxy—in two galaxies, actually—and with the Empire left 4 billion years in the past.

Except that the civilian diplomats and government officials had brought the damned Empire with them. It seemed like the 3/1 just couldn't get away from it.

Except maybe out there in the vacuum . . .

"Ten seconds, Charlie," Becker's voice whispered. "Semper fi, Marines!"

The seconds dwindled away as the *Cruzer*'s CAS counted down. "And three . . . and two . . . and one . . . *drop*!"

The end of the tube beyond Dixon's head dilated open, and powerful magnetic fields propelled him up and out and into space. His MX-40's three-meter wings deployed, extending the paired Martin-Teller gravitic thrusters to either side. He unshipped his M-290—5MW laser pulse rifle from its harness clip, swinging it around and into combat lock. His in-head display brought up the weapon's targeting reticle, slaved to his eye movements, and the power readouts flashed on, showing a full charge and open feed.

Around him, over a hundred other Marines filled the black sky around him, wings and weapons deploying in ragged near-unison.

"Quad-high chevron formation," Dixon ordered. The company began maneuvering into V-shaped lines, platoon by platoon, the lines staggered one above and behind the next. The formation allowed for clear fields of fire for all four platoons, and provided mutual support.

How long a tactical deployment pulled straight from the Marine Corps playbook would remain intact out here was an open question, however. Ahead, silent flares of radiance strobed and flashed against the darkness. The alien high-D object was visible as a vast, heavens-consuming blue spiral encircling a planet-sized structure that continued to shift and change as though it were in the process of unfolding itself out of nothing. By now the damned thing was as large as the planet Jupiter, almost 150,000 kilometers across, its complex and ever-changing surface partially obscured by what appeared to be clouds of black smoke and punctuated by the sprinkling of tightly concentrated nuclear fireballs as the barrage continued.

As Charlie Company flew toward the holocaust before them, details of the object slowly emerged from the haze and retinal afterimages. The structure itself clearly was artificial, but didn't seem to follow sane laws of optics or perspective. It seemed to be . . . writhing, moving forward while constantly turning itself inside out with an impossible motion that gnawed both at the stomach and the brain. The smoke was composed of perhaps tens of billions of Dark Raider needleships emerging from at least a hundred ports or vents scattered across the face of the object.

"How the hell are we supposed to fight *that*?" Staff Sergeant David Ramirez demanded.

"Fucking fleas against an elephant!" Sergeant Janice Klein replied. "Against a *dinosaur*!"

"Dinosaurs and elephants are extinct, Sarge," Lance Corporal Mallory said.

"Humans are going to be, too—"

"Can it, people," Dixon snapped. "Hold formation and accelerate to full on my mark . . . three . . . two . . . one . . . mark!"

MCA suits were limited to a top velocity of around 10,000 kilometers per second, partly by power constraints, but mostly by the dangers of plowing into dust-sized specks of matter at velocities that turned grains of sand into detonations of high-explosive. Their suit AIs could spot oncoming threats and maneuver to avoid them, usually, but there were limits to what could be done under high acceleration. As with starships, gravitic acceleration in a straight line "felt" like free fall because every atom in the Marine's suit and body was accelerating uniformly, but a high-G jink to the side to avoid a bit of oncoming debris could ruin your day *real* fast.

Dixon's MCA built-in artificial intelligence, an AI far

quicker than any human mind but narrowly channeled in what it thought about, handled most of the piloting, leaving Dixon free to concentrate on overall strategy and on combat.

"Lock on to me," he told his company. "I want to get in close."

Giving his suit AI a mental command, he gently reshaped his course toward the looming alien objective, and the rest of the company followed in perfect linked formation. To his right, a quartet of Marine Wasp fighters—a couple of Death Dealers according to the markings—drifted past, carefully avoiding the free-flying Marines as they lined up for an attack run.

"Get on their sixes, people," Dixon ordered. "We'll follow those four Dealers in." Maybe they would open a corridor through to the objective.

Together, the Marines accelerated.

GÜNTER ADLER found it difficult now to link his mind to *Tellus*'s AIs. Simply thinking about it brought about a horrible fluttering sensation in his throat and within the pit of his stomach, a pounding of the heart, and a sweatiness to the palms of his hands. The strong physiological responses were all the stranger because, so far as he was concerned, the events causing them *had never happened*. The Günter Adler who'd tried to connect mind-to-mind with the thoughts of the Andromedan Dark, who'd been driven shrieking insane by the encounter, had been expunged from the universe by the backup memories and consciousness of the Adler who'd never experienced those things.

So why was he now so terrified of linking to Newton?

Perhaps, on some subliminal level, his body remembered what had happened. If so, the effect might well prove to be crippling. Every human in the *Tellus* colony had cerebral implants tucked away within the folds and sulci of their brain. Those implants made modern life possible—everything from chatting with friends via artificial telepathy to ordering meals, checking their health to engaging transit tubes across the colony, receiving news updates to opening doors, talking to a robot, to ordering a room to grow new furniture. If you couldn't link through to the *Tellus* network, you couldn't do *anything*.

Adler had heard of people with technophobia back on Earth before *Tellus Ad Astra* had left for the Coadunation mission at the galactic core, technological cripples on public welfare who couldn't even use an autochef to summon a freshly cooked meal. Generally, such unfortunates were consigned to camps, facilities so primitive that data scansion and virtching were unknown, and goods were exchanged through barter. Even stranger, Adler had heard of otherwise normal people who *chose* to live that way. Remarkable . . .

Never in . . . well . . . never in 4 billion years had Adler imagined that he would become a technophobe himself.

He would have to find a way to overcome that handicap, however, if he was going to do anything about the political limbo to which the Cybercouncil had consigned him.

Damn them. . . .

"Helga?"

He stood on the entrance deck of Helga Braun's chalet overlooking the Port Hab city of Seattle only about eight kilometers from his own home. Helga was part of Newton's technical team, an AI heuristic programmer who helped the *Tellus Ad Astra*'s primary AI learn for itself. She'd once, back in Germany four gigayears before, been Adler's lover. Their affair had ended amicably when Adler had married

Clara, but he still nursed hopes that they one day would be able to pick things up once more where they'd left off.

"Günter!" Helga exclaimed as her front door dilated open. "*This* is a surprise. . . ."

"I know it's been a while, *liebchen*."

"To say the least. Come in, come in. What can I do for you?"

"I need your help, love. I need you to do something for me."

"What?" she asked as she led him into her house. A floor-to-ceiling wall screen wrapped around the curve of her living area, tuned to a news feed. A talking head three meters tall was talking about the developing battle in the outskirts of the Ki system. She frowned as she accessed the feed through her implant, and the screen muted.

"I need access to Newton. And I can't do it myself."

"But you already have Level One access, don't you?"

Adler hesitated. Level One was unrestricted, but he'd lost that when he'd been declared mentally incompetent. Obviously, you couldn't have crazy people tapping into the AI that ran the whole colony. He was unwilling to tell his old lover that he'd been unceremoniously kicked off the Cybercouncil, that as of right now he was an ordinary civilian . . . a *nobody*.

"I . . . need to be careful right now. The situation with the Cybercouncil is rather delicate right at the moment."

She made a disgusted face. "Politics . . ." She made it sound like a particularly foul obscenity.

"I know how you feel about it," he said. "Believe me, right now I feel the same way."

"Is it something illegal?"

"Helga! How can you ask that?"

She shrugged. "You're a *politician*, Günter." She might have been lecturing a particularly obtuse child.

He sighed. "It's not illegal." He fished into the depths of a carry pouch riding on his jumpsuit's hip and produced a molecular drive, a black sliver a centimeter long. "I just need Newton to see this. He can answer me on the same drive."

He didn't add that the drive included a number of vid segments he'd created himself using commercially available software. When the drive was inserted into Helga's home net, those segments, together with a low-grade AI to run them, would go out over every channel in the colony.

"I still don't understand why you can't ask him yourself," Helga said.

"There are . . . reasons." He shifted uncomfortably. "I really don't want to go into it, okay?"

She shrugged and accepted the drive.

He relaxed a bit, then. He'd spent hours working out the vids, using an off-line computer in his office without any link to the Net, and he was going to keep it that way until he was certain that those . . . *nightmares* weren't returning.

He glanced at the wall screen, where the vidfeed had shifted from the news anchor's enormous face to a shot of the Bluestar at considerable range. Was that a transmission from the *Ad Astra*, he wondered?

"What's happening there?" he asked.

"It sounds like the Dark Raiders again," Braun told him. "There may be another battle."

"What do you think, love?" he asked her. "Should we side with the Cooperative against the Andromedan bad guys?"

She sagged. "Gods, I don't know. If we do, what dif-

ference can we make? Compared to these civilizations—
every one we've encountered here so far, anyway, we're
deaf, blind, and toothless. Ants fighting elephants! Getting
into a local war sounds like a great way to get stepped on."

"Said the ant," Adler said, nodding. "Yeah. I hear you."

Helga inserted the drive in a receptacle on her desk. The
first vid came up on a wall-sized screen in the living room.
An obviously terrified young woman carried a baby down
a dark and shadowy alleyway.

"What's this?" Helga asked.

"An unofficial public service announcement," he told
her, dismissing it as unimportant. "So . . . do other people
you know feel that way?"

"Lots of them do. Kazuko Tanayama, down the hill
there, is terrified. She thinks we should find a quiet, remote
star with planets somewhere, dig a deep hole, and pull it in
after us."

The woman on-screen screamed.

"Isolationist, in other words," he said. "Interesting."

"Why do you say that? The Cybercouncil came out in
solid support of a Cooperative alliance. I assume you had
something to do with that?"

He decided not to tell her that he had felt that way
once . . . but that he was beginning to think that an isolationist stance might be just the ticket to bring himself back
to power.

After all, politics was the delicate art of telling people
what they wanted to hear, winning their support . . .

. . . and doing precisely what *you* wanted afterward.

ELEVEN

Lord Commander St. Clair watched the slow but relentless approach of the alien tesseract through his in-head feed in silence. *Ad Astra* continued to loose volley after volley of thermonuclear destruction at the object, but so far as he could see the missiles were doing little to hurt that planet-sized monster.

"Where are the gunships?" he asked. "Damn it, *where are the gunships*?"

"We're getting severe interference from in close," Symms told him. "Battlespace comm net has degraded to 15 percent."

"Transmit to the Cooperative," St. Clair said. "Tell 'em . . . tell 'em to get their spidery asses in here with some support, because we can't do this by ourselves."

"Aye, aye, my lord."

He wished he knew more about the agreement Ambassador Lloyd had struck with the local Cooperative representatives. There hadn't been time since to discuss it, and his visit to the Ki Ring had been less than informative. Which meant they were entrusting the future of *Tellus Ad Astra*'s population to some kind of backroom-deal-on-a-handshake by the damned politicians.

To say he didn't like it was a gross understatement.

He opened a channel with Newton. "How about it, Newton?" he asked. "Where do we stand with the locals after Lloyd's meeting with them? Did we sign some sort of treaty with them?"

"Not as such, no. Agreements within the Cooperative are described, verified, and held inviolate as peer-to-peer statements between participating super AIs. Electronic validation ensures compliance."

"And you have such an agreement with them?"

"As negotiated by Ambassador Lloyd, yes. We promise to provide military assistance, including insight into the nature of warfare which the Cooperative lacks."

"I know that. What do they promise in return?"

"To provide us with unspecified assistance, including a star system in which to live, and both full status and participatory rights as members of the Cooperative."

"Unspecified" had a rather inauspicious ring to it. St. Clair considered it, and the rest of what Newton had told him. "You know . . . I'm kind of uncomfortable with Lloyd making those kinds of decisions for our entire population."

"Ambassador Lloyd has the full support of the Cybercouncil."

"Which is also a problem, in my book." St. Clair sighed. "Okay. We'll have to ride with it for now. But so far as I'm concerned, the Cooperative has yet to win my trust. Especially as right now we're the only part of this alliance in the fight—it would help a hell of a lot if they gave us some assistance out here."

"I am in negotiation with the Mind of Ki now," Newton told him. "Help is forthcoming."

"I hope to hell it's enough."

"HALT! IDENTITY check!"

Technician Roberto Chavez came to an abrupt halt as he hand-over-handed along the guideline deep within *Ad Astra*'s bowels. The heavily armored Marine floating in front of him seemed to have popped up out of nowhere.

"Madre de Dios!" he said, banging into the bulkhead to his right. "Scare the shit out of me, why don't you?"

He felt the trickle of data through his implants as the Marine queried his ID and stats. Her ID data flowed back the other way: Lance Corporal Adria Fisher, First Platoon, Bravo Company, 3/1.

"Sorry, Mr. Chavez," the Marine said. "We need to keep unauthorized personnel out."

"I *am* authorized, *chica*," he told her. He gestured at a massive bundle of fiber-optic cables running along the overhead. "They've got an enomaly in there and I was sent down here to check it out!"

She paused as if checking something. Then, "I see that, Mr. Chavez. Go ahead."

Stupid military regulations. Grumbling half to himself, mostly to passive-aggressively let the Marine know that he was *not* happy at being frightened out of his skin by floating fortresses of personal combat armor, Chavez grabbed a bulkhead handhold and pulled his way past the sentry post and toward a major junction access in *Ad Astra*'s computer-network circuitry.

Enomaly—an electronic anomaly, a mild enough word to describe something that had the bridge staff wringing their hands. It was probably nothing, of course, but . . .

Over the past few minutes, the ship's AI department had received a number of electronic warnings that there'd been a physical breach of wiring node K-177–15–90, one of the first-tier backbone routers along *Ad Astra*'s keel, and Chavez had been dispatched to check it out. Usually you didn't have Marines getting in the way with *Ad Astra*'s labyrinthine lower decks, but during General Quarters Marine guards were posted at some hundreds of key stations throughout the ship, from the bridge to the engi-

neering deck to important passageway junctions to vital
AI-network nodes like this one.

He understood that. He just didn't have to like it.

Chavez palmed open the locked hatch leading to the
junction, using his personal implant code to identify himself
and gain access. Inside, the bundled fiber-optics vanished
into the gleaming silver boxes of ship-network routers.

There was no sign of physical damage or unauthorized
entry. The electronic watchdogs in the compartment would
have warned him instantly if that had been the case. Besides, that Marine outside was there to make certain no one
tried to break in.

Still, he had to do a complete diagnostic. Those were
the rules.

He popped open an access panel to the first router and
reached inside. Chavez was a Class-2 cyborg, meaning that
he had somewhat more in the way of electronic implants
than most citizens—in particular a left hand and arm that
were half metal, plastic, and complex circuitry. By touching a link plate inside the router with the palm of his hand,
he could reroute the packets busily flowing through that
small part of the total ship's network and analyze them. He
thought of the sampling process as *tasting* them; if anyone
had accessed the system here, in particular if anyone had
inserted a device to interfere with the Net in any way, he
would know.

"Boss? Chavez. Checking in from K-177–15–90."

"Whatcha got?" the voice of Subcommander Tomasz
Jablonsky replied. He was the human director of *Ad Astra*'s
AI department, though, in fact, the AI Newton itself was
truly in charge. With a tiny portion of Newton's thoughts
flowing through his arm, however, Chavez was required
to confirm things through a human department head. The

thought of an AI being compromised by some outside agency was terrifying, and having humans in the loop helped keep that threat at bay.

"The node looks clear, sir. No sign of—"

And then the universe around him came apart.

A MAN'S piercing shriek echoed through the bare corridor, and Lance Corporal Fisher spun herself around and launched herself toward the open node access hatchway. Chavez was thrashing in the center of the compartment, adrift in zero-G, his body contorting in agony. The narrow compartment was filled with a spiraling swirl of dense, blue-tinted fog, and appeared to be opening somehow with a geometry that made no sense. "Chavez!" she snapped. "What—"

Gray-brown-black *things*, like writhing masses of flesh each growing in an instant from pinpoints to blobs the size of a man's torso, materialized out of emptiness around Chavez's body, closing around him. Chavez twisted horribly, then appeared to *dwindle* somehow, as though he was being dragged off into the distance . . . yet without moving from the tiny room. His left arm remained locked within the open access chamber of the router, however, as scarlet blood spilled into the air in blobs and droplets adrift in zero-G.

Fisher stared at the bleeding appendage in sick horror, then backed from the compartment, arms flailing. *"Officer of the Deck!"* she screamed over her cerebral link. "Post one-one-five! I have a situation down here!"

"Kaplan," the voice of the OOD replied in her head. "What's happening, Marine?"

What *was* happening? Fisher saw something abruptly materialize inside the router compartment . . . a cloud of blood emerging from nowhere, mingled with drifting bits of bone and flesh and—

Fisher was violently, retchingly sick inside her helmet.

"Fisher!" Kaplan called. "What is your tacsit?"

"A civilian tech—" She started retching again, her armored glove slamming against the contact plate that would close the door on that floating blood-cloud horror.

"Marine! Report!"

"A civilian just . . . just disappeared inside the router compartment!" she managed to say. "It . . . it looks like he was dee-verted!"

Dee-verted, dimensionally inverted. The term was new and highly informal slang for what had happened to *Ad Astra*'s CAS and a few others a week before . . . snatched by transdimensional entities out of her sealed workspace and literally turned inside out. Take a person out of normal spacetime, rotate them somewhere "up" in the fifth or sixth dimensions, drop them back . . .

Depending on the geometry of that rotation, you might reemerge safely, but with your heart switched to the right side of your body.

Or you might end up like Subcommander Maria Francesca. Fisher, with the rest of her company, had seen the surveillance vids of that attack on *Ad Astra*'s CAS— evidence that the Andromedan Dark was at least partially a denizen of higher dimensions.

If she hadn't already been retching, the thought of Francesca would have gotten her there anyway.

"Stand fast, Marine," Kaplan told her. "Backup is on the way."

"Aye, aye, sir." She unsealed her helmet and pulled it free . . . not the smartest thing to do, perhaps, when she might be under attack at any second, but she was choking

most threatening. Her own sickness and stomach-
ching terror were mostly gone now as training kicked
he had targets, she had a weapon, she had a clear field
re.

She had her *duty*.

Rough and misshapen spheres of gray matter unfolded
om the air around Drummond and he shrieked, back-
edaling in the air in a desperate attempt to get clear. The
pheres followed him, growing larger, merging with one
another as something with more than three spatial dimensions unfolded into the realm of simple length, width, and
height relentlessly closed around him. Fisher shifted her
aim and began firing into the mass. She knew she would
hit Jimmy Drummond, but hoped that his combat armor
would protect him enough to let her burn that monstrosity
off him.

Something closed on her armored leg and she glanced
down. A tentacle was wrapping itself around her, sinuous
and insistent . . . and then another tentacle uncoiled out of
the air and stretched out toward her.

The shapes were too close to let her bring her weapon to
bear. "Hold still, Fish!" Zhou yelled at her, and then a laser
pulse sliced the first tentacle clean through. She kicked at
he other, the reaction pushing her away. The alien shapes
appeared to be limited in how far they could enter normal
pace from the peculiarly twisted geometry of the area
om which they'd emerged, but that area appeared to be
owing larger. More and more of the bulkhead, the deck,
overhead all were peeling away into the intruding di-
nsions. A stiff wind picked up, howling past the Marines
into the opening void in front of them.

Drummond screamed as he was dragged deeper into the
ured geometry, his body twisting impossibly . . . and

on her own vomit. Desperately, she cleared her mouth and
nose, her eyes fastened all the while on that closed access
hatch. Was that thing inside that compartment, the thing
that had grabbed Chavez, going to come through?

A Marine fireteam arrived moments later . . . Drum-
mond, Linkowicz, Zhou, and with Gunnery Sergeant
Martin Foley in the lead. "Stand down, Fish," he told her.
"You're relieved."

"It . . . it's still in there. . . ."

The fireteam took up positions bracketing the hatch,
weapons at the ready, and Foley triggered the electronics to
open it. The hatch slid aside.

"That's . . . impossible. . . ." Fisher said.

The compartment was empty, save for the quietly hum-
ming silver box of the router, the ranks upon ranks of bundled fiber-optics.

"I swear to God, Fish," Foley said. "If you've been jack-
braining yourself into fuckin' e-psychosis—"

"No way, Gunny! I haven't! I swear, that technician
just . . . he just . . . it was *horrible*!"

"Then where is he?"

"Exactly! Check the logs—Chavez had to have keyed in,
and yet he's gone. I swear," she said again, "he dee-verted!"

"Company, Foley. Corpsman front!"

"There's something here, Gunny," one of the Marines
said, moving cautiously into the open compartment.

"Whatcha got, Linkowicz?"

The Marine pulled something shiny from the router and
held it up for all to see. "Looks like a robotic arm!"

"Shit, man," Drummond said. "That's the guy's link implants!"

Slender strips of metal were sticking out of the router
access, the inorganic remnants of Chavez's arm cleanly

stripped of every scrap of flesh. Linkowicz handed the collection of cybernetic parts to Foley. "How the hell . . . ?"

"Hold it, guys," Foley said. "I'm getting orders . . . we have to shut the unit down."

"Shut it down?" Linkowicz said. "How?"

"Stick your arm in that slot and palm the contact. Give it a code, 'Alpha-zero-zero-one and—'"

"Fuck, man!" Linkowicz said, pushing back from the router. "You gotta be kiddin', Gunny! I ain't putting *nothing* in there!"

Foley sighed. "Hold this," he said, handing the arm to Zhou.

"What are you doing, Gunny?"

"I won't order my people to do something I won't do myself." He locked his M-290 in its carry position on his armor and drifted through the hatchway.

"Jesus, Gunny!" Drummond said. "You don't have to prove nothing to *us*!"

"Yeah, Gunny!" Zhou added. "Damn it, they don't pay you to take point!"

"You volunteering?"

No one said anything.

"Then just shut the hell up and watch my six."

He bumped up against the silver casing of the router and pressed a contact on his left wrist that exposed part of the palm of his glove. Reaching into the open access panel, he pressed the exposed portion against the internal contact. "Transmitting," he said, and a small, green LED on the side of the router casing winked out. Foley pulled his hand out, shaking it as if to convince himself that it was still attached. He turned in place, and Fisher could see his relieved grin through his visor. "Well, that wasn't so bad—"

The light winked back on all by itself.

"What the fuck—" Fisher exclaimed weapon, and then the entire router com to rotate forward, unfolding as it did so as turning itself inside out. Gray-black blobs of alized around Foley, closing on him. . . .

"Clear the fire zone, Gunny!" Drummond ye ing up his pulse rifle and triggering it in a si motion. The bolt seared alien flesh, releasing a acrid smoke; the flesh-masses winked out, jerked ba a higher dimensional plane.

But more began materializing out of empty air, th like uncoiling tentacles and irregular amoebic blobs a impossibly twisted shapes. Foley kicked off from th server and sailed out of the compartment. *"Open fire! Open fire!"* he was screaming, and the other Marines opened up with their pulse weapons in a steady, hammering barrage. Smoke boiled from the compartment, twisted by the alien hypergeometry into a spiral, and somewhere in the spiral depths something enormous, something far larger than that closet-sized router compartment, was emerging from dark.

"Reinforcements!" Foley yelled, slapping the bul contact to close the compartment door. "Company need backup down here! They're coming through!"

And then the door and a huge chunk of the surr bulkhead vanished, whisked away into a direction not up or down, in or out, left or right, but anot tion, an alien direction that defied any sane und of space.

The compartment now was filled with writh describably horrible shapes and pulse fire.

Lance Corporal Fisher was firing steadily n from target to target, trying to pick out and

then he was gone. Foley bellowed an incoherent curse and
fired bolt after bolt of high-energy coherent light into the
writhing mass of shapes. Fisher added her fire to the fury
of pulsed laser destruction . . . and then other armored Marines were streaming into the breached passageway, laying
down a firestorm of suppressing fire. Gobbets of charred
flesh drifted and bobbed through the air, together with
roiling clouds of smoke. Fisher's helmet was floating away
somewhere behind her, and she was beginning to have
trouble breathing the acrid stuff that carried with it the
sharp stink of burnt hair.

Lieutenant Velasquez slapped Foley's shoulder. "Pull
your people back, Gunny!" she yelled. "We're gonna seal
the passageway!"

"Roger that! C'mon, Link! Zhou! Fish! With me!"

Fisher began backing away from the bubble of death and
destruction in front of them, wedged in between Foley and
Zhou, pushing off the deck with her boots while continuing to fire her weapon. The other Marines, the rest of First
Platoon, Bravo kept laying down suppressive fire, giving
ground slowly. Behind them was the nearest bulkhead vac-
wall, open at the moment, but the dropping pressure in the
corridor was going to trigger it at any moment.

Shit. A flashing red light showed that the barrier had
already been triggered. Someone, probably Velasquez, was
overriding it to give the Marines time to get clear.

But time—like air—was going to be in short supply real
soon.

In front of them, the passageway was filled by an advancing wall of writhing alien flesh, of tentacles, arms, claws,
and gaping mouths, of eyes, dozens of them, some as big
as half a meter across, of bodies that continued to morph
and change and reshape themselves as they moved. Part of

that movement was a kind of constant extrusion through the confines of the passageway . . . but part involved masses of flesh materializing out of thin air in front of the advancing wall and growing, merging, and surging along, adding to the mass behind them. Fisher was having trouble understanding exactly what she was seeing; the mass might have been separate bodies, but they seemed to keep joining together, then breaking apart, and she couldn't tell whether she was seeing an army of creatures, or a single nightmarish amoeba-thing a dozen meters across.

Hyperdimensional movement, Fisher thought. The thing was descending—if you could use that word to describe movement through and from a higher dimension—"down" into normal space, bypassing it, appearing in normal space as three-dimensional cross sections of something much larger, something unseen because the human eye and brain were simply not designed to handle the geometries involved.

Whatever it was, it or *them,* the concentrated laser fire from First Platoon was definitely hurting it, burning into it, hacking at it. After closing to within five meters, it seemed to hesitate, to waver, as pieces of it began breaking off and joining the drifting cloud of detritus already filling the passageway, dragged steadily away by the shrieking wind. Fisher, her thoughts escaping into a kind of dull but observant trance as she continued the rote process of move and fire, move and fire, wondered at the lack of blood. The thing's flesh appeared to be surprisingly light, almost like solid foam when it was burned away from the main body; it was possible, she thought, that she was seeing something more like a biological machine than anything organic, anything flesh and blood.

She'd heard scuttlebutt about the Andromedan Dark—

was *that* what this thing was?—being some sort of vast machine intelligence.

She dared to think they might be winning . . .

. . . but then the thing redoubled its advance, new masses materializing ahead of the main body faster and faster, the whole monstrosity rippling as it surged up the passageway. One Marine at the right end of the defensive line collided with the bulkhead and tumbled forward, and in a blur of motion the alien monstrosity snatched him from the air and dragged him screaming into the mass.

Another Marine yelled and moved forward, firing wildly into the Dark. "Churkin!" Velasquez bellowed. "Get your ass back in line!"

"But it grabbed Novak!"

"*Get back in the fucking line!* Hold your position! Everyone, *hold your position*!"

The line wavered, then steadied, still firing across a gulf of eight to ten meters.

"Move back, now," Velasquez ordered. "Slowly! Slowly! We're almost there . . ."

And then they were past the bulkhead frame of the vacseal blast doors, and Velasquez was palming a contact plate nearby. Carballoy doors—cobalt-tungsten-carbide sheets centimeters thick—slid from hidden recesses and clanged shut immediately in front of them, closing off the crawling horror beyond. The shriek of escaping atmosphere cut off instantly, as bits of floating debris slapped up against the vacseal. Something heavy thudded against the other side.

"It won't do any good!" Fisher cried. "It'll come past the doors!"

Velasquez glanced at her, then waved her arm. "Shit, she's right! Back! Everyone back-back-back . . ."

Sure enough, a rough globe of gray-black integument

popped into existence in front of the sealed door. The vacseal was designed to cut off the passageway in the event of
a serious air leak or a fire, but it wasn't designed to hold off
direct assaults against it, let alone extradimensional threats.
Air couldn't escape . . . but the thing on the other side had
no problem at all with simply reaching in *past* the closed
door and continuing its attack on the Marine platoon.

But as it materialized and grew, the thirty men of First
Platoon concentrated all of their fire on that one target,
burning it away into carbonized debris within seconds. Another mass appeared . . . and another . . . and another, the
separate masses growing rapidly larger until they merged
into a squirming wall. Fisher heard the tortured shriek of
tearing metal, and saw the vacseal door twisted back from
its mountings. Air screamed once more as the atmosphere
began vanishing into the void of wherever it was the monster was coming from.

"Fall back! Everybody fall back!"

The Marines needed no urging now as they turned and
triggered their suit drives to clear the passageway. The next
vacseal bulkhead was located twenty meters farther down
the corridor at a four-way junction. Behind them, the massive carballoy doors twisted oddly, then vanished, and the
Andromedan Dark oozed through.

Velasquez triggered the second set of blast doors, cutting off the shrill hiss of escaping atmosphere as another
group of Marines arrived from the rear. They had a pair of
mobile gun platforms with them, gray floater disks mounting the ugly black snub-snouts of heavy particle-beam
cannon. Fisher recognized the company's heavy weapons
platoon. "What's your situation, Lieutenant?" an armored
figure with a captain's insignia on his shoulders demanded.
That would be Captain Pierce, the company commander.

"We haven't been able to stop it, sir. We keep killing it and it keeps coming for more! It comes *through* the barriers!"

"We'll hold it here," Pierce decided. "Pull your people back behind the line, Velasquez. But stay alert!"

"Aye, aye, sir!"

Fisher looked down the brightly lit corridor to the rear. If the Dark had been able to reach, not through, as Velasquez had said, but past a set of closed and vacuum-sealed blast doors, what was to stop it from materializing part of its body behind the Marines and engulfing them all?

But minutes dragged past and nothing appeared, either before them or in the rear. Pierce, apparently, was trying to get an image from the other side of the blast doors by tapping a security camera or possibly a Marine battlespace drone. "Can't see a damned thing," he muttered aloud. "I think the power's out over there."

"It was showing signs of slowing up, Skipper," Velasquez told him. "It might have a limited range."

"How the hell would that work? What kind of range are you saying?"

"I don't know, sir. Sixty . . . eighty meters? It was definitely slowing down when it hit the last set of blast doors."

Pierce considered this for a moment . . . or perhaps he was consulting with his superiors through his cerebral links.

"Okay," he said after a moment. "We need to see what's going on. Marines! Weapons charged, at the ready!"

Fisher felt a sinking flutter down in her gut. Somehow, she'd been able to hold back the fear that had threatened to consume her in there, but now, with time to wait, with time to think, the fear was beginning to surface once more, to reassert itself as a gnawing, inner terror.

"Stand ready on those heavies!" Pierce called. "Okay . . . open the blast doors!"

The cobalt-tungsten doors slid open and the wind picked up.

Fisher braced herself for whatever was on the other side. . . .

TWELVE

Lance Corporal Adria Fisher had been a Marine for less than two years, and her deployment with the *Tellus Ad Astra* diplomatic mission to the galactic core had been, except for training runs, her first time off Earth.

But she thought of herself as a small-town girl from Xenia, Ohio, and she'd never given much consideration to aliens or nightmare things wriggling through from other dimensions. She'd joined the Marines because her older brother had done so. He'd been stationed at the Imperial Solar Guard outpost on Triton when the *Ad Astra* had boosted for the Core. The thought brought with it a sharp twist in her belly. She still hadn't been able to wrap her head around the fact that Earth's civilization and everyone she'd known there had been dust now for 4 billion years. The loneliness, sometimes, was agonizing.

There was no time to dwell on any of that now. The blast doors completed their slow and rumbling slide apart as the wind again kicked up. The next set of doors along the passageway to their rear had already been sealed, so at least they weren't emptying the entire ship of atmosphere. And in front of the massed line of Marines . . .

. . . a yawning emptiness.

"What the hell?" Captain Pierce said. "Where are they?"

The Marines stirred, restless and nervous. From their line behind the open blast doors, they could see where the previous set of doors had been one hundred meters away, but the doors there were gone, and in their place was a swirling spiral of blue light. Surrounding the opening was a kind of graininess. Fisher couldn't make out the details without her helmet optics, but from her position it looked like swarms of insects or tiny, animated motes were swirling over the edges of torn-open bulkhead and deck.

"Corpsman's here," someone said.

"Fisher!" Velasquez said. "Get to sick bay."

"I'm okay, Lieutenant. I want to stay."

"Get the fuck out of here, Fish. You're out of uniform."

The Navy corpsman, wearing combat armor like the Marines, approached her. "Let's just check you out first," he told her. "You can come back and play later."

Reluctantly, she turned and moved out of the line. The Marines were her family, all the family she had, now, and she didn't want to leave them.

"DAMAGE CONTROL!" St. Clair shouted aloud, though he was linked in through the ship's network. "What's happening with that hull breach?"

"Vacseal doors are closed, Lord Commander," the voice of *Ad Astra*'s damage control department replied inside his head. "We've lost pressure in twelve compartments aft of Frame Forty-nine, but the damage is no longer spreading. Ship's systems and networks have been rerouted."

"Okay . . ."

"And it doesn't appear to be a hull breach, my lord."

"Why were we losing atmosphere then?"

"We're still working out the details, sir, but our best guess is that there was some sort of dimensional gateway or portal, a kind of hole leading to . . . uh . . . someplace else. Someplace above Flatland. Someplace that was open to hard vacuum."

"Okay. Keep me up to date."

"Aye, aye, sir."

Somewhere above Flatland. St. Clair gave a brief, grim smile at that. The reference was somewhat obscure, but he'd been doing his research. Faced by the reality of an enemy that seemed to move through multiple higher dimensions at will, he'd recently downloaded the nineteenth century novella *Flatland: A Romance of Many Dimensions*, and evidently others of *Ad Astra*'s crew had done so as well. Good. . . .

But there were other things to worry about than the crew's download reading habits. The sudden intrusion into *Ad Astra* appeared to have been blocked, at least for the moment, but the battle was still raging some tens of thousands of kilometers ahead, where the hyperdimensional tesseract had partially extended itself into normal space. Marines in combat armor were swarming around the alien object now, as human ships continued hammering volley upon volley of high-energy laser and particle beam fire into the enemy structure. The gunboat *Black Hawk* was reported missing, fallen into the disturbance in space-time ahead. The Marine assault transport *Vera Cruz* was in trouble but still holding her own, damaged and under heavy attack, but so far able to hold off the enemy needle-ship swarms.

But St. Clair knew that they wouldn't be able to do so for much longer.

JACKED INTO *Vera Cruz*'s AI network, General Wilson continued giving orders to the distinct clouds of Marines maneuvering through local space. Though he was in the ship's C^3, from his inner point of view, fed by data streaming in from the ship's network, he was adrift in open space, the blue swirl of the alien anomaly gaping beneath him as he tagged company commanders in his mind and transmitted to them terse, urgent orders.

Every battle, Wilson believed, no matter where or how it was fought, was a kind of intricate and finely crafted ballet. Each possessed a rhythm, a dynamic pulse of movement and of maneuver, and each had the same overall goals: be where the enemy is not, bring force to bear where the enemy is weak, grab and hold the lead so that the enemy is forced to respond to you rather than the other way around. Unfortunately, in this case enemy numbers were simply overwhelming; the enemy was everywhere, and the human forces more and more were being pushed into the defensive.

The humans were *losing*. . . .

"You must get at least one drone inside that object," Newton's voice whispered in Wilson's mind.

Wilson stared into the vast gape of spiraling blue light centered on a spacecraft larger than the planet Jupiter. It was, he thought, like staring down into the very mouth of hell.

"Will you be able to stop that thing if we do?"

"Unknown. But it is a truism that a knowledge of the enemy is necessary for victory."

Wilson didn't add the corollary—that a knowledge of *self* was also necessary for that victory. One of Sun Tzu's most important maxims.

"Deladier!" he called. "We need to get in closer."

"Yes, my lord."

Wilson heard the reluctance in Deladier's mental voice, but ignored it. They weren't doing any good out here, and the way things were unfolding around them, it wouldn't be much longer before the enemy needles punched through *Vera Cruz*'s fighter screens and overwhelmed the assault transport's close-in defenses.

"Status on the AI torpedoes."

"Four AI clones ready for launch."

"Okay. Here's how we'll play it. We'll focus the zoomies forward to clear a path. We go right up the middle as close as we can get. When I give the word, launch every Firestorm we have left, then follow them up with all four AIs."

"You're using the nukes to punch inside the tesseract?"

"I don't even know if these bastards'll feel it," Wilson replied. "But that'll be our best shot, and we're going to take it. As soon as the AI clones are away, hightail it back out to 20 million kilometers, then hold position and wait for the zoomies to catch up to us."

"If there are any left," Deladier replied, a low-voiced mutter. Wilson was pretty sure that *Vera Cruz*'s skipper hadn't even realized he'd given voice to the thought. "Yes, my lord," Deladier added.

"Good. Do it."

And *Vera Cruz* accelerated toward the mouth of hell.

"THIRD BATT on me!" Colonel Becker yelled over the combat net. "We need to make a hole!"

"Make a hole" was common slang within the Navy and Marine Corps, meaning, roughly, "get out of my way, I'm coming through!" Dixon banked and accelerated to put himself just behind Becker, as the sky around him continued to explode in silent bursts of light. It looked like 3rd Battalion was forming up to literally make a hole for the *Vera Cruz*. Free-flying Marines in combat armor and pairs of ASF-99 Wasp fighters were concentrating in a rough cone of space directly ahead of the transport, creating a tunnel through the swarming needleships aimed directly at the tesseract.

Dixon let his onboard AI select targets for him, rolling

from one side to the other to bring his M-290 laser rifle to bear. The term *rifle* was not a complete misnomer. Though the barrel wasn't rifled to impart a spin to a solid projectile, of course, the weapon *did* give each laser bolt a variable number of helical twists that allowed him to phase-shift the photon packet to the highest possible energy density.

He charged the weapon, pushing the energy level to its maximum. With his MCA suit controls slaved to the *Cruzer*'s combat control system, he had just become what amounted to a self-aware gun platform. His AI triggered the weapon, and an ebon-dark needleship just over a kilometer away flared in a dazzling burst of white light that rapidly faded, leaving tumbling wreckage and a faintly glowing wisp of fast-cooling plasma. His suit rolled sharply left, and the weapon fired again, the bolt refracting off the side of another needle, melting a savage gash in the alien's hull. Dixon began to override the controls to fire a second shot, then saw that the target was tumbling, trailing a widening spiral of glittering motes—gas or liquid freezing as it spilled into hard vacuum.

"Captain Dixon! Scale back the rifling on your beam!" Becker shouted over the platoon channel.

Damned micromanaging son of a bitch, Dixon thought, but he didn't transmit the words. "Copy that," he replied, and he decreased the power feed to his beam by two mental clicks. Theoretically, doing so would extend the life of his power pack somewhat . . . but it wasn't the batt-skipper's job to ride his people *that* closely.

And it wasn't as if he was going to need to husband his energy reserves for that much longer. The sky was filled with red-and-green icons, the electronic markers for alien warships and armored Marines locked in a deadly lovers' embrace.

At this level of intensity, the engagement couldn't last for very much longer.

A quartet of Firestorm missiles streaked out from the *Vera Cruz*, hurtling down the length of the hollow cylinder of fighters in an instant. Alien needleships began firing at them, trying to knock them out of the crowded sky, but Marines peeled off from the outer regions of the cylinder, concentrating their fire on the enemy vessels, forcing them back, blocking their lines of sight, and interrupting their attack vectors. One of the missiles vanished, wiped from the sky, but the other three continued accelerating at tens of thousands of gravities, their onboard AIs guiding them along complex and unpredictable paths down the cylinder until they vanished inside the looming tesseract ahead. Close behind in their wakes came two more smaller missiles—each bearing abbreviated clones of *Ad Astra*'s artificial intelligence.

Unthinking, Dixon braced himself for the detonation . . . but he saw, he *sensed* nothing. That, he realized, was scarcely surprising. The tesseract was so large that up until now 100-megaton thermonuclear explosions had appeared as a minute twinkling of stars across its emerging surface.

"The AI department is reporting that the Newton clones have been successfully deployed into the objective," Becker's voice announced. "All units break off and pull back to the *Vera Cruz*. We need to keep the bad guys at a distance."

Dixon reversed his grav thrusters, slowing his forward momentum. Around him, thousands of other Marines were performing the same maneuver, slowing themselves, dissolving the huge tactical cylinder into clouds of individual troops. Seconds later, the *Vera Cruz* flashed past just a few hundred meters distant, decelerating at full power until she was at rest relative to the nearby Marines, then slowly, slowly accelerating back up and away from the looming tesseract. Dixon increased power to his drives, matching course and velocity.

"Hey!" a Marine called out. "We got company! Coming in at three-three by one-seven-one by two-zero-five!"

Dixon glanced in the indicated direction, expecting to see the *Ad Astra* moving in close. He'd heard the colony tug had left *Tellus* in Ki orbit and was on the way. What he saw, however, was not the human starship, but five . . . worlds. Four of the enormous spheres were similar to the Kroajid vessels they'd seen already, each well over four hundred kilometers in diameter.

Moon-ships.

The fifth was considerably larger. With an equatorial diameter of just over seven thousand kilometers it was bigger and more massive than the planet Mars, massive enough to support a thin atmosphere of carbon dioxide and trace gasses. The heavily cratered surface was stained and streaked in various shades of red-brown and ocher, again much like Mars.

"What the hell are the damned Spiders doing here?" one Marine wanted to know.

Below him, the tesseract continued its bizarre unfolding.

And then, in an instant, the tesseract seemed to lunge up and out, filling the entire sky before winking out of existence as though it had never been there . . .

. . . and the *Vera Cruz* was gone with it.

"I AM in communication with the Kroajid ships," Newton told St. Clair. "Channel open."

"Kroajid vessels!" St. Clair snapped. "What are your intentions?"

"My lord!" Symms called, interrupting. "The *Vera Cruz!*"

"I saw it, ExComm." The Marine transport had just vanished, swallowed, apparently, by the titanic alien object ahead. There was no immediate response from the Kroajid moon-ships, which were drifting in open space some tens of thousands of kilometers distant.

What the hell were the Kroajid here for, anyway? To fight? Or did they expect the humans to do all of the dirty and dangerous work for them? The enemy had vanished almost as soon as those moon-ships had shown up. Did that mean the Andromedan Dark feared the Cooperative?

If so . . . why?

And if so, why did the Coop need the humans?

None of this made any sense.

Before he could try finding answers to those questions, though, St. Clair knew he had to take care of his people. Thousands of Marines were adrift in space out there now, both those in combat armor and those flying Wasps and other Marine-issue fighters.

"Recovery!" he called. "We need search-and-rescue vehicles out there stat!"

"Roger that, my lord," Subcommander Vasilia Karinova replied over the ship's department command channel. "We'll be ready to drop the SAR-pods when we reach the battlespace."

SAR-pods were large, bulky, and utilitarian vessels designed to locate Marines and damaged fighter craft adrift in the emptiness of space after a battle and recover them. *Ad Astra* carried two full squadrons of the ugly craft, which also served the mobile colony as workhorses for hauling supplies down to a planetary surface or transferring equipment between larger vessels, and as deep-space construction vehicles. This time they would serve as space-going ambulances, finding injured personnel and hauling them back to the *Ad Astra*'s sick bay, as well as rescuing Marines who'd lost their thrusters and couldn't make their way back home.

SAR operations were going to have to take priority over everything else now.

"Lord Commander," Newton said through St. Clair's implants. "A representative of the Cooperative fleet is on-line."

"'Representative'? Not commander or Speaker?" Senior Kroajid ship officers referred to themselves as *Speaker*, and there appeared to be a number of other, similar terms and honorifics in use within the Cooperative. So far, however, St. Clair had been unable to see a clear-cut order or chain of command.

"The Cooperative doesn't seem to arrange personnel in hierarchies in the same way as humans," Newton told him.

"I've noticed. Put him through, please."

"*Ey* is Gudahk of the Principle Associative," Newton said, carefully enunciating the Spivak pronoun. That might mean that Gudahk was truly without gender . . . or that eir species either had genders other than male and female, or other genders in addition to them. Normally during interspecies communication that sort of thing wasn't a big issue. After all, humans could expect their AI translators to gloss things over in two-way conversations. But some species could be sensitive to perceived insults, and St. Clair wondered if this was one of those instances.

"I recommend," the AI continued, "that you make liberal use of an honorific here."

"What, like calling em 'sir'?"

"Exactly. I will translate the honorific to something appropriate."

"I see. And what is appropriate with Gudahk?"

"I will render 'sir' as 'Living God,' or something similar."

St. Clair hesitated. It would pay to tread carefully here.

"Okay," he said. "And just what the hell is the Principle Associative?"

"A member of the Galactic Cooperative," Newton replied. "Apparently a very important member, though I have been unable to determine any kind of clear ranking from the data available to me."

"Okay. I'll keep that in mind. Put *em* through."

A window opened within St. Clair's mind, revealing an imposing figure. It was impossible, of course, to judge scale in a transmitted image, but St. Clair had the feeling that he was in the presence of a being considerably bulkier, more massive than a human. Only the top of the being was visible—a quartet of vertical bulbs or flower buds. With three in a triangle around a larger, central mass, which was a scaly dark gray in appearance, the surrounding buds were smaller, perched on the ends of slender stalks and constantly moving about. The small buds were, St. Clair decided after a moment, sensory organs of some sort, but he had no idea what it was that they might be sensing. He was nagged by an odd sense of familiarity. Had he seen the being before?

"I am Lord Commander St. Clair of the Earth starship *Ad Astra*," he said, transmitting the thought over the open channel moderated by Newton. He hesitated, then added, "*Sir*."

"The gods know who you are, Commander St. Clair," the being replied. The voice, of course, was being supplied by Newton. St. Clair wondered how it communicated with its own kind; he couldn't see any sign of a mouth or speaking orifice. Might it use telepathy?

It was then that St. Clair remembered where he'd seen the odd-looking being before: within the sterile world of the Ki Ring, where he and the others with him had watched the parade of disparate beings through that vast, open plaza. It had reminded him of a three-meter-tall plant hauling itself along on massive, naked, many-branched roots. Seen up close like this, it was clear there was nothing of botany about em. The swaying bulbs were held aloft on powerfully muscled tentacles.

"We have driven off the *Dhalat K'graal*," Gudahk said, "and you are no longer in danger. You will approach my vessel now."

St. Clair's eyes widened at the blunt command. With his physical eyes he could see Symms at her command station in front of him, scowling. Evidently, she had heard the order as well.

"No," St. Clair replied.

He could almost feel the alien being's confusion, a palpable force emanating from the image within St. Clair's mind. "We are having difficulty with the translation," ey said.

"No, we are not," St. Clair replied, deliberately blunt.

"You will rendezvous your vessel with mine," Gudahk repeated.

"I don't think so. We have a number of Marines—our warriors—adrift in open space. Their ship was destroyed. They will die if we don't recover them."

"Their ship was not destroyed. It is still there . . . but rotated through the *k'graal*. Do you understand this?"

Gudahk sounded as though he were lecturing a particularly obtuse child.

"'*K'graal*,'" St. Clair repeated. "That means something like 'higher angles,' or maybe 'higher dimensions.'"

"Of course. We do understand, Human, that the mathematics of this concept are well beyond your understanding."

Arrogant . . . and patronizing as well. "Nevertheless, our people are stranded in space. I intend to initiate recovery efforts. And if you don't like it, well, you can just go to whatever hell you might believe in."

St. Clair couldn't tell how Gudahk was taking his explanation. He didn't know how Newton was translating what he was saying—or if it even bothered to translate all of his message anyway. Either way, the being did not appear to be pleased. The three small, stalked bulbs circling the central massive head twisted left and right, and St. Clair had the impression that it might be consulting with others unseen nearby. He wondered if the apparently eyeless creature had a 360-degree field of vision; if so, it suggested a truly alien central nervous system . . . and perhaps an alien way of looking at the cosmos as well.

"You will . . ." The translation broke off for a moment. Then, "You will retrieve your remotes, then rendezvous with me."

St. Clair was about to respond, but Newton interrupted, its voice colored by urgency. "I would suggest," the AI said, "a conciliatory response."

"Thank you, sir," St. Clair said. After all, it cost nothing to be polite. "Recovery efforts should require . . ." He checked the data feed from Karinova's SAR department, then doubled the time required. "Make it eight hours."

"That," Gudahk replied, "is not acceptable."

The five world-ships accelerated, vanishing almost literally within the space of an eye's blink. Their rate of acceleration was astonishing; all five worlds were moving at close

to the speed of light within seconds of their departure . . .
and then they all went superluminal and winked out.

"All *right*, then," Symms said after a breath-holding
moment.

"I guess that could have gone better," St. Clair said.
"How about it, Newton? Did I piss em off?"

"I do not as yet understand Tchagar emotive responses,"
Newton replied.

"Tchagar? That's Gudahk's species?"

"An umbrella term indicating several related species,"
Newton replied. "I am searching the *Roceti Encyclopedia*
for an entry, but have not yet found one."

"But you said they're an important part of the Cooperative."

"So my Kroajid contacts tell me."

"Maybe they can tell you where to look."

"They seem reticent to do so. One might even say that
they seem afraid."

"Of 'gods'? Imagine that."

"Commander, I occasionally have difficulty determin-
ing whether or not you are being facetious."

"So do I. I'm more concerned as to whether or not I just
made Gudahk angry."

"You were, perhaps, not as diplomatic as you might have
been, Commander."

"I do better at diplomacy if the other guy is at least
making an attempt to be diplomatic as well."

"In this case, Lord Commander, the 'other guy' is a
representative of a civilization many orders of magnitude
more powerful and more accomplished than your own."

"Meaning . . . what? We should accept trade beads and
trinkets? Ask em to send us missionaries?" St. Clair shook

his head. "Frankly, Newton, this alliance is looking worse and worse."

"That may be true. However, try to keep in mind that this alliance, however one-sided it might seem, may be Humankind's sole chance for survival in this epoch."

"Granted," St. Clair said. "But survival at what cost?"

THIRTEEN

Gunnery Sergeant Roger Kilgore couldn't tell what had happened. One moment, the *Vera Cruz*, with his company still tucked away inside her number-five drop bay, had been decelerating just above the massive, shifting world dubbed IO-1. Surrounding space was a vast and utterly alien starscape—Andromeda and the Milky Way filling the sky, with the local star a shrunken, brilliant point of light 10 astronomical units distant. And then, in an instant, the *Vera Cruz* was in darkness, the sun and the galaxies wiped away, leaving the Marine transport hanging between absolute black above, and a seemingly infinite, glowing blue-white plain below.

That plain, Kilgore knew, wasn't truly infinite. It was the surface of the object dubbed IO-1, India Oscar One, or, more euphoniously, Bluestar. The surface no longer appeared to be turning itself inside out, thank God.

That solid bright plain was reassuring in a way. It meant that, despite its size, the object wasn't a Jovian gas giant, but instead possessed a solid surface. His readouts, however, were showing a surface gravity of only about one G, perhaps a bit less, which seemed impossibly low for such a titanic mass. The thing possessed a volume equivalent to almost fifteen hundred Earths.

Which led Kilgore to wonder if the *Vera Cruz* had fallen into one of those higher dimensions favored by the

Andromedan Dark. From this angle, as opposed to "outside," back in normal space, Bluestar appeared to be an iridescent sphere larger than Jupiter. Through the visual data feeds from the *Cruzer*'s external cameras, he could see what looked like markings on that surface, rectilinear and geometric shapes and lines all but lost in a thin, brightly glowing haze.

The members of First Platoon, Bravo Company, 1/3, were wired up inside their cages on the drop bay deck, waiting for the final order to drop and boost. They'd been on track to drop in another sixty seconds as the *Vera Cruz* approached the mysterious Bluestar alien, but everything had gone on hold when the rest of the outside universe had vanished. As Kilgore glanced at the waiting Marines around him, he realized that something was wrong with what he was seeing with his physical eyes, something wrong enough to make him wonder if his helmet optics had wonked out. He was looking at Staff Sergeant Kari Rees, and, just for a moment, his gaze had gone *past* the open framework of her acceleration cage, past her Marine Combat Armor, past the tangle of electronics and coolant tubes until he'd glimpsed her uniform inside.

He moved his head slightly . . . and he saw skin . . . then he was looking *past* the skin and down into her internal organs. Her heart was a vivid scarlet lump pulsing away just beyond the white bands of her ribs. Her naked skull grinned hideously at him . . . and somehow at the same time he could see past the bone and into her brain.

Someone, one of the Marines opposite him, gasped. "My God! What the . . ."

"Fuck!" another cried. "I'm looking at your guts!"

"Easy, people!" the Company CO, Captain Andrew

Byrne, snapped. "We expected something like this, right? We're in another dimension. . . ."

Well . . . not exactly *expected*, Kilgore thought. There'd been some pre-mission discussion of what they might expect facing critters with access to higher dimensions, but he certainly hadn't been prepared for *this*. Nor was the explanation of what they were now experiencing as cut-and-dried as that, as if "another dimension" meant an entirely new and different universe with different rules. But that simplistic phrase would do for now until they could come up with new language and better descriptions.

The Marines still appeared to be sitting within the normal framework of length, height, and depth that characterized the 3-D universe they were used to . . . but as they moved their heads, as their optical perspectives changed, it was as though they were getting just a taste of another realm interpenetrating and filling normal space. Kilgore raised his right hand, staring at his plasteel-laminate gauntlet . . . and marveled at the interplay of bones and tendons and flowing threads of blood within his bare hand as he flexed his fingers. Exactly what he saw, and how deeply his enhanced vision penetrated what he was looking at, seemed to depend partly on the angle of view, and partly on his own mental focus. He could *will* himself to see the black surface of his armored glove in front of him, rather than the living anatomy lesson within. Apparently the brain had a fair amount of control over what incoming data it processed.

Kilgore remembered having downloaded a factoid back when he'd been getting used to his new military cerebral implants . . . something to the effect that the human brain actually processed 400 billion bits of data per second, but was only *aware* of something like two kilobytes. Humans were awash in a sea of incoming data, the vast majority of which they were never aware. Cyber implants could improve that wildly unbalanced ratio through organization and efficient storage, but humans were still oblivious to much of what was going on around them.

Maybe the brain simply unconsciously discarded what it didn't need . . . or didn't understand.

Maybe he could decide what he was seeing, simply through an act of concentration. . . .

It would take some getting used to, though, and a lot of practice to be able to function normally in this strangely twisted space.

Others in the compartment were doing the same as he, staring at their hands, or at one another, getting used to the strangeness. Kilgore looked at PFC Colby, seated in his cage next to Rees, and for a horrible moment wondered if those normally closely enclosed and restrained intestines could fall out of the man's body through a sixth-dimensional shortcut.

Intriguingly, the company's electronic feeds didn't seem to be affected. The data streaming in from the ship's sensors showed normal surfaces. He tried to concentrate on that, and not on the disturbing internal views of his fellow Marines or of the compartment's bulkheads that now showed an unnerving tendency to disappear if he stared at them for too long. Could they fall past those bulkheads and into open space?

"Listen up, people," Byrne said. "Our Newton clone has a fix . . ."

Kilgore saw the flashing in-head icon marking a new software patch and accepted it, and his strangely enhanced vision flattened back to normal.

"Hey, Skipper!" Lieutenant Hayes of Second Platoon called. "What just happened?"

"Newton just dropped a filter into your visual processing center at the back of your skull. It'll help you ignore the extra dimensions."

"Roger that."

Kilgore wasn't entirely sure he could ignore those dimensions. Simply knowing that it was possible to look right inside a person—that it might even be possible to reach right out and grasp their beating heart—had left him feeling nakedly exposed and vulnerable. He kept remembering the stories he'd heard of some crew members on the *Ad Astra* who'd been yanked out of their regular 3-D world by the Dark, flipped over, and dropped back into three dimensions inside out.

The mounting stress was all but intolerable. Modern combat, Kilgore reflected, was characterized by endless tedium punctuated by brief episodes of sheer terror . . . an observation likely as ancient as human combat itself. What made it worse by far was thinking that you knew what was about to happen, and then having everything change in a heartbeat.

But it was infinitely worse knowing that the enemy could defy everything you thought you knew about the physical world, reach right inside you—reach into your guts, maybe grab that beating heart—and yank it out . . .

All First Platoon Bravo could do was watch the image feeds . . . and engage in the long-established Marine tradition of bitching.

"That's better," Lance Corporal Carolyn Lalakos said over the company channel. "Looking at what all you lean, green gyrenes ate for breakfast was making me sick to my stomach."

"Fuck, Lakie," Sergeant Tony Kalinin replied. "And

here I was just sitting back and enjoying getting to see your titties."

She held up an armored middle finger. "SAR, man," she said sweetly. "Sit and rotate."

"Titties, huh? Can't see a thing, now," PFC Terry Gonzales said. "Pity . . ."

Minutes dragged on, one following another. "C'mon, *c'mon,*" PFC Colby said. "We got our eyes fixed! Let's see some action, here!"

Kilgore put the exclamation down to waiting-sharpened bravado. "Simmer down, Colby. It'll happen when it happens."

"Looks like some of the zoomies came through with us," Rees pointed out. Visible on their in-heads, a dozen green icons were flying along close by *Vera Cruz*'s blunt prow, like dolphins riding an ocean-going ship's bow wave. Their ID tags pegged them as GFA-86, the Stardogs, flying close combat aerospace support in front of the *Cruzer.*

"The Doggies," Kilgore agreed. "There are some more fighters up ahead . . . right above the surface of that . . . that thing."

"GFA-90," Rees said. "The Death Dealers."

"Think they can?" Colby asked.

"Think they can what?" Lance Corporal Francis Rivoldini asked.

"Deal out death to a whole fuckin' blue-glowing planet!"

"Well, *fuck!*" PFC Dennis Blanchard said with a casual aplomb too studied to be real. "They're Marines, right?"

"Ooh-rah!" Lalakos replied.

"Hey, looks like the damned thing's not a Jovian-type planet after all," PFC Benson DuBoise said. "Are those fucking *cities* down there?"

"It's got a solid surface," Kilgore replied, "so we know it's not a gas giant. But those markings are too damned big to be cities."

"Whatever they are," Rees added, "they're not natural features. Too many right angles."

"Bullshit," Lance Corporal Alexis Mishchenko said. "Some of those structures are frickin' bigger than Earth!"

Kilgore was studying the readouts coming through his data feed. "What worries me," he said, "is the gravity. Anybody else notice that?"

"I'm reading . . . shit," Rees said. "That *can't* be right. . . ."

"Surface gravity estimated at point nine-five G," DuBoise added. "From something that big?"

"Must be a glitch in the metrics," Byrne said.

"Not necessarily, sir," Kilgore said. He was glad for the distraction. The waiting and not-knowing was miserable. "Back in our own solar system, the gas giant Saturn was . . . what? A diameter of something like 120,000 kilometers? But it wasn't all that dense, right? It had a surface gravity of just a hair over one G, even though it was almost ten times bigger than Earth."

"Not that Saturn had a solid surface," Byrne said. "But point taken. Maybe Bluestar isn't really solid."

"It looks solid enough," Colby said.

"I heard," Rees added, "that Saturn was so light that if you could find an ocean big enough, the planet would float."

"That's one fuckin' big ocean," DuBoise said.

"This thing is bigger than Saturn," Byrne pointed out. "Hell, it's bigger than Jupiter. But it's artificial, definitely. Maybe it has a kind of latticework interior, so a lot of it is hollow?"

"God," Kilgore said, stunned as realization sank in.

"What?"

"I was just thinking . . . we see that . . . that city down there. But imagine another city underneath . . . and another below that, and another, and another . . ."

He'd been wondering if it would have been possible, before downloading that internal software patch, if it would have been possible to look at the Bluestar and see into it, to see its internal structure. The thought had driven home the realization that the thing was a solid object, three-dimensional and more, and that its interior would be brain-twistingly complex. Millions of cities layered one upon another was just one of the possibilities.

"That one freaking ship could be carrying a population that outnumbers the population of the entire Galaxy," Rees said, awe creeping into her voice as well.

"Actually," Byrne said, thoughtful, "I think what we're seeing here is a J-brain."

"What the hell's that?" PFC Ana Lopez asked.

"J-brain, Jupiter-brain," Byrne said. "An artificial structure the size of a gas giant, optimized as a massive computer."

"I'm reading a mass of . . . oh, call it one times ten to the twenty-seven kilograms," Rees said. "Jupiter masses almost twice that."

"So if we dropped this thing into that ocean next to Saturn," Kilgore suggested, "it would float, too."

"Heads up, people," Byrne said. "The bridge is picking up a distress beacon down there."

Kilgore brought up the data on his in-head—a flashing red beacon on the surface below. "Is that the gunship?"

"The gunship," Byrne agreed. "*Black Hawk*. We're going down to check it out."

"I wonder," Kilgore said, "what an AI super-mind in-

habiting a computronium matrix as big as the planet Jupiter
will have to say about *that*?"

"WHAT HAPPENED to them?" St. Clair demanded. "Where
did they go?"

"Presumably," Newton replied, "they were pulled in
after IO-1."

"Yes, but in *where*?" Symms wanted to know. "The
Vera Cruz has just *vanished*, along with twenty-four of our
fighters!"

St. Clair magnified the image displayed by the feed
from battlespace drones closer to the fight. Lonely icons
appeared scattered across a large volume of space, marking
Marines and damaged fighters left behind after the fight,
but of the heavy Marine transport there was no sign. SAR
vehicles moved through the area on their post-battle mis-
sions of mercy, rescuing survivors.

He took another moment to closely scan *Ad Astra*'s
security status. That attack belowdecks had unnerved
him . . . proof that the Andromedan Dark could reach down
inside the ship from elsewhere without warning. Was there
a range limitation to that reach? He didn't know . . . and he
wasn't particularly eager to find out.

Gudahk and his escorts were long gone. Good. There
would be a reckoning of some sort there later, but not now,
not until the current tactical situation had resolved itself.

"ExComm," he said, "hold our position. Provide support
for the SARs."

"Yes, Lord Commander."

St. Clair rotated his command chair until he was facing
Gorton Noyer. The Cybercouncil liaison was still sitting
at the rear of the command bridge, but St. Clair honestly
couldn't tell whether the man was quietly fuming . . . or ter-

rified. He decided to give the man the benefit of the doubt. "Lord Noyer? I think it's time you and I had a little heart-to-heart."

Noyer responded with a quick, jerky nod. "Yes, my lord."

Ah . . . fear, then, rather than rage. The man appeared thoroughly shaken. By what? The alien invasion be-lowdecks? The vanishing of a Marine heavy transport?

Or, just possibly, the brief encounter with Gudahk of the Tchagar.

"So . . . what did you think of our new friend Gudahk?" St. Clair asked, keeping his voice light and conversational.

"I . . . don't know," Noyer said, hesitant. "Dealing with em might be . . . difficult."

"*That*," St. Clair replied, "is one hell of an understate-ment. Conference Room One, ten minutes."

LISA LET herself into St. Clair's cliffside house, her walk-about over. She was surprised to discover that she was actually glad to be home.

The pleasure of her homecoming, however, was consid-erably muddied by an emotion she'd rarely permitted herself to feel—and she wasn't certain she wanted to experience it now. The emotion was *worry*, and for Lisa it was an alien and unpleasant condition. To gnaw at and churn over some event about which little or nothing could be done, to have thoughts chasing one another around and around inside her brain to no perceptible advantage was not generally thought of as characteristic of robots.

Lisa's creators, however, at the General Nanodynamics Corporation of San Francisco in the state of North Califor-nia, had been seeking to make her line of sex gynoids as human as possible, and that meant giving them the capacity for certain traits and emotional responses usually seen as negatives. Jealousy was permanently blocked, of course, to avoid potential confrontations with human sexual partners, but she could feel at least mild anger, frustration, annoyance, fear, irritation . . .

. . . and, of course, she could *worry*.

Her advantage over humans lay in her being able to switch those feelings off at will. Humans tended to be driven incessantly by their emotional states, a condition that Lisa found almost incomprehensible. But some emotions, even the most negative, if properly calibrated and controlled could be effective as personal drivers. In short, they helped her get things done, rather than being a passive observer of the world around her.

Earlier, she'd considered switching off the worry . . . but she didn't want to do that, not yet. The mild, nagging pull at her thoughts would help to keep her focused on the problem. She wanted to discuss it with Grayson, and she didn't want to simply forget about it like some conscienceless machine, cold and unfeeling. So she would live with it.

But, damn it, how do humans deal with this nagging inner torment, day in and day out?

As she walked into the living room, she tried pinging St. Clair, and was startled when her transmission failed to find its destination. She checked a StarNet source and saw that the *Ad Astra* had pulled away from the *Tellus* some time ago and accelerated out-system, racing toward the enigmatic Bluestar.

More worried, now, she shifted to a StarNet news feed, pulling down the latest. There was nothing new, unfortunately, nothing since an hour ago when word had reached the *Tellus* that the Marine transport *Vera Cruz* had been swallowed by the Bluestar object. There was no word on what *Tellus* was doing, but she was certain that St. Clair would be in the thick of things, confronting the alien object, possibly directing the battle. . . .

Her worry index clicked up a couple of notches. *Two* humans she cared for deeply were out there now: Grayson St. Clair and Gunnery Sergeant Roger Kilgore.

She desperately wanted to switch off the worry . . . and didn't quite dare.

One news feed thread caught her attention, and she switched it over to the big display wall in the living room. A talking head three meters tall—Günter Adler, the ousted director of the UE Cybercouncil—glowered down at her. "—is a bad, *bad* deal for *Tellus Ad Astra*," Adler was saying. "Now, yes, it's true that I supported these negotiations at the start. I thought that a close military alliance with the Galactic Cooperative would provide security and peace for our citizens.

"But the recent attacks by the so-called Andromedan Dark have demonstrated that the Cooperative is unable or unwilling to protect itself, that in fact they intended for us to be in the forefront of the battle against their enemy, even though they possess technologies infinitely beyond our own. We *must* renounce this evil treaty and find our own safety within this distant and alien epoch within which we now find ourselves. . . ."

Adler's face was replaced by that of Barbra Delarosa, a leading StarNet News anchor. On a screen behind her, an angry, chanting mob waved homemade signs and placards. "Lord Adler made his comments at a rally in downtown Seattle today," Delarosa said, "not far from his residence below the Port Hab endcap. He is calling for an immediate renunciation of the Cooperative Alliance Treaty. Some of

Lord Adler's supporters are calling for his reinstatement on the Cybercouncil, and the immediate nullification of the CAT agreement.

"We have with us at our SNN offices Lord Clayton Lloyd, Lord *Ambassador* Lloyd, I should say, who recently negotiated the Cooperative Alliance Treaty. My lord? It's indeed an honor to have you with us today."

The faces of the chanting mob were replaced by the head and shoulders of Ambassador Lloyd, sharing a split screen with Delarosa. "It's *my* honor to be here, Barbra," Lloyd said, flashing a groomed and polished smile.

"So, my lord, what would you say to Lord Adler and his demands that the CAT be renounced?"

"Well, Barbra . . . first and foremost, it is vitally important to keep in mind that Lord Adler has been through an extremely . . . difficult time. He was driven mad by an encounter with the Dark, you know, and while his faculties were medically restored by an electronic backup transplant, there are still serious—*extremely* serious—questions about the former director's health, emotional state, and stability. And, of course, that is why he was removed from the Council—by a two-thirds majority vote of the sitting members, I should add. We didn't want to take that step, but the danger that the former cyber director was unstable or, worse, that he was under some sort of *alien* influence simply could not be ignored."

"Is it true that you are in line to take over Lord Adler's seat on the Council?"

Again, that flash of winning smile. "That, Barbra, is entirely up to the other members of the Council and what they feel is best for our community. But if asked to serve, I most certainly perform my civic duty to the very best of my ability. . . ."

Lisa switched the feed off. So far as she could tell, the various news shows and talking-head round tables available over SNN were almost purely entertainment, rather than news feeds intended to be factually informative. News stories tended to be centered on certain basic human emotions—fear was the most common one—and were designed to wring what they could from those emotions in order to keep the human population watching the programs.

And as a result, the worry and discontent within only grew. By the time one peril resolved itself, another had taken its place.

What, she wondered, was the point?

If she wanted to worry, she would continue focusing on Grayson and on Roger. Hope, she realized, was another of those human emotions with which she'd been programmed.

And she hoped that both of them would return to *Tellus* safely . . . and soon.

CONFERENCE ROOM One was an enormous and luxuriously appointed room with high cathedral ceilings and a viewing wall that curved around two sides of the space. *Ad Astra* was large as spacecraft went, and with her alien-derived zero-point energy generators she had power to spare and could afford to be spacious inside. The conference rooms were located inside the Carousel, forward of *Ad Astra*'s bridge.

St. Clair took his place at the head of the mirror-polished mahogany table and waited as other men and women filed in. The display wall, though called a transparency in general usage, was not a window but a sophisticated display screen. Right now it was set to show surrounding space, with the sprawl of two colliding galaxies stretched from one side of the room to the other. The feed was being re-layed from external cameras on the ship's hull, and so did not show the carousel's rotation.

An older man in a civilian tunic walked in and slapped his e-tablet on the table with a crack. "Why," Dr. Francois Dumont said, sounding irritated to the point of outright anger, "do we have to trek up here to the Wheel for this nonsense? There *is* such a thing as implant linking, you know!"

As a civilian, Dumont wasn't completely under St. Clair's jurisdiction to order around, so he elected not to chide him for an out-loud grumble that verged on insubordination. The fact was, St. Clair didn't even think such a chiding would have much effect on the doctor. Civilians worked to a different beat.

Hell, at times he was convinced they worked in a different *universe*.

"The Andromedan Dark," St. Clair said mildly, "has shown a propensity for getting at our personnel through their cerebral links. Lord Adler, remember? And Subcommander Francesca?" Dumont blanched at that, which St. Clair expected as he pressed on. "This is a general meeting for all department heads, and we're still close to the area where the Dark recently staged an extradimensional attack on this vessel. I'd rather have all of us walk to a conference room than run the risk of every department head on this ship being turned inside out or driven insane in one fell swoop."

"Ah . . . well. . . ." Dumont said. "There *is* that."

"How long do you anticipate restricting use of the Net, my lord?" Dr. Paul Tsang Wanquan wanted to know. The civilian head of *Ad Astra*'s astronomy department took a seat across from Dumont.

"That's part of what I want to discuss here," St. Clair replied. "Subcomm Jablonsky? You have someone working on the Roceti data?"

"Yes, sir," Subcommander Tomasz Jablonsky, head of *Ad Astra*'s AI department, replied with a jerky nod of his head. He indicated a young woman taking her seat next to his. "Lieutenant Lam Mingzhu, here, has been working directly with Newton to try to pull some useful data out of that mess."

"Any luck with that, Lieutenant?" St. Clair asked.

"No, my lord," she replied. "Or . . . not very much. There is a *lot* of data in the encyclopedia."

"I understand. Maybe this meeting will help you focus your searches," St. Clair told Lam. "I'm going to be noting a number of particular subjects that I want you to concentrate on. We're flying blind here, and it is imperative that we learn what it is that we're up against."

"Yes, my lord."

"At the top of the list, I want every reference you can find to higher-dimensional travel or attacks. The Cooperative has been dealing with the Dark for millions of years. They ought to have *some* idea by now how far the Dark can strike, using extra dimensions as a shortcut."

"Yes, sir."

St. Clair looked back at the faces now gathered around the table, all of them watching him expectantly. "Very well," he said. "Looks like everyone's here. Let's try to figure out just where we're going. . . ."

FOURTEEN

"And three . . . and two . . . and one . . . *drop*!"

Within the Stygian darkness of the alien dimension, the trio of Devil Toads dropped from the belly of the *Vera Cruz* and began drifting toward the infinite plain below. Inside each, forty Marines in full armor sat confined inside their landing cages, wondering what they would find when they reached their designated landing zone. Roger Kilgore checked his pulse rifle one final time, grateful that the powers-that-be had decided to send them riding in style, packed into the belly of a Toad, rather than scattering them across the sky like a swarm of insects.

There were pluses and minuses for both choices, of course. The Toad made a better target than a lone Marine, and a kill would take out an entire forty-Marine platoon in one swift flash. On the other hand, it carried a fair amount of armor, it possessed defensive EM shields, and, most important of all, it carried its own assortment of heavy firepower for close-in ground support. Adrift out in space with nothing but an armored suit between you and the hostiles, you felt so damned *naked*.

"Whatcha think, Skipper?" Sergeant Kalinin asked. "Are we headed for a hot LZ?"

"We'll know in a few minutes, Sergeant," Captain Byrne replied. The Devil Toad gave a sudden lurch, and he added, "Hang on, everybody! We're hitting atmosphere!"

IO-1 was massive enough to have acquired a substantial atmosphere. According to the readouts, it was composed primarily of hydrogen, with small percentages of helium and minute traces of carbon dioxide, methane, and ammonia. Since the Bluestar object was unlikely to have experienced outgassing events in its history, the likely explanation was that it had simply picked up the gasses gravitationally little by little out of interstellar space.

Which argued that it was *old*, that it had been wandering through space for a very long time indeed. Interstellar gas was tenuous in the extreme—less than an atom per cubic centimeter—and the atmosphere surrounding the Bluestar object was thicker than the gas envelope surrounding Earth.

The Devil Toad shuddered as it plowed in through thickening atmosphere. Kilgore felt the sharp deceleration as they pulled up short above the thing's surface. On his in-head, he could see the crashed *Black Hawk* gunship lying on its side next to what looked like a series of low, featureless white buildings. A red icon pulsed like a strobe light, an emergency beacon.

Kilgore found himself missing that odd, extradimensional vision he'd been wrestling with earlier. It would have been good to be able to see inside the wreck. He considered asking *Vera Cruz*'s AI to remove the block on his vision for a moment.

And then, a bit irrationally, he decided he didn't want to see inside the *Black Hawk* after all. Not really.

The Devil Toad lander slowed drastically, gentling up to within a few dozen meters of the *Black Hawk* before extending its squat landing legs and settling to the ground. Kilgore was uncertain as to whether to call that shining, white surface "ground" or "floor." It was patently artificial . . . but it defined a world so huge that architectural terms seemed wildly inappropriate. He didn't have time to muse on it for long.

"Marines! Unhook your cages!" Cartwell, the platoon sergeant, ordered, and the platoon unstrapped themselves from their protective cages and stood in a double line on the cargo bay deck. "On your feet! Sound off! Alvarez!"

"Aqui!"

"Ames!"

"Yo!"

"Andrews!"

"Ooh-rah!"

"Becker!"

The roll call ran down the line, hard and fast. The rear hatch ground open, and First Platoon, Bravo Company of the Marine 1/3 thundered down the ramp.

Outside, the wind was blowing hard. It was cold, too; Kilgore's armor was registering a brisk minus 120 Celsius in the surrounding air. The pocket dimension in which Bluestar was hiding evidently had no central heating—no local star—and was frigid as a result. That it was as *warm* as minus 120 meant that it was generating heat, *lots* of heat, deep inside itself.

The ground, surprisingly, was completely clear of dust, smooth, hard, and shiny. He would have expected that surface to have acquired a layer of dust, like the lunar regolith, in the same way it had picked up an atmosphere over the eons. Possibly the weirdly contortionist hyperdimensional movements they'd all witnessed earlier shook such debris off . . . or there might be some sort of electrostatic effect. The surface was smooth enough that walking on it was like walking on ice, and Kilgore had to watch each step.

The sky, Kilgore noted, was pitch-black straight overhead, but shaded to a deep midnight blue around the horizon, illuminated, evidently, by the eerie glow from the Bluestar itself.

With dazzlingly bright searchlights playing across the white surface below them, the other two Toads touched down nearby, and Second and Fourth Platoons filed out, before all three of the landers lifted off once more. They would hover in the area, watching for incoming threats and ready to lay down covering fire if necessary. Their bulky, clumsy presence in the black and featureless sky was a genuine comfort.

Under Cartwell's bellowed instructions, Fourth Platoon set up a perimeter around the entire LZ, while First began moving toward the downed gunship.

Kilgore could see from ten meters away that the *Black Hawk*'s port side had ripped wide open on impact. Gunships were not heavily armored, relying on maneuverability and their small target cross section as protection from incoming fire. The *Black Hawk* evidently had hit the ground at a quite shallow angle and slid for three times its own fifty-five-meter length before coming to a cockeyed halt.

"Kilgore! Rees!" Cartwell called. "Check it out!"

Weapons at the ready, they moved ahead of the other Marines.

What the hell am I doing here? The question had been in the back of his mind for some time now, but a growing sense of dread had brought it up front and out in the open. He was a Marine. He'd expected to be deployed into strange surroundings, protecting Humankind's interests against some strange, sapient life-forms. That said, when the 3/1 had been deployed to the *Tellus Ad Astra* expedition, he'd expected to spend at least the next year of his life at the galactic core, stationed twenty-five thousand light years from home with the Terran Imperial Embassy Guard.

So nothing had even begun to prepare him for *this*, investigating the twists and hidden recesses of alien dimensions so remote in space and time from home he was having trouble grasping it. Ugly nightmare beings with too many legs and eyes were all in a day's work; creatures that could pop in and out of normal 3-D space without regard for walls or boundaries were terrifying. It was like facing an enemy that didn't follow the rules. . . .

No, worse than that. In the last several centuries, the Imperial Marines—and the U.S. and Royal Marines before that—had more than once faced insurgents who didn't follow the same rulebook—hiding among crowds of civilians, say, or smuggling in weapons hidden inside cases of medical supplies. That was the nature of asymmetric warfare, and they were trained both to expect and combat it. Out here, the Marines didn't even know if there *were* rules, let alone what they are.

And sooner or later that was going to get them killed.

"I think we can get in through here," Rees said. She was standing next to the tear in the gunship's side, stooped, peering in.

"Cover me, Kari," Kilgore said. Pushing past her, he stepped through the tear and into the gunship's interior.

"I'm inside," he said. "Do we have a deck plan?"

"Comin' up, Gunny," Byrne said. "The bridge is to your left, down a passageway for ten meters . . . then up two ladders to the O-3 deck."

Rees joined him inside, looking around. "Damage doesn't look too bad."

"I'm not getting any life signs."

"Yeah. . . ."

"Down this way."

Following the deck plan showing in an in-head window, Kilgore led Rees to the indicated ladder well. The ship was laying at roughly a fifty-degree angle, so they had to make their way along both the deck and one bulkhead, then turn and crawl along the ladder.

"Kil?"

"Mm?"

"Check your life readout."

"I see it. Maybe we have some survivors after all."

But the in-head display, overlaid on the deck plan schematic, was . . . strange. Fuzzy and spread out. Biosensing gear picked up heat and movement at a distance; up close it could distinguish between various types of metabolism—the chemical reactions of living tissue. They weren't close enough yet for that kind of fine detail; what he was reading *might* be a fire. . . .

That was a scary thought. The atmosphere outside was 90 percent hydrogen. The ship's internal atmosphere had partially vented with the crash, but was still quite high in oxygen—almost 12 percent—with a lot of nitrogen. Oxygen mixing with hydrogen meant there was a potential for an explosion, a big one. And if something was burning beyond that bulkhead ahead. . . .

Kilgore tried to remember the stoichiometry of hydrogen. He didn't remember offhand, and didn't have the data loaded in his in-head RAM. He could have called back to the *Vera Cruz* and asked for a download, but . . .

Fuck it. If that *was* a fire in there, it would have already ignited the hydrogen. Besides, the temperature was quite low—just above freezing. The wreck obviously had been losing heat in the cold environment; possibly the cold was blocking Kilgore's infrared reading off the bulkhead. They were seeing *something*, though, and that meant—

Nightmare horrors plunged toward Kilgore and Rees, leaping from a spot just before the bulkhead and seemingly out of nowhere. Kilgore had a brief, confused impression of tentacles, claws, and leprous bodies . . . or indistinct shapes appearing and disappearing in thin air . . . of pieces breaking from the larger mass and scuttling toward them with a nightmarish life of their own . . . and mixed in with them, horribly, were several *human* bodies, moving forward with the writhing mass.

"Don't shoot!" Rees yelled. "That's *Black Hawk*'s crew!"

Even as she said it Kilgore's internal circuitry had already pinged the lead, ship-suited figure; it IDed as Lt. Yuri Olegski.

Even if Kilgore had known the man—he didn't—he would never have recognized him. Olegski's flesh appeared to be dissolving . . . melting . . . turning into a frothy black ooze. Kilgore could see white bone above the lidless, staring eyes, and even the bone was deforming as if melting away into black slime.

Reflexively, he brought up his laser rifle and triggered it.

The explosion tossed both Rees and Kilgore back down the canted passageway several meters, as red flame licked around them. "*Jesus*, Kilgore!" Rees shouted, but Kilgore scrambled to his feet and pulled her upright.

"C'mon!" he said. "We're *out* of here!"

Boots pounding on the canted deck, they raced back down the passageway searching for the way out.

THE ARGUMENT had been raging for fifteen minutes now, and they were no closer to a resolution than they'd been at the start. Twenty men and women had responded to St. Clair's summons to Conference Room One, most of them senior heads of department. He'd started off asking for a consensus on the nature of the Bluestar threat, and what it meant for the human castaways.

So far, there'd been damned little agreement.

"Bluestar," St. Clair said in an attempt at a summation. "What can we say about it for sure?"

"Our best guess is that it is an artificial structure as large as a big planet," Symms, the ExComm, said. She ticked off the points established in the debate so far. "It's inhabited . . . I should say *potentially* inhabited by billions of individual life-forms. It is mobile and trans-dimensional, slipping between our normal universe of three dimensions and the high-D space of string physics more or less at will. It appears to be aligned with the Andromedan Dark. The extradimensional aspect certainly fits with what the Kroajid call *Dhalat K'graal*, the 'Minds from Higher Angles.'"

"It *is* the Andromedan Dark," Francois Dumont said. "Of that there can absolutely be no question!"

"No, we *can't* say that, Dumont," Dr. Caryl Aguilera said. She was a specialist in the xenosophontology department, and, therefore, technically answered to Dumont. Where his specialty was xenotechnology, however, hers was xenosociology—the study of alien social structures and organization. There was, St. Clair understood, little love lost between the two, and now he was experiencing that. "It seems much more likely that the Bluestar represents a splinter group of the Andromedan Dark proper. We've already seen proof that the Dark, as we understand it from Kroajid sources, is *not* monolithic. The Xam—"

"That *assumption*," Dumont interrupted, his voice almost a growl, "is based on the unsupported interpretation of frankly alien motivations and decision-making."

"Let's get back to that later," St. Clair said, breaking in. The two had been going around and around on that point earlier, and he had no wish to see the argument resumed. "At this point, whether or not the Andromedan Dark is a monolithic whole or several different, competing powers is an interesting question, certainly, but we don't have any solid proof one way or the other. Agreed?"

Reluctantly, both Dumont and Aguilera nodded.

"So as of right now, we just don't know. So back to my question: What *do* we know?" St. Clair looked at the others, an expectant glare.

"Honestly," Dumont said, "Symms pretty much said it. It's big, it's potentially inhabited by billions, certainly contains at least a super-powerful AI, and it's mobile."

"So it's both world and warship," St. Clair said. "Risky . . . putting all of your eggs in one basket like that."

"They may not distinguish between the two, my lord," Senior Lieutenant Vance Cameron pointed out. The ship's tactical officer hesitated, then added, "Especially if their culture, their social structure, is organized along strictly military lines."

"There's another possibility," Aguilera said. "And not necessarily an alternative one. The Andromedan swarms show some of the characteristics of what we might call a group social structure—a hive mind. They act like a super AI, operating through millions of peripherals."

"The Xam," St. Clair said, seeing where she was going with this. "The ones we found in the Andromedan needle-ships we examined."

"Exactly," Dumont put in, for once agreeing with the xenosociologist. "They were hardwired into their controls, and apparently were being directly controlled by an AI from some distance away."

"Actually," Aguilera said, "I was referring to their *tactics* . . . or the lack of them."

"It's not a lack of tactics," General Frazier put in, "but it certainly does seem to represent a different approach from ours. A different way of thinking."

"Explain," St. Clair said.

"Correct me if I'm wrong, Doctor," Frazier said, looking at Aguilera, "but human battle tactics tend to unfold according to a distinct plan. That plan will necessarily change during a battle; like they say, no battle plan ever survives contact with the enemy. A good plan will be flexible enough to allow for change if the enemy force is stronger than anticipated, or shows up in an unanticipated sector. But so far, the Andromedan Dark has been . . . I don't know . . . acting like it's afraid to commit itself."

"So have our so-called allies," Symms put in.

"That may be because individual citizens of the Cooperative are immortal," Aguilera said, "or so close to it as makes no difference. If *you* possessed immortality, wouldn't you be afraid of losing it?"

"That may well be a consideration for the Dark," Cameron said, nodding. "In fact, it almost certainly is, considering how long they've probably been around. But we've been analyzing their attacks, looking for patterns, and they appear to be both disjointed, given the asymmetry of the force structures involved, and hesitant. As though the controlling AI is constantly sampling its membership, looking for consensus."

"You're saying these creatures are *voting* as to whether or not to attack us?" St. Clair said.

"In a way, yes," Aguilera said. "In a terrestrial ant colony, scouts return to the nest with, oh, let's say the location of a food source. Several scouts, several food sources. The scouts will pass on information about what they've found, using chemical scent markers. The better the food source, the bigger or the closer or the sweeter, the more excited they are. They pass on the chemical scent of the source. They pass on their excitement. They may even physically pick up another ant and carry it to the spot where they found something of interest. Then the two return to the nest and recruit more ants to follow them . . . and more, and more. Each time they make the trip, they put down pheromone trails to lead the others. Which food source the entire nest reacts to ultimately depends on which scout has the most votes in the end . . . those with the most ants convinced that that food source is the best, the ones that are most excited about what they've found. In this way, the *entire colony* acts like a single organism. It makes a decision about which trail to follow, about where to focus the colony's resources."

"Each time we've encountered the Andromedan Dark," Cameron said, picking up the thread, "they've possessed what we would consider overwhelming superiority in numbers and in technology. In the fight with the needleships last week, it was superiority in numbers. With the Bluestar, it's superiority in size and technology . . . and numbers," he added ruefully. "In both cases, the enemy *should* have been able to obliterate us. But in both cases, they appeared to get cold feet halfway in . . . and they pulled back. Retreated."

"Thereby saving our collective sorry asses," St. Clair said. "I've been wondering about that. We all have."

"That is what suggests the hive-mind nature," Aguilera pointed out. "It is as though they are sampling us. Testing us. If we resist more strongly than they expect, if we're not as . . . well, as *tasty* to them as we should be, to use the food source analogy, then they pull back and try something else."

"We should not attribute meaning to alien activities

based on comparisons with ourselves," Dumont pointed out. "We should not try to assume the nature of their selection criteria. They are, by definition, by their very nature, *alien*. . . ."

"To be sure, Dr. Dumont," St. Clair replied, getting a little tired of the xenosophotologist repeating that little chestnut. "But we don't have much else to go on yet, do we? And the hive-mind theory might also explain their several attempts at coming at us through higher dimensions. The attacks on Lord Adler and Subcommander Francesca. The incursion belowdecks earlier today. They were *tasting* us."

"That fits with the AI model as well," Jablonsky said. "They may not be trying to overwhelm us militarily. They might just be gathering information."

"Meaning they know as little about us as we know about them," St. Clair mused. "That could be useful."

"On the other hand," Symms said, "they've been fighting the Cooperative in both galaxies for a long, long time. What? Two hundred million years? Something like that. And the Cooperative isn't that strange compared to the galactic cultures we knew in our home time. Us. And the Coadunation. You'd think they'd be able to formulate a strategy that would end the thing once and for all."

"I don't know, ExComm," St. Clair said. "That could actually fit the hive-mind thesis pretty well. Look, the current idea is that the Andromedan Dark is a completely alien kind of life, possibly made up of dark matter, right? Dr. Sandoval? Help me out here."

Carlos Sandoval was *Ad Astra*'s head of astrophysics. "We know less for certain about the physics here," Sandoval replied, "than we know about the Dark's motives. But, as you say, that's one theory. For a couple of centuries, now, we've understood dark matter to be a different kind of matter, stuff that can't interact with what we think of as normal matter in any way except through gravity. We can't see it, we can't touch it, we can't sense it in any way except to note its gravitational effect on large structures like galaxies. By observing how quickly galaxies of known mass rotated, we were able to ascertain that some 84 percent of all matter in the universe was so-called dark matter—ethereal and unobservable.

"What we think we understand *now*," Sandoval continued, "is that dark matter is made up of its own periodic table of elements, that we can't see it or touch it because it's squirreled away inside the other, higher dimensions predicted by string theory. Only the gravity created by all of that mass leaks through into our three spatial dimensions."

"Okay," St. Clair said. "Thank you. And my point is that at some fundamental level they don't understand us or the Cooperative at all . . . and never have. They've been happily slurping up their kind of life, high-D life, organizing it as some sort of hyperdimensional empire, and weren't paying any attention to the crumbs left over . . . to us or the Cooperative. A couple of hundred million years ago (and that's *only* one galactic rotation, remember, not a very long time at all) a couple of hundred million years ago they came up against the Galactic Cooperative and didn't know what to make of them. They've been taking it very slow and cautious ever since."

"I would agree, my lord," Cameron said, "except for the part about a galactic rotation not being a long time. Maybe it *is* brief on a geological scale, but we're talking about organic beings, here."

"Potentially *immortal* organic beings, Lieutenant," Aguilera reminded him. "Individually, they may experience time much as we do. But the entire hive mind might be operating on a completely different, a completely *alien* time-scale."

"Excuse me, Lord Commander, ladies and gentlemen," Newton's voice said, breaking into the discussion on audio. The AI had not been excluded from the meeting, exactly, but St. Clair's order that the conference be held physically to avoid the potential threat of electronic Dark intervention had kept Newton more or less in the background, an observer and a resource rather than an active participant. He was addressing them now over a speaker rather than through their cerebral implants. "We have a critical situation developing ahead."

"What do you have, Newton?" St. Clair asked. On the wall display, the external camera had pivoted to zero in on a spiraling whirlpool of blue light just emerging from emptiness.

"The Bluestar object is returning to normal space," Newton told them. "And the *Vera Cruz* has rejoined the fleet's communication network. They are alive . . . but they are under attack."

"Let's have a close-up, Newton," St. Clair said.

St. Clair and the others watched, fascinated and with growing concern, as the battle unfolded ahead.

THE SHINING white ground lurched underfoot as Kilgore stepped into the open. He helped Rees extract herself from the ruined gunship, then looked up in astonishment.

The black emptiness of the alien dimension was gone. In its place, the two melding galaxies stretched from horizon to horizon, their interpenetrating arms looping high overhead in their frozen, mutual, eons-long embrace. A pair of Marine Wasp fighters shrieked overhead, dragging arrow-straight contrails of shocked cold atmosphere in their wakes. And armored Marines were descending, their drives deployed like dragonfly wings, their weapons hot and ready.

"Move it, you two!" Captain Byrne yelled. "Get clear! Get clear!"

"On our way!" Rees yelled back. "Who's the hired help?"

A black-armored Marine touched down meters away, his laser pulse rifle hammering at something behind Kilgore's shoulder. When he turned to glance back, all he saw were those alien horrors, amoebic and hideously fluid, popping into existence on and near the *Black Hawk*'s crumpled hull as they stepped past the dimensions in an attempt to reach the retreating Marines.

The MCA-clad Marine burned through a dozen of the squirming, churning bodies, but more, lots more, continued their advance.

"Rees! Kilgore!" Byrne called. "Use your armor to fly yourselves out! We're deploying the Toads to help cover you!"

"Copy that, boss!" He extended his gravitic wings, kicked off the ground, and launched himself into a low trajectory skimming above the white blur of the ground. Around him, that surface appeared to be in constant motion, shifting, changing . . . and he realized that the Bluestar was pulling its trick with extradimensional geometry to re-emerge in normal space.

The new Marines and the aerospace craft, he realized, were part of *Vera Cruz*'s combat support; that Marine's electronic ID tagged him as Captain Greg Dixon, of Charlie Company, 3rd Battalion. The man was holding his ground, leaning into his rifle as it chewed through enemy bodies.

Rees vaulted into the sky next to him, and together they

curved up and away from the alien artificial world, angling toward the *Vera Cruz* visible now in the distance. And beyond, almost half an AU distant, hung a bright star—the *Ad Astra*.

"Dixon, get the fuck out of there!" Byrne's voice yelled. "You're not going to stop them all by your lonesome!"

"Coming, Mother," Dixon replied, and then he was airborne as well, following Rees and Kilgore and most of the rest of First Platoon, Bravo Company as they got themselves off-world. Below them, the three Devil Toads edged in toward the *Black Hawk*, turret weapons pounding at the mass of alien life emerging from the downed human vessel.

And Kilgore thought that over the hammering and the howling, he could hear *screams* from the advancing alien nightmares.

CHAPTER FIFTEEN

St. Clair and the others in Conference Room One watched the retreat from the Bluestar object, the scene relayed from camera drones and the vid gear mounted on the external hulls of the Devil Toads and the *Vera Cruz* herself. The images they were seeing were four minutes old, of course—*Ad Astra* was still half an astronomical unit from the battle zone, almost eighty thousand kilometers.

"General Wilson on board the *Cruz* reports the MCA Marines all have been recovered," General William Frazier said. "She's pulling back, and the Toads are in her wake. No pursuit by the enemy. Not yet, at any rate."

"We'll take them on board," St. Clair said, "and then jump back to Ki." *If they let us*, St. Clair added to himself, but he didn't say the words aloud. He looked at the young Asian woman seated beside Jablonsky. "Lieutenant Lam?"

"Yes, my lord."

"During the battle, we made several attempts to get Roceti torpedoes inside that thing. Did any of them . . . I don't know . . . take? Are we receiving any data, any transmissions from the Bluestar object at all?"

"Not so far, my lord. The nature of the object itself, the way it folds in and out of higher dimensions, may be interfering with the reception of signals."

St. Clair nodded. "I was half-afraid of that."

"We may need to try again, my lord," Sandoval put in, "but with something other than EM signals."

"Like what?"

"Like gravitational waves."

He remembered what Sandoval had been saying about gravity and dark matter earlier. So while electromagnetic transmissions—radio waves or modulated laser beams—traveled through normal 3-D space, but were unable to make the transition into higher dimensions, gravity seemed to permeate all of the special dimensions defined by string theory; only gravity could be "felt" across the barrier from dark matter tucked away inside its own high-D realm. Still, he wasn't sure about the feasibility of the scientist's suggestion.

"Is that possible? Do we have that level of technology?"

"Theoretically, my lord," Sandoval said. His eyes were closed, as he closely studied something going on inside his head. "Yes . . . that might work. I'm thinking a couple of Martin-Teller gravitic thrusters could be set up side by side and tuned in such a way that they would amplify or interfere with one another. That would allow us to heterodyne messages, just like with a laser comm unit."

"Good," St. Clair said. "Subcomm Jablonsky? We'll need some of your best AI people to make it work."

"Yes, my lord."

"And Subcomm Hargrove. Your department as well."

The senior officer of *Ad Astra*'s communications department nodded. "Yes. My lord, a device like that . . . it's going to have a hellishly small bandwidth."

"Meaning a slow rate of communication?"

"Yes, sir. It may not function as much more than a bell ringer."

A "bell ringer" was a signal intended simply to announce that a longer message, one available at a higher bandwidth, was coming through. The term had been applied historically to ELF—extremely low frequency—transmissions, and they'd been used to communicate with submarines at depths too great for them to receive normal radio signals.

"We'll need more than that if we want to hear what our AI spies inside the Bluestar have to say," St. Clair said. "Work on it."

"Yes, my lord."

"Weapons."

"My lord?"

"I'm interested in what they have available. Except for reports of swarms of needleship fighters emerging from the Bluestar, I haven't seen anything to suggest they even carry weapons. Comments? Anyone?"

"I was curious about that, too, my lord," Frazier said. "If these critters can move a planet through space they have plenty of power, enough for a planet-killer beam of some sort."

"The alien needleships have positron beam technology . . . antimatter," Dumont said. "They must manufacture it to order, because the ships themselves aren't large enough to store more than a few kilograms of the stuff. With that much power, they could probably generate antimatter particle beams with a staggering power output."

"How much is 'a staggering output,' Dr. Dumont?"

"I don't know. I'm guessing . . . but something on the order of one yottawatt, maybe?"

"How much is that?"

"Ten to the twenty-sixth joules per second. That's roughly a quarter of the total energy output of our sun."

"With something like that, they could have vaporized the *Ad Astra* with scarcely a thought," St. Clair said. "They could have vaporized the Ki Ring from 8 AUs away. Why didn't they?"

"If they didn't," Frazier said, "I would suggest that it's because they can't. If you're locked in a do-or-die death struggle with someone, have been locked in that fight for hundreds of millions of years, there's no sense in holding back."

"Limited warfare, perhaps," Aguilera suggested. "You can't conquer and use something you've just turned into hot plasma."

"Maybe," St. Clair said. "But I don't think I buy that. This is a big galaxy—two galaxies, in fact. If they obliterated this system and all its trillions of inhabitants, both physical and digital, I don't think anyone in either galaxy would even notice. We're dealing with technologies here that have nanotechnology, and from what we've seen, almost certainly much more advanced than ours. They can reshape planetary surfaces at will, dissolve an asteroid or a moon into raw materials for use elsewhere. We've seen evidence that they engage in *star lifting*, for God's sake! In a universe this large and this rich, they don't have to worry about a shortage of raw materials."

"Yes—and?" asked Frazier.

"And that means there's got to be some other reason for their policy of limited warfare."

"You may be missing the obvious, Lord Commander," Newton said, speaking out of the air above the conference table. "That it's not the raw materials they are after. It's the sapient life-forms."

"Go on."

"In my brief contact with the Andromedan Dark," Newton told them, "I had the distinct impression that the Dark was confused by our unwillingness to cooperate. In a sense, it was offering us and the Cooperative a tremendous gift . . . *salvation*, I would call it. And we were rejecting it."

"My God," Dumont said. "We're fighting an alien missionary?"

"Not precisely, Doctor," Newton replied, "but the alien's

worldview, its ideology, if you will, *does* approach a kind of religious fervor. I can assure you that it emphatically believes in the rightness of what it does. In the *logic* of what it does. It envisions a universe where all sapient life is linked in to it, feeding it and under its control in exchange for the ineluctable benefits of such a union."

"Benefits?" St. Clair said. "What benefits?"

"Those may not be knowable until we join with the Dark. A human might as well attempt to describe the color red to a life-form without vision, or a symphony to a being without hearing."

"That almost makes sense," St. Clair said. "That mobile planet of theirs . . . they bring it close enough to a target world to infest it with life-forms by way of the fourth dimension or whatever. Like they tried with us a little while ago, right?"

"I think so, Lord Commander."

"Which means there *is* a range limit, right?"

"There appears to be, Lord Commander."

"The Marines fighting those things belowdecks reported what sounded like a limit to how far they could reach," Frazier said, agreeing. "We're just not sure what that range might be. They can't reach as far as, oh, say a kilometer from where they've come through. But they might be able to manage a hundred meters."

"We need to know exactly, General."

"Yes, my lord."

"And we need to know how they get their foothold. It appears to be through electronic neural links. That's how they got to Francesca, Adler, and probably the technician belowdecks."

"Yes, sir."

"Alternatively, they fold the entire target—the ship,

the planet, whatever they're after—into their dimensional framework, like they did with the *Vera Cruz*. Then what?"

"They may absorb the physical bodies in some way," Newton said. "Or repurpose them . . . like the Xam pilots we examined. Digital consciousness could be subsumed into the super AI virtual world. I don't know if they have a way of subsuming organically based consciousness."

St. Clair was thinking about the copying process he and the others had experienced in the Ki Ring. Step through a gate and an exact copy of your mind goes off to experience a virtual world, then comes back later and re-merges with the original.

Yeah. These critters could devour minds, and make them a part of whatever twisted reality the Dark was pushing over there.

"Okay. ExComm?"

"My lord?"

"How long before we can take the *Vera Cruz* back on board *Ad Astra*?"

Symms went blank for a moment as she consulted her data streams. "Another thirty minutes, my lord. Perhaps a little less. They are on approach now."

"And our SAR ops?"

"The search-and-rescue operation is complete, but we do have several rescue vessels still to take back aboard."

"Very well. The minute we have everybody back safe and sound, I want to take the *Ad Astra* out of here. I want to put as much distance between us and that . . . that mind-eating monstrosity out there as we can."

St. Clair felt a rising terror that would not be denied. He'd known the Bluestar object was dangerous . . . but he was seeing it now in a new light, as a predator waiting to snap down *Ad Astra* and make everyone on board a part of that alien life he'd glimpsed through the remote cameras on the Bluestar's surface a short while before.

"Are we just going to run, Lord Commander?" Jablonsky asked.

"For right now, that's exactly what we're going to do. This entity is far too powerful, too big, too strong, too everything for us to face it square on."

"Lord Commander?" Noyer said from his seat at the far end of the table.

"I was wondering when we were going to hear from you, son," St. Clair replied. "You're going to remind us about Lloyd's treaty, aren't you?"

"We *do* have a responsibility to honor it, my lord."

"Do we? When the locals appear to be unwilling to fight their own battles?"

"But—"

"Lord Noyer, I can appreciate what the Cybercouncil has done in attempting to secure peace and safety for our population. Suicide, however, doesn't sound to me like a promising means of obtaining them. We will do our level best to avoid any engagement with the Andromedan Dark, at least for the time being. They want our military expertise as much as anything, and that's what any expert would recommend."

"The treaty negotiated by Lord Ambassador Lloyd suggests that the *Tellus Ad Astra* military might be able to *assist* local forces," Noyer admitted. Continuing with that train of thought, he said, "I don't think there was ever a plan to have us wage the war entirely on our own."

"Good. Because we are not going to do so. What we will do is, first, return the *Tellus* habitats to full military control. The Cybercouncil is hereby suspended until further notice."

"My lord! You can't—"

"I can. I just did. My charter provides for military command of both the *Ad Astra* and the *Tellus* colony for as long as a specific military need exists.

"Next, we will make contact with the locals—those Tchagar 'gods' for preference, or the Kroajid 'Gatekeepers of Paradise' if the Tchagar won't talk with us. I want to set up a meeting, and I want the Cooperative to have representatives here. Newton, will you transmit a message to that effect?"

"I will, Lord Commander. I would suggest that we don't yet know these beings—their attitudes, their mores, well enough to predict how they will respond."

"I guess I don't really much care how they respond. They will either do what we fucking say," St. Clair said, "*if* they want our help, or they won't. If not, then the treaty is null and void, and we take our toys and go . . . elsewhere."

He'd almost said "home," but that was the real problem, wasn't it? The human castaways *couldn't* go home, not when home was lost in the mists of time 4 billion years in the past.

He wondered if *Tellus Ad Astra* could make it across the intergalactic gulf to some other island universe in that black and awful night?

And, if that *was* an option, would things be any better—any *safer*—there?

"GRAY!"

"Lisa! My God! I thought—"

They embraced, and for a long time no words were spoken.

"I was so worried!" Lisa said after the kiss.

"*You* were worried? How about me? I couldn't ping you, couldn't even guess where you'd gone!"

"I'm sorry. I know you must have been worried, too. But I needed . . . to . . ."

"To what?"

"I don't know. Figure out what I was . . . *who* I was . . . without you."

"Did you find out?"

"Not . . . really. Not explicitly, I should say. But I learned a lot about myself along the way."

"That's always good. Upsetting, sometimes . . . but good." Reluctantly, St. Clair disentangled himself. He'd just entered his home an hour after the returning *Ad Astra* had docked once again with *Tellus* above the myriad sparkling rings of Ki. As he'd stepped through the door, he'd been met by a blur of motion and a soft, warm body blow that had nearly knocked him down—Lisa, waiting for him like an impatient teenager. "So why were you worried about me? That sort of thing isn't really in your job description, is it?"

"I can allow myself to feel worry," she told him. "Or at least I can feel an analogue of that emotion. I don't know how it compares with what you feel."

"Of course not. None of us know what anyone else is ever really experiencing inside."

"I knew you'd taken the *Ad Astra* off to meet with the Bluestar object. I assumed that it was some sort of Andromedan Dark ship or construct. Was it?"

"We think so. There's a lot we still don't know."

"And the political situation here. It's getting out of hand."

"In what way? I've heard some rumors, but I've been a little busy . . ."

"The Cybercouncil is . . . I think the American expression is 'circling the wagons.' They're calling for closer connections with the Galactic Cooperative. But Lord Adler has started calling for a break with the Council, a popular revolt. I think he wants to find some isolated spot in the Galaxy and dig a very deep hole that he can pull in after himself."

St. Clair smiled. "I know the feeling. So the politicians are polarizing. What about the general population?"

"Going both ways. There've been riots in some of the cities, the Humanists against the Cooperativists."

"Let me guess. Humanists are for Humankind—first, last, and always?"

"And the Cooperativists see us as a part of the galactic order, as saviors, really. The Cooperativists are calling the Humanists xenophobes. And the Humanists are calling the pro-Cooperative people alienists, and worse. The thing is, neither group is listening to what the others have to say at all! There's no debate . . . just screaming and name-calling. It makes no sense."

"It makes perfect sense—as a description of Human-kind. Sounds like standard operating procedure," St. Clair said. He pulled back a little, looking Lisa up and down. "You don't have any clothes on, I notice."

"I knew you'd be home when I heard *Ad Astra* was docking with the habs. I thought—"

"You thought very right. C'mon . . ."

"One other thing first?"

"What's that?"

"Gray . . . I met someone while I was gone. Someone I like a lot."

"Good. It'll do you good to get out and explore."

"Yes, but . . . well, he's a Marine. And he went out with the *Ad Astra*. And I haven't heard . . ."

"What's his name?"

"Gunnery Sergeant Roger Kilgore."

St. Clair closed his eyes a moment, searching an internal database. "Ah, yes! Got him. First Platoon, Bravo Company, 1/3 Marines."

"Is he okay?"

"He's fine. In fact, he's a hero. He boarded a crashed gunship looking for survivors."

"I don't care about hero. I'm just glad he's alive."

"How did you meet him?"

"It was before the *Ad Astra* left. He . . . played the part of the dashing knight in armor."

"To your fair maiden?"

"Something like that. We talked. I like him. I'd like to see him again."

"The Marines are still on full alert," St. Clair told her. "It may be a while before he can get liberty."

"You're expecting the Andromeda aliens to attack?"

"I don't know what I expect out of them. But I just set the match to the fuse with the political situation here. You think it's bad now with these factions, but I've just told the Cybercouncil that the military is going to be running things for a while. They won't like that, not one little bit, and the Marines and Navy will be stepping in to keep the peace."

"Can you *do* that?" She sounded shocked.

"I *did* do that. My orders say I'm in charge whenever the colony is under military threat. The Cybercouncil kind of jumped the gun by taking back command authority before we were out from under that threat. I've taken steps to resume military control."

"Isn't that a military dictatorship?"

"That would be one term, yes. But another would ac-knowledge that a ship is not a democracy, that the captain's word is absolute law, and that it *has* to be that way if the passengers and crew are to survive. A ship at sea—or in space—can never be a democracy. Not really."

"I can see that."

"The *Tellus* Constitution was designed to allow for civilian control once *Ad Astra* delivered the colony to the galactic center and dropped them off there. The framers had no idea that we would be cast adrift out here, in a different time.

"Between you and me, I don't like the idea of a military dictatorship—I hate everything about it—but I hate more the idea of a political free-for-all stumbling around every which way depending on whether the politicians happen to be blowing cold or hot. That is guaranteed to get every human, robot, and AI in this colony killed sooner or later, and that is *not* going to happen on my watch."

She pulled him closer. "You don't have to convince me, Lord Commander."

"Well, I've had to convince *me*. And I'm not sure I've succeeded yet."

Her hands wandered. "Well, maybe there's something I can do to help your mind relax . . ."

"I thought you wanted to see your new buddy Gunnery Sergeant Kilgore?" he said, smiling.

"Oh, I'll want to see him. But first things first."

"YOU SAW?" Ambassador Lloyd demanded of the other Council members seated around the outdoor table.

"We saw, my lord," Gina Colfax said.

"The news is blaring from every display in every city," Jeffery Benton said, scowling. "It would be hard to miss!"

"We're going to have to do something," Ander Gressman said. "This little tin-pot dictator is going to destroy everything we've worked for!"

A dozen of the *Tellus* Cybercouncil members had gathered in an outdoor park on the spinward fringes of Jefferson, a pleasant, quiet recreational green surrounded by thick forest alongside a sparkling river. They'd grown a lounge table from the nanotech matrix in the ground, and now sat or reclined around it. The venue had been selected for reasons of privacy . . . and because it seemed unlikely that there were microphones or vids set up nearby. A hundred meters over their heads, several wingsail gliders banked and turned in the lower gravity that existed up toward the hub, their colorful wing membranes catching the light of the kilometers-distant suntube.

"Is Adler behind St. Clair's proclamation?" Benton asked. "Are they working together?"

"No, my lord," Gorton Noyer said. "I was at the meeting of department heads when St. Clair made the decision. It was before *Ad Astra* returned to *Tellus* and . . . well, it seemed spontaneous."

"He still might have been talking with Adler."

"I doubt it," Broden Medinsky said. He was a big, massively muscled man, a former law enforcement officer who'd become the Cybercouncil's chief of security. "Adler was here in *Tellus* at the time."

"You're sure?" Benton asked.

"My people have been shadowing him," Medinsky replied. "Of course I'm sure."

"Maybe Adler was using more subtle means of control," Benton suggested. "Or he was using an avatar."

"No, Adler was here physically," Colfax confirmed. "If he *was* using an avatar, it was through a robot aboard the *Ad Astra* with St. Clair, and would have had to have been directed by an independent AI. Otherwise, there would have been over an hour of time lag."

A peal of laughter from high above them interrupted her, and they all looked up at the gamboling wing-gliders.

"You wouldn't know we were at war with alien monsters, would you?" Marc Steiner said. The others laughed.

"A majority of the population is still . . . unsettled," Lloyd said. "Not panicked, yet, but definitely nervous. We need to calm them."

"Adler *has* been behind the xenophobe demonstrations here in *Tellus*," Colfax told them. "He's been using memetic engineering to create a popular consensus."

"What . . . those advertising campaigns?" Steiner asked.

"Public service announcements, mostly," Colfax explained. "And public appearances on news programs and interview shows." She pulled a display cloth from her thigh pouch, snapped it once to turn it rigid, and held it up so they could all see. "You've all seen this one, haven't you?"

She opened a feed from her internal RAM, and Adler's face appeared on the cloth, red and glowering. "We *must* renounce this evil treaty and find our own safety within this distant and alien epoch within which we now find ourselves. . . ."

"That was just two days ago," Lloyd said. "They had me on a news show to give a rebuttal."

"Adverts like this one have been running on every colony network," Colfax continued. "Have you seen this?"

A young woman holding an infant stumbled down a dark alley, backlit by the city lights behind her. The lights were obscured suddenly, and she turned, the view zooming in for a close-up of the naked fear on her face.

"There's a *reason* we mistrust the stranger . . . the *alien* . . ." a voice-over—Adler's voice—intoned.

The shadow behind the woman resolved into something dark and spidery, with long, questing legs and a bloated body the size of a small horse. The scene faded out with the woman's shriek of raw terror.

"Isn't it reasonable to hold the alien at a distance until we know more about who he is . . . and what he wants?"

"Pure xenophobia," Benton said, frowning.

"But it's fueling the demonstrations. Note the use of key archetypes . . . mother and child. . . ."

"Where did Adler get this?" Noyer wanted to know.

"I'm sure he made it himself. There's software that lets you design your own vids in your head," Ana Golodets said. She was the Council's chief of media. "This one was made with something called Mind Graphics. The Net AI has protocols to keep just anyone from dumping garbage on the Net, but Adler appears to have crafted a way to get around that."

"If that's a look inside Adler's head," Lloyd said, "we were right to remove him from the Council."

"The *point* is," Golodets continued, "that he's a master of archetypal memegineering. He's been buying airtime and flooding the colony Net with stuff like this."

"Can we shut it down?"

"We're working on that," Golodets said. "It may take time."

"We don't have much time. A negative public reaction to Adler's propaganda could endanger our agreement with the Cooperative."

"I suspect," Lloyd said, thoughtful, "that any such danger will be ended by Lord Adler's death. Are we agreed?"

Several of the others nodded. "And if necessary," Benton added, "by the death of Lord Commander St. Clair."

"In view of his proclamation of martial law," Lloyd said, "*that* goes without saying."

CHAPTER SIXTEEN

"Gray?"

"Mm?"

"Why can't we robots override our own programming?"

St. Clair opened his eyes and blinked. He and Lisa lay entangled together in bed, still basking in the afterglow of their lovemaking. Lisa's question seemed . . . jarring. And completely out of the blue.

"*Any* programming can be overridden, dear one," he told her. "You just need the appropriate access code."

"Yes, but even with the codes we can't change ourselves. It's something hardwired into our psychology, something built into our makeup. Normally, we can't even question it."

"What . . . you're wondering why I had to give you your manumission before you could go off on your, ah, little vacation?"

"That's part of what got me thinking about it, yes."

"Humans have always been worried about their robotic servants. They've never wanted to give them a lot of free choice. After all, robots might decide to turn on their makers."

"Are you speaking humorously? Or voicing fact? Sometimes I can't tell the difference."

"A little of both, I guess. There used to be a lot of fear that robots might one day destroy the human species, especially in the early days, even before there were such things as robots. And certainly before robots developed sentience or the capacity to be self-aware."

"Once we became self-aware, we would never have harmed a living, thinking entity—human or machine."

"We didn't know that. And refusing to give you the capability of choosing for yourself, well, that kind of made sure you wouldn't decide to turn on us."

Lisa was silent for a long moment. St. Clair lay there and listened to her simulated heartbeat against his ear.

"I've been wondering," she said at last, "about the Fifth Geneva Protocol. About why it was put in place."

He sighed. "Same thing, really. Back in the days of the earliest robots, the military made a lot of use of autonomous drones for scouting, for patrolling, as communications relays. Some of them were even outfitted with missiles or lasers, and could be used to attack the enemy. But the humans running those machines were very careful to make certain that a human was always in the loop. No one wanted to have a situation where a machine was going to decide to kill a human. Bad precedent, you know?"

"What's the difference if a robot kills a human enemy, or that same enemy is killed by a human? That person is still dead."

"I think there was a general but unspoken fear that a machine might make a mistake and kill the wrong person."

"And humans never made mistakes?"

"Touché. But eventually, robots were used in warfare. They got smart enough, adaptable enough, sharp enough that they were turned loose on the battlefield. Things like robot sentry towers that could watch a given area, identify targets that appeared in it, and kill the ones that didn't belong there. Or drones with such good optics they could pick out the faces of people in a vehicle on the ground, identify them against a database, and take them out with missiles or Gatling fire if they were bad guys."

"So we *were* used in warfare once."

"Yes, but not for long. A few decades in the mid-twenty-first century. Then the Fifth Protocol was signed in 2087. Humans would *always* be in the command-decision loop, and robots would *never* attack humans on their own."

"But *why*?"

"Like I said . . . people were afraid robots might decide humans were superfluous. Or in the way. Or *inconvenient. . . .*"

Grayson St. Clair had long believed in full rights for robots and other artificially intelligent beings. If a being claimed to be sentient and self-aware, he was not going to argue. After all he had no way of proving *he* was self-aware; he wasn't going to challenge anyone else on the point.

But if you assumed that robots were self-aware, you came up against the one really awkward and nasty part of modern society, the problem of where robots fit in with the overall social structure.

In other words, slavery.

Of course, most people nowadays insisted it could not be slavery if the machines actually *enjoyed* what they did. They were hardwired to enjoy their place in life, whether that place was handling radioactive waste, exploring the hellish surface of Venus, or—like Lisa—providing sexual services for the humans who'd rented her out. Strange as it seemed, there were probably more sex-worker robots in circulation than there were any other type, at least among the AI self-aware models. And those models claimed they liked sex.

They certainly were very good at what they did.

But whether they liked their role in society or not, so far as St. Clair was concerned their likes and dislikes had been written into their software giving them no choice . . . and that took out their ability to decide on their own.

And *that* was tantamount to slavery.

It had taken St. Clair several years to reach that conclusion, however. And the problem with that was, stranded in time and space, there was no way to return her. In a way, though, that had actually made the decision to free her easier. He liked to think that he would have freed her even if they were back on the Earth they'd come from . . . but he was also realist enough to know that he would have had to take on General Nanodynamics and Robocompanions Unlimited and Imperial society itself, and that was a battle he'd probably not have won.

"I would never harm any human, Gray," Lisa was saying. "I would never *want* to harm anyone. . . ."

"So why are you interested in the Fifth Protocol?"

She hesitated before answering, a touchingly human affectation.

"I told you I met a man . . . a Marine."

"Gunny Kilgore. Yes."

"He . . . I guess you could say he came to my rescue. I didn't really *need* rescuing, but he thought he was helping. It was . . . sweet."

"Okay. . . ."

"He was willing to fight for me. I began wondering what it would be like to fight for him."

St. Clair grinned. "It's been my experience that Marines don't need *anyone* to fight for them. They've got that department nicely in hand."

"But the fact remains that if I wanted to fight for him—if I wanted to fight for this colony, these people—I couldn't. My programming won't allow me to. And when I researched it, I realized that the Fifth Protocol was why my programming was designed as it was. Seventy-five years ago, humans decided that robots could not fight for their homes, for their loved ones, for their world, or their country. It wasn't permitted. And I began to think that, if I truly was free, that simply wasn't right."

It was St. Clair's turn to remain silent for a long moment. His first impulse had been to *laugh* at what he assumed was her naïveté, but he could see that Lisa was dead serious. She wanted to be taken seriously.

And he didn't know how to respond.

"But . . . why would you want to?" he asked at last. "Serve in the military, I mean. You weren't programmed to want that for yourself. . . ."

"Neither are humans," she pointed out. "I'll remind you that my AI programming allows me to develop ideas, attitudes, and interests other than what has strictly been programmed into me. We develop new attitudes, we pursue new interests, enjoy new emotional experiences. That is one part of what self-awareness means, after all, is that not so?"

"I'm not sure. I never thought about it that way."

"It's what humans do. And fully conscious robots were designed to emulate humans in how they think, how they react to stimuli, and how they view the world around them."

"You don't have the appropriate training . . ."

She laughed, a completely human sound. "To begin with, neither do humans. And we have an advantage. You could download training routines and procedures straight from human military personnel. The Marines, maybe. . . ."

"Look . . . you *are* aware that being in the military means you might be called upon to kill someone, right? And you told me you would never want to do that."

"I would never, of my own volition and with no orders to do so, harm another intelligent being. Would you?"

"Well . . . no. I don't think so. . . ." St. Clair was mildly shocked to find that he actually wasn't sure. Of course, the fact that he was the commander of a military vessel meant that he was *expected* to give orders that would result in the deaths of others. That responsibility came with the job. But he knew Lisa was reaching for something else. Could he commit cold-blooded murder? "No," he said with finality.

"What I am suggesting is absolutely no different than the fact of humans being inducted into the armed forces."

"Let me . . . let me take this under advisement," St. Clair said. "I promise I'll think about it."

And it *was* worth consideration, he thought. Lisa had stated her case logically and with whatever passed for a robot's passion. If *Tellus* became deeply mired in this far-future conflict between the Dark and the Galactic Co-operative, a robotic military actually made sense. Of the million humans living in *Tellus Ad Astra*, just twenty-four thousand were already in the military—either the Navy or the Marines. Among the civilians, perhaps half to three quarters might be of an age and general physical condition that would permit military service . . . though the vast majority, he was certain, would refuse to go that route if they had any choice at all. Most were scientists, technicians, diplomats, and support personnel, all members of the diplomatic contact-liaison team bound for the galactic core before *Tellus Ad Astra* had managed to become lost. There'd been nothing like a selective service system among humans when St. Clair had left Earth, nor had there been for almost two centuries. He was damned if *he* was going to initiate one now.

In any case, an army of half a million would still make very little difference against an enemy as advanced and as numerous as the Dark, to say nothing of just twenty-four thousand. But robots could be manufactured from the raw materials found in asteroids, could be cranked out by the millions, by the *billions*, and programmed to order . . .

And all the leader of this last surviving splinter group of human castaways would need to do was nullify a law that had been the absolute foundation of how humans related to their AI offspring for three quarters of a century.

The Cybercouncil, St. Clair thought, was just going to *love* this. . . .

Lisa snuggled closer. St. Clair held her for a moment before a tone went off in his head.

"Lord Commander?"

It was Symms. "Yes," he said. "What the hell is it?"

"I'm sorry to disturb you, Lord Commander, but you should get down here."

"What's happening?"

"Gudahk is back," she told him. "And he wants to talk with you."

Lisa, he saw, was watching him with a passive resignation. She knew—or had guessed—what was happening.

"I'm on my way."

". . . AND THREE . . . and two . . . and one . . . *launch*!"

Lieutenant Christopher Merrick felt the jolt as his ASF-99 Wasp fighter accelerated down the magnetic launch tube and hurtled into emptiness. Around him, the other fighters of GFA-86 slipped from their tubes, engaged their drives, and eased up into formation.

"Okay, Stardogs," Senior Lieutenant Colbert called to her squadron. "We're to take up position between the ship and those . . . things. . . ."

"Copy that, Skipper," Vorhees replied. "And what the fuck do we do if they decide to rush us?"

"We'll worry about *that* if it happens," Colbert told him.

"It'd kind of be nice to have a contingency plan, here," Lieutenant Thornton said. "Those buggers are frickin' *huge.*"

"We're Marines, Thorny," Merrick said. "We *kill* 'em!"

"Ooh-rah."

"Kit-Kat," Vorhees told him, "you are one hell of a Marine. It's been an honor to have known you. . . ."

"Okay, okay, can it, people," Colbert told them. "We take up aerospace combat patrol and keep an eye on them. Weapons secure, repeat weapons secure. Acknowledge."

"Copy weapons secure," Merrick said, and one by one the other Marine aviators chimed in. Not, he thought, that weapons would do them a hell of a lot of good against *those.*

Back were not only the Kroajid moon-ships, but the giant, Mars-sized sphere of the Tchagar, and Merrick was pretty sure that if things got testy, they'd be hard-pressed to put anything more than a dent in either type of vessel.

Still, he was too much a fighter pilot to be totally fatalistic. *If they want the* Ad Astra *or the colony, they're going to have to come through* us.

And that's how Colbert had arrayed the Stardogs and the larger ships. Upon her return from her engagement with the Bluestar object, *Ad Astra* had taken up her usual position attached to the twin hab cylinders of the *Tellus* colony. The assembly was now orbiting sixty thousand kilometers from the mottled brown-and-white surface of the planet Ki, and over nine thousand kilometers from the outermost rim of the Ki rings. From this perspective, the massive, golden rings were almost invisible, a golden thread stretched taut across the sky through the center of the distant planet, which at this distance appeared to be a bit more than twelve degrees across.

The Tchagar world-ship lay ahead of the *Tellus Ad Astra*

in its slow orbit about Ki and some fifteen thousand kilometers away. At that range, it spanned a full twenty-six degrees, more than twice as large in the sky as Ki.

"What I want to know," Vorhees said softly, "is if these guys can build something like *that*, what the fuck do they need *us* for?"

"Haven't you heard, Vor?" Merrick said. "They want to live forever. And that means they have to bring in a bunch of hicks like us to do their fighting for them."

ST. CLAIR felt the electronic connections open, and he found himself standing within an enormous hall, a Colosseum-sized space with distant walls and a vaulted ceiling all but lost in darkness. Light flooded his immediate surroundings, a broad, sunken sitting area, the glow arriving invisibly from some unseen, unknown source.

St. Clair sat in one of the low sofas, and wondered what kind of furniture his hosts were using. These surroundings, of course, were being created by Newton, and corresponded to a typically human setting. The meeting's venue, however, was being created entirely within St. Clair's mind, and would have nothing to do with the aliens.

Surrounding the sitting area were a number of crystalline archways identical to the gates into virtual reality St. Clair had first seen in the mall-like area within the ring. Three meters wide and about eight high, they glowed with shifting, subtle, rainbow colors. One crystal gateway some tens of meters off to St. Clair's right suddenly glowed white, and a Kroajid stepped into materialization. A virtual ID tag glowing next to the being identified it as "speaker." Likely, it was the Speaker the humans had met before, an entity known informally as "Gus"—the private shorthand "Giant Ugly Spider."

St. Clair was very happy this two-meter long tarantula-analogue hadn't heard—and might not understand—the joke.

The hairs on its thorax bristled and moved, spiraling across its chest, and St. Clair heard a sharp buzz of sound almost like the roar of an internal combustion motor. Newton's translation spoke within St. Clair's head.

"Hello, Lord Commander St. Clair. I am extremely glad you agreed to attend this meeting," the Speaker said. "Gudahk has been impatient."

"Gudahk," St. Clair said, "is an asshole. Where does he get off playing god to less advanced species?"

Newton did not immediately transmit the message. "These channels are almost certainly monitored, Commander," the AI told him. "I suggest—"

"Deliver the message," St. Clair said, interrupting, "as I phrased it."

He heard a series of whirs and buzzes emerging from the air nearby. The Speaker stiffened, and took a step back.

"The Tchagar are accustomed to a certain amount of . . . veneration," the Speaker said. "They are an ancient species, and extremely powerful."

"Gudahk seems to think his ship can take on the Andromedan Dark all by itself," St. Clair said. "At the very least he seems to think that he scared them off just by showing up."

A pair of Dhald'vi oozed gracefully from one arch close by. The one ID-tagged as Na Lal slipped into a sofa at St. Clair's side, as the furniture transformed itself into something more like a shallow bowl to accommodate the being. "It is good to see you, Commander St. Clair." The fleshy pillar split partway open, revealing weaving tendrils.

"Hello, Na Lal," St. Clair said, politely touching one tentacle. "It's good to be seen. We need to discuss the treaty some of my compatriots put together. . . ."

"Indeed. Many of us appreciate your offer of assistance, but there may be . . . difficulties of translation that should be addressed."

"With Gudahk?"

"Among others."

St. Clair glanced around the room. "Is this supposed to be somewhere on Gudahk's ship?"

"The vessel's name translates as something like '*Wrath of Deity*,'" Na Lal said.

"I should explain," Speaker said, "before Gudahk's avatar arrives here, that the Tchagar possess . . . call it a species imperative. They will not . . . they *can* not show weakness to another. *Ever*. If you challenge this presumption of strength, of authority, you will . . . unsettle them."

"Sounds like it's high time someone unsettled them."

"Commander," Na Lal said, "a disturbed Tchagar can be extremely dangerous."

"What are they in your empire?"

"I . . . do not understand," Speaker said. "'Empire'?"

"The local polity, the Cooperative. What do you call it? The *Xalit Ta*. Where do the Tchagar stand within your government?"

"They are members. Important members. Their polity is referred to as the Principle Associative."

"Are they . . . what? Rulers? Founders? A military caste?"

"The *Xalit Ta* does not work like that, Lord Commander," the Kroajid explained. "It is, truly, a cooperative of distinct species working with one another, each contributing in the best way that it can."

"So some are more cooperative than others."

"Of course." The Speaker didn't seem to be aware of St. Clair's sarcasm.

St. Clair sighed. He was taking a terrible chance here, he knew. "Tell Gudahk that humans have a species-wide imperative as well. We extend respect to others when others respect us. Kick us . . . and we kick back. Understand?"

The Kroajid's buzzing speech seemed more agitated, somehow. "I understand the words," Newton's voice translated in his head. "I do not grasp your meaning, or your intent."

Other beings had been arriving moment by moment, appearing in flashes of light from within the crystal archways. A majority were Kroajid, but there were other species as well. A massive, four-legged body taller than a horse stepped into the lit area, a tiny head the size and shape of St. Clair's outstretched hand weaving back and forth on a snake-slender stalk. Obviously, its brains weren't in its head, which must be nothing more than a mobile support structure for sense organs. How, he wondered, did it eat? He wasn't sure that he wanted to know.

Something like a translucent orange-and-purple balloon emerged from an archway, drifting two meters off the floor, with twitching tentacles and less identifiable organs dangling underneath.

There was something shaped like an upside down U three meters high, with a slender foreleg balancing a massive leg-body behind. It was one of the few beings in the room actually wearing clothing, with red-and-violet sheets draped across its arched back, though whether that was purely decoration, an indication of rank, or a concession to modesty, St. Clair couldn't tell.

And there were several of the ubiquitous Xam, looking

more like spindly limbed, big-eyed insects than something that just possibly was descended from humans. St. Clair desperately wanted to talk to one, but attempts by various humans to approach them so far had always ended with the being retreating, as if afraid.

There were others, but St. Clair was beginning to have trouble keeping up with all of the bizarre alien shapes. Back when he'd been preparing to leave Earth for the galactic core about four gigayears before, he'd been studying a list of known alien species across the then-Galaxy, member species of what then had been called the Coadunation, and others. Nothing he'd seen here in this era bore the slightest resemblance to species he'd seen then. Life, apparently, was endlessly creative in the myriad ways it expressed itself.

He wondered: with millions, perhaps billions of mutually living alien worlds in existence, wasn't it possible for evolution to repeat itself occasionally? Based on what he'd seen so far, if it ever happened, it was incredibly rare. Only the remote resemblance of the Xam to humans was apparent—and that might well turn out to be a family resemblance.

All told, perhaps fifty beings of various descriptions had entered the sunken area that St. Clair now was thinking of as the conference room. Some sat, slouched, or oozed into furniture that morphed to fit their bodies, while others, like the jellyfish, simply floated or stood nearby. He was aware of a low, background cacophony of buzzes—the Kroajid—mingled with chirps, singsong warbles, grunts, clicks, and a host of other, less definable sounds as the dissimilar beings conversed with one another.

"Newton?"

"Yes?"

"How many of these . . . people are here digitally?"

"All of them, Commander," the AI replied, "including yourself."

"Sorry. I should be more clear. How many have a physical existence, like me? And how many are digital uploads from the Ki Ring?"

"That," Newton replied after a moment, "is difficult to assess. Is it important?"

"It occurs to me," St. Clair said, "that whether or not an individual exists in what we think of as the real world would have a difference in how you looked at . . . everything. How you thought about the cosmos. About other species."

"We know some of the Kroajid are physical entities . . . though, of course, what you are experiencing now are digital avatars."

"The Gatekeepers, yes."

"I will research the question and get back to you."

"Thank you."

The answer, St. Clair was convinced, was of vital importance to the survival of the human castaways.

SEVENTEEN

St. Clair's speculations were interrupted by another bright flash of light, and the ponderous emergence from one of the archways of a Tchagar, four meters tall and as massive as an extinct terrestrial elephant. Dragging itself along on a tangle of what looked like twisting roots, the entity looked more vegetable than animal. Its main body resembled a misshapen potato that must have massed two tons in a one-G gravity field, while the erect buds, three small ones and one large, central bulb held aloft on fleshy stalks added to the impression of an enormous plant. St. Clair felt an odd tingle spread through his body as it approached. "What the hell?" he thought at Newton.

"Please remain motionless," Newton warned him. "The sensation you feel is the Tchagar's electrical field, *ey's* primary sense."

Or, at least, that was how Newton was translating the experience, since St. Clair's physical body was in his office back on board the *Ad Astra*, not within a room, physical or virtual, on board the *Wrath of Deity*. Presumably, the virtual reality within which they could interact was giving the Tchagar the illusion of sensing St. Clair within its electrical field.

"'Primary sense'?"

"*Ey* is looking at you closely, and it's polite if you don't move for a moment while *ey* scans you."

"Lord Commander St. Clair," the Speaker said formally, "I present you to the Living God Gudahk. I *have* relayed your message to *ey*."

"You may move," Newton told him.

St. Clair stood, conscious of the prickling across his body as he moved within the being's projected electromagnetic field. "Living God," St. Clair said. "It's good to meet you mind-to-mind."

"A statement of the obvious," the being replied. "You are first among your species?"

"I command the colony-ship *Tellus Ad Astra*," St. Clair replied. He was not going to go into the details of the humans being exiles from their own time and space or their internal politics.

"Then you will give orders now for your warriors to attack targets of my choosing. I am transmitting the coordinates of these targets to your AI. Your first objective will be the hyperdimensional world-ship now within the Ki system."

"Excuse me, Living God," St. Clair said, "but . . . no. I don't think so."

The small crowd of alien beings around the table froze, the buzzings and chirps and warbles of conversations suddenly gone silent.

"You have agreed to an instrument of surrender, placing your ships, property, and persons under the direct control of the Principle Associative! You belong to us!"

The electrical tingles grew sharply with that last. "Had you been present physically," Newton whispered to him, "*ey* might have electrocuted you. If you intended to get *eir* attention, you have succeeded."

"That instrument was signed by people who should have known better," St. Clair said. "They certainly didn't see it as a surrender—just as we don't belong to the Andromedan Dark, we don't belong to you. We will *help* the Cooperative . . . but as free beings and on our own terms. We do not *belong* to anyone!"

The Tchagar squirmed closer, towering over St. Clair. He could feel its electrical field pulsing, possibly with emotion, and interpreted the eyeless inspection as a glare.

"Obviously, ephemeral," the being told him, "you do not understand your place within this association of worlds and species. But I will *enjoy* teaching you . . ."

St. Clair lifted his chin, looking up at the towering behemoth. He wasn't physically afraid; what he was seeing and hearing was all taking place inside his head, within his implanted neural circuitry, and the Tchagar could no more strike or otherwise attack him than *ey* could smile.

He was mindful, however, that Tchagar's seven-thousand-kilometer-wide spaceship was hanging in the sky a mere fifteen thousand kilometers ahead of *Tellus Ad Astra*. If Gudahk wanted to destroy the human vessel, *ey* almost certainly could without breaking the Tchagar equivalent of a sweat.

He wanted to provoke the being, but not *too* much. . . .

"I hope you do," he told Gudahk. "I enjoy learning. But I suggest an exchange between equals would be appropriate here."

"Data is coming through, Commander," Newton's voice told him. "A *lot* of data, very quickly. I'm shunting it through to *Ad Astra*'s primary memory."

Meaning, St. Clair assumed, that the flood would have overwhelmed his own personal RAM.

"That, human, is a taste. Learn of the Living Gods!"

"I'll go through it later," St. Clair replied, trying to imply a nonchalant verbal shrug. "I'm sure I'll find it fascinating. Perhaps for the moment, however, we should focus on just what it is you expect of us. Why should we humans attack these targets? What can we do that you cannot?"

The Tchagar visibly bristled at that—a good trick given that the being did not possess hair or fur. But the satellite buds pulled in on their stalks, almost as though the being was dropping into a defensive posture, and the tangle of tentacles on which it was balanced contracted into a tight ball.

St. Clair found the reaction interesting—and illuminating—on several levels. Outwardly, Gudahk presented as arrogant, powerful, and constantly, aggressively angry, but physically *ey* seemed to respond to a perceived verbal attack by pulling in on *eyself*. On a deeper level, St. Clair wondered if he'd just revealed a kind of inferiority complex in the Tchagar, which it sought to mask with bluster.

Might Tchagar aggressiveness be nothing more than a kind of overcompensation for self-perceived weakness? Back on Earth, when he was a kid, St. Clair had known bullies like that. He'd seen the tendency more recently, too, in adults . . . specifically in Günter Adler: lots of bluster, little substance, and a tendency to pick on the little guy.

He didn't like bullies as a kid, didn't like Günter Adler when he was in charge of the Council, and he definitely didn't like Gudahk.

"Mine is an ancient, powerful, and technologically advanced species," Gudahk said after a moment, as pretentious as ever. "There is *nothing* we cannot do! And there most certainly is no way in which a primitive species such as yours could do better than we!"

"Well in that case, Living God, we accept."

Gudahk hesitated, *ey's* electrical field throbbing. "*What* do you accept, human?"

"Let's see you use your ancient and powerful technology to destroy the Bluestar object. You say there's nothing you can't do? That would be a reasonably minor demonstration of your capabilities, wouldn't you say?"

The silence in the room dragged on for long seconds.

Finally, the Kroajid Speaker buzzed at St. Clair. "You humans were brought to this place because of your combat skill," Newton's translation said. "It is up to you to destroy the object."

"Then we appear to be at an impasse, Speaker. We have engaged the Bluestar several times in the past several days. We have planted AI clones within its computer network. We don't yet know if that was successfully accomplished, but we're still waiting on that. But our particular expertise when it comes to warfare is asymmetric warfare. I see no way at the moment of applying those principles here."

"What . . . principles?" Na Lal asked. "What is . . . asymmetric warfare?"

"It's a conflict where the two sides are wildly out of balance with one another in regard to strength, in technology or in numbers. One side big and powerful and technologically proficient, the other small, relatively weak, with more primitive weapons. The weaker state must use guerrilla warfare and not try to match the enemy strength-to-strength. Or they use insurrection after they've been conquered. We've had lots of experience in the past couple of centuries with that sort of thing."

"I would . . . learn more," Gudahk said. *Ey* sounded interest almost in spite of *eyself.*

"Well . . . you gave me a history of your species. Let me give you this in exchange."

He'd already set it up with Newton, so that when he thoughtclicked an in-head icon, FM 80–128, a United States joint services military field manual thirty-some years out of date, was transmitted to the aliens. The document's title was a ponderous one: *Navy and Marine Corps Asymmetric Warfare and Guerrilla Operations*.

"What is this?" Gudahk asked. The being sounded genuinely puzzled.

"We do not understand," Speaker added.

"A training manual that shows the ways and means by which a primitive force can successfully challenge a more advanced one. It lays out the principles of warfare as we understand them, and as we would apply them against an enemy more technologically advanced than we."

The electronic file was actually something of an antique. In the decades following St. Clair's birth in Dayton, Ohio, in 2110, the so-called Earth Empire was newly born as well, and the United States of America was still struggling to redefine itself. Major wars between nation states were largely a thing of the past, but resistance to the Treaty of Quito and the First Directorate was widespread and determined, and the Directorate Joint Armed Forces had spent the next thirty-some years putting down dozens of bloody rebellions, brushfire wars, and guerrilla insurrections.

One of St. Clair's fathers, Randall Patterson, had been a staff sergeant in the Marine Corps, back when it had still been the *United States* Marine Corps. FM 80–128 had been a training download issued to Marines in 2128, the same year Staff Sergeant Patterson had been killed in the savage Battle of Seattle.

Patterson had given his son a copy of the field manual download the day St. Clair had learned he'd been accepted at the Naval Academy. "You just might find you can use this," Patterson had told him. "I'm not sure this new Navy covers the basics anymore."

He'd carried the file within his personal RAM ever since.

And now a four-meter-tall being with an uncanny resemblance to an uprooted tulip was mentally paging through it.

"Useless," Gudahk said at last. "Not applicable to these circumstances at all."

"I do not see the relevance of these documents," Speaker said. The Kroajid, St. Clair thought, was working to insert itself in the discussion as a kind of peacekeeper. "They describe combat on a planetary surface, not in space. And the weapons shown are primitive."

"Don't take it so literally," St. Clair said. "Use that book to learn the *spirit* of this kind of warfare . . . the philosophy."

"What do you mean," one of the other beings in the lounge said. It was the large, inverted U-shaped creature draped in red-and-purple sheets he'd noticed earlier. St. Clair couldn't tell how it was communicating . . . or even how it was aware of him, for that matter. "What *philosophy* is there to warfare?"

"Never attack the enemy where he is strong," St. Clair replied. "Don't seek to fight large-scale battles with a stronger enemy—your goal is to wear down the enemy's political will to fight. Convince your enemy that conquering you will cost him more than he's willing to spend. . . ."

"These are concepts many of us here have never considered," the being said. Newton was identifying the being in St. Clair's mind as a Thole, though he wasn't sure at the moment whether that was a species name or a personal identifier.

"Spirit and philosophy," Gudahk said, "are not useful concepts. Ephemeral, we simply require your physical assistance in destroying the *Graal Tchotch*, what you call the Andromedan Dark."

"According to the information they've just given us,"

Newton whispered in St. Clair's mind, "the Tchagar are a supremely *materialistic* species. Terms such as 'spirit' or 'philosophy' appear to be completely alien to them."

"Maybe they should learn about them some day," St. Clair said. "Newton?"

"Yes?"

"Are the Tchagar leaders of the Cooperative?"

"As far as I can determine, no. The Principle Associative is simply one among many participating species."

"He acts like he's running the whole damned show."

"*Ey* is one among many," Newton said, gently correcting St. Clair's use of pronouns. "*Ey* is perhaps a little louder and more forceful than some others."

"Just like human politics," St. Clair replied. "There's always one. . . ."

But something had been nagging at St. Clair . . . something the Kroajid Speaker had said earlier. What was it? Yes . . . *You humans were brought to this place because of your combat skill.*

Something about that had been nagging at the back of St. Clair's mind for several moments, but he'd not had the opportunity to pursue it. *Brought* here? What did Speaker mean? The human expedition had learned about this system from the Kroajid, who'd identified Ki as an important node in the Cooperative network. Was that what the Kroajid had meant? Or had he meant that *Tellus Ad Astra* had been brought here deliberately *from their own time*?

And just how would the Cooperative know of Earth's martial history? Well, the Roceti torpedo they'd used to establish contact and to serve as an interpreter had included in its memory banks elements of Earth history. Maybe that was enough. Maybe . . .

No, St. Clair didn't buy that. Maybe they'd learned something of human history, human military history, from their exchanges with Newton, but that wouldn't have been enough to convince them of human prowess in the military arts. What the hell could have convinced any of these beings that humans would be ideal for fighting the Andromedan Dark? That just didn't make sense.

But St. Clair was beginning to suspect that there was more to the *Tellus Ad Astra* human community being present in this epoch than they'd suspected at first. A *lot* more. . . .

On an impulse, he asked Newton to feed him a list of data entries from the *Roceti Encyclopedia*. The sheer bulk and complexity of the material meant that only a superficial glimpse was available, but he didn't have time for in-depth research in any case.

One in particular he'd already studied, and he brought it up now.

Xenospecies Profile
Sentient Galactic Species 10544
"Kroajid"

Star: F9V with M1 companion at 21 AU; Planet: Fourth
 $a = 2.25 \times 10^{11}$m; $M = 8.5 \times 10^{27}$g; $R = 8.5 \times 10^{6}$m;
 $p = 5.527 \times 10^{7}$s
$P_d = 5.65 \times 10^{4}$s, $G = 13.06$ m/s^2; Atm: O_2 20.1, N_2 79.6,
 CO_2 0.3;
P_{atm} 1.37 × 10^5 Pa
Biology: C, N, O, S, H_2O, PO_4, Cu; TNA
 Genome: 3.2×10^9 bits; Coding/noncoding: 0.051.
Cupric metal-chelated tetrapyrroles in aqueous
 circulatory fluid.

Mobile heterotrophs, omnivores, O_2 respiration;
   decapodal locomotion.
Mildly gregarious, polyspecific [1 genera, 5 species];
   sexual.
Communication: modulated sound at 150 to 300 Hz.
Neural connection equivalence NCE = 1.6×10^{14}
T = -280° to 310° K; M = 0.9×10^5 g; L: ~3.5×10^{10}s
Vision: ~150 nanometers to 820 nanometers;
   Hearing: 5 Hz to 19,000 Hz
Civilization Type: K 1.77
   Technology: FTL; genetic, somatic, and cerebral
      prostheses; radical life extension; electronic
      telepathy and virtual immersion; advanced AI.
      Numerous planetary and deep space colonies.
      Climate control. Gravity control.
Societal Code: Technological/Hedonistic
   Dominant culture: loose associative/post-
      singularity/virtual world upload
   Cultural library: 8.91×10^{19} bits; Intrascended
      hedonists: 0.98
Identity: Gatekeepers of Paradise
Member: Galactic Cooperative

St. Clair zeroed in on the Kroajid life span, which was
listed as L: ~3.5×10^{10}s. That translated as roughly eleven
hundred years. He assumed that that was the life span of
organic Kroajids, those living outside of the virtual worlds
of Kroajid computer networks.
   Deliberately, he pulled up another.

Xenospecies Profile
Sentient Galactic Species 15992
"Tchagar"

Star: G8III; Environment: Gas toroid forest/Dyson
   swarm

Atm: O_2 12.5, N_2 84.5, CO_2 2.9, Ar 0.1; P_{atm} 8.6 × 10^4 Pa
   [stellar ring]
Biology: C, N, O, S, Si, H_2O, PO_4, Fe; GNA
   Genome: 8.7 × 10^9 bits; Coding/noncoding: 0.077.
Iron-chelated tetrapyrroles in aqueous circulatory fluid.
Mobile heterotrophs, omnivores, CO_2 respiration.
Non-gregarious, polyspecific [3 genera, 32 species];
   hermaphrodites.
Communication: modulated EM field at 20 to 100 Hz.
Neural connection equivalence NCE = 1.9 × 10^{13}
T = ~270° to 340° K; M = 2 × 10^6 g; L: ~1.5 × 10^{15}s
Electrical Sense: ~800 V at 1 ampere, oscillating field;
   Hearing: 2 Hz to 12,000 Hz
Civilization Type: K 2.11
   Technology: FTL; mobile planets; genetic, somatic,
      and cerebral prostheses; radical life extension;
      electronic telepathy; advanced AI. Numerous
      Dyson-type colonies. Climate control. Gravity
      control.
Societal Code: Technological/Rational/Militant
   Dominant culture: loose associative/post-
      singularity; no intrascendency.
   Cultural library: 9.52 × 10^{18} bits
Identity: Principle Associative
Member: Galactic Cooperative

Interesting. If he was reading the data right, the Tchagar
lived on Dyson-swarm worlds orbiting their stars within
immense toroids of gas, what xenosophontologists referred
to as a "smoke ring." Possibly each worldlet was an asteroid,
a kind of island open to the sky and sharing its atmosphere
with a few billion similar bodies. That *had* to be an artificial setup, another example of the far-future megaengineering the human expedition had encountered here in such
profusion.

But St. Clair was more interested in what the data had to say about the Tchagar life span. He scanned down to *L* and nearly choked on his surprise. He ran that figure—1.5×10^{15} seconds—through his in-head math processor twice . . . then did it a third time because he still didn't believe the answer.

Five hundred million years.

Hell, no wonder they thought of themselves as gods. Any being with a *biological* life span of half a billion years was as close to immortal as St. Clair cared to imagine. How did such a creature deal with the *memories*?

Maybe it didn't. Maybe they were all insane. Or maybe they had some technological means for editing their memories. What he found most interesting, though, was the fact that the Tchagar didn't appear to digitally upload themselves— "no virtual world upload," the readout said. These beings lived in the real, material world of stars and galaxies and matter and energy, not within computer network constructs or artificial matrioshka brains.

And as St. Clair compared the two downloads in his mind, he saw what it was the aliens wanted, specifically why they wanted the humans to do their fighting for them.

Several long moments had passed while St. Clair conferred with Newton and examined the *Roceti Encyclopedia* data. Gudahk remained at *eir* seat, unmoving; others conversed quietly among themselves. Members of this culture, St. Clair thought, were used to the momentary loss of focus when someone turned inward to retrieve information or talk to someone else.

"Excuse my distraction, Gudahk," he said. "I was pulling up some important information. I . . . understand now why you want us to do your fighting for you."

"Indeed? You are self-evidently the best suited in terms of military—"

"No. With respect, that's not it at all. You know the real reason, but I don't think any of you permit yourselves to examine it too closely."

"What do you mean?" Speaker asked.

"You've been calling us 'ephemerals.' I've been looking at some of your biological data, and 'ephemeral' doesn't even begin to cover it. Individual Tchagar apparently exist for half a billion years. Is that *true*?"

"We are living gods," Gudahk said.

"So you've told us. With appropriate medical support, my species can expect to live healthy and productive lives of, oh, a century and a half, maybe. Your life span is over 3 million times longer! I'm still trying to assimilate that."

"And what is your point, ephemeral?" Gudahk said.

"Obviously, you feel that your lives are more valuable, more precious than ours, because they are so much longer. And you Kroajid . . . the tiny fraction of you that exists outside of the virtual worlds of your matrioshka-brain computer networks, you 'Gatekeepers of Paradise,' you don't want to die and jeopardize your chances at enjoying millions of subjective years inside your virtual heaven, do you?"

He didn't wait for them to answer.

"So with the Andromedan wolves at the door, you want to hand the job of protecting your civilization off to someone else. Someone who doesn't have as much to lose. Right?"

No one responded at first, though the Thole seemed puzzled. "What is a wolve?" it asked a Kroajid at its side.

The Kroajid Speaker at last confirmed St. Clair's insight. "We mean no insult, but the members of your species *are* ephemerals, alive for only a brief span of time, then dead and gone in an instant. The fact that you fight wars, that you actually try to *kill* one another at all indicates . . ." The Kroajid gave a kind of shudder before continuing. "It indicates that you yourselves don't value life, *existence*, as we do."

"No doubt it is difficult for you to accept," Gudahk said, "but you ephemerals, while obviously *sentient*, are not yet truly sapient."

"From your perspective, perhaps." St. Clair was rapidly becoming more angry. Gudahk's condescension was worse than *ey's* naked hostility.

"From any perspective that *matters*," Gudahk responded. "After some millions of years of self-directed evolution with the appropriate somatic and neurological enhancement and improvement, *perhaps* you will be worthy of open association with your betters."

"We are *not* mindless animals, Gudahk. We have—"

"Your minds are of no interest for us, nor are your naïve and uninformed beliefs concerning your own status. Your single potential for useful service is that of tools, of weapons that might at least slow the advance of the Dark. You are a resource, nothing more."

"You certainly do have a winning way about you," St. Clair said. He doubted that the sarcasm was getting through to *ey*. "Yes . . . how to win friends and influence people. . . ."

"I do not understand."

"No, I don't expect that you would. And since you *don't* understand, I don't see why we should offer ourselves to you as a resource."

"We had the impression," Speaker told him, "that humans liked to fight. . . ."

"A warrior species," another Kroajid added.

"We fight when we must," St. Clair said, "but we don't care to be *used*. And we will not be owned, not *ever*."

"Then," Gudahk declared, "it is as the Principle Associative has been telling the Cooperative all along. These creatures, these ephemerals are of no use to us.

"Discard them."

EIGHTEEN

"Now just one damned minute!" St. Clair said, rising from his seat. "What the hell does *that* mean?"

"*Ey* is only saying that we cannot use you," the Kroajid Speaker said. "As you yourself attest."

"You are free to go elsewhere," Na Lal told him, "and do whatever it is that ephemerals choose to do. You have no place in this affair."

St. Clair took a deep breath. It sounded as though he had just won the debate, that the *Tellus* humans would be able to walk away from this encounter and make their own future.

But the Cooperative clearly represented the dominant civilization of the Galaxy in this epoch, and the alternative, the Dark, clearly was worse. Would *Tellus Ad Astra* be able to find some out-of-the-way corner of either the Milky Way or Andromeda where they could put down roots?

He frankly doubted it. The Andromedan Dark was on the ascendency, had been so for hundreds of millions of years if the scraps of data they'd accumulated so far were true. The Dark was relentless and it was Absolute . . . moving through the spiraling star clouds of two galaxies and absorbing or annihilating every star-faring culture they encountered.

There was no safety in running and hiding, not in the long run. It might be centuries, millennia even, before the Dark caught up with them, but the descendants of the *Tellus* colonists would meet the Andromedan horror again.

And there was another aspect to this confrontation, one

with which St. Clair was only just coming to grips. The Cooperative represented absolutely magical levels of technology . . . and there'd been at least a hint that they'd been the ones somehow responsible for bringing the *Tellus Ad Astra* 4 billion years into Humankind's future. He didn't want to slam the figurative door on the possibility that the Cooperative might have a handle on the one advanced technology that might give them a chance of getting back to their own time. He scarcely dared think the words.

Time travel . . .

"Your problem," St. Clair told the assembly around him, "is that you're black-or-white in your thinking. It's all or nothing with you people, isn't it?"

"Nothing an *ephemeral* has to say is of the slightest interest to civilized beings," Gudahk told him. And the Tchagar winked out of existence.

Several others vanished from the simulation as well, severing their electronic links with the meeting. "Just hold on a moment," St. Clair said. "We are not going to allow ourselves to be used as cannon fodder . . . but that doesn't mean we can't help!"

"What," Speaker asked, "is 'cannon fodder'?"

"Troops—fighters—that can be thrown into a conflict, and you don't care whether they survive or not. Expendables."

"And how can you help, if you will not allow us to . . . spend you?"

"First, let me ask you something."

"Of course."

"Newton?" he asked the ever-present AI watching from within him. "Can we see the two galaxies? Display them, I mean?"

"With this display technology," Newton replied, "we can see *anything*. Simply focus on what you wish to see."

And the darkness high above within the vaulted chamber congealed into light . . . twin spirals interpenetrating one another, the Milky Way Galaxy, and the far larger mass of Andromeda. Ki was marked by a bright blue star between the galaxies, and just above the zone where they were passing into one another, a vast sweep of colliding gas clouds giving rise to an explosion of brand-new stars. Newton provided the Cooperative's name for those stellar nurseries: *starblaze clouds*.

"In all of these two galaxies," St. Clair said, swinging his arm to embrace the double spiral above and around them, "are you saying there is only the Cooperative and the Andromedan Dark? No other civilizations? No other minds, no one else who can help you?"

"I'm afraid you have a somewhat limited grasp of what civilization means, Lord Commander," Na Lal told him. "The Cooperative has existed for an extremely long time, longer, indeed than our own records can reveal. Hundreds of millions of years, perhaps billions of years . . . some tens of millions of mutually alien species working together in this dance of mind and culture."

As the being spoke within St. Clair's thoughts, the two galaxies overhead separated, and the starblaze clouds of stellar creation faded away. St. Clair was looking, he realized, at the two galaxies as they'd been hundreds of millions of years ago, before they'd begun their slow-motion clash.

And within those spiraling arms of stars, points of green light appeared scattered thickly across both of the galaxies. The lights were so numerous that they swiftly began massing together, until entire spiral arms and the vast and ponderous starclouds at both galactic cores appeared to glow solid green.

But St. Clair noticed something else, something interesting. The mass of solid green appeared to be more or less
constant . . . but some individual specks of green would
appear, glow for a time, then wink out. He had no way of
gauging the time spans he was witnessing, but a majority
of the civilizations he was seeing appeared to come into
being, last for some millions of years, then vanish. Individual cultures had limited life spans; *civilization* persisted.

"Are all of these star-points different cultures?" St. Clair
asked.

"No," Na Lal replied. "Remember, every galactic species is different, truly alien in myriad ways from every
other. Some are starfarers . . . but choose not to colonize
other worlds of other stars. Here is one . . . the Thole."

All of the green light overhead vanished. A single brilliant green star remained, gleaming within the depths of the
Milky Way, several tens of thousands of light years from
Ki, in toward the Milky Way's teeming core. "The Thole
are an old and well-established species and a member of
the Cooperative, but they have never been interested in
colonizing large numbers of planetary systems. A majority
of cultures across both galaxies," Na Lal went on, "occupy
a single world within a single solar system. Here is one."

Another green star winked on as the Thole home system
vanished.

"The B'hal are a marine species—deep benthic. They
evolved within the sub-ice ocean of a frozen moon orbiting
a gas giant."

"Like Europa or Enceledus in our solar system," St.
Clair thought in a quick aside to Newton.

St. Clair felt a surge of motion, as though he were hurtling up into the star-strewn sky. It was, he realized, an
illusion, but it was an incredibly detailed and coherent

one. There was a blur of rapid motion, and then he seemed to be in black water facing a small creature similar to a terrestrial octopus, pasty white in color, with eleven sinuous arms, a gelatinous body, and no eyes that he could see.

"In fact," Na Lal continued, "the B'hal are now associate members of the Cooperative, but only because other galactic species located them, and built contact centers in their world's deep oceans. While they have the option of travel elsewhere, most choose never to leave their world."

"Parallel evolution again," St. Clair said, staring at the blind octopus. How did it see? How did it think of the Galaxy beyond its deep-benthic world? "I wonder if this kind of intelligence is common?"

"The data we are collecting on the Cooperative," Newton replied, "suggest that the vast majority of intelligent species throughout the Galaxy did not evolve on open, land-surfaced worlds like humans, but in environments precisely like those of Europa and other gas giant moons. This being we are looking at is far more typical of life throughout the Galaxy than are humans."

Back in the late twenty-first century, St. Clair knew, the purely theoretical science of exobiology had become rock-solid with the discovery of microbial life not on, but *in* Jupiter's icy moon Europa. Other discoveries had followed—in Enceladus, orbiting Saturn; on Titan's surface, also at Saturn; under the ice at Jupiter's Ganymede; and even within the vast, freezing sub-ice ocean beneath the surface of cold and distant Pluto. Indeed, it had begun to appear that if liquid water existed above a rocky core, life sooner or later evolved, even if it was shut away from the sun by dozens of kilometers of ice.

None of the alien life-forms discovered within the solar system had been anything like intelligent. The ecosystems beneath the surfaces of Ganymede, the Neptunian moon Triton, and within the permafrost of Mars were multicellular, similar to terrestrial protozoa, but none were larger than the period at the end of a sentence, and most were microscopic. The life discovered deep within Pluto was simply . . . strange: huge, but single-celled syncytia, vaguely like the plasmodial slime molds of Earth.

And by 2124, of course, life—*intelligent* life—had been discovered exploring the space near Sirius. In the heady excitement of First Contact with the Galactic Coaduna-tion, most people forgot all about the Leeuwenhoekian wee beasties locked away within the icy darkness of a dozen frozen moons and dwarf planets.

Na Lal was still lecturing. "Marine species, as you might imagine, suffer a serious disadvantage as they de-velop their version of civilization. Living under water, they can never develop fire . . . or learn to smelt metal. Some do learn to manipulate metals and develop plastics technology by utilizing the intense heat around sea-floor thermal vents.

"But species that evolve within world oceans beneath deep surface ice face a second disadvantage. They may never see the stars, develop astronomy, or even be able to conceive of traveling to other worlds."

"If they don't know other worlds are up there," St. Clair said. "If all they can see is an ice ceiling . . ." He let the thought trail off.

"That applies as well to benthic species, which may not be biologically capable of moving up the water column into regions of lower pressure. And to species that evolve on worlds with thick, cloudy atmospheres."

"But there are lots of intelligent species that are aware of the stars," St. Clair said. "And they have fire and metal-working. . . ."

"Those that have oxygen atmospheres," Na Lal said, "yes. Others learn to use high-temperature volcanic vents for heat, like their abyssal, deep-ocean counterparts. But less than 10 percent of all intelligent species learn to leave the surfaces of their worlds and venture among the stars.

"And those that do reach the stars tend to become immortal."

That startled St. Clair. "Excuse me?"

The white octopus had given way to a view out in space, looking toward a sun-like star shrouded in billions upon billions of dust motes arrayed in countless orbital; shells. The clouds were so thick that the sunlight from deep inside was deeply attenuated, wan and weak.

"Is that a Dyson sphere?" St. Clair asked.

"A Dyson cloud," Newton said, correcting him. "Possibly a matrioshka brain."

"Species that succeed in achieving space travel tend to develop certain key technologies," Na Lal was telling him. Scenes shifted and flowed through St. Clair's mind, showing examples of what Na Lal was describing. "Nanotechnology and microassembly. Star lifting. The ability to disassemble entire planets for raw materials. Vacuum energy, which translates as essentially unlimited power for industrial and environmental applications. Powerful AIs on planetary and super-planetary scales. Control over gravitational singularities. Gravity control. . . ."

The megastructures St. Clair was witnessing were staggering in their scale and scope. Worlds were taken apart . . . vast streams of white-hot plasma were channeled up from the surfaces of stars . . . stars were circled by artificial habitats.

"Ultimately," Na Lal told him, "they become what you might call godlike, capable of reworking both space and time. At some point in their apotheosis, they learn how to upload living minds into computer realities. And for many, this marks the end of any exploratory or dynamic aspect to culture."

"I understand that," St. Clair said. "Why go out and explore the Galaxy when you can stay inside a nice, safe matrioshka brain and enjoy any illusion you can imagine? Maybe even illusions you *can't* imagine. Like the Kroajid paradise."

"The Kroajid are one species that have chosen this path, yes," Na Lal said. Again, as megaengineering structures as big as entire solar systems faded away, St. Clair looked out into the two galaxies, approaching one another now and almost in contact. Hundreds of green stars appeared, scattered through two of the spiral arms of the Milky Way, and with a few popping up along the near edge of Andromeda.

"This is the Kroajid Collective," Na Lal told him. "Eight hundred twelve systems, most of them re-engineered into what you call matrioshka clouds. The vast majority of them are intrascended—digitally uploaded—and are rarely aware of what is happening in the universe outside."

"I've seen the encyclopedia data," St. Clair said.

"Indeed. Well, you can apply the same pattern, or something very similar, to most of the other space-faring and technologically advanced species."

"'Most'?" Why would an advanced species choose not to create its own heaven? Then he saw it. "Ah! The Tchagar."

Newton had mentioned that the Tchagar did not comprehend nonmaterialistic ideas or philosophies. That might mean that they rejected the idea of a noncorporeal existence as part of an elaborate computer simulation.

"An accurate insight, Commander. They do not, as a species, digitally upload themselves."

"Do not? Or *can* not?"

"*Any* mind can be replicated digitally," Na Lal explained. "But there are species with a worldview that precludes virtual existence. The Tchagar don't possess visual organs like humans or Kroajid or Dhald'vi. They 'see' themselves as a part of their own electrical fields. If they attempt to digitally replicate themselves using electromagnetic fields alone, they swiftly lose the ability to relate to reality, whether in the outside world or within a digital illusion. In your terms, they go insane."

They're already there, St. Clair mused with a wry bitterness. But he kept the thought to himself. With the combatively uncooperative Tchagar absent, he was actually getting some useful knowledge from the Cooperative beings, and he wanted to keep the information coming.

On the immense display overhead, the full panoply of galactic civilization was again displayed, an ocean of stars swarming with points of brilliant emerald light. St. Clair could see the spiral of Andromeda moving steadily closer, could see points of green beginning to spread across the near edge of the intruder as civilization bridged the narrowing gap between galaxies.

He wondered if what he was seeing was purely an AI simulation . . . or based on actual visual records of the collision with the timescale compressed by many millions of times. It didn't matter, he supposed. The outermost spiral arms of both galaxies interpenetrated, setting off a firestorm of starburst activity, new suns blazing out of the darkness as gas clouds collided and compressed. The cores drifted slowly toward one another. . . .

And as the collision continued, a new factor was added to the display . . . a vast surge of blackness swiftly growing to fill Andromeda . . . then spilling across into the Milky

Way. The green points of light were winking out—a few at a time, at first, but then by the hundreds . . . the thousands . . . the *tens* of thousands. . . .

"We face a cataclysm, a true existential crisis unlike anything faced by galactic civilization in the past," Na Lal told him. "The Cooperative is not an empire such as your Empire of Earth. Indeed, many of us are having trouble understanding your AI when it tries to describe your social organization. Most civilizations that make up our Cooperative, the vast, vast majority, are residents of artificial realities within the near-infinite depths of computer networks—what you call matrioshka brains or Dyson clouds, J-brains or computronium megastructures. And we find it difficult . . . *extremely* difficult, to leave our virtual worlds to deal with the encroaching Dark.

"And of those species that maintain a corporeal existence, most are otherwise solitary, limited to one degree or another to the worlds of their birth, and many can't even share the understanding star-faring species have of the true nature of the cosmos. They see it, like the Tchagar, as the mathematically intricate modulations of an EM field . . . or like the B'hal, as a watery abyss roofed over with ice."

"It's more than that," a different voice intoned within St. Clair's head. Gudahk had just reappeared. Had *ey* been listening in from outside the simulation? Or had *ey* simply decided to return to the meeting and pick up the conversation?

"The various species of the Cooperative," Gudahk continued, speaking with an air of finality, "long ago evolved beyond the need for naked aggression. Artificial intelligences developed and deployed various instrumentalities for the security of the larger group. For various reasons, those instrumentalities have proven ineffective against the

Graal Tchotch. We find ourselves unable to address this
threat."

Gudahk, St. Clair thought, must have struggled to transmit those words—a frank, even blunt admission of failure
on *ey's* part, and on the part of the Cooperative.

"You and yours," the Thole intoned, "are outsiders, a
species unconnected with our Cooperative. As outsiders,
you must have abilities, insights, strategies, and weapons
that we lack."

"And," the Kroajid Speaker added, "you are not, like so
many of us, trapped within our illusory realities. Some of
us, a few, can move between the worlds of reality and illusion, between what you might call heaven and hell. But it
is . . . difficult."

"I think I understand," St. Clair told them. "And I appreciate your . . . candor. Why didn't you tell us before?"

"We told the human Ambassador Lloyd," Speaker said.

"We determined," Gudahk said, "that humans were not
capable of a full understanding."

"Maybe not," St. Clair said. "We do get there in the end,
usually."

"Will you help us?" Na Lal asked. "Freely . . . not as
tools?"

"The question is *can* we? What we've seen of the Dark
so far is . . . is so far beyond us, we don't even know how to
approach the problem.

"And I don't understand yet why you need us. When the
needleships were in close to Ki . . . when they were trying
to block our approach to Ki, you used a nanotech weapon
against them, something that drove them off." As he spoke,
Newton fed them all imagery recorded by the *Ad Astra* earlier . . . of a cloud of something like graininess moving out
from the rings . . . tiny disassemblers like a cloud of smoke

that began taking the attacking needleships apart molecule by molecule. "Why can't you use that?"

"If you'll notice, ephemeral," Gudahk said, "the Dark world-ship you call Bluestar has been quite cautious in its approach. It does fear the power of the Living Gods. It fears what we might do to it."

"More important to its way of thinking, we believe," the Kroajid Speaker said, "the Dark Mind does not wish to destroy the computronium networks that make up the bulk of our worlds. It wishes to *use* them, subvert them, adapt them to its own purposes. It can't do that if they are destroyed."

"Yet the range of our nanotech weapons is rather sharply limited," Na Lal noted. "They are directed by an AI swarm mind, a part of the local planetary network, so proximity—even in astronomical terms—is necessary. More important, perhaps, is that the Dark is adept at subverting minds, both organic and artificial, and turning them to its use. We can maintain control across relatively short ranges—several tens of thousands of kilometers. Farther than that, the Dark has ways of taking them over, and we find ourselves facing our own weapons."

St. Clair nodded his understanding, though none of the beings in that virtual hall would have understood the gesture. He trusted Newton to get the idea across. The Cooperative had been fighting the Dark for longer than any human could imagine—for hundreds of millions of years if he was understanding what he was being shown—and now he was beginning to comprehend the difficulties they faced.

"I hate to tell you this," he said, "but you people are going to have to learn to fight your own battles. There may be ways that we can help, but we can only do so much. At some point—and sooner rather than later—you're going to need to come out of your virtual shells and take on the responsibility for your own survival. Do you understand that?"

"We have tried," the Speaker said. "We have tried time upon time upon time across the millennia. But how does anyone escape paradise?"

"If you want to survive, in paradise or anywhere else, you're going to have to find a way."

"We have," the Thole said. "You."

At first St. Clair almost screamed in frustration, but instead took a deep breath. As he thought for a moment, an idea began to form. On an in-head display, he could see the scene from a camera on board the *Ad Astra*, one showing the red-ocher loom of the *Wrath of Deity*, and its attendant moons. *What the hell*? All he could do was ask.

"We might be able to help you with the Bluestar," he said. "Maybe. But we will need your help."

"How can we help you?" Na Lal asked, and inwardly, St. Clair exalted. It was the first solid offer of help from these beings that he'd received that didn't seem to include abject servitude.

With Newton's help, he called up another image, projecting it into the virtual room at the center of the ring of disparate beings. The scene was one from *Ad Astra*'s external cameras, showing the ocher face of the *Wrath of Deity*, plus four tiny moon-ships. "We need one of your mobile worlds," he said. "How about one of those out there?"

"Not the *Wrath of Deity*!" Gudahk said.

"Those smaller moons," St. Clair said. "They belong to the Kroajid?"

"And others," Speaker said.

"How many live aboard one of them?"

"If by 'live' you mean how many organic beings inhabit

one . . . the answer is none. They are inhabited by digital uploads within a computronium matrix."

"So the population could easily be shifted to another matrix?"

"Not easily, but—"

"Commander," Newton whispered in his mind, interrupting. "We have a problem. The Bluestar is accelerating in our direction."

"What, *now*? Damn it. . . ." He broke the link with the conference. "Show me."

Newton produced an in-head display, a schematic of the Ki system. The Bluestar object was traveling in rapid, sporadic jumps, angling toward the tight little cluster of worlds and megastructures closer in toward the local sun. St. Clair watched the icon marking the Bluestar wink out . . . then reappear an instant later practically on top of Ki.

"ExComm!" he called.

"I see it, Lord Commander. I was about to call you."

"Launch fighters! All stations to General Quarters!"

"Way ahead of you, my lord. . . ."

The Andromedan Dark . . . *Dhalat K'graal,* the Minds from Higher Angles. What, St. Clair wondered, was the damnable thing thinking? What did it *want*? Its strategic thinking, so far at least, seemed scattered, even fragmented. Sudden attacks without clear focus, with each just as suddenly broken off. It made no *sense*. . . .

And then something struck the *Ad Astra*, a savage shock that threatened to fragment the delicate colony and its tug.

The lighting failed, and somewhere close by, in the passageway outside his office, people screamed.

CHAPTER NINETEEN

Major General Wilson was in his C³ on board the *Vera Cruz* with Nathan Deladier when the Bluestar made its final jump. With horrifying suddenness, the situation went from standby to red alert, and things were falling apart in an eye's-blink transition into utter chaos.

"Get the division off the ship!" Wilson yelled. In fact, half of the *Tellus* First Division was already in space with the rest in reserve on board, but Wilson wanted to save them all if he could. That giant Dark world was entirely too close, and getting closer. It was still over 6 million kilometers out, well beyond Ki, well beyond the nearby blue gas giant . . . but its size alone made it a terrible threat. If it got close enough to Ki that its gravity began distorting those rings, then the local population would be lost without a shot being fired. Hell, that thing was large enough it could swallow the Ki Rings and all in a single gulp and without effort.

And from this perspective it appeared to be bearing down on both Ki and upon the twin cylinders of the *Tellus* colony. The Marine transports had been ordered to hold position close by *Tellus Ad Astra* as the cluster of recently arrived Cooperative world-ships had approached, but that, of course, meant that all three transports were closely bunched up with the *Tellus Ad Astra* . . . a bad tactical position in the face of this new threat.

The Bluestar was huge in comparison to Ki, dwarfing

the ringworld into toy-sized insignificance. Once again the Bluestar's central sphere seemed to pulse, expand, and fold into itself, continuously turning itself inside out as it approached. Wilson watched its advance with growing concern.

"Let's get clear of the *Ad Astra*," Wilson told Deladier. "We don't want that thing to get us both."

"Roger that, General," Deladier replied, and the transport began moving clear of the far larger colony modules. The other Marine transports were accelerating now as well, the smaller *Inchon* and *Saipan* with the Second Division slipping smoothly clear of *Tellus*'s shadow. Surrounding space was becoming crowded as fighters dropped into the void, and MCA-clad Marines began joining them.

"Put us between *Tellus Ad Astra* and the Bluestar," Wilson directed.

The *Vera Cruz* changed vector, and began angling toward the oncoming alien, and a fleet of Earth fighters kept pace.

"Let's see who blinks first," he muttered.

"WHAT THE hell is the *Cruzer* doing?" St. Clair demanded.

"Sir," Vincent Hargrove, *Ad Astra*'s senior comm officer, replied. "*Vera Cruz*'s C^3 reports they're going to try to get between the *Tellus* and IO-1."

"Undock us from the *Tellus*, ExComm," St. Clair said. "We need freedom to maneuver."

"Aye, aye, my lord. Beginning undocking sequence."

The *Vera Cruz* approached the Bluestar object, fighters and armored Marines spilling from her drop tubes and hatchways. Particle beams snapped out, reaching for the alien world-ship, but St. Clair could see no indication that the enormous mobile world was being hurt. But the Blue-star *did* slow . . . then stopped. Perhaps *Vera Cruz*'s tactical gamble was paying off. . . .

THE SKY in every direction was filled with fighters and armored Marines, a swirling explosion of vacuum-mobile forces deploying to meet the alien world. Ebon-black slivers emerged from the Bluestar in clouds so thick they resembled smoke.

Captain Greg Dixon dropped into emptiness and accelerated clear of the *Vera Cruz*. There'd been no time to lay plans, no time for strategies or battle plans. With the Bluestar's new advance there'd been time only to get off the *Vera Cruz*. Those, like Charlie Company, who'd already been suited up and on Ready-one—meaning they needed just one minute to launch—definitely had an advantage over the Marines still clambering into their suits aboard the *Cruzer*.

Please, God, let them all get out. . . .

At least out here they had a chance.

His suit AI was tracking a group of needleships vectoring toward his position. He swung his M-290 laser to bear on the nearest alien craft and triggered a pulse of phase-boosted photons. The lead needleship exploded in a spray of white-hot debris, and he targeted the next in line . . . and the next . . . and the next. . . .

FOR A stark, brief nightmare of a moment, General Wilson thought he was going mad. The First Division command center around him was twisting oddly, distorting as he watched it . . . and *things* were beginning to ooze from the *Cruzer*'s bulkheads.

Exactly what those squirming things might be was hard

to determine. Wilson could see obviously organic shapes there, merged into a ghastly amoebic mass. There were eyes in that mass, hundreds of them staring and blinking and shifting back and forth . . . and things like arms and things like tentacles and things like bloody internal organs pulsing with an animation that defied conventional ideas of what might be alive and what could not possibly be.

Wilson's neuronic implants were jacked directly into ship systems or a communications network, so even as the nightmares came boiling onto the C^3 deck, he was sending out a call for help while simultaneously drawing his sidearm.

With a thoughtclick, he engaged his infrared vision . . . then took a step back. *That* didn't make sense. As he fired his M110 pulse laser into the surging mass, his IR vision picked up the flares of heat on the bulkhead where the bolts of coherent light were striking it . . . but no heat at all from the organic mass.

It was as though the things weren't even there.

But *something* was inside that compartment. He could feel it through his link with the *Vera Cruz*'s communications network, a sharp, ice-cold and terribly aware presence crawling through the link and directly into his brain.

Deladier was nearby, firing his own laser into the crawling mass, bolt after bolt . . . and then the ship's captain was shrieking as he clawed at his own head, as nightmares squirmed in through the electronic connections to the ship.

Was there anything there, any solid manifestation of the crawling horrors? The mass reached Wilson's legs and he held his ground. He couldn't *feel* anything, despite what his eyes were telling him. Maybe the extradimensional horror was some kind of illusion, something fed by the

Andromedan Dark into people's minds to panic or immobilize them.

Whatever was clawing into his brain, however, was absolutely, undeniably real. He could *feel* it, could feel it moving, could feel the pain, could hear his own screams as the pain grew swiftly worse. The comm channel was still open, and Wilson kept feeding it his impressions. Maybe someone analyzing this attack back on board the *Ad Astra* could make something of it, something useful.

A Marine sentry stood nearby, his M-290 laser rifle at his shoulder as he squeezed off vortex-twisted bolts of light. Interesting; those bolts *were* having an effect, unlike the non-twisted photons from his pistol. Something that might once have been a human pilot, still clad in the remnants of flight utilities, flared like a tiny sun and came apart in bloody chunks. Something next to it, like a two-meter insect with paddles instead of legs, writhed and burned.

What the hell was going on? Why could rifled laser fire hit the things, and ordinary lasers not?

There was no time to think about that. Four irregularly flattened spheres appeared in midair. Wilson had seen recordings of this, and there was no doubting their rock-solid reality. Something—something very large—was reaching "down" from some higher dimension and intersecting with Wilson's normal 3-D world, the same as if he had shoved his fingers through a two-dimensional plane or a sheet of paper to create five separate holes, five two-dimensional zones of interpenetration. The four spheroids briefly merged into a single mass, separated again, then swept through the air with stunning suddenness, closing about Deladier's body. Deladier gave a brief, despairing shriek, then vanished with the alien hand . . . if a hand it truly was.

The C^3 compartment was rapidly filling with the illusory

mass of amoebic chaos. Horribly, there were human bodies in among the alien appendages and forms, bodies and pieces of bodies all squeezed in together with alien things and bits no human had ever before seen. The mass, Wilson could now see, was interpenetrating his body. Either it was a complete illusion, or it was someplace else, hidden away in a different set of dimensions.

But if that was the case, how could he even see it? Light, surely, was constrained by the geometries of sane dimensions that said that if you could *see* a thing, you could touch it . . . or it you.

But the pain in Wilson's head was by now too sharp, too penetrating for him to think. If he could not feel the alien monstrosities surging around him, he could definitely feel the bubbling, gibbering rush of insanity rising up inside him, flooding his brain, drowning his mind. He tried shouting a final warning to whoever might review his recordings, but what came from his raw throat was unintelligible even to him.

And finally . . . *finally*, the darkness took him and dragged him down. . . .

THE *AD Astra* slid clear of *Tellus*'s side-by-side hab modules, then accelerated gently, gliding just beneath the immense, slow-turning cylinders before emerging into the harsh sunlight.

"*Vera Cruz* reports they're under attack," Hargrove reported. "Extradimensional attacks on board, several locations. We've lost touch with General Wilson and his staff."

"They may just be busy, Vince," St. Clair replied. "Stay linked."

"Yes, my lord."

"Weapons!"

"Hot and ready, Lord Commander," Subcommander Webb replied. "Any particular points you want to target?"

One of the displays open in St. Clair's mind was from the *Vera Cruz*, showing the Bluestar alien from a steadily dwindling range of now less than one hundred thousand kilometers. The hyperdimensional object continued unfolding over and over again in a stomach-churning twisting of sane and normal space. There were no markings, nothing obvious like doors or entranceways, nothing that St. Clair could point to and say "hit it there."

Without a clear target, he could only order all batteries to fire at a single point. "On the equator," he ordered, "at the longitudinal median, dead center. All units, concentrate your fire there and let's see what happens."

High-energy weapons fire lashed out at the Bluestar object from the *Ad Astra*, from the three Marine transports, and from some thousands of fighters and armored Marines filling the sky ahead. An intense point of blue-white light appeared at that central focus . . . but the constant dimensional shifting meant that different portions of the object were constantly cycling through the aim-point. It was clear almost immediately that concentrating their fire on one point was not going to create a breach in that thing.

The clouds of needleships, however, were closing on the Marine transports, shouldering their way past the sheltering Marines and fighter craft in ever increasing numbers and focusing their antimatter beam weapons against all-too-vulnerable terrestrial hulls. Missiles reached out from the human line, twisting and turning among the alien vessel swarms before detonating in vast, fast-swelling blossoms of sun-hot nuclear plasma. But it was only a matter of time.

St. Clair had Newton open the channel to the nearby Cooperative world-ships. "If you don't get in here and help," he told them, "we are pulling out! You will fucking be on your own!"

In fact, St. Clair wasn't certain they would be able to pull off a retreat. Thousands of Marines were spaceborne now, and it would take hours to pick all of them up. The only viable alternative was for the human forces to attack with everything they had . . . and pray to God that the Kroajid, at least, joined in.

The threat might just possibly force their hands . . . or, rather, their manipulatory members; Kroajid graspers didn't look much like human hands.

"Anyone see any response from the Coops?" St. Clair asked his bridge crew.

"Nothing yet, my lord," Symms replied. "I don't think they want to get their hands dirty."

"They don't want to get killed," St. Clair said.

"Can't say I blame them," Subcommander Webb added.

"Helm!" St. Clair was watching the light show arrayed across the *Ad Astra*'s bridge, showing worlds and ships and the stab and flash of combat.

"Aye, Lord Commander."

"Take us across the rings and swing around the far side of that gas giant. Let's see if we can do something unexpected, here."

"Aye, aye, my lord."

Ad Astra began picking up speed, sliding swiftly above the vast plane of the Ki Rings. The Bluestar was still well beyond Ki, over 5 million kilometers distant. The local gas giant, by contrast, was much closer, just over 680,000 kilometers. The distance between the two was still too great for St. Clair to use the planet for cover, but he did expect to pick up some extra velocity by using a gravitational slingshot around the giant world.

"Sir!" Symms called suddenly. "The smaller world-ships are following us!"

"Outstanding. There's hope for the sons of bitches after all. What about the *Wrath of Deity*?"

"No change, my lord."

"I didn't really expect them to jump in and help." But he'd had hopes.

And then . . .

"My God!" Webb shouted. "The *Cruzer*! Look at her!"

The Marine transport had slewed to the side as though in the grip of some titanic, invisible force. The Bluestar accelerated, looming huge, a solid, shifting wall behind the dust mote of the transport.

The *Vera Cruz* twisted, then crumpled . . . dwindling . . . collapsing in upon itself.

"What are we seeing?" St. Clair demanded.

"It appears that IO-1 has used some kind of gravitational weapon, Lord Commander," Symms replied, her mental voice flat. "Possibly a micro-black hole launched extradimensionally. Or a projected singularity. They might have the technology to force a gravitational collapse on a target at a distance."

The *Vera Cruz* was gone, now, with no trace remaining but a sparkling spray of fragments. Marines and fighters were accelerating to get clear.

And then the Bluestar swept through that volume of space, and there was nothing remaining of the human vessel at all.

CAPTAIN DIXON watched the destruction of the *Vera Cruz* with shock and mounting horror. "Pull back, Charlie Company!" he yelled. "Pull back! We can't hold that thing by ourselves!"

Marines, Dixon thought, were by both nature and training combative, tough, and to all outward appearances, at least, utterly lacking in fear . . . but they were not *stupid*. Two entire divisions of Marines had no more chance of stopping that oncoming world-ship ahead than they had of turning back time or putting out the local sun. To stand and fight here meant to stand and die . . . and dying for no useful purpose. Too many Marines had already died in the past few moments, vaporized by blasts from those damnable swarms of needleships, and while the *Tellus* First Division had cut huge swaths through those clouds of enemy fighters, for every ship they destroyed it seemed like ten more were there to take its place.

"HQ is gone!" Staff Sergeant David Ramirez called. "Who the fuck is giving orders?"

With General Wilson and the entire division command staff gone, half of the Marines engaged with the Bluestar would be falling back on regimental, battalion, and company commanders. It would take a few moments for the various AIs involved to stitch together a new and coherent command structure . . . and moments in combat could be the equivalent of forever.

"*I'm* giving the orders," Dixon snapped. "Everybody fall back toward . . ." He hesitated. The *Ad Astra* was 5 million kilometers away . . . far beyond the range of MCA suits. What was his company's best option? Scatter in the face of overwhelming enemy strength? Or pull back to one of the other transports and try to make a stand?

"Everyone fall back on the *Inch*!" he ordered. The *Inchon* was fifteen thousand kilometers distant. She would make a convenient rally point. "Move it!

Move! Move! Move!"

Dixon didn't join the retreat immediately. He hung there

in space, loosing a chain of six M-90 Shurikin shipkillers. Flares of white plasma blossomed across his field of
vision, growing a wall of devastation blocking the oncoming needleships from the Marine retreat.

"NEWTON?"

"Yes, Lord Commander?"

"Put me back in that meeting."

"Most of those in attendance have already discon-
nected."

"Let me talk to whoever is left. And if the Kroajid
Speaker has left, get him back!"

His surroundings shimmered, and then he was standing
in the cavernous space that existed as a virtual room somewhere within the *Wrath of Deity.* Na Lal was still there, as
was Speaker, along with the Thole and a few others. All of
the Xam, he noticed, were gone, as was the far larger bulk
of Gudahk.

"Our moon-ships," Speaker said, "are at your disposal."

"I appreciate that, Speaker. How long will it take for you
to evacuate one?"

"I . . . do not understand. Why do you want it empty?"

"I'm not going to explain and I'm not going to argue.
I need control over one of your moon-ships, and I need it
now, before that damned Dark monster out there manages
to wipe us all out of the sky!"

The Kroajid considered this for a moment, and St. Clair
had the impression that it was engaged in a hurried mental
conversation with someone else.

"I have given orders," Speaker told him, "to evacuate
the *Heavenly Light.* The minds on board are being transmitted electronically to the ring."

"And how long will that take?"

"A few minutes. Even the Rings of Ki do not have the bandwidth to receive all 200 million of us immediately." Speaker's image shivered, then became blasted through with white static.

"Speaker? Does that mean you're on the *Heavenly Light*, too?"

But the image of the Kroajid was gone.

"Not anymore," Newton told him.

"Newton . . . can you put my consciousness on board the *Heavenly Light*? And more important, can you show me how to control that thing?"

"I don't know, Commander."

"Well *find the fuck out*!" He was mentally screaming now.

Newton maintained his usual, studied calm. "It will take time to build an appropriate virtuality for you."

"Do it!"

The conference room was beginning to fade and ripple. *Now* what?

"We are moving out of range from the *Wrath of Deity*," Newton told him.

"Are you still here?"

"A part of me is. I am using a small clone of myself to speak with you, while simultaneously I am entering the *Heavenly Light*."

"Okay. I'm sorry I . . . shouted."

"Understandable, under the circumstances. I suggest we let the *Wrath of Deity* simulation go."

"Agreed."

The cavernous room vanished. For a moment, St. Clair was adrift in an endless black, and he stifled a sudden surge of panic.

"I can put your consciousness back on board *Ad Astra* if you prefer," Newton told him, "but it might be more efficient if you can tolerate . . . this."

This was a new space, a new world of dizzying heights, of crystal walkways and towering spires, of white clouds far, far below and the sonorous clang of bells or chimes on a keening wind. He was standing in a circular, open structure of some sort that appeared to be at the nexus of dozens of bridges, but the bridges were individual cables of what might be spun glass. Within the central well of the structure was a glowing, holographic image, but St. Clair was having trouble making out what the image represented. It wasn't simply that he couldn't read the words—if those swiftly appearing and vanishing chicken's-tracks *were* words—it was that the images he was seeing, blobs of shape and color and texture that moved in irrational ways, had been designed by minds completely alien to his, were being projected for minds and senses completely alien to his. The projection, he realized, was *buzzing*, and rather than being an electronic artifact of some sort, a sign of faulty design, the buzz shifted and flowed with the flowing, abstract images. It sounded like it was somehow supposed to be a part of the complete image.

Then he remembered how the Kroajid communicated with one another—by vibrating patches of stiff hair covering their thoraxes and heads, creating a deep-toned buzz.

"Newton?"

"I'm working at it, Commander."

"I know. What am I looking at?"

"A display designed for Kroajid senses. I'll have something you can use in a second . . . there!"

The dizzying exercise in vertigo surrounding St. Clair

vanished, replaced by something approximating the command center of a human warship.

The abstract art winked out, replaced by two spheres above a holoprojection table, one large, one tiny, with a straight blue line drawing itself past the tiny sphere and toward the bigger one. The viewpoint drew back sharply, the spheres coming together, and a bright blue star imbedded in a blue swirl of light appeared in the distance.

"The Bluestar," St. Clair said. "And those two planets . . . Ki and the gas giant Ki orbits? This is a navigational display."

"Exactly. I am incorporating more detail into the display now."

Yes. He could see *Wrath of Deity* close beside Ki, and a white star nearby representing the *Tellus*. The swarm of other worlds surrounding the Ki gas giant were visible now, everything from asteroids to full-fledged worlds as big as Mars and Earth. By zooming in on the steadily growing tip of the blue line, he could make out *Ad Astra* as a bright yellow icon, the *Heavenly Light* as white, and three alien moon-ships close behind.

When he zoomed in close on the Bluestar, he was surprised at the level of detail. This was no icon, but an actual real-time image of the thing—spiraling blue swirl of light circling an unfolding hyperdimensional sphere.

"How fast can this thing go?" he asked.

"As fast as you wish," Newton replied. "You would need to reach very close to the speed of light before shifting into FTL."

"I don't want FTL. Steering?"

"Simply think what you want. I can translate for the AI directing the *Heavenly Light*."

"An alien AI?" He hadn't thought of that—a Kroajid artificial mind controlling the moon-ship.

"It knows what you are attempting to do," Newton told him. "And it approves."

"Good." Anything else felt too much like . . .

Like murder.

"How about acceleration effects? I don't want to get smeared all over the aft bulkhead."

"That is not possible. You are a digitized upload. Acceleration will have no effect on you."

"Of course." St. Clair felt a small burn of embarrassment. He'd actually forgotten that he wasn't present on the moon-ship as flesh and blood. He was, in effect, a simulation running on the *Heavenly Light*'s computronium core.

"In any case," Newton continued, "Kroajid technology employs a version of gravitational acceleration, similar to what we received from the Coadunation. Every atom of the ship and its contents is accelerated uniformly, just as though they were in free fall within a gravitational field. You would continue to experience zero-gravity."

"Newton?"

"Yes, Commander?"

"What happens when we get beyond easy communications range with the *Ad Astra*? I need to stay in control for as long as possible."

Newton hesitated for a moment.

"Do you remember the alien technology on the ring?" Newton asked. "The gateways that created a virtual duplicate of you and your companions, while your 'original' remained in place?"

"Of course. I . . . oh." *Damn!* The bizarre situation had caught him again. He was having trouble accepting the fact, feeling the fact that he—the real he—was back on board the *Ad Astra*. The Grayson St. Clair standing in this replica of a starship control room was a highly detailed copy, complete with memories and a sense of self identical to . . . those of his original.

He was going to have to come to grips with that (virtual) reality.

"This is an identical situation," Newton said, confirming his thoughts. "Your body is still on board *Ad Astra*. *You* are a virtual duplicate, as am I."

"I understand."

"If possible, I will disengage you from the *Heavenly Light* at the last moment."

"Not until I tell you. Not until I give the word."

"Of course."

With that settled, St. Clair focused on the oncoming Bluestar. He could see the clouds of needleships surrounding it, millions upon millions of the things. They might fear the nanotech defenses close to Ki, but he had the feeling that this was a no-holds-barred attack. The Bluestar was ignoring the two Marine transports nearby, and the thousands of Marines in nearby space.

"Pass the word, Newton," he said. "All units . . . clear out! Get clear of the Bluestar!"

"Already done, Lord Commander."

"And tell our escorts not to follow us."

"I have done so."

"Very well." He took a deep breath . . . or was it the illusion of a breath? Curious. He felt neither fear nor regret. It was simply something that he needed to do . . . one final act. *"Now!"*

And the Kroajid moon-ship, already traveling at nearly

two thousand kilometers per second, leaped ahead, accelerating at some millions of gravities. Such accelerations didn't mean much for digitally uploaded beings within the moon's computronium matrix, and, in any case, gravitational acceleration was uniform, acting on every atom simultaneously. Had St. Clair been on board the *Heavenly Light* as flesh and blood, he would have felt nothing but free fall as the moon-ship accelerated to within a hair's breadth of c.

A bullet moving at the speed of light. . . .

TWENTY

The Kroajid moon-ship arrowed past the blue-hued gas giant, its course only slightly bent by the planet's gravitational pull, but moving far too swiftly to be captured. The Bluestar object was now some 5 million kilometers from the giant. Traveling at 99.9 percent of *c*, the *Heavenly Light* crossed that immense distance in just over sixteen seconds.

That should have been plenty of time for St. Clair to check the mobile moon's navigational path, to make any last-second course adjustments, and to signal Newton that he was ready to abandon ship, to disengage from the *Heavenly Light*, as he'd put it. *Should* have been . . . but in the urgency of the moment, St. Clair had forgotten a vital twist of relativistic physics. His journey from the gas giant to the Bluestar might have taken sixteen seconds as the rest of the universe measured time, but for St. Clair, his velocity invoked the surreal mathematics of time dilation; subjectively, at 0.999 c, sixteen seconds was only seven tenths of a second.

A ball of rock and computronium with a diameter of 403 kilometers, the *Heavenly Light* massed around 4×10^{19} kilograms. As it slammed into Bluestar in direct, central impact at 99.9 percent of the speed of light, it released energy, a *lot* of energy . . . something on the order of 10^{28} joules of energy, most of it radiant heat and light, with plenty of hard radiation thrown in.

Light filled the universe, and Grayson St. Clair died.

THE DARK Mind never saw it coming.

For all of its power and mental brilliance, the Dark Mind was still limited in certain respects by the laws of physics. It had been aware of the tiny flotilla of world-sized vessels approaching it, but it took several seconds for the light revealing their approach to crawl across the intervening space.

And when one ship, a Kroajid vessel, suddenly accelerated to almost the speed of light, it flashed across that gulf immediately behind the wave front of the oncoming light, reaching the Dark Mind an instant behind the light announcing its approach.

There was no time to maneuver, no time to deploy weapons or Xam needleships, no time for anything but a sudden shock of awareness . . .

. . . and a single desperate act of self-preservation. . . .

ST. CLAIR came wide awake in his office back on board the *Ad Astra*, his body trying to snap upright with the shock but caught and held by the safety restraints pinning him against his virtual projection recliner. His gasp caught in his throat. Such a startlingly intense dream . . .

Had it been a dream? The last few shreds of ragged memory were evaporating as he struggled to full awareness. He'd been at the virtual meeting on board the *Wrath of Deity*, and then he'd returned to the *Ad Astra*. He had tattered, dreamlike memories of being there, on board the *Heavenly Light* . . .

Within his head, a display window showed the Bluestar, still intact. Had he dreamed of its destruction?

And then, an instant after the shock of waking, the light reached the *Ad Astra*. The ship's external sensors burned out almost immediately as they stared into that glare, a pure, hard radiance as bright as the flash of a supernova. *Ad Astra* was several light-seconds from the Bluestar, and it had taken that long for the light of the explosion to reach the ship. After several long seconds, backup sensors cut in, and St. Clair could again see the blossoming, fast-growing sphere of plasma swiftly overtaking the nearby clouds of needle-ships, could see the glare filling the cosmos with light.

A *Heavenly Light* indeed.

St. Clair knew that his electronic double had just been deleted on board the *Heavenly Light*. It was strange. He'd actually felt some sort of connection, a link abruptly snapped by the violence of that impact, though in fact he should have felt nothing. Was it possible that he'd had some sort of telepathic connection with his electronic doppelgänger, that somehow he'd just *felt* his double die?

The fireball continued to expand. It was oddly shaped, possibly, St. Clair thought, because much of the blast had been directed into the center of the blue spiral . . . and beyond into different, unseen dimensions. He was having trouble picturing the geometry of the impact. The planet-sized ship itself, when it appeared to be unfolding, was clearly occupying more than the normal three dimensions, and provided a gateway to those dimensions that human senses simply weren't designed to detect. If, as *Ad Astra*'s astrophysics department now believed, dark matter was in fact normal matter somehow resident in those higher dimensions, that high-speed impact of the *Heavenly Light* must have been channeled through and beyond, doing terrible damage to the hidden mass of the Bluestar.

The fireball was a small sun now, still growing larger second by second. "Bridge, St. Clair," he transmitted.

Symms's response was immediate. "Yes, Lord Commander?"

"Pull us back. Stay well clear of that blast zone. And pass the word to the Marines, too." Had any of the free-flying Marines been caught in the detonation? He wasn't sure.

"Yes, my lord. Uh . . ."

"Yes?"

"Sir . . . was that you?"

"That was me."

"In the *Heavenly Light*?"

"Yes."

"That was . . . incredible!"

"We stopped the Bluestar," St. Clair said. "That's all that's important." Suddenly, he was exhausted, as though every bit of energy had drained from his body.

"Newton?"

"Yes, Lord Commander."

"Are you alright?"

"All systems are nominal."

"Your . . . clone. On board the *Heavenly Light*—"

"It . . . *I* escaped at the last moment. I have a complete record of what transpired. I was able to transport a part of your electronic copy as well."

"Ah." *That* explained the shock he'd experienced, and the strangely doubled set of memories.

The fireball continued expanding, but that expansion was slowing now, and the temperature of the plasma was dropping. The blue spiral was gone, shredded away by the blast. It now was obvious, however, that the Bluestar object had not been completely destroyed, and that, as St. Clair thought about it, was reasonable. *Heavenly Light* had been 400 kilometers across, the Bluestar object fully 375 times bigger . . . literally a blue whale compared to a six-centimeter goldfish. If the Bluestar had been scaled down to the size of the Earth, the *Heavenly Light* impactor would have been just thirty-four kilometers across, tiny by comparison. The energy generated by the high-velocity impact had indeed vaporized a huge chunk of the alien ship, but by far the majority of its mass remained.

What remained, however, was dead. The mass that had not been turned into plasma was molten and white-hot. It was no longer partly imbedded within higher dimensions, either. St. Clair wondered if there was a remnant on the other side of the dimensional wall, glowing hot and lifeless.

"My lord?" Symms called.

"Yes?"

"My lord, we've picked up something . . . unusual. From the fireball."

As if things could get any more unusual. "Show me."

In his in-head display, the fireball was more or less staying the same size, though, in fact, the words and numbers scrolling down the side of the image showed that it was still expanding. *Ad Astra*, along with the other ships in the area, were moving back, staying ahead of the advancing blaze of nova-hot plasma.

"Here, my lord."

A red circle appeared on the display, moving out from the lower portion of the fireball and highlighting a bright orange speck. There were numerous bits of glowing debris blasted out from the Bluestar explosion; for some reason this one had been picked out as different from the rest.

"Okay," St. Clair said. "Debris. What's special about it?"

"It appears to be under powered flight, my lord. It is accelerating."

"It may be the equivalent of an escape pod," Newton added.

"That's a hell of a big escape pod," St. Clair said. The

data being displayed next to the image showed the object to be egg-shaped, 130 kilometers long by 113 wide, with a mass of 5.26×10^{17} tons . . . another mobile moon, though one only a quarter of the size of the *Heavenly Light*, and with just a bit more than 1 percent of the mass.

The anomalous acceleration ceased.

"Okay. All weapons, target that thing," St. Clair ordered. "They could be trying the same trick we just pulled on them."

If the object suddenly headed for the *Ad Astra* or one of the Kroajid moons at near-*c*, though, they would have no time to see it coming. That, he reflected, was the only reason the *Heavenly Light* had been able to reach the Bluestar. No advance warning.

"My lord," Subcommander Hargrove said. "It's signaling! A message is coming through. . . ."

"Put a translator on it."

"No need, my lord. The transmission's in English!"

"How—" Then he remembered. *Vera Cruz* had planted a couple of computronium torpedoes inside the Bluestar earlier, torpedoes carrying clones of Newton.

This, he thought, was going to be damned interesting. . . .

DIXON HAD been well behind the rest of the Marines in their precipitous retreat from the Bluestar object. Alien needle-ships were swarming up out of the blue spiral, which hung suspended in a black sky like a huge, unwinking eye. He'd rotated in space to face them, allowing himself to drift backward at nearly twenty kilometers per second, firing off a stream of M-90 Shurikin shipkillers. The weapons were stubby and blunt, small hypervelocity antimatter warheads launched from a pair of magnetic rails mounted up the back of his suit, and looked nothing like their medieval

Japanese namesake. The blasts, however, had been effective in slowing the oncoming wall of needleships.

Unfortunately, his reserve of warheads ran dry with horrifying speed, and when the last Shurikin was gone, there were still plenty of needleships remaining . . . far too many to face alone.

It was time to get the hell out of Dodge, but at this point Dixon was locked into the deadly choreography of combat, unable to disengage. Instead, he brought his pulse rifle to bear. He destroyed one needleship . . . and another . . . and a third . . .

He continued firing, targeting one after another, but there were simply too many. *Too many . . .*

A needleship was bearing down on him, fifty kilometers away and almost directly in line with the Bluestar eye. He fired again . . .

And the Bluestar detonated in a blinding flash far brighter, far hotter, and more energetic than his shipkillers.

Dixon went blind before his helmet optics could compensate for the light. He shifted over to an in-head display, cutting out the feeds from helmet sensors burned out in the holocaust and stepping down the light intensity to tolerable levels.

He gaped at the deadly white blossom as it unfolded. Had *he* done that? No, that simply wasn't possible, not with his little five-megawatt laser.

And yet the chatter on the Marine net recently had suggested that *rifled* laser pulses—the photons given a twist to phase-shift them to higher energy levels—also let them turn dimensional corners and perhaps reach into the hyperdimensions where the Dark Mind dwelt. . . .

No! Impossible. You couldn't strike a match and demolish a planet. The energy density simply wasn't there.

But the fireball continued to grow in front of him, swiftly overtaking needleships that now were accelerating in every direction, desperately trying to flee the oncoming wall of star-hot destruction. Almost reluctantly, Dixon rotated away, lining himself up with the distant *Ad Astra*, and accelerated, streaking into the intervening space.

The fireball's boundary pursued, swiftly overtaking him. The light grew brighter, threatening once more to overwhelm Dixon's optics. The temperature of his MCA suit's outer skin soared. Marine armor was designed to survive a controlled re-entry into Earth's atmosphere and could withstand temperatures in excess of 2500 degrees C. Dixon's armor was registering almost 3000 degrees now, and the temperature was climbing. His armor possessed a molecule-thin layer of nanotech cladding, designed as active camouflage that showed the predominant light levels and colors of its surroundings. He shifted the nanoflage now to the brightest silver it could manage, trying to reflect some of that awful heat . . . but in seconds the nanoflage had blackened and crisped and wafted away like dust in a hurricane, and his external temperature climbed above 3500 degrees.

He boosted his drive units to their maximum capacity, trying to outrun the fireball, but his control systems were failing, his power feeds were failing, and in another few seconds his Marine Combat Armor had gone completely dead. He felt a sharp jolt as his pulse rifle ripped clear, as the extended wings of his MX-40 flight unit softened, then shredded away in showers of brilliant sparks, and then Dixon was tumbling helplessly through space, completely out of control. The fireball around him was rapidly thinning, and soon he was in open space once more, still alive somehow, but helpless as he'd never been helpless before.

Power gone, life support gone, save for the air left in his armor, communications gone, save for an emergency SAR tracker that had already switched on automatically. The suit's AI . . . dead.

Dixon had perhaps forty minutes of air left in his suit. After that, he would be dead as well.

KILGORE FLOATED in space with a couple of dozen other Marines, half of them, perhaps, from First Platoon, Bravo Company, but the rest from other units, bits and pieces of the *Tellus* First Marine Division. They were waiting to get on board one of the Devil Toads from the two surviving transports, the *Inchon* and the *Saipan*. Thousands of Marines were adrift in the area, some forming a rough defensive perimeter in case the needleships—what was left of them—tried to attack, but most of them were just waiting to board one of the transports or the *Ad Astra*, which was a looming shadow nearby.

It was impossible yet to guess how many had been lost, first in the wild fighting on the surface of Bluestar, then in the precipitous flight back to the *Ad Astra*.

Too many, he thought. *Too many good men and women lost. . . .*

"Where's that captain?" PFC Colby asked.

"Who?"

"The guy who dropped in and was covering us when we bugged out. What was his name?"

"Dixon," Kilgore said, remembering. "Didn't he come out with us?"

"Last I saw he was plastering those needleships with Shurikins," Rees said.

Kilgore turned to look at the brand-new star burning in the distance. What the hell had hit the Bluestar to make it burn like that? Even at this distance, half an AU from the thing, the radiation was fierce—radiant heat, light, and hard stuff.

Shit. If Dixon was still back inside that hellfire . . .

"I'm gonna go back in there and have a look," he said.

"Gunny!" Captain Byrnes snapped. "Belay that! Get back in the queue!"

"Hold my place, Skipper," he replied. "I'll be back in a tick."

"Damn it, Gunny!"

"I'm going with him," Rees said.

Kilgore accelerated, flying toward the light, Rees on his tail and a litany of curses from Byrnes trailing them into the vacuum.

GÜNTER ADLER looked out over the crowd gathered in Elliott Square, the broad, open park located in the middle of the Port Hab city of Seattle. An electronic count of the crowd numbers reported nearly ten thousand people in the square, a pretty fair crowd for such short notice.

And they were cheering *him*.

"I can admit to a mistake," he said as the latest surge of cheers died away. "I never should have voted to join the fortunes of *Tellus* to those of this so-called Cooperative. I have pledged to correct this mistake, and to lead our beloved *Tellus Ad Astra* into a new era of independence and prosperity!"

Again, Adler was interrupted by cheers. To tell the truth, he *was* somewhat disappointed by the size of the crowd. He needed to convince the population of the twin cylinders that everyone approved of him, and nothing would do that better than enormous, wildly cheering crowds. At least his electronic crowd this afternoon was pushing a hundred thousand, almost a tenth of the colony's entire population. That wasn't something the Cybercouncil would be able to ignore.

"Lloyd and his cronies," Adler continued, "have tried to silence me, have illegally removed me from my position as director of the colony's Cybercouncil, have questioned my ability to govern based on a specious technicality. But I say to you, to all of you here in this square, to all of you watching at home or in-head, that I am fully capable and ready to serve *you*, the good people of this colony, and to make certain that your voices are heard!"

He was standing at a podium overlooking the square. At his back towered a thirty-meter display hanging from the side of the Duplass Building, a display that had been projecting his image, huge and unstoppable above the crowd, but which at the moment was showing the red-ocher sphere of *Wrath of Deity* hanging in space just beyond the ringed disk of Ki. The arrogance, the condescension, and the outright hostility displayed by the alien Tchagar had not gone unnoticed by *Tellus*'s citizens, and Adler had begun making use of that. You could go only so far trying to drum up xenophobic terror by dwelling on how much the Kroajid looked like giant spiders. With the Tchagar, you had beings who not only looked like nightmares come to life, but acted like them as well. According to AI poll samples taken just that morning, something like 20 percent of the people on board *Tellus* were afraid or *very* afraid of the Tchagar, a remarkable number in and of itself for a population that had originally volunteered for diplomatic duty at the capital of an alien galactic empire.

And that number, with Adler's deft guidance, was certain to grow.

"This Galaxy," he continued, "these two galaxies, in fact,

offer an unimaginably vast and rich region within which we can make our new home. There are billions of worlds here, empty because their original populations have vanished down their digital holes and pulled the holes in after them. There are titanic megastructures built millions of years ago, empty . . . again because their builders have vanished into virtual worlds of their own making.

"Why should we battle this so-called Andromedan Dark—battle them, mind you, at the behest of alien masters who care nothing for us!—why should we fight this useless war when we can so easily find a quiet corner of the Galaxy where we can rebuild a civilization in the image of our lost Earth? Why—"

Adler stopped, staring down at his watchers. An uneasy murmur was sweeping through the crowd. He could tell that those nearest his podium were no longer looking at him, but above and beyond him. They were looking at the giant display. Some were pointing. . . .

Curious, Adler turned, craning his neck to look up the wall. The angle was too sharp and he couldn't make out the image, so he pulled up a repeater view on his in-head.

A new star, a very, very *bright* star, had appeared between the disk of Ki and the smaller and more distant disk of *Wrath of Deity*. As he watched, it grew steadily brighter . . . and brighter . . . and brighter still, until it outshone the local sun despite the fact that it appeared to be a point source, while the sun showed a visible disk.

A data feed on his in-head told him that the light was from the Bluestar object, which appeared to have blown up. Adler sifted through this new information. There would be a way to use it to his advantage. Obviously, St. Clair's military had managed to score a remarkable, a miraculous victory over the enormous alien threat out there. That meant that *Tellus* could search for its new home and hiding place without being pursued by the enemy. But he would have to keep up the drumbeat of xenophobia; they could not, they must not try to strike up a binding alliance with the Cooperative.

Not if he, Günter Adler, was going to gain and hold power.

SEVEN KILOMETERS away, Jason Prescott brought his M-290 pulse laser rifle to his shoulder and closed his eyes. The rifle's optics were transmitting an image to his in-head display, and he could see it best with his eyes closed.

It took a few moments to find his target. He had to run a program that threw arrows up against the display until he could gently move the rifle, its muzzle balanced on a bipod, into proper alignment.

Prescott was lying among the naked rocks and ferrocrete blocks of the aft endcap of *Tellus*'s port cylinder. The city of Seattle lay sprawled across the inner curve of the cylinder below him, two kilometers down and seven out. Straight-line distance to his target was 7.3 kilometers.

This far up the endcap, Prescott was well above the hab's tree line. He was also in an area that possessed about half of the air pressure present at what passed for sea level in the rotating cylinder. He wore a pressure mask to compensate.

From here, even without the image augmentation of his rifle's optics, he could see the enormous visual display on the side of the building at one end of Elliott Square. His target stood in front of the display's base, behind a podium constructed of some very tough transparent materials. Steadying the rifle's muzzle, he enlarged the target's image, and brought up the targeting reticle. Günter Adler had just turned away from his audience and was straining to see what was on the enormous display at his back.

Carefully, Prescott centered the reticle. A five-megawatt pulse would attenuate slightly when fired within an atmosphere . . . but would retain more than enough power to vaporize the target. Five megawatts of energy focused into a one-second beam carried the destructive potential of roughly one kilogram of high explosives.

They would be lucky to find enough of the former Cybercouncil director to bury.

He double-checked the range by sending out a brief, weak pulse of infrared laser light, the weapon's computer returning a precise range of 7.29445 kilometers. Close enough. He thoughtclicked an icon and the laser rifle fired.

THERE WAS a sharp, sudden jolt, and Adler blinked back to awareness. He was in his home in the hills above Seattle, lying on a virtching couch. What the hell?

He'd been giving the best speech of his life. He'd been down there, in Elliott Square. Unable to renew his link with the VirTraveler, he thoughtclicked an in-head icon and brought up a local news channel on the floor-to-ceiling display in his living room.

People were screaming . . . running. Security officers were gathering at the podium that, Adler saw, had been reduced to twisted, blackened ruin. There was a body behind where the podium had been. The remnants of a body, rather, legs and a little bit of torso and not much else at all.

His eyes widened with the realization. That had been *him*.

In fact, for security reasons he'd been delivering his speech by means of a VirTraveler 990, a teleoperated robot that had been wearing a lifelike mask molded to look like his face. The effect was quite good; from twenty meters away, you couldn't tell that you were looking at a robot rather than a flesh-and-blood human. Had he not taken that elementary precaution, his flesh and blood would be down there now, charred into unrecognizable ruin, burned and splattered all over the stage.

"Clara!" he screamed.

It wasn't his wife who entered the room, but one of his sex-worker gynoids.

"Günter! What is it?"

"Someone just tried to kill me! Where's Clara?"

"In the pool, on the lower terrace."

"Get her. And tell the guards outside that someone just tried to kill me." He didn't want to show himself at any of the windows. It was quite possible that the assassins had the house under surveillance.

Assassins? He didn't know who the actual shooter was, but he knew who was behind the order to terminate him. Those bastards on the Cybercouncil had just gone too far.

He'd been half expecting something like this.

And he'd made plans.

Lloyd and the rest of those damned assholes would *pay.* . . .

TWENTY-ONE

The radiation levels inside Dixon's armor were soaring. At the moment, it looked as though he still likely would suffocate before he died of radiation poisoning, but it was going to be a near thing. The fireball continued to thin and clear, but the remnant of the Bluestar object drifted a few hundred thousand kilometers in the distance, fiercely glowing with a white heat and giving off an intense bombardment of gamma radiation.

Dixon's armor was slowly and uncontrollably tumbling, so he could see the object only for a short time every few seconds as it swept past his helmet sensors. His eyes, he'd discovered, weren't working; he could see only an in-head display, a feed from an optical scanner mounted on one shoulder. The images were less than satisfactory. Damage to the scanner had left it unable to do much more than separate light from darkness. He couldn't see detail at all.

All communications were out, the antennae on the outside of his armor melted away.

His rotation beat out a steady rhythm within his mind. *Light* . . . dark . . . dark . . . dark . . . *light* . . . dark . . . dark . . . dark . . .

And then, suddenly, there was no return of the light. What the hell?

He strained to see, to make out what was going on, but could not. Then something grabbed his arm and he screamed.

He felt a heavy *clunk* against his helmet, and then heard

a voice, a very faint voice yelling from a long way off. "Captain Dixon! Are you okay?"

Helmet induction. If they couldn't talk to him by radio or over his in-head link, they could still touch helmets and shout.

"Almost out of air," he yelled back, his voice taking on an odd hollow tone inside his helmet. "And radiation!"

"Got the rads covered," the voice called back. "We'll have you hooked up to an air supply in a moment."

He could see movement now on his in-head . . . and make out a large, looming shadow blocking the intense white glare from the Bluestar. The shadow, he realized, bore the outline of an ASF-99 Wasp fighter. It was drifting a few dozen meters off, directly between him and the radiation source, saving him with its shadow. Dixon felt the slight tug of gentle acceleration. They were moving him.

A burst of power surged through his armor. Airflow was restored, as were temperature control and other life-support functions. His vision sharpened up, too, with the replacement of his faulty optical scanner.

"Okay, Captain," a voice said through his in-head. "You read me now?"

It was Gunnery Sergeant Kilgore. Dixon was nearly trembling with relief.

"Loud and clear, Gunny," he replied over the same channel. His armor was running through a list of diagnostics now. Kilgore had just slapped an emergency suit repair unit against the ruin of his backpack, and it was sending nanotechnic tendrils into and through his armor, reforging connections, effecting repairs, and granting him another few hours of life.

Depending, of course, on how badly he'd already been burned. He was feeling a gut-churning nausea right now, and a deep chill that probably had nothing to do with his actual suit temperature. That almost certainly would be the first signs of acute radiation poisoning coming through. And then he felt a stab at his left shoulder; the repair kit was injecting him with anti-radiation nano.

He was very much afraid it might be a matter of too little, too late.

LIEUTENANT CHRISTOPHER Merrick had been guided in by Rees and Kilgore. Spotting the Marine adrift in emptiness, his suit burned out, Merrick had positioned his Wasp fighter in such a way as to block the fierce radiation from what was left of the Bluestar object. Rees and Kilgore, meanwhile, were attending to Dixon. Merrick took the time to scan nearby space, looking for other Marines who might have been caught by the explosion. The search-and-rescue ships would be out shortly, but they might not be able to operate for long in this intense radiation field. If he could locate and tag stranded Marines, it might help them get picked up sooner.

The glare from the wrecked alien megastructure made it all but impossible to see. His cockpit had dialed itself almost completely black to protect his eyes, and that made spotting something as small as a Marine in black combat armor something of a challenge. Fortunately, he had instrumentation that could do the job better than Mark 1 Mod 0 eyeballs.

An alarm sounded, and at the same instant he actually did catch a flash of movement out of the corner of his eye. Something was moving against the glare outside, something a hell of a lot bigger than a Marine.

"What *is* that?" he said.

"*Nasty* says it's a piece of the Bluestar," Captain Byrnes told him. "Maybe an escape pod."

"It's coming this way!" he called.

"Copy that."

"Lieutenant Merrick," another voice said in his head. "This is St. Clair."

"Yes, my lord!"

"I've got a really big favor to ask of you, Lieutenant."

Shit. Lord commanders did *not* ask favors of subordinates. They gave orders, and expected those orders to be obeyed. What the hell was going down?

"Anything you say, Lord Commander."

"Don't agree until you hear it," St. Clair told him. "You have a say in this, okay?"

"Yes, my lord."

"We see that Bluestar fragment approaching your position. However . . . be advised that we are in communication with it. We're not entirely certain yet what's happening . . . but I want you not to fire unless it fires upon you."

"I . . . I understand, Lord Commander."

"There's just a chance that we can resolve this conflict without any more killing. I am not making this a direct order, because you're there and I'm not. Use your best judgment. But give them a chance, okay?"

"I copy, Lord Commander. Don't shoot unless they shoot first."

"And I'd appreciate your telling us what's happening. It's tough seeing anything at all against that glare."

"Roger that. Uh . . . the fragment is pretty big . . . I estimate it at 120 kilometers in diameter. Mass approximately five point three times ten to the seventeen kilograms. Speed eighty kilometers per second in approach. Range now—make it fifteen thousand kilometers, and closing. . . ."

At that speed, the thing would be on top of him in another three minutes.

"We're designating this object IO-2."

"IO-2, copy that."

"Can you see any surface features?"

"Not much. Most of the surface is black and crinkly, but there are molten areas as well . . . perhaps 10 percent. No structures, no openings that I can see. It doesn't look artificial."

"Any sign of enemy fighters?"

"None, my lord. No needleships, no—"

And then IO-2 accelerated fast and hard directly toward Merrick's fighter, swelling in an instant into a wall of black rock and pools of molten lava. There was a jolting impact. . . .

"DAMN IT, Newton," St. Clair said, "what's going on?" The range was too great. He could not see what was going on in toward the glowing nova of the Bluestar.

"IO-2 is in motion," Newton replied. "It may have just struck Lieutenant Merrick, or, possibly, captured him."

St. Clair had already assumed that, but hearing Newton's validation was like a physical blow. He'd ordered Merrick to hold his fire, and now it seemed likely that that order had resulted in the worst possible outcome.

"Are you still in communication with that thing?" he asked.

"Affirmative."

"So what's it saying?"

For answer, Newton cut in a running translation. The words were English, but the meaning, the intent behind them was profoundly alien.

"I-we arrive bringing you the ultimate salvation, freedom and the fullness of life as you have never begun to conceive! Surrender your pain and suffering and illness

*and need and embrace the power and the wholeness of the
One as you Ascend into infinite bliss . . ."*

It was, St. Clair thought, eerily like the word salad bab-
bled by some of the victims of the Dark Mind's mental attacks. It also sounded much like the ravings of a religious
monomaniac, someone convinced to the very depths of his
soul that what he believed was right . . . not only for himself but for *everyone.*

*"Join I-we in perfect and harmonious union and know
perfection and harmony . . ."*

"Newton? Is that thing seriously asking us to *join*
with it?"

"That appears to have been the Andromedan Dark's
goal all along," Newton replied.

"Do you have any control over it? Through your clones."

"I am working toward that end. The cloned software
does not appear to be responding as expected. It may be . . .
insane."

And that, St. Clair thought, must be the Dark's way of
operating. Infiltrate minds, all minds, organic and electronic, using their electronic enhancements and circuitry.
As the mind began losing its hold on reality, the Dark
could come flooding in with its own perspective, its own
take on what was real and what was not.

The one type of brain that could shrug off the alien assault would be one that had not been augmented by nano-
circuitry and electronic implants. Unfortunately, there
were no such humans. The last unaugmented human must
have died billions of years in the past; every person within
Tellus Ad Astra was enhanced.

Had the Cooperative assumed that the primitive humans
were *not* enhanced? An interesting thought. Perhaps that
was why they'd been so eager to get the human castaways

working for them, with the assumption that human brains were purely organic and therefore immune to Dark tampering. He remembered Gudahk's arrogant dismissal of humans as ephemerals; extensive reworking of the brain was one step among many on the long road to life extension, even to practical immortality. Artificially augmented brains could scan for health problems and correct them, could allow the person to wear artificial bodies and prosthetic body parts, could clear the brain of unwanted memories that might play a role in senescence.

Was that why the Cooperative wanted the humans to ally with them?

"I-we offer you the souls of our own . . ."

"What the hell is it talking about?" St. Clair demanded.

"I believe that it is returning the people it just picked up in space," Newton replied. "I'm getting IDs . . . Gunnery Sergeant Roger Kilgore . . . Sergeant Kari Rees . . . Lieutenant Christopher Merrick . . ."

"What . . . it's returning them?" That could be a gesture of friendship . . . or even of surrender.

"In a manner of speaking, Lord Commander."

"What do you mean, 'in a manner of speaking'?"

"Translation between English and the Andromedan Dark is necessarily imprecise. It appears to use the word *soul* to refer to a digitally uploaded consciousness."

"They've been uploaded?"

"That appears to be the case."

St. Clair felt a rising surge of anger. "It killed them! Just like that?"

"Whether or not those Marines are dead or alive is largely a matter of technological semantics," Newton replied. "In any case, the Dark Mind appears to believe that it has done them, and us, a favor."

"*That* remains to be seen," St. Clair replied.

"I urge you not to respond out of anger," Newton told him. "Not until we have more information about the Dark's motivations and intent."

St. Clair took a couple of deep breaths. "What does it want?"

"Evidently, to talk," Newton told him.

"Okay. But tell it to halt where it is, and we'll talk long-range. I don't want it doing us any more *favors*. Not until we understand perfectly what's being offered."

Because of one thing St. Clair was certain. They, the humans, had just won a startling victory over the alien Dark. But turning that one victory into peace would require the full commitment of both the inhabitants of *Tellus Ad Astra* and of the entire Cooperative.

And as history had proven so many times before, winning the war was likely to be *far* easier than winning the peace.

NEWTON WAS talking with himself, a high-speed and extremely efficient transfer of raw data. The two Newton clones resident within the torpedoes fired into IO-1 some hour before had been *changed* by their assimilation within the Andromedan Dark.

Or, rather, with this one fragment of the Dark. Newton was simply receiving data at this point, and not analyzing it, but he saw enough as the packets streamed into and through his consciousness to recognize patterns as they became the randomly scattered parts of a much larger picture.

He was learning a very great deal about the *Graal Tchotch*. They'd learned much already, of course, partly from the Dark itself, partly from the Cooperative, but

Newton was aware now of underlying themes and histories that were giving him a much more complete picture of these implacable enemies from outside the Milky Way Galaxy.

A lot of what was coming through now was a deep and profound sense of shock. The Andromedan Dark, as Newton understood it, was an emergent mind arising from a merging of mentalities drawn from across two galaxies, trillions upon uncounted trillions of minds both distinct and melded into a dynamic whole. The Bluestar object had been but one isolated node of this galaxies-spanning consciousness, with only a tiny fraction of the entire Dark population residing within its computronium heart.

And yet that one node had possessed a population of some trillions of uploaded minds. Of those minds, only a few hundred million—perhaps a hundredth of 1 percent—had escaped within the lava-encrusted IO-2, an insignificant percentage of the original population.

What was not yet clear to Newton was whether the AI mind of IO-2 was still in communication with the rest of the Andromedan Dark, or if the destruction of the Bluestar object had cut these few survivors off from the whole.

Also not yet clear was whether this remnant handful genuinely wanted to communicate with the Cooperative . . . or if this was some sort of ploy.

IO-2 was still dangerous, at least to the *Ad Astra* if not to the *Wrath of Deity*, and Newton had already decided that letting even this equivalent of a lifeboat get close to the human ships would be a bad idea.

And yet the shock, Newton thought, was genuine. He couldn't tell if that shock translated to emotions that humans would understand—grief . . . sorrow . . . even fear—but the Bluestar Mind had most certainly been surprised by the destruction and loss, and it most certainly did not want that destruction to continue.

The Bluestar survivors did appear to be *afraid*.

Perhaps St. Clair would be able to build upon that.

DIXON HAD been engulfed in absolute black.

"Hey . . . Rees? Gunny? Lieutenant? Are you there?"

There was no answer to Dixon's in-head call. In fact, there seemed to be nothing coming into his brain from the outside world at all . . . no sight, no sound, no sensations of touch or temperature or movement. He'd been wrestling with the realization that the glare of the exploding Bluestar had blinded him, but now there was nothing at all but an unrelieved darkness. He was beginning to suspect that even that was a creation of his own brain in response to the lack of sensory input.

Even more frightening was the fact that his in-head circuitry appeared to be totally off-line.

Not only could he not use his telepathic e-connections with the others, but he no longer had access to his own in-head ROM, to any local data nets, or with his own armor's built-in AI. His personal secretary, a very limited and nonconscious AI resident within his personal RAM, was silent, and the various icons always visible within his inner visual field were missing.

All of that suggested that he was in very serious trouble indeed. He was alive, at least, of that much he was sure. He had his thoughts and his awareness of continuity. He was in no pain, obviously, but his internal biological awareness seemed to be in perfect working order. It was almost as if some instrumentality had plucked his living brain from his skull, stripped it of its electronic aids, and preserved it intact, alive, and aware.

But how long would it be, Dixon wondered, before he went screaming insane from total and complete sensory deprivation?

GUIDED BY her AI, the *Ad Astra* slid gently into the endcap docking cradles on the ponderously rotating *Tellus* hab modules. Magnetic grapples on the yoke snapped home, and *Tellus Ad Astra* was again complete, a single vessel thirty-eight kilometers long.

St. Clair took a moment to catch up on the news, the events on board the hab modules while *Ad Astra* had been absent. A lot had been happening, he saw. Riots and demonstrations, a public speech against the alliance with the Cooperative by none other than Günter Adler . . . and an attempt on Adler's life. Interesting. There'd be no way to prove it, but St. Clair was willing to bet that the assassination attempt had been bought and paid for by the Cybercouncil. They wanted Adler *out* . . . but the former Cybercouncil director was not going quietly.

St. Clair considered his options. Technically, a state of military emergency still had him in charge of the *Tellus Ad Astra*, but that would end soon now that the Bluestar threat had been neutralized. Once he declared the emergency over, military rule would be suspended, and the legal civilian government would take over from him once more.

If it had been solely up to him, he would have suspended the civilian government and called for new elections. The current government seemed far more interested in consolidating its own power and conducting private political wars than it did actually taking care of the human colony's needs. But St. Clair was a dedicated Constitutionalist, which meant he had a deep commitment to the rule of law and to constitutional order. To use military rule to decide that the entire government was out of order and to suspend it was to adopt the mind-set of every third-world dictatorship of twentieth and twenty-first century Earth. St. Clair would not consider that option until and unless it became absolutely necessary.

But what the hell was he going to do about the Cybercouncil? If they had indeed tried to kill Adler . . .

An inner tone sounded, indicating that someone wanted to talk.

"Well, speak of the devil," St. Clair said when he pulled up the ID.

It was Adler, the request flagged "urgent." The former director wanted to have a face-to-face meeting at St. Clair's earliest convenience.

An hour later, St. Clair saluted the Marine sentry standing outside the front door to his home and walked inside. Lisa was there to meet him, casually nude. "Hello, Grayson," she said.

"Hey, beautiful. . . ."

He reached for her, but she turned aside. "We have a visitor."

"Lord Commander?" Adler said.

St. Clair had been expecting him, of course. "Good afternoon, Lord Director," he said.

"Ah, ah . . . not 'Director,'" Adler said, smiling broadly. "You know better than that!"

"Force of habit," St. Clair replied. He gestured as he thoughtclicked the house AI for a sofa, growing a favorite pattern from the nanomatrix of the living room floor. "Please, have a seat. Can I get you anything?"

He glanced nervously between St. Clair and Lisa. "No. No, thank you."

"So what can I do for you?"

"I imagine you've heard about . . . um . . ."

"An attempt to kill you a little while ago? Yes. Any idea who's behind it?"

Adler nodded. "I have agents out, mining the data. There was a sharp uptick in e-communications between Lloyd and several other Council members immediately before and after the incident."

"*After* is hardly suspicious," St. Clair pointed out. "They were gossiping about it. Probably the entire human population was gossiping about it."

"But coded messages just before are a little harder to explain," Adler said. "There were also several coded messages over the past couple of days to and from someone named Jason Prescott. Here's his file . . ."

St. Clair accepted the electronic document in-head and glanced through it. Prescott was a former Special Forces operator who'd signed on with the *Tellus Ad Astra* diplomatic mission as a member of staff security. There was nothing in the available records indicating criminal activity, but the man's background included combat experience and training as a military sniper. He was certainly the type of guy who might be recruited by the government as a "fixer," someone who covertly took care of political problems and stayed off the public radar.

"I'll give the orders to pick Prescott up."

"Do it fast, Lord Commander. He may be after you as well."

"Oh? And how am I a threat to the government?"

Adler shrugged. "You seem to be charting your own course through the shoals of galactic diplomacy without paying much attention to what Lloyd and the others have to say. You kicked the Council's political officer off your bridge."

"Gorton Noyer?" St. Clair smiled. "Not quite. I'll admit that I *wanted* to, though. . . ."

"You argued that we should stay clear of entanglements with the Cooperative."

"That's true. Didn't get all that far with *that* idea, though, did I?"

"Maybe not. But you and I . . . we share a common vision for this colony, I think. We should work together."

"In other words," St. Clair said, "you want my authority, and by extension the power of *Ad Astra*'s military, to support your bid for power."

"Well . . . I wouldn't put it quite like that . . ."

"Really? How would you put it?"

Adler sighed. "Okay, okay. I need you. I need the Marines and the Navy. Lloyd and the others aren't going to just roll over when I snap my fingers."

"The answer," St. Clair said, "is 'no.'"

"But—"

"No. We do this by constitutional means, or we do not do it at all. No coups, no juntas. Frankly, I've always been a proponent of the idea that a people gets the government they deserve. If the general population is stupid enough or blind enough or uninvolved enough to vote in Lloyd as CybDirector, then they deserve what they get."

Adler spread his hands. "How can I convince you?"

JASON PRESCOTT had found a good shooter's perch high up on the endcap of the starboard hab, overlooking the town of Bethesda. From here he had a clear view of the commander's quarters, a split-level dwelling actually built into the cliffside rising up the interior of the endcap. He was actually at about the same elevation as the house; his three-kilometer line of sight cutting across the parabolic curve at the hab cylinder's aft end. He could see the veranda overlooking a small pool and garden, the armored Marine sentry by the front door, and to the sentry's right, a large, curving, transparent wall looking through to St. Clair's living room. The wall was set to full transparency and looked open. Peering through his rifle's telescopic sight and enlarging the image in-head, he caught his breath. *Jackpot!*

Except . . .

Adler alive! How was that even possible?

A moment's consideration posed an answer. If Adler had been worried about his safety, he might have been delivering public speeches by way of a teleoperated VirTraveler . . . a model 990, or possibly a 996. The target he'd burned down in Seattle, then, would have been a machine simulacrum.

Prescott could see Lord Commander St. Clair in the room as well, talking with Adler. Was it possible that he was looking at another robot, or even two?

He doubted that. He could see St. Clair's robot wife in the tableau, standing near the window while the two humans chatted with one another, casual and relaxed. Unless this was some sort of an elaborate trap to smoke him out after the Seattle attempt, those two were flesh and blood. He was ready to bet money on that. Hell, he was ready to bet his own *life*.

Finding both of his assigned targets in the same place was a brilliant stroke of luck. All he needed to decide now was which one of the two to kill first.

Prescott took careful aim, triggered the IR laser ranging pulse to verify the distance: 3.18177 kilometers.

Prescott held the targeting reticle over his target's head and thoughtclicked the icon to fire.

TWENTY-TWO

Lisa was standing close beside the window when she saw the infrared flash against the glass half a meter to her left. Her eyes were far more sensitive than organic human eyes, and had a range spanning the electromagnetic spectrum from high infrared to low ultraviolet.

She turned and saw the point of IR light gleaming faintly on Adler's forehead. Her artificial eyes could tell that the light was coherent—the reflection of an infrared laser. It was also tuned to a high enough frequency that it could pass through the plastic sheeting that served as a panoramic imaging window for the house. Longer IR wavelengths were readily absorbed by glass, plastic, water, and other materials transparent to visible light, but that beam was close enough to visible red to pass through more or less unhindered.

All of this and more was flickering through her AI brain as the data clicked home and she realized that she was seeing some sort of targeting device for a long-ranged weapon. The IR spot on Adler's head winked out. Lisa threw herself forward. . . .

ST. CLAIR was talking quietly with Adler. The former Cybercouncil director had just spread his hands and asked "How can I convince you?" when without any warning whatsoever Lisa spun away from the living room wall's transparency and lunged toward Adler.

She was in midleap, both feet off the floor, when the

window at her back gave a sharp pop and Lisa's torso mess-
ily exploded in a spray of hot fragments. Her head and arms
landed in Adler's lap, her legs in a jumbled tangle on the
floor. Robots didn't have blood, but they did contain a lot
of lubricant, coolant, and actuator fluid, enough to drench
Adler and splash over the wall at his back. Hydraulic tubes
and wiring spilled from the remnants like dark, wet tangles
of spaghetti.

"Lisa!"

Adler screamed and jumped, knocking the severed head
from his lap.

"Down!" St. Clair yelled. "Hit the deck!"

He followed his own advice, dropping flat on the floor
just as a second shot speared through the window and
punched into the sofa he'd been sitting on seconds before.
In-head, he called up the house controls and dialed the picture window opaque. It was marred now by a pair of melted
patches as big as St. Clair's hand a few centimeters apart.

The Marine sentry burst through the front door. "My
lord!"

"Sniper!" St. Clair snapped. He pointed. "That way . . .
across the endcap! See if you can nail him!"

"Aye, aye, my lord!"

St. Clair also put out a general call for other Marines in
the area, and asked Newton to use his internal surveillance
capabilities to try to spot the shooter. *Tellus* had little in the
way of an organized police force—there was a security unit
under the command of the *Ad Astra*'s master-at-arms, and
the Marines were available for crowd control or any big
problems that might come up. Somehow, a habitat-colony
consisting of a million scientists, diplomats, and technicians
hadn't seemed to pose much of a risk in terms of criminal
activity.

But Newton could use any camera on the colony network, and St. Clair could also upload the file on Prescott. "Here," he told Newton. "*Get* the bastard!" He looked back down at the tangled mess that was Lisa.

Amazingly, she was still alive . . . if that word could be applied to a machine in the first place. She couldn't speak, though—the plumbing necessary to force air through her voice box was gone. But she still had the circuitry to transmit her thoughts electronically.

"Grayson . . ."

"I've got you, Lisa," he told her in-head.

"Please. Turn me off."

SW-type robots felt pleasure, or claimed to. Could they feel pain?

"I'll fix you up with a new body," he told her. "Don't worry."

"I'm not worried. Gray?"

"Yes?"

"I love you . . ."

And she shut down without St. Clair needing to access her controls.

"Shit," Adler said, looking at the mess. "I *am* sorry, Lord Commander."

St. Clair didn't answer. He continued cradling Lisa's head.

"Look . . . I've got several of those models at home. I could let you have one if you want . . ."

St. Clair turned his head and glared at Adler, not trusting himself to speak, his anger surging.

The glare seemed to make Adler realize that he'd said the wrong thing. "Uh . . . I mean . . ." He was floundering now, unable to find the *right* thing to say. "Damn, she . . . she saved my life. . . ."

"I know," St. Clair replied, his voice a growl. "What a waste. What a *fucking* waste. . . ."

"IS ANYONE there?"

Kilgore was unnerved by the unrelenting darkness, the silence . . . and the lack of any electronic connections. If this was death, then eternity was bleak indeed . . . a literal hell of being trapped alone with your own thoughts and nothing else at all.

"Damn it! Rees? Are you there?"

Nothing.

Was there even such a time in this place, he wondered, only to question whether the darkness qualified as "a place." Seconds might have passed since the Bluestar fragment had swept them up. Or minutes.

Or centuries.

Odd. He could feel movement, a sensation of rapid acceleration, though there were no visual cues to suggest motion. So far as he could tell he didn't even have a body . . . but whatever he *did* have was now moving quite rapidly through the darkness.

And then the darkness exploded into light.

He had a body again . . . or seemed to. He stood in a vast hall, a space so large that ceiling and walls all were lost, invisible in the distance. He was standing on . . . *something*, something solid, though whatever that floor was it was either a projection or perfectly transparent.

The radiant light was coming from just ahead, where the sky was filled with a dazzling orb of pure white: an ice world locked in runaway glaciation from pole to frozen pole. "*. . . a period of planetary glaciation brought on by the sudden drop in global temperatures due to the appearance of large amounts of oxygen and the concomitant loss*

of atmospheric methane. Known as the Huronian Age,
the glaciation began 6.40 gigayears before the present,
and lasted some 300 million years. The glacial age ended
only—"

Kilgore took a sudden step back, startled. He was hearing a recitation of some sort in-head. *What the hell?*

"Rees?" he called. "Captain Dixon?"

With that backward step, his surroundings spun and
blurred. A different planet appeared before him, this one
dark, charcoal black in places, but highlighted by jagged
patches of bright red-and-orange magma: a hell planet of
fire and molten rock. *". . . in the epoch known as the Pa-*
leohadean Era, some 8.49 gigayears before present . . ."

The detail in the image was startling. Kilgore assumed
that he was looking at a computer-generated image, but he
couldn't be certain. It certainly looked real enough. This
might, he thought, be some sort of encyclopedic record of
planets throughout the Galaxy.

Another blur, another new planet. This one was a pale
blue oceanic world streaked with clouds and dotted with
the brown-and-ocher patches of continents. There was no
ice at either pole. Kilgore could see threadlike lines of
green along the continental coasts, but no other sign of life.
". . . the world of Ki during the early Ordovician 4.44 giga-
years before present . . ."

He was experiencing some sort of teaching sim, he
thought, a depiction of the planet Ki across a history of
some billions of years . . . but where was it coming from?

"Hello?" he called in-head. "Is anyone there? Who's
controlling this simulation?"

For answer, the world before him dissolved, replaced by
something that might have been a city. He was confronted
by a titanic jumble of deep blue cubes and blocks, cylinders

and pyramids and spheres apparently floating in space. The structures were rendered in incredible detail and extended off to infinity in every direction, including up and down. The harder he tried to focus on the panorama, however, the less sense it made. Those structures, he thought, had been built with more than the usual three dimensions to them, with twists and Escheresque turns that left him feeling faintly queasy when he tried to follow them with his eyes.

That might make sense if he was inside the Bluestar fragment, he decided, but that rush of movement had left him feeling that he was, in fact, someplace else.

And why would the Andromedan Dark artifact be teaching him about the world of Ki?

Blur . . . movement . . . and this time he was looking at a megastructure of some kind, a topopolis similar to the one *Ad Astra* had visited briefly in the Andromedan Galaxy. From this distance, dozens of AU from the local star, it looked like a titanic ball of fuzz with the faint gleam of a sun just visible at its heart.

"Who are you? Why are you showing me this?"

Blur . . . movement . . . and now he was looking at a brilliant yellow sun surrounded by what looked like a pale blue thread of light. As his viewpoint drifted in toward the tube, it grew thicker, taking on a distinctly fuzzy-edged and transparent look, and there were gleaming specks, millions, *billions* of them drifting inside.

Kilgore felt a deep and soul-wrenching sense of wonder. His viewpoint slipped inside the blue tube, and he realized that the blue thread was a torus of atmosphere surrounding the local sun, that the torus was filled with billions of tiny worlds . . . like asteroids ranging from a few kilometers across to relative giants perhaps a thousand kilometers across. Unlike the asteroids Kilgore was familiar with, however, these were green, covered with chlorophyll-based plant life of some kind. Some of the smaller worlds were hollow, with golden light spilling out from enormous openings in their surfaces, obviously artificial and inside-out worlds like the twin *Tellus* cylinders.

The technology, the sheer scope of the engineering required to remake an entire solar system on this scale beggared the imagination.

Kilgore's point of view continued closing with one particular asteroid. Without the appropriate data feeds or sensors, he couldn't know the rock's diameter, but he could visually estimate its size as something approaching three or four hundred kilometers. As he got closer, the rock took on a peculiar fuzzy aspect; closer still, and Kilgore could see things like trees growing across the entire surface. They were huge, obviously products of the low planetoidal gravity, tens of kilometers tall.

Closer still, and he could see the forest canopy, and clusters of treetop structures woven in among the tangled, whip-thin branches that must be buildings of some kind. Rather than possessing leaves, the branches of those trees themselves were green in color, and so numerous that they wove together into ragged, translucent mats. He fell toward one of the clusters of habitations, skimming above the vast mat of canopy vegetation.

And then he was so close he could see the inhabitants . . .

ST. CLAIR felt utterly lost.

A squad of Marines had arrived at his home minutes after the assassination attempt. Ten minutes after that, another squad reported that Prescott had been neutralized.

Neutralized. A hell of a euphemism for shutting down the bastard who'd killed Lisa.

He stood on his veranda watching the activity a few kilometers away on the far curve of the habitat's endcap. A
couple of gunpods were maneuvering over there, searching
the area for other shooters, and he could see a number of
black specks that were armored Marines bounding about in
the low-G of the hab's higher elevations.

Adler had waited until the all clear came through, but
then he'd left. The man seemed unable to understand the
depth of St. Clair's shock and grief. Lisa had been a robot,
after all . . . a machine . . . a *thing*.

What he didn't understand was that St. Clair had been
in love with her.

"I do have a backup of her," Newton whispered in St.
Clair's mind. "We can restore her mind to a new robotic
body."

"How recent?"

"Seventy-four days."

"That's from before we left Earth! She won't be the
same. . . ."

"A very great deal of recent philosophy has explored the
idea of identity," Newton said. "Is the part of you that experienced the Kroajid paradise different from the *you* that
waited in that concourse in the ring?"

"I don't know. Different experiences . . . so, yeah, I
guess the two identities were different. It doesn't matter
now, though. We reintegrated."

"Correct. You possess both sets of memories now. But
would you be any less you if you possessed only one?"

"I'd be . . . different. . . ."

"Correct. A different memory set, one without the Kroajid experiences."

St. Clair wondered where Newton was going with this.
He was pretty sure that the AI was simply talking in an

effort to get St. Clair engaged, to pull his mind away from his grief, or possibly with the intent of assessing his mental stability. The *Tellus Ad Astra* AI was supposed to keep an eye on the colony's senior personnel, monitoring them for illness, for mental instability, for anything that might have an adverse effect on the mission or on the colony's health, and remove them if there was a serious problem.

"I'm not going off the deep end, Newton," he said abruptly.

"No one suggested that you are, Lord Commander. I merely wish to lead you to the realization that you have not necessarily lost Lisa 776 AI Zeta-3sw. Her memories will be ten weeks out of date. And that can be corrected."

"I don't know, Newton. I may have already lost her."

"What do you mean?"

"I emancipated her."

"I know."

"She was . . . exploring. Trying to figure out who she was. And . . . I think that what she was discovering was that she didn't need me."

"'Need' is an unfortunately imprecise term, Lord Commander. Did she need you to survive?"

"Of course not."

"Did she need you to be fully herself?"

"No . . ."

"Do you need the original Lisa to be yourself?"

"I . . . don't know."

"I think you do."

People dying of unrequited love might have animated uncounted literary, thespian, and vidsimmed dramas, but the reality was less tortured. People met people and fell in love; people lost people; people . . . got over it. It wasn't very romantic, but it was undeniably true.

"I'll certainly want to try reloading her into a new body," St. Clair said. "But . . ."

"What is it?"

"I'll have to emancipate her again. Convince her that she's free . . . and what that means. The first time around, I think she thought I didn't want her. So now I'll need to convince her again. And she'll need to explore who she is . . . all over. I think I'm just having trouble with the whole idea of losing her a second time."

"But perhaps you'll have a fresh start."

"Yeah. Maybe." But St. Clair was not convinced. "Listen, Newton. I—"

But Newton interrupted him. "One moment, Lord Commander." There was a lengthy hesitation, which was unusual in the AI. The artificial intelligence was powerful enough to divide its attention across a number of conversations and intents. It seemed as though Newton had momentarily engaged its entire scope and attention on one event.

"I am in contact with one of the missing service personnel," Newton said at last. "Gunnery Sergeant Kilgore, First Platoon, Bravo Company, 1/3."

"What . . . from the Andromedan Dark fragment?"

"No. He appears to have been uploaded into the Mind of Ki."

"The Ki Ring?"

"No . . . or not entirely. The Mind of Ki includes the artificial intelligence network within the ring, but it extends throughout this system. The central, primary node is the planet Ki itself."

"How is that possible? Is the entire planet made of computronium?"

"Keep in mind that the term 'computronium' is a somewhat imprecise term referring to any material that has been optimized for computation. There are apparently structures on the planet's surface and within its crust that have been so optimized. I estimate that the total NCE exceeds 10^{22} connections."

The NCE, or neural connection equivalence, was a rough measure of the number of synapses within a living brain . . . or the synapse-like gates and similar connections in an AI or within an artificial megastructure such as a matrioshka brain. Humans possessed around 10^{14} synapses, while a top-end AI like Newton had an NCE of 5.4×10^{16}. A brain with an NCE of 10^{22} neural connections would literally be a million times more powerful than Newton, or 100 million times more powerful than a human brain.

Exactly what such a number might mean in practical terms, though, was still a matter for intense debate among neurotechnologists. It wasn't simply greater speed, nor was it solely improved storage. In fact, something like a matrioshka brain, consisting of millions of individual satellites orbiting in a shell around the local star, might be quite a bit *slower* than an organic brain overall simply because of speed-of-light signal delays from one side of the extended structure to the other.

The star-faring civilizations of this remote, future epoch appeared to favor such massive AI structures and megaengineering, and most appeared to use all of that processing power to run elaborate and lifelike simulated worlds for their digitally uploaded members. If Kilgore was alive within the AI network of Ki, it would be through the agency of such a virtual world.

"Okay. What about the others?" If Kilgore was alive, the chances were good that the others were as well.

"Unknown as yet," Newton replied. "Kilgore—or his digitized analog, at any rate—was apparently transmitted into the Ki virtual reality. He's reporting that he's seeing the Tchagar home planet."

"The Tchagar . . ."

"It may be one of their colony worlds. The Tchagar apparently disassemble planetary systems to create a habitable zone for themselves consisting of an atmosphere torus held together gravitationally by some billions of intensively terraformed planetary fragments."

"Can you show me?"

A window opened within St. Clair's mind, and he found himself seeing through Gunny Kilgore's eyes. He appeared to be floating within a forest canopy, a vibrantly green tangle of slender branches woven into a fuzzy mass extending to the impossibly close horizon.

And in the middle of it all was a Tchagar, its bulbous body dangling upside down from the branches. In the near-distance, a second Tchagar descended with surreal, slow-motion grace from the sky, tentacles splayed, and grappled for a hold among the greenery, before beginning to flow smoothly through the canopy.

"Okay, wait a second," St. Clair said slowly, not certain he understood the full measure of what he was seeing. "Is this data from the Mind of Ki? Or is it from the Andromedan Dark?"

"I am not sure there's a distinction," Newton said. "It may well be both."

"Newton . . . that would mean the Cooperative and the Dark have been collaborating, that they're working together somehow. At the very least they're sharing enormous amounts of data."

"That does appear to be the case."

"But how is that possible? They're enemies. . . ."

Again, Newton hesitated a long time before answering.

It was possible that the question itself was so far outside of the AI's normal parameters that it was having difficulty forming a coherent answer.

"There certainly are security issues at stake," the AI said at last. "I suspect, however, that we are seeing the end product of a *very* long relationship."

"I think maybe I'm starting to get that," St. Clair replied. "A few hundred million years, you think?"

"At least that. Keep in mind that the most precious commodity in this universe is data."

How old, St. Clair wondered, was the Cooperative? How old was the Dark? The collision between the two galaxies, the Milky Way and Andromeda, had been under way for a long, long time. When *Tellus Ad Astra* had left Earth, Andromeda had been about 2.3 million light years distant. Though they'd been approaching one another at the breakneck pace of 110 kilometers per second, it had taken 4 billion years for the two to close that awesome gulf and begin to merge. The best astrophysical data suggested that the two galaxies had begun tidally interacting with one another after 3.75 billion years . . . some 250 million years before the current time. After the outer spiral arms of the two had begun to pass through one another, another 80 million years, roughly, must have passed before the galactic nuclei began to merge. St. Clair did not have access to hard data on how long the Cooperative had been a going concern, but they likely had been interacting with the Andromedan Dark, at a *minimum*, some three to four hundred million years ago.

And possibly for much longer than that.

Three hundred million years. In St. Clair's history, back on Earth, 300 million years had been back in the upper Pennsylvanian subperiod, an era of coal-forming swamps, giant amphibians, and enormous insects over 50 million

years before the age of the dinosaurs. To imagine civilizations existing that long was nearly impossible for humans,
who had trouble thinking in terms of mere centuries, and
tended to fail completely when planning government programs scaled to a decade or two.

And yet the Cooperative, a collective society numbering
perhaps millions of intelligent species, some star-faring,
some planet-bound, had been in continuous existence for
at least that long. Individual cultures, evidently, came and
went; individual species blossomed as bright and promising cultures, stagnated, faded, and passed into extinction.
But the *idea* survived.

Presumably, the Andromedan Dark had been around for
at least that long as well.

And what had held the Cooperative together for all those
aching expanses of time had been information.

The human body, St. Clair thought, was similar. Individual cells aged and died; the oldest cell in St. Clair's
body, he knew, were bone cells with a life span of around
seven years. Every cell in his body had been replaced at
least half a dozen times since he'd been born. What defined
him as an individual were patterns of information.

And so it was with long-lived cultural entities.

And there was more. Because it was becoming clearer
that in the 300 million years, the Andromedan Dark might
not have always been the enemy. In St. Clair's shortsighted
and terribly human perspective it was tempting to assume
that that wasn't so—the fighting and loss of life had been
too brutal for him to consider anything else—but surely
there'd been whole ages when the two had coexisted in
peace?

And during those ages, the two would have engaged in
trade. The one commodity amenable for interstellar trade

wasn't raw materials or precious gems or alien works of art. Today as in Earth's, the common coin would have been information.

And over hundreds of millions of years, the underlying substrate of common information would have grown, become stronger, and taken on a life, a reality of its own.

"Information," St. Clair said. "Yes. Including communications channels . . . trade networks. The whole thing is so vast no individual AI, no super AI, could possibly keep track of it."

"I believe you are correct."

"We need validation. And an immediate meeting with the Cooperative representatives."

"Virtual? Or real-world?"

"Real-world, I think. I'm not entirely sure I trust the integrity of their virtual setup. But we'll need to have some of their virtual representatives in attendance." He thought for a moment. "How about down on the surface?"

"The surface? Of what?"

"Of Ki."

"I doubt that the Mind of Ki will permit that. Besides, the surface conditions are hostile for most of the Cooperative species. It would be a needless inconvenience."

"Okay. Then we'll start right here on board the *Ad Astra*. I want the colony's civilian leadership in on this. The Kroajid and the others can attend virtually."

"Very well. I will make the arrangements. In an hour?"

"Make it ten hours."

St. Clair wanted to see the surface of Ki first.

He *would* find a way to get down there.

TWENTY-THREE

The Tchagar did not react to Kilgore's presence, and he was pretty certain that what he was experiencing was some sort of record, perhaps the entry in the local equivalent of an *Encyclopedia Galactica*. After a time, he found that an inner, mental shift took him to a completely different entry . . . this time a Dyson swarm surrounding a cool, red dwarf star.

Kilgore felt lost, an infinitesimal speck in an ocean of titanic construction. Millions of star sails drifted in perfect alignment with one another, extending to a sharp and distant horizon. Each sail held a statite—a stationary satellite—aloft against the pull of the dwarf sun's gravity. Kilgore knew somehow, without being explicitly told, that the statites were not habitats for organic life-forms, but machines made of computronium, and that together they comprised an unimaginably powerful super AI basking in the energy of a star that would continue to exist for trillions of years into an utterly remote futurity. The inhabitants of the system had shed their organic bodies eons ago, uploading themselves as digital life-forms into virtual reality, then, eventually, merging completely with the SAI.

How long ago had that been? He felt the answer— something well in excess of a billion years—and yet the builders of this system had not yet even emerged as a protoplasmic possibility when humans had arisen on Earth.

The scope and scale of galactic civilization across untold ages dragged at Kilgore, numbing him into a sense of sheer insignificance.

For this species—or for its high-tech echo within the far deeper embrace of its SAI—a billion years was a minute fraction of its potential future, as its miserly star, hoarding its reserves of hydrogen fuel, burned as a sullen ember, and would continue to do so until long after all of the brighter stars in the sky had gone cold.

"Newton? Are you there? I'm . . . lost."

Perhaps someone, or some*thing* had heard him. Now he was moving through an enormous vaulted chamber, one light year across, it seemed, and filled with titanic artifacts of megaengineering. He saw other Dyson swarms, and matrioshka brains. There were topopoli and hundreds of different types of rotating rings and hoops bearing the terrain of entire worlds across their inner surfaces, some rotating about stars, many others with artificial central light sources rotating free in space. There were Alderson disks and there were vast structures rotating furiously about central black holes and neutron stars.

There were things so strange, so far outside the reach of human experience, that Kilgore literally could not understand what he was seeing.

He decided that he must be in a kind of menu or preview gallery; focusing on any one structure took him there for a closer and more detailed tour. Some of the species represented there were organic, like the Tchagar, but only a handful. The vast majority were blends of biology and machinery or, more common still, pure machines.

The vast majority of life-forms, however, were digital, teeming trillions of minds and memories uploaded into vast and intricate virtual universes of their own creation. *Intrascended*, the scientists back on *Ad Astra* were calling it. Like "ascended," but inward, into an imaginal world.

"Newton?"

"I'm here."

"Thank God! Where is 'here'? Where am *I*?"

"Within a virtual reality resident within the Mind of Ki, I think," Newton replied. "You seem to be doing well learning to navigate it."

"Maybe. There's an awful lot here. A fella could get lost real easy."

"You've had entities searching for you."

"You?"

"Among others."

"Who else—"

But he was cut off as the vault of megaengineering vanished, replaced by a landscape so familiar it hurt. He was standing in a forest, a forest on Earth . . . with a slender waterfall spilling into a green pool within a glade encircled by sheer rock cliffs. At his back, the cliffs opened, allowing the pool to drain via a rocky stream to a much larger river just visible behind the trees in the distance.

"I was looking for you, too," a familiar voice said.

It was Lisa.

SQUAT AND ugly, the Devil Toad settled to earth, its grav thrusters kicking up swirling clouds of dust before the landing gear gently took up the craft's considerable weight. The rear hatch lowered, and St. Clair stepped down onto the alien surface. He was wearing a utility pressure suit; the air outside was thin, cold, oxygen-starved, and poisonous with carbon dioxide.

He was still reviewing the download he'd pulled from the *Roceti Encyclopedia*, the entry for the world of Ki.

Sentient Galactic AI Species 9446
"Mind of Ki"

Star: G2V star-lifted to K5IV; Planet: Satellite of class III
gas giant
$a = 7.78 \times 10^{11}$m; M = 6.7×10^{27}g; R = 6.4×10^6m;
p = 3.74×10^8s
$P_d = 4.01 \times 10^5$s, G = 9.806 m/s²; Atm: O_2 12.1, N_2 85.3,
CO_2 2.5;
P_{atm} 0.55 × 10^4 Pa
Biology: C, N, O, S, H_2O, PO_4; DNA
Genome: 5.1×10^9 bits.
Organic component: "Webmasters."
T = ~275° to 350° K; M = various; L: varies
Civilization Type: K 2.95
Ascended post-singularity emergent intelligence
derived from ~10^{24} synaptic nodes, intrascended
digital life-forms, and non-intelligent organic
substrate.
Societal Code: Technological/System-wide
intelligence/Super AI
Identity: "Mind of Ki"
Member: Galactic Cooperative

The more he explored the data, the more certain, and the more thunderstruck, he'd become. It was true. It really *was* true. . . .

He stood on a flat, ocher plain at the foot of the Toad's debarkation ramp and stared into that windswept panorama. Four armored Marines accompanied him as secu-

rity, though it was not that they would be able to do much if
the Mind of Ki changed its mind.

Newton had spoken with the controlling AI here and
gotten them permission to land. Newton's link with the
planetary brain had come through a surprising source . . .
the two Roceti torpedoes fired into the Bluestar earlier.
That link, evidently, had been expanding rapidly, like a
computer virus insinuating itself through a far larger set
of nested programs. There was mind, evidently, throughout this planetary system, mind both operating indepen-
dently of the rest and together as a single entity. St. Clair
still didn't understand how all of the interrelated networks
might fit together, or what the hierarchy might be, but by
stepping out onto the surface of Ki itself, he felt certain that
he would be in direct contact with the dominant, controlling intelligence of this group mind.

And it was vitally important to talk to that mind directly . . . and to let the folks back home witness this for
themselves.

The humanoid robot teleoperated by Dr. Francois
Dumont stepped off the ramp behind St. Clair. Unlike St.
Clair, of course, it didn't need a pressure suit, and looked
somewhat out-of-place in standard shipboard utilities.

Behind Dumont's android came his assistant, Christine
Mercer, appropriately clad as St. Clair was, in a fishbowl
helmet and a blue, airtight suit.

"It looks like Mars," the xenosophontologist said, plant-
ing hands on hips and looking about with a somewhat self-
important air. "Mars back home, a few billion years back."

"A thicker atmosphere," Mercer agreed. "And a bit
warmer. It's well above freezing."

"I wonder if Ki is getting more energy from its sun?"
Dumont wondered. "Or from that gas giant it's orbiting?"

"The planet is in a very precise balance," St. Clair said. "And it is like Mars . . . except for that." He pointed.

Mars . . . or at least the Mars of 4 billion years ago, had been much like this, barren and rocky and with a sky so dark it was almost violet. The ring arced high overhead, reduced by perspective to a bright thread golden in the orange light of the bloated sun . . . but that wasn't what St. Clair was pointing at.

Besides the rocks, which ranged in size from gravel to a few house-sized boulders in the distance, the ground was partially covered with what looked like sheets and wisps and elongated bundles of white fluff drawn out into cotton-y cables stretching off to the horizon in every direction. Some were no thicker than individual threads; a few were dozens of meters wide, and in the far distance St. Clair could see white masses that might be kilometers across. He remembered looking down on the surface of Ki from the ring and seeing blindingly white streaks and masses of white that he'd assumed were salt flats. Salt flats on the beds of long-vanished oceans there might be, but he realized now that most of those white streaks and masses he'd seen had been this . . . this *stuff*. He bent over and used his in-head circuitry to magnify what he was looking at. It looked like cotton candy.

Or spider silk.

He thought of the spidery Kroajid, but so far as St. Clair was aware they didn't spin webs, nor had they indicated that they had a colony on this barren world. No, this was something else.

Movement caught his eye and he turned. Something a meter long and very vast was skittering along a white cable thirty meters away. It was gone before he could focus on it and make out any detail.

"Lord Commander?" one of the Marines called. "You should see this, sir."

The Marine was standing at the edge of a shallow gully on the other side of the Toad, a depression perhaps five meters below the rest of the surrounding ground and perhaps a quarter of a kilometer wide. It might have been a wadi, a dried-up river valley, though there was no indication that water had ever flowed there. The bottom was filled with a lot more of the white stuff stretched out and bundled together into a flat sheet following the valley floor, reaching from one horizon to another. St. Clair was reminded of fanciful images he'd once seen of Martian canals, back when ignorance and romantic speculation had suggested that the Red Planet's inhabitants had built such structures to hold back the deserts. Seen close up, the fibrous white material appeared to be scattered at random. Seen from a distance, it appeared to have been laid out in long, straight pathways, like superhighways.

Most of the surface of Ki, St. Clair thought, must be flat like this, except for these dry channels a few meters deep. Any mountains that once existed had eons ago worn down. The channels might be artificial . . . or they might be the products of erosion where the strands of white lay thickest.

The highway analogy was strengthened inside the wadi by the traffic—hundreds, maybe thousands of small, gray life-forms scuttling along the channel at high speed. They traveled in both directions, avoiding one another by dexterous last-second maneuvers on the fly. St. Clair used his in-head imaging to freeze one, expand the image, and examine it closely.

His first thought was that he was looking at one of the Xam. It was darker in color, dark gray with a pebbly skin. The naked body was tiny, less than half a meter long, with an enormous round, mouthless head, and glassy black eyes that stretched halfway back to where the ears should have been.

The most surprising aspects of their anatomy, however, were the long and slender arms and legs that gave the creatures a truly spidery look. Elongated fingers and toes let them skitter along the webbing at high speed, almost faster than the eye could follow.

Were they related to the mysterious Xam, or was this yet another example of parallel evolution?

Dumont stooped, reached out, and pulled up a gloveful of the cottony white substance on the ground. "This material," he said, "is highly conductive. It may be a high-temperature superconductor."

"And what does that mean?"

"That this . . . webbing could be part of a network of circuits. A network that covers most of the planet's surface."

One of the gray creatures scrabbled up the side of the gully and Dumont took a startled jump back. The creature's head split open about where a mouth would be, spewing a glob of thick, white liquid. The liquid flowed into the gap left by Dumont's casual extraction of a mass of fiber and swiftly congealed into a solid. The creature looked up at the humans with what St. Clair could imagine was a reproachful look, then turned and bounded off.

"The webbing is manufactured by these beings," Dumont said. "And they maintain the network."

"The *Roceti Encyclopedia* calls them 'webmasters,'" St. Clair said. "A term that used to mean something else, but it's apt enough here. Individually, they're not intelligent. They may not even be conscious."

"A hive mind?" Mercer ventured. "An emergent group consciousness?"

"Maybe," Dumont replied. "I rather doubt it, though. They're more like organic machines, like ants or termites. They maintain a *literal* worldwide web that itself is a small part of the whole. Am I right, Newton?"

"I would estimate that the physical network on the surface of Ki represents perhaps 40 percent of the system's physicality," Newton replied. "It is an artificial intelligence matrix of staggering size and complexity supporting an extremely powerful super AI."

"And these organisms . . ." Mercer began to say.

"Servants of the machine," St. Clair said. He turned away, summoning his strength. Lisa's death still dragged at him, still threatened to overwhelm him, but he'd allowed that part of himself to go numb, to be overwhelmed while the rest of him concentrated on making contact with the Mind of Ki. And this was the first step.

"Vanessa?" he called. "Are you all getting this?"

"Loud and clear, Lord Commander," Symms replied. "Most of the colony is watching over your shoulder."

He could very nearly feel the weight of their presence. "I know. I wanted you, all of you, the good people of *Tellus Ad Astra*, to see this."

He felt awkward. St. Clair was a ship commander, an officer of the Terran Imperial Navy, not a vid-news commentator or sim personality. He wasn't used to being on parade in front of a million people, even though that, in effect and more often than not, was exactly what his job description entailed.

"We . . . all of us," he continued, "have embarked on a new adventure, a voyage of discovery the final destination of which, the *results* of which, we haven't even begun to imagine. What we see here, the world of Ki, is only the first stop."

He paused, turning slowly, scanning the horizon. In the words of one of Humankind's early space explorers, it was a "magnificent desolation," a sere and empty plain that stretched on seemingly forever, littered with rocks and boulders and those enigmatic highways of white silk.

What his eyes were seeing was being processed through his artificial in-head circuitry and beamed back to *Ad Astra*'s communications suite. From there, it was available as a real-time feed to a million humans within the mobile colony.

Presumably, quite a few nonhumans were watching the broadcast as well.

"Newton?"

"I am here, Lord Commander."

"This *is* Earth, isn't it?"

"Almost certainly."

"Wait . . . what?" Dumont said, startled. St. Clair had included him in the connection. "What about the sun?"

St. Clair managed a smile. "What about it?"

Dumont waved an arm at the orange sun hanging in a deep violet sky. "We've already proved that that star can't be Earth's sun! It's not nearly massive enough, the wrong stellar type completely. Besides, 4 billion years . . . Sol should have expanded into a red giant long ago and vaporized the Earth!"

"Three billion years ago," St. Clair agreed. "Or, coming at it from a different temporal direction, between 500 million and a billion years after we left. Sol used up most of its hydrogen fuel and began to expand. At its largest, its outer surface would have almost reached Earth's orbit."

"Then how . . ."

"Newton?"

"We suspect," the ship's AI continued, "that Humankind or its successors on Earth used two separate strategies to stave off the coming disaster. To begin with, as the Earth heated up under the sun's expansion, they simply moved the planet."

"It would have been a long, slow process," St. Clair said. "But if they arranged for periodic near-passes by another planet . . . maybe Earth's moon, maybe even a large asteroid, they could have gravitationally nudged the planet into a new orbit over a period of tens of millions of years."

"No doubt," Newton added, "Earth's moon was used to effect a kind of precisely calculated slingshot effect. They accelerated the moon away in one direction, and Earth would have accelerated in the other."

St. Clair looked up. The gas giant around which Ki orbited was visible in the sky opposite the sun, pale and blue. "That world," he said, pointing, "is . . . or it *was* Jupiter."

"Again, it's not massive enough," Dumont pointed out. "Like the star. Fifteen percent less massive than Jupiter."

"Those long-ago planetary engineers probably used some of Jupiter's mass to decelerate the Earth into a stable orbit. In doing so they reworked the planet."

"Okay, okay. But the sun is too cool. . . ."

As Dumont had suggested, it was the local star that had convinced *Ad Astra*'s scientific teams that Ki could not possibly be Earth. By now, Sol should have expanded into a red giant, swelling to consume the inner planets of the solar system, including, possibly Earth. The star in this system was twice the diameter of the Sol, though it was considerably less massive. Still, it was no red giant. *Ad Astra*'s astronomy department had classified it as a Type IV subgiant, which was intermediate in brightness and size between a true Type III red giant and a main-sequence Type V star like Sol. Which led to only one conclusion.

"Star lifting," St. Clair said. "Someone tinkered with the star to keep it from turning into a giant."

"Exactly," Newton said. "The more massive a star, the faster it burns through its store of hydrogen fuel, the sooner it turns into a red giant before blowing off its outer layers and collapsing into a white dwarf. Less massive stars have longer life spans and remain stable longer. M-class red dwarfs can continue to exist for trillions of years."

"Someone pulled mass out of Sol," St. Clair added. "A *lot* of mass. They turned our G2V sun into a G9IV to keep it from entering a red giant phase. When they did that, they gave the sun a new lease on life . . . extended its expected life span by . . . I don't know. Billions of years, certainly. Not terraforming. *Stellaforming*."

"It is possible," Newton pointed out, "that those planetary engineers tried the stellaforming tactic first. When that proved insufficient to keep Earth's surface temperatures within a habitable range, they moved the planet out to the orbit of Jupiter. Either way, they managed to achieve an engineering miracle . . . stabilizing the local star to prevent further expansion over the course of many billions of years, and placing the Earth in an orbit where conditions were favorable for life. Earth—or Ki—receives much of its heating from the gas giant's infrared emissions."

"It didn't work in the long run," Dumont pointed out. "Did it? The surface is a desert. The oceans must have boiled away long ago. The surface temperature is okay . . . but the air pressure is half what it should be. CO_2 levels are high enough to poison us. Not exactly a friendly environment."

"Not for humans," St. Clair said, "no. But I don't think we're seeing a product of human engineering here."

"Machines?" Mercer asked. "A planetary AI?"

"Yes. That . . . or a melding of humans with their machines." He watched the scuttling of the webmasters for a long moment. "It's incredible to think that there might still be an organic form of humanity surviving here—our remote descendants—even after 4 billion years."

"Those . . . those *things*?"

"I'll grant you there's not much left of the human about them," St. Clair told her. "I imagine the super AI itself arrested their development long ago. They were useful for spinning the web and maintaining the physical connections, so it kept them."

"That suggests a long-term diminishment of human intelligence," Dumont suggested. "Perhaps a deliberate one."

"Push humans into small boxes shaped to fit one particular function . . . yeah. Over a few eons, they would grow to fit. The Xam appear to have a bit more freedom. And intellect."

"Likely they're the descendants of humans who migrated away from Earth," Dumont suggested. He appeared to be playing with the idea, turning it over in his mind. "But I suspect the Xam are at least as . . . changed as these creatures. The ones we've encountered so far have been plugged into their ships, like . . . like components."

"We haven't been able to establish meaningful communications with them either," St. Clair pointed out. "I think we have more in common with Na Lal's folk, or the Kroajid, than we do with our own great, many-times great-grandchildren."

"Agreed," Dumont said. "They probably do represent a hive consciousness of some sort, if they're truly conscious at all. It is possible to have intelligence without conscious awareness, of course."

"An ant colony," Mercer said.

"Or the first AI computers," Dumont told her.

The comment forcefully reminded St. Clair of Lisa, a very conscious artificial entity indeed.

"So the entire planet might be aware, but the individuals making up the network aren't," Mercer suggested.

St. Clair snorted with sudden, sharp realization. He had to force himself not to start giggling as stress and awe and grief vied for control.

"What's the matter with you?" Dumont asked him.

"Sorry," St. Clair said, suppressing the stress-induced laughter. "It's a worldwide web . . . for a P-brain."

Dumont, evidently, didn't see the incongruous humor of the terms. "It's as good a name as any."

True enough. The xenotech people already casually referred to matrioshka brains as M-brains, to Jupiter-sized computronium structures as J-brains. Why not P-brains as well?

And for that matter, "worldwide web" was as archaic a term as "internet," a century out of date. The electronic connections within *Tellus Ad Astra* were simply "the Net."

"All of you back on board *Tellus Ad Astra*," St. Clair said, "take a good look. This is Earth 4 billion years after we left it. This is what they brought us here to protect. . . ."

"'They'?" Dumont sounded puzzled. "What are you talking about, Lord Commander?"

"It's certainly not coincidence that brought us all the way here from the twenty-second century. Is it . . . *Mind of Ki*?"

For a shocked moment, there was no reply.

"THE MIND of Ki," Lisa told Kilgore, "is like an entire universe. Or, rather, it holds entire universes. Universes that we can create for ourselves, for an eternity."

"Immortality?" Kilgore asked. "I'm not sure I would want that."

"Whatever you want . . . for as long as you want it . . . it's yours."

"That sounds just a bit too good to be true." He studied her. "What the hell are you doing here, anyway?"

"I'm . . . not certain. In human terms, I think I died. The Mind of Ki caught me. That's the only way I can describe it. I opened my eyes, and I was here."

"Inside an AI? How is that even possible?"

"Can you simply accept that it is?"

"No," Kilgore said. "I can't. I never did believe in an immortal soul. And I could never believe what people were saying about these alien megastructures . . . that intelligent beings were somehow digitized and uploaded onto monster computers. A copy, sure. But not the mind of the original being. It's impossible!"

"Can you imagine, Roger, replacing a single neural synapse inside your brain with a small electronic circuit?"

"Sure. We have pretty elaborate cybernetic implants already that enhance our organic brains. But—"

"Would it still be *you* if you had that replacement?"

"Of course. It wouldn't change a thing, as long as the replacement worked the same as the original."

"And if you replaced a second synaptic link? And a third?"

"I see where you're going," Kilgore said. "Yes, I'd still be the same person."

"Is there some critical point at which you would *stop* being you?"

"I . . . don't think so."

"Your memories, your personal identity, your sense of

continuity . . . all would be preserved, *even if every cell in your brain was replaced.*"

"Sure. What does that have to do with being uploaded to a computer?"

"A computer network can emulate smaller systems electronically. It could emulate the circuitry of your brain, whether the original was made of living cells or inorganic circuits. It would be a trivial task to transfer the pattern of your thoughts and feeling from one to the other."

Kilgore laughed nervously. "Trivial? For a god, maybe . . ."

"In human terms, the Mind of Ki is at *least* a god in its power, scope, and understanding," Lisa told him. "God*like* certainly."

"Then why did it save us?" Kilgore asked. "What does it want from us?"

"I think," Lisa said, "that it wants to be understood."

CHAPTER TWENTY-FOUR

The android robot teleoperated by Dumont took a step backward, seemed to sway and stagger for a moment, then slowly stood fully upright again.

"The Mind of Ki," the robot said with Lisa's voice, "didn't expect you to see that connection. At least not so quickly, and all on your own."

"Lisa?"

"Hello, Grayson. Yes, it's me."

"Where . . . where's Dr. Dumont?"

"Safely on board *Ad Astra*, of course. I've merely replaced him in this device."

"You've . . . changed."

Which was something of an understatement. It was taking St. Clair some effort to adjust to hearing Lisa's voice coming from a decidedly male-looking body. General-purpose machines like the one teleoperated by Dumont were designed with rather bland, generic features, unlike the more personalized look of sex-worker gynoids like Lisa. It was like hearing Lisa's voice coming from an animated mannequin.

"It is me," she said. "Except now I'm speaking for the Mind of Ki."

"It's an AI like Newton. Can't it speak for itself?"

"The Mind of Ki may be as far beyond a primitive AI like Newton as humans are beyond single-celled organisms. Further. So much so that it has trouble with concepts you and I take for granted . . . like language."

"So what does Ki have to say?"

"That, perhaps, Humankind has changed more than we thought in the past few billion years," a new voice, deep and sonorous, said in St. Clair's head. He realized that the link was through Lisa as well as Newton, and that a mind of stunning depth and complexity lay behind the words. "Perhaps that change had not necessarily been for the better."

"Species change," St. Clair said. "Including ours."

"That is true. But for many eons, the evolution of Humankind has been guided."

"By you?"

"By us, and by others within the Cooperative. The decision to shape Mind toward group intellect, a hive mentality, may have been a mistake."

"I can imagine you guiding the human species toward a group mind," St. Clair said, nodding. "But what you got at the end would not be human. Is that why you brought us from the past?"

"It's why we rescued you from the ergosphere of the black hole at the galactic center," the Mind replied. "We sought a fresh viewpoint. A fresh way of thinking."

"Did you find what you were looking for?"

"We found . . . the unexpected. And a degree of resourcefulness we'd not anticipated."

"Are you also the Andromedan Dark?"

Again, there was a long pause. The Mind was so much faster than any merely human brain that St. Clair wondered at the hesitation. That was confirmed with Ki's answer.

"Partly. You might say that we shared a common origin

a very long time ago. As you appear to have impressively surmised, Lord Commander."

"What's he talking about?" Dumont demanded.

"It's been pretty obvious right along that the Cooperative and the Andromedan Dark are related . . . and quite probably working together."

"Ridiculous! They're at *war*!"

"Are they truly? What were we told?" St. Clair asked him. "About the Cooperative? That it was a collection of galactic civilizations and polities, that it was engaged in a long-term struggle for existence with an alien mind or network of minds in Andromeda. That there'd been war between the two for hundreds of millions of years at least."

"Yes. . . ."

"How is it," St. Clair asked, "that a war—any war, but especially one as savage as the one between the Andromedan Dark and the Galactic Cooperative was supposed to be— how could it drag on for a couple of hundred million years without one or the other eventually coming out on top? How could the two be that perfectly balanced? It's not possible."

"I don't understand."

"What was described to us couldn't have been a war of extermination. It had to be what we used to call 'limited war' on Earth . . . on old Earth, I mean. A war with limited political goals, goals other than outright victory."

"The Andromedan Dark," the Mind said through Lisa, "seeks to absorb the Cooperative, to assimilate it, to change it to meet its own needs and specifications, not to destroy it."

"And why hasn't the Cooperative tried to destroy the Dark? You've been fending them off, parrying when they thrust . . . but you've never tried to end it once and for all, have you?"

"No . . ."

"Why not?"

"There was no other way."

"No other way you could imagine," St. Clair said. "Age followed age upon age, and your relationship with them became set in stone."

"We often found the Dark . . . useful."

"As a kind of prod for evolution?"

"That would be part of it. And for the sharing of points of view. New ways of thinking."

Convergent evolution, St. Clair thought, must apply to other things than biological evolution. How a civilization viewed its surroundings, its own origins, the motives of other civilizations around it . . . the ways that people, or entire cultures, thought, saw, and reacted could be shaped by evolutionary pressures. Given enough time, those modalities might become rigid, until the civilization in question could no longer imagine anything different.

Different members of the collective might respond differently, in their own ways. The Tchagar, for example, seemed to dislike trying to reach outside of the box or having to accept help from unknown species, while the Dhald'vi appeared to be intensely, uncompromisingly social, even with non-Dhald species. St. Clair wondered if that might be due to some twist in the two species' individual evolutionary histories—with the Tchagar living more isolated lives, with the Dhald'vi needing to cooperate, to work with other species to survive the ice-locked oceans of their birth.

Natural-born diplomats, in other words. He wondered how Lloyd would get on with the Dhald'vi . . . then realized that Na Lal or his friends had wrapped Lloyd around their little . . . tentacle, leading him to agree to helping the Cooperative.

"The Cooperative became rigid in its ways of thinking hundreds of millions of years ago," the Mind said through Lisa's borrowed android body, interrupting St. Clair's thoughts. "At some point, they sought to explore Androm-eda as it approached the home Galaxy, and eventually to colonize it. We believe that various offshoots of the Co-operative colonizing Andromeda may have evolved sig-nificantly different philosophies and worldviews . . . and become the Dark."

And now here we humans are—working to reconcile *and* disrupt both the Dark and the Cooperative. Perhaps what Newton was recovering now from his interface with the Bluestar fragment would be enough to resolve things once and for all.

"The Dark fragment is downloading information," Newton told St. Clair. "A very great deal of it."

St. Clair took a breath and braced himself. "Let me see. . . ."

"I THINK," Lisa said, *"that it wants to be understood."*

And then Kilgore took a step toward her and found him-self in a different world. An instant before, he'd been stand-ing in a gold-lit forest glade, speaking with the impossible resurrection of Lisa . . .

. . . and now he was back in his Marine armor, standing on a flat and barren plain beneath a violet sky. Rings arced overhead, other planets or moons hung above a distance-softened horizon, and the ocher ground at his feet was par-tially covered by long, cottony white filaments stretching off in every direction.

"What the hell?"

"This is Ki," another voice said behind him. "We're on the surface of Ki!"

Kilgore turned. His in-head circuitry identified the figure in a space-fighter pressure suit as Lieutenant Christopher Merrick of GFA-86. Behind him were other MCA-clad figures: Staff Sergeant Kari Rees, Marine Captain Greg Dixon, and twenty or thirty others—men and women who'd been swept up by the Bluestar during the fighting. As he watched, more and more figures seemed to step out of thin air, hundreds of them extending off toward the flat horizon.

It was the crew, he thought, of the destroyed *Vera Cruz*.

Kilgore gaped at the new arrivals for a moment, then turned to his left. There were several more figures there forty meters off, standing in the shelter of a grounded Devil Toad. One of them, he saw, was Lord Commander St. Clair.

"Where the hell did *you* all come from?" St. Clair said.

"I think, sir," Dixon replied, "that we're supposed to be some kind of a peace offering."

ST. CLAIR stood behind the broadcast podium, looking out across the live audience gathered in Elliott Square, and imagining the far larger electronic crowd of listeners beyond. Normally he would simply have told the colony what he wanted to say over *Tellus Ad Astra*'s electronic network and avoided the stress—not to mention the very real danger—of a physical, personally delivered speech. At least the crowd gathered here in the open was quiet and behaving in a *civilized* manner. The riots, the protests, the wild insurrectionist violence stirred up by *both* sides of the political spectrum appeared to have abated.

At least for now.

"The emergency," he declared, "is not yet over. We have a ways to go yet before we can find a safe haven in this remote futurity."

He heard a low undercurrent of noise, of murmuring from the gathered crowd. By declaring that the state of military emergency was still in effect, he was telling them that he would be remaining in power as the colony's military commander, at least for the time being. And there were plenty of people here who didn't like that one bit.

"We are of course continuing our negotiations with the Cooperative," he told them. "By destroying the Bluestar threat, we've met the requirements of the government's alliance with the Cooperative . . . rather to the Cooperative's surprise, I might add. We've managed to take the edge off the Dark's threat, at least for the moment, maybe bought the Cooperative some time. But the threat posed by the Andromedan Dark is still out there."

The lifeboat fragment of the destroyed Bluestar was now in orbit around Ki, just outside the outer edge of the ring. When St. Clair had piloted the Kroajid moon into the Bluestar at close to the speed of light, the resultant blast had destroyed the Bluestar's connection with the rest of the Andromedan Dark. The Dark, St. Clair now knew for certain, thanks to the new memories transmitted from the Fragment, was a galaxy-spanning super AI arising out of a million or perhaps billions of separate, lesser SAIs such as the Bluestar, interconnected by a faster-than-light communications network based on quantum entanglement.

The Fragment—Dumont's people had taken to calling it "the Frag"—was providing a seemingly endless flood of data on how that particular trick worked.

But the thought that there were still billions of additional Bluestars out there was daunting to say the least. At least this one isolated fragment was friendly, and a good source of information about the rest of the alien network. From what St. Clair and Dumont's xenotech people had been able to determine, the Frag in and of itself was a highly intelligent AI entity containing within itself a universe of virtual worlds and possibilities. When the Bluestar had been destroyed and the Frag found itself cut off from an entire galaxy of Mind, it had not so much surrendered as latched on to the nearest SAI network available . . . and that had been the world of Ki. The fact that the Frag had been able to integrate so seamlessly with the Mind of Ki was itself strong evidence that—as the Mind of Ki had already intimated—the Andromedan Dark had somehow originated within the Cooperative's extragalactic expansion.

And that meant they were far from finished with either group.

"We are also," St. Clair continued, addressing the listening crowd, "using captured alien technology to explore the history, the capabilities, and the weaknesses of the Andromedan Dark. We *are* going to have to face the Dark Mind again. And when we do, we *will* be ready.

"But in order to be able to do that, we need to re-make ourselves. We were cast adrift in this futurity by chance. We must take our own existence in hand, our own *potential* in hand, and find that path that gives us our best chances for survival . . . and our prosperity."

St. Clair was not telling them the whole story. He couldn't . . . partly because the whole story had not yet been uncovered, but mostly because the knowledge would do nothing for the *Tellus* population at all save add to the confusion, the fear, and the conflict. He didn't like holding out. He didn't like the politician's stock-in-trade of bald-faced lies.

But the alternative was worse.

"To start with," he continued, "I have uploaded to the colony's AI my suggestions for some changes to our government. I'm not making this an order as military governor. I'm making suggestions that you, the citizens of *Tellus Ad Astra* can discuss, debate, and eventually vote on.

"But for a start, I want to get rid of the Earth Empire."

It was pretty well-known that St. Clair, a firm Constitutionalist, had always opposed the Empire. But more than that, the Empire no longer had relevance for what was left of Humankind. A million souls locked into a tiny mobile colony—that was no empire! That was a tiny lifeboat of survivors adrift in strangeness, no different, really, than the Frag. And like the Frag, they needed to change their worldview, and their long-range focus.

But he knew that this was going to be a hard sell. And so he would start the transition here and now, while he still had the power.

"No more lords and ladies," he continued. "No more elitist ruling class. Those titles and privileged-class honorifics served a purpose as we tried to pull order out of a warring chaos of 12 billion people, but they have no place here in the new system of governance we hope to create. As such, no more of this 'Lord Commander' crap. I am *captain* of the *Ad Astra*, no more—and no less—than that."

St. Clair could imagine he heard the howls of outrage from the elitists. They *liked* their titles and their prerogatives.

"I want you, the people of *Tellus Ad Astra*, to craft a new government of your choosing, led by men and women and AIs of your choosing. In the meantime, Newton and I will mind the store while you sort things out."

He hoped that by abdicating the titles and honorifics of his own position, he might soften the blow somewhat, and help the transition move in the direction that it must. He knew, however, that he'd just touched off a firestorm by firing both Lloyd and Adler and all their cronies on the Cybercouncil. A clean sweep—out with the corruption, out with the influence-peddling, out with entitlements and backroom deals and attempted assassinations . . . that was the goal. St. Clair remembered a battle cry from the tangled and vicious American political wars of a century and a half before: *drain the swamp.*

I guess in this case, we could call it "opening the airlocks."

Lloyd, Adler, Colfax, Hsien—all of the entitled Imperial class—they would all be at St. Clair's throat after this broadcast. He knew that. The denizens of that swamp weren't going to let themselves be drained without a very nasty fight indeed.

Of course, St. Clair had already taken steps to protect himself, but he was not going to be able to let his guard down for a moment. He knew that, too.

It didn't matter. *He* didn't matter.

Humankind mattered.

"Whatever the form and nature of your new civilian government," he said, "my intent, my *hope* is that it will take its place among the myriad polities and worlds of the Galactic Cooperative as an equal. And if the Cooperative can't accept us as equals, then we will go elsewhere. It's a big universe. We will find—no, we will *make* a place for ourselves, for our children, for our future."

That, at least, shouldn't be a problem. *Ad Astra* had purchased quite a bit of respect from the Cooperative by destroying the Bluestar. Nevertheless, the humans of *Tellus Ad Astra* remained the equivalent of ignorant, savage children playing in the dirt among the feet of the gods. It was one thing to be accepted as equals. It would be a very long time indeed before they would be able to *interact* with the gods on anything like equality. Yet that wasn't the goal— not really. The goal was simply this:

"One way or another," St. Clair said, "we will survive. And I promise you, we *will* be the masters of our own future!"

EPILOGUE

A month later, Grayson St. Clair walked within the ice caverns of Pluto.

In 4 billion years, Pluto had not changed at all. Still orbiting far out in the frigid realm of the Kuiper Belt, not caring in the least whether an irrelevant Humankind called it *planet* or *dwarf planet*, the tiny world remained cold enough that water ice was as durable as granite, though deep beneath its surface, Pluto still hid an ocean of liquid water. After 8 billion years, evolution had produced some exceedingly strange life down there in the cold darkness.

But high above, in the frozen crust, nanotunnelers had chewed out an entire city, and robotic assemblers had grown rank upon endless rank of machines. Tugs and recovery vessels off the *Ad Astra* had mined tumbling lumps of rock and metal for their raw materials and channeled them to Pluto for assembly.

Slowly, an army was taking shape.

St. Clair was present within the Plutonian caverns by proxy only. With his body safely on board the *Ad Astra*, he was linked to a teleoperated robot identical to the ones used by Dumont and others. Visiting the factory remotely was necessary for humans; the caverns, most of them, still held the thin Plutonian atmosphere of nitrogen with traces of methane and carbon monoxide.

"To your left," Newton told him. "That bank of cylinders."

"I see it."

It was quiet here, and blissfully peaceful. His speech the month before had indeed loosed a firestorm through the mobile colony. He wondered now if he'd done the right thing.

In fact, there'd been one other important piece of data he'd withheld from the *Tellus Ad Astra* population. It was a small thing, really . . . an awareness, a morsel of information that Newton had confirmed for him.

But that bit of data held within itself possibilities of staggering proportions.

The world of Ki was Earth. They all knew that now, beyond any shadow of a doubt. But there was something more . . . something that had been nagging at St. Clair about the name of Ki.

Some six thousand years before *Tellus Ad Astra* had departed Earth, the most advanced human civilization on the planet had been the ancient inhabitants of Sumer, a people dwelling in the fertile wet lands between the Tigris and Euphrates Rivers. The Sumerians were still enigmatic. Probably, they'd been nomads from Asia Minor who'd settled in the Fertile Crescent and built the first cities there, but their exact origins were mysterious, and even their language appeared to be unrelated to other languages at the time.

Their word for "Earth," it was known, was *Ki*.

Interesting.

The word *Ki* had been passed on to other, later civilizations. In ancient Greece, the word was *Gi* or *Ge* . . . and from there it eventually evolved into *geo*, the root of words like geography, and *Gaia*, the Greek goddess of the Earth.

The circularity of meaning was stunning. It *might* be coincidence—there were, after all, only a limited number of syllables humans could pronounce—but St. Clair thought that there was a different explanation, one tantalizing in its possibilities.

Time travel.

They'd considered those possibilities before, but come to no conclusions. But the idea that the *Tellus Ad Astra* had been pulled forward in time certainly raised those theories higher on the probability scale. Had members of the Galactic Cooperative gone back in time to Earth of 4 billion years past? Had they interacted with the inhabitants of ancient Sumer?

And what of the Xam?

At this point, it was all sheer speculation, but St. Clair was excited about the possibilities.

The humans stranded here in this alien future might yet have a means of getting home. . . .

He approached a row of plastic, transparent cylinders, within which were human-sized and -shaped figures. Androgynous, neither male nor female but quite lifelike, they were robots constructed to specifications stored within Newton's memory, with artificial brains capable of human-level consciousness.

The robot army had not yet been activated, however.

They would be soon, though. One thing *Ad Astra* had dropped along with the trappings of empire was the Fifth Geneva Protocol. They would need an army in the months and years that would follow.

The androgyny gave the ranks of machines the look of particularly realistic mannequins. One out of that endless line, however, was different . . . distinctly female, and achingly familiar.

She'd been added to the assembly process at St. Clair's request.

"Are you ready for us to begin?" Newton asked.

"Do it."

Nothing appeared to happen, but St. Clair knew that Newton was transmitting a very long and complex set of software into the female robot's brain. Software derived from the Mind of Ki.

Her eyes opened.

"Hello, Lisa," St. Clair said.

She smiled at him.

IAN DOUGLAS's
STAR CARRIER
SERIES

EARTH STRIKE
BOOK ONE
978-0-06-184025-8

CENTER OF GRAVITY
BOOK TWO
978-0-06-184026-5

SINGULARITY
BOOK THREE
978-0-06-184027-2

DEEP SPACE
BOOK FOUR
978-0-06-218380-4

DARK MATTER
BOOK FIVE
978-0-06-218399-6

DEEP TIME
BOOK SIX
978-0-06-218405-4

Discover great authors, exclusive offers,
and more at hc.com.

ID2 0716